Philip Lutley Sclater, George Brown Goode

The Published Writings of Philip Lutley Sclater

1844-1896

Philip Lutley Sclater, George Brown Goode

The Published Writings of Philip Lutley Sclater
1844-1896

ISBN/EAN: 9783337062637

Printed in Europe, USA, Canada, Australia, Japan

Cover: Foto ©Andreas Hilbeck / pixelio.de

More available books at **www.hansebooks.com**

SMITHSONIAN INSTITUTION.

UNITED STATES NATIONAL MUSEUM.

BULLETIN

OF THE

UNITED STATES NATIONAL MUSEUM.

No. 49.

BIBLIOGRAPHY OF THE PUBLISHED WRITINGS OF PHILIP
LUTLEY SCLATER, F. R. S., SECRETARY OF THE
ZOOLOGICAL SOCIETY OF LONDON.

Prepared under the direction of

G. BROWN GOODE.

WASHINGTON:
GOVERNMENT PRINTING OFFICE.
1896.

ADVERTISEMENT.

This work (Bulletin No. 49) is one of a series of papers intended to illustrate the collections belonging to the United States, and constituting the National Museum, of which the Smithsonian Institution was placed in charge by the act of Congress of August 10, 1846.

The publications of the National Museum consist of two series— the Bulletins, of which this is No. 49, in continuous series, and the Proceedings, of which the eighteenth volume is now in press. A small edition of each paper in the Proceedings is distributed in pamphlet form to specialists, in advance of the publication of the bound volume.

The Bulletins of the National Museum, the publication of which was commenced in 1875, consist of elaborate papers based upon the collections of the Museum, reports of expeditions, etc., while the Proceedings facilitate the prompt publication of freshly-acquired facts relating to biology, anthropology, and geology, descriptions of restricted groups of animals and plants, the discussion of particular questions relative to the synonymy of species, and the diaries of minor expeditions.

Other papers, of more general popular interest, are printed in the Appendix to the Annual Report.

Full lists of the publications of the Museum may be found in the current catalogues of the publications of the Smithsonian Institution.

Papers intended for publication in the Proceedings and Bulletins of the National Museum are referred to the Committee on Publications, composed as follows: Frederick W. True (chairman), Marcus Benjamin (editor), J. E. Benedict, Otis T. Mason, Leonhard Stejneger, and Lester F. Ward.

S. P. LANGLEY,
Secretary of the Smithsonian Institution.

WASHINGTON, D. C., *August 1, 1896.*

THE

PUBLISHED WRITINGS

OF

PHILIP LUTLEY SCLATER,

1844-1896.

Prepared under the direction of

G. BROWN GOODE.

WASHINGTON:
GOVERNMENT PRINTING OFFICE.
1896.

CONTENTS.

INTRODUCTION.

Many years ago the publication of a series of bibliographies of representative American naturalists was begun in the Bulletins of the United States National Museum. The series was intended to include analytical discussions of the writings of the men who have been especially prominent in the study, classification, and naming of the animals and plants of America, with a view to facilitating the use of the very extensive, widely scattered, and very complicated literature which has grown up in connection with American systematic biology.

Five bulletins have been published in this series: No. 20, The Published Writings of Spencer Fullerton Baird, 1843–1882, by G. Brown Goode; No. 23, The Published Writings of Isaac Lea, LL. D., by Newton Pratt Scudder; No. 30, Bibliography of Publications Relating to the Collection of Fossil Invertebrates in the United States National Museum, including complete lists of the writings of Fielding B. Meek, Charles A. White, and Charles D. Walcott, by John Belknap Marcou; No. 40, The Published Writings of George Newbold Lawrence, 1844–1891, by L. S. Foster, and No. 41, The Published Writings of Dr. Charles Girard, by G. Brown Goode.

The scope of this series would seem appropriately limited to the work of the naturalists living and working in America, but there is one exception which no one can doubt the propriety of making—that in the case of Mr. Philip Lutley Sclater, the secretary of the Zoological Society of London, who has confined his work for the most part to American ornithology, and whose contributions to the systematic ornithology of the American Continent have far exceeded in extent those of anyone working in this country. His opportunities have been almost unlimited, and his utilization of these opportunities has been wonderfully effective.

The ornithology of Neotropical America was but little known when he began his work. Mr. George N. Lawrence, of New York City, also an indefatigable worker in the same field, has left an extensive record in his bibliography already published. His studies were carried on, however, in the intervals of an active business life, while Mr. Sclater has been able to devote his entire time for more than half a century to systematic work, and has given most of his attention to the bird fauna of Central and South America, with results the extent of which is well shown by the analytical catalogue of his writings now published.

It is believed that this bibliography will materially lighten the labors of everyone engaged in the study of American birds or of the problems of geographical distribution.

Since Mr. Sclater is not an "American naturalist" in the same sense as the others whose bibliographies have already been published, the present work is not included in the series of "Bibliographies of American Naturalists." He is, however, in another and a broader sense, one of the most eminent and prolific of American naturalists.

The plan adopted in the present volume is essentially different in its entirety from any previously used, although many of its features are familiar. The method of citation is essentially that of Coues, but the annotations to the titles are made as brief as possible. The object of such annotations is understood to be simply to describe each paper so that a person consulting the bibliography can determine without further research whether the paper cited is one which he needs to consult. The customary practice of analyzing the paper and enumerating under its title all the species, genera, and families which it describes is not followed. It is thought that a much more satisfactory plan has been adopted, namely, that of combining this enumeration of species with the alphabetical index, so that a person desiring an exact reference for use in synonymy, or indeed for immediate use in consulting the literature, can find in one alphabetical series all the names for which the author is responsible, each accompanied by an exact statement of place of description, the locality of the specimen, and the place where the type is to be found.

A separate list of species figured, with an exact bibliographical citation for the plate and the page related to it, is also given. The reason for including a separate list of the species figured is obvious, since a large number of Mr. Sclater's figures relate to forms not for the first time described by him.

Much care has been given to the typography of this bibliography, with the purpose of securing compactness as well as clearness. The material here included, if printed in the same style as the bibliographies previously issued by the Museum, would have occupied at least four times the space. Notwithstanding this compactness of typography, the arrangement of the matter and the contrasts secured by the choice of type and by the system of spacing and indentation adopted has, it is believed, produced a page which is clearer and easier of reference than any previously used, at all events in the publications of the Museum.

Special acknowledgment is due to Mr. George Arthur Doubleday, clerk in the library of the Zoological Society of London, by whom the titles have been copied and arranged. Mr. Charles W. Richmond, of the National Museum, has done excellent service in reading proof and verifying the citations.

BIOGRAPHICAL SKETCH OF PHILIP LUTLEY SCLATER.

Mr. Philip Lutley Sclater, secretary of the Zoological Society of London, is one of the best known of living zoologists. Few men have contributed so much as he to systematic ornithology, and none have done so much in the identification and description of new forms from the Western Continent. His work has been largely in connection with the luxuriant fauna of Neotropical America, little known at the time when he began his researches. Nearly every year since he began work in 1853, his correspondents in tropical America have laid at his feet new wealth in the form of collections from regions hitherto unexplored.

He has characterized 1,067 new species (245 in collaboration with Osbert Salvin), 135 new genera (25 with Salvin), and two new families of American birds.

Remarkable as has been his industry and his accuracy in diagnosis and description, the fact should be recognized that but for his energy and his skill as an organizer many regions now well known to the ornithologist would doubtless still remain unexplored.

The labors of Mr. Sclater have also resulted in great additions to our knowledge of the geographical distribution of vertebrates. Not only has he worked out many local faunas, but his generalizations upon the distribution of life and the division of the globe into zoogeographical regions have had great influence upon scientific opinion. He was one of the pioneers in this field of investigation, and his writings upon the subject have always been full of suggestion and have stimulated many others to engage in similar inquiry. His views as to the geographical distribution of birds are undoubtedly more widely accepted throughout the world than those of any other authority, and though, with increasing knowledge, modifications in the scheme proposed by him long ago will doubtless become more and more numerous, his studies of geographical distribution will always be considered as of fundamental importance, and the terms which he suggested for the principal divisions of the earth's surface will doubtless remain in ordinary use.

For more than thirty years the chief executive officer of the most wealthy and vigorous zoological society in the world, his influence upon the progress of natural history exploration has been very great, and his relations with American naturalists have always been cordial and cooperative.

Notwithstanding the great bulk of his technical publications, he has for four decades been prominent in the activities of scientific London and a noteworthy figure in the midst of every important scientific gathering.

At the age of sixty-seven he is still productive and adding each year a number of titles to the already remarkable assemblage of papers which have been published under his name.

It is the object of this bibliography to render thoroughly available to American naturalists all the results of the work of this eminent scholar, who has done for the ornithology of Central and South America what has been done by Nuttall, Wilson, Audubon, Baird, Allen, Merriam, Ridgway, and their associates for that of the Northern continent.

Philip Lutley Sclater was born November 4, 1829, at "Tangier Park," in Hampshire, the residence of his father, William Lutley Sclater, Esq.; and his boyhood was passed chiefly at "Hoddington House," another estate in the same county, belonging to his father, who died there in 1885 at the age of ninety-seven.

In beautiful Hampshire, close to the home of Gilbert White at "Selborne," he acquired early in life a love for outdoor life and a taste for the study of birds.

At the age of ten, he was sent to a well-known school at Twyford, near Winchester. In 1842 he went to Winchester College, and in 1845 was elected scholar of Corpus Christi College, Oxford. Being at that time under sixteen years of age, he was not called into residence at the University until Easter, 1846.

At Oxford his attention was given principally to mathematics, though his spare time was occupied by the study of birds and of the excellent series of natural history books then in the Radcliffe Library.

Hugh E. Strickland, the well-known ornithologist, who was at that time resident in Oxford as reader in geology, became interested in young Sclater and took him under his protection. At Strickland's chambers he met John Gould, shortly after his return from his great journey to Australia. From Strickland he received his first instruction in scientific ornithology. He began his collection of bird skins at Oxford, making British skins for himself and buying foreign species at a shilling apiece, whenever he could get to London for a run among the bird shops.

In December, 1849, he received the degree of Bachelor of Arts, obtained his first class in the mathematical school and a "pass" in classics. At that time these were the only two recognized subjects for study in the university, no sort of encouragement being given to natural history.

After taking his degree he remained at his college in Oxford for two years, devoting his time principally to natural history. He also gave much attention to modern languages, studying with masters at home and always visiting the Continent in vacation time, and thus soon made himself familiar with French, German and Italian.

At this period of his life he was often in Paris, where he made the acquaintance of the great ornithologist, Prince Charles Bonaparte, at whose house, until his death in 1858, he was a frequent visitor.

In 1851 he entered himself for the bar, becoming a student at Lincoln's Inn, occasionally visiting Oxford, and passing his leisure time at Hoddington, but always enthusiastically engaged in natural history pursuits. The winter of 1852–53 was given to travel in Italy and Sicily.

In December, 1855, he was admitted fellow of Corpus Christi College, and having in the previous June completed his legal education and been called to the bar by the Honorable Society of Lincoln's Inn, he went the Western Circuit for several years.

In 1856 he made his first journey across the Atlantic, in company with the Rev. George Hext, a fellow collegian. Leaving England in July, they went by New York up the Hudson to Saratoga, and there attended the meeting of the American Association for the Advancement of Science. After that they went to Niagara, and thence through the Great Lakes to Superior City, at the extreme end of Lake Superior. Here they engaged two Canadian "voyageurs" and traveled on foot through the backwoods to the upper waters of the St. Croix River. This they descended in a birch-bark canoe to the Mississippi. Mr. Sclater subsequently published an account of this journey in the third volume of "Illustrated Travels." (See paper No. 576.)

Returning by steamboat and railway to Philadelphia, he spent a month in that city studying the splendid collection of birds belonging to the Academy of Natural Sciences, where he formed the acquaintance of John Cassin, Joseph Leidy, John Le Conte, and other then well-known members of that society. He returned to England shortly before Christmas, 1856.

For some years after this he lived in London, practicing occasionally at the bar, but always at work on natural history. He was a constant attendant at the meetings of the Zoological Society, of which he was elected, in 1850, a life member and in 1857 a member of the council.

In January, 1859, he made a short excursion to Tunis and eastern Algeria, in company with Mr. E. C. Taylor and two other friends. They visited the breeding places of the vultures and kites in the interior and gathered many bird skins, returning to London at the end of March.

At this time Mr. D. W. Mitchell, secretary of the Zoological Society, was about to vacate his post in order to take charge of the newly instituted Jardin d'Acclimatation in Paris. For this position Mr. Sclater was selected by Owen and Yarrell, then influential members of the council. He was formally elected to it on April 30, 1859, and he has been re-elected annually ever since.

He found it necessary to devote himself entirely for three years to the reorganization of the affairs of the Society. The "Proceedings" and "Transactions" were at that time several years in arrears—they were brought up to date; the Garden Guide, which was out of print, was rewritten; the large staff at the gardens was rearranged and divided into departments under the superintendent, and various other reforms were introduced.

For thirty-five years his life has been almost entirely spent in work connected with natural history.

In 1874, when his brother (then the Right Hon. George Sclater-Booth, M. P., and afterwards Lord Basing) accepted office in Mr. Disraeli's administration as president of the local government board, Mr. Sclater became his private secretary, a position which he occupied for two years. But when subsequently offered a permanent place in the civil service he declined it, because he could not make up his mind to give up his dearly loved work in natural history.

His most engrossing duties have been in connection with the Zoological Society of London, to which, as principal executive officer, he has, of course, devoted most of his time. It is conceded by all that its affairs have prospered well under his direction. The number of fellows of the society, in 1859 about 1,700, has increased to over 3,000. The income of the society, which in 1858 was a little over £14,000, is now seldom under £25,000. Besides this, nearly all of the principal buildings in the society's gardens have been rebuilt during the past thirty-five years and fitted up with every sort of modern convenience for animals. The old office building (No. 11 Hanover square) has been sold and a larger and more convenient one (No. 3 Hanover square) bought in the same vicinity. A debt of £12,000 to the society's bankers, originally secured upon its house, has been paid off, and this property is now entirely the property of the Society without any sort of incumbrance.

The first floor of the society's house is devoted to the accomodation of a large and very valuable zoological library, under the care of a librarian and his assistant, and is the constant resort of the working zoologists of the metropolis. This library has been almost entirely accumulated since 1859.

The publications of the society, consisting of Proceedings, Transactions, Lists of Animals (of which eight editions have been published), the "Garden Guide" and "Zoological Record," are all issued from this office, with almost unfailing regularity. The scientific meetings of the society are held here during the eight months of the scientific session, and an abstract of their proceedings is always printed and issued within a week after each meeting has taken place.

Mr. Sclater was selected by the British Ornithologists' Union as the first editor of "The Ibis," in 1859. He finished the first series in 1864.

Professor Newton took his place as editor of the second series, and Mr. Salvin as editor of the third. In 1877 he was associated with Mr. Salvin as joint editor of the fourth series, and in 1883 commenced the editorship of the fifth series, with Mr. Howard Saunders as co-editor. When the fifth series was completed, in 1888, he became sole editor of the sixth, which he finished in 1894. In 1895, having again obtained the assistance of Mr. Howard Saunders, he commenced work on the seventh series, of which two volumes are already complete.

When the British Ornithologists' Club was established in 1892, he joined heartily in the movement inaugurated by Dr. R. Bowdler Sharpe, and has usually had the honor of occupying the chair at its meetings and of delivering an inaugural address at the commencement of each session.

With the British Association for the Advancement of Science he has had a long connection, having become a member in 1847 at the second Oxford meeting, and having attended its meetings with few exceptions ever since. For several years he was secretary of Section D, and at the Bristol meeting in 1875 he was president of that section and delivered an address "On the present state of our knowledge of geographical zoology" (Paper No. 743). In 1876 he was elected one of the two general secretaries of the association, together with Sir Douglas Galton, and served in that capacity for five years, thereby becoming an ex officio member of the council, at the meetings of which he is a constant attendant.

Ever since the scientific journal "Nature" was started by Professor Lockyer in 1869, he has been a frequent contributor to that most important periodical.

In 1886 he began the transfer of his private collection of American bird skins to the British Museum. This collection contained 8,824 specimens, representing 3,158 species, belonging to the orders Passeres, Picariæ, and Psittaci. It may be remarked that when he began his collection at Oxford in 1847 he intended to collect birds of every kind and from all parts of the world, but after a few years resolved to confine his attention particularly to the ornithology of South and Central America and to collect only in the orders just mentioned, which were at that time generally less known than the others and of which the specimens are of a more manageable size for the private collector.

At the time of the beginning of this transfer, which was only completed in 1890, he agreed to prepare some of the volumes of the British Museum "Catalogue of Birds," relating to the groups to which he had paid special attention. In accordance with this arrangement by the expenditure of fully two years of his leisure time for each volume, he prepared the eleventh volume in 1886, the fourteenth in 1888, the fifteenth in 1890, and half of the nineteenth in 1891.

When the *Challenger* expedition started around the world in 1873, at the request of his friend, the late Sir Wyville Thomson, he agreed to work out all the birds. Soon after the return of the expedition in 1877 the specimens of birds collected were placed in his hands, and with the assistance of his ornithological friends were speedily reported upon in a series of papers contributed to the Zoological Society's "Proceedings." The whole of these papers were reprinted with additions and illustrations, and now form part of the second volume of the "Zoology" of the *Challenger* expedition.

Geography, being very closely connected with zoology, has always commanded Mr. Sclater's hearty interest. He became a life member of the Royal Geographical Society in 1880, and has attended its meetings regularly ever since. He has also served two years on the council, and is a member of the Geographical Club. He has assisted in promoting many researches in foreign parts, chiefly, however, with a view to obtaining collections of natural history from strange places. Among these may be especially mentioned Sir H. H. Johnston's expedition to Kilima-Njaro in 1884 and Professor Balfour's visit to Socotra in 1880. He also took a leading part in sending out naturalists to Kerguelen Land and Rodriguez, along with the transit-of-Venus expeditions of 1874–75, and in many other similar efforts to explore little-known parts of the earth's surface. At the present time he is serving on two committees of this kind—one for the investigation of the fauna and flora of the Lesser Antilles, and the other for the further exploration of the fauna of the Hawaiian Islands. In both of these countries collectors are actively at work.

In 1884 he took advantage of the opportunity of the visit of the British Association to Montreal to cross the Atlantic a second time, and after the meeting to visit the United States. He was not in good health at that period, and did little, if anything, in the way of zoology. But he had the pleasure of seeing several of his former friends, especially Lawrence and Baird, and of making the personal acquaintance of Mr. Ridgway, Mr. Allen, Mr. Brewster, Dr. Merriam, and many other naturalists.

One of his closest friends was the late Professor Huxley, long a member of the Council of the Zoological Society, where he was one of Mr. Sclater's most constant supporters. Professor Huxley, it may be said, was the chief advocate of the project of employing an anatomist at the society's gardens, and invented the title "prosector" for the new office. A. H. Garrod, who became prosector in 1871, and W. A. Forbes, who succeeded him in 1879—both very talented and promising young naturalists,—were dear friends of Sclater, and the unfortunate death of Forbes during the excursion to the Niger in 1883 was a most severe blow to him. Notable among his other friends was Charles Darwin, who frequently visited him in his office, bringing long lists of memoranda for conference.

Mr. Sclater married in 1862 Jane Anne Eliza Hunter Blair, daughter of the late Sir David Hunter Blair, baronet, of "Blairquhan," in Ayrshire. He has five children, of whom four are sons. The eldest,

William Lutley Sclater, has inherited his father's tastes: he was for four years an assistant in the Indian Museum in Calcutta, and after a short term of service as science master at Eton College was appointed director of the South African Museum at Cape Town, a position which he now occupies.

The second son, Capt. Bertram Lutley Sclater, is an officer in the Royal Engineers, and is now on duty in British East Africa, constructing a road to Uganda from the coast.

The third son, Lieut. Guy Lutley Sclater, an officer in the Royal Navy, is a specialist in torpedo work; while the youngest, Arthur Lutley Sclater, is a tea planter in Ceylon.

In 1887, after a continuous residence of more than twenty-five years in London, he gave up his residence in Elvaston Place, where so many American naturalists visiting England have received a hearty welcome. He has since lived in Hampshire at his country house, "Odiham Priory," about forty miles from town, taking a house for his family in London for three or four months at the beginning of each year. In summer he constantly visits the Continent, making excursions to see the various zoological gardens and museums.

Mr. Sclater received the degree of doctor of philosophy *honoris causa* from the University of Bonn in 1860, and in 1861 was elected a fellow of the Royal Society, on the council of which he has twice served. As has already been said, he has long been an active member of the Council of the British Association for the Advancement of Science, as well as of that of the Royal Geographical Society.

A list of the other scientific and learned societies of which he is a member is as follows:

Fellow of Linnean Society of London (1856); member of Allgemeine deutsche ornithologische Gesellschaft (1856); corresponding member of Academy of Natural Sciences, Philadelphia (1856); corresponding member of Lyceum of Natural History, New York (1857); corresponding member of Dublin University Zoological and Botanical Association (1859); member of British Ornithologists' Union (1859); member of Academia Germanica Naturæ Curiosorum, cognomine " Bechstein " (1860); honorary member of Sociedad de Naturalistas Neo-Granadinos (1860); honorary member of Royal Zoological Society of Ireland (1861); member of k. k. zoologisch-botanische Gesellschaft in Wien (1862); member of Philosophical Club (1862); honorary member of Zoologische Gesellschaft in Hamburg (1863); honorary member of Zoological and Acclimatization Society of Victoria (1865); honorary member of Rotterdamsche Diergaarde (1866); corresponding member of the Gesellschaft für vaterländische Naturkunde in Württemberg (1867); honorary member of the Sociedad de Ciencias Físicas y Naturales of Carácas (1869); corresponding member of Academia Scientiarum Instituti Bononiensis (1870); honorary member of Koninklijk Zoologisch Genootschap " Natura Artis Magistra " of Amsterdam (1871); member of Geologists' Association, London

(1873); corresponding member of Senkenbergische naturforschende Gesellschaft zu Frankfurt-am-Main (1873); fellow of American Philosophical Society of Philadelphia (1873); honorary member of New Zealand Institute (1876); member of Royal Society Club (1876); fellow of Geological Society of London (1878); foreign honorary member of the Nuttall Ornithological Club (1878); corresponding member of the Verein für naturwissenschaftliche Unterhaltung in Hamburg (1879); honorary member of Hertfordshire Natural History Society and Field Club (1880); corresponding member of Academia Nacional de Ciencias, República Argentina (1880); honorary member of Sociedad Zoolojica Arjentina, Buenos Ayres (1881); foreign member of American Ornithologists' Union (1883); honorary member of Ornithologischer Verein in Wien (1883); corresponding member of Biological Society of Washington (1884); honorary member of Zoological and Acclimatization Society of South Australia (1885); honorary member of Newport Natural History Society (1885); ordinary member of the Societas Cæsarea Naturæ Curiosorum Mosquensis (1885); corresponding member of Royal Academy of Turin (1885); honorary corresponding member of Geological Society of Australasia (1886); member of the Hampshire Field Club (1887); fellow of Imperial Institute (1892); member of British Ornithologists' Club (1892); honorary member of Societas Cæsarea Naturæ Curiosorum Mosquensis (1894); honorary member of Bureau Central Ornithologique Hongrois (1894); corresponding member of Société Scientifique du Chili (1894); honorary fellow of Corpus Christi College, Oxford (1894); corresponding member of Boston Society of Natural History (1895); honorary member of Museu Paraense de Historia Natural e Ethnographia (1896).

His prominence in zoology has received frequent recognition in the naming of new forms. Among the animals which bear his name are the following: *Anabates Sclateri*, Pelzeln (Sitz. Akad. Wien, XXXIV, p. 132); *Attila Sclateri*, Lawrence (Ann. Lyc. N. Y., VII, 470); *Barbus Sclateri*, Günther (Cat. Fish. Brit. Mus., VII, 93); *Calliste Sclateri*, Lafresnaye (Rev. Zool., 1854, 207); *Casuarius Sclateri*, Salvadori (Ann. Mus. Civ. Genov., XII, 422); *Chætura Sclateri*, Pelzeln (Orn. Bras., 16, 56); *Chrysomitris Sclateri*, Sharpe (Cat. Birds Brit. Mus., XII, 200); *Crax Sclateri*, Gray (List Gallinæ Brit. Mus., 14); *Cyanocorax Sclateri*, Heine (Journ. für Orn., 1860, 115); *Doliornis Sclateri*, Taczanowski (Proc. Zool. Soc., 1874, 136, 541, pl. xx); *Erinaceus Sclateri*, Anderson (Proc. Zool. Soc., 1895, 420); *Euchlornis Sclateri*, Cornalia (Contr. Orn., 1852, 133, pl. 101); *Eudyptes Sclateri*, Buller (Birds New Zealand, II, 289, 1888); *Euphonia Sclateri*, Bonaparte (in Mus. Paris; Sundevall, Œfv. Vet. Ak. Forh., 1869, 596); *Goura Sclateri*, Salvadori (Ann. Mus. Civ. Genov., XII, 325); *Heliomaster Sclateri*, Cabanis and Heine (Mus. Hein., III, 54); *Hirundinea Sclateri*, Reinhardt (Fuglef. Camp. Bras., 147); *Hirundo Sclateri*, Cory (Auk, 1884, 2); *Icterus Sclateri*, Cassin (Proc. Acad. Nat. Sci. Phila., 1867, 49); *Leptocalamus Sclateri*, Boulenger (Cat. Snakes Brit. Mus., II,

251, pl. xii, fig. 1); *Lophophorus Sclateri*, Jerdon (Ibis, 1870, 147);
Loriculus Sclateri, Wallace (Proc. Zool. Soc., 1862, 336, pl. xxxviii);
Loxigilla noctis Sclateri, Allen (Bull. Nutt. Orn. Club, V, 166);
Megapicus Sclateri, Malherbe (Picidæ, I, 22, 156, 165, pl. viii, fig. 1;
pl. xxxv, fig. 8); *Micropygia Sclateri*, Bonaparte (Compt. Rend.,
XLIII, 599) *Myiarchus Sclateri*, Lawrence (Proc. U. S. Nat. Mus., I,
357); *Myzomela Sclateri*, Forbes (Proc. Zool. Soc., 1879, 265, pl. xxv,
fig. 2); *Ornithion Sclateri*, Berlepsch and Taczanowski (Proc. Zool. Soc.,
1883, 554); *Penelope Sclateri*, Gray (Proc. Zool. Soc., 1860, 270); *Phile-
mon Sclateri*, Gray (Ann. Mag. Nat. Hist., V, 1870, 327); *Picumnus
Sclateri*, Taczanowski (Proc. Zool. Soc., 1877, 327); *Plectropterus
Sclateri*, Sousa (Jorn. Ac. Sci. Lisb., II, 157); *Polioptila Sclateri*,
Sharpe (Cat. Birds Brit. Mus., X, 449); *Psittacula Sclateri*, Gray (List
Psittacidæ Brit. Mus., 86); *Pternistes Sclateri*, Bocage (Jorn. Ac. Sci.
Lisb., I, 327, pl. vi); *Synallaxis Sclateri*, Cabanis (Journ. für Orn.,
1878, 196); *Tanagra Sclateri*, Berlepsch (Ibis, 1880, 112); *Thripophaga
Sclateri*, Berlepsch (Ibis, 1883, 490, pl. xiii); *Thryothorus Sclateri*,
Taczanowski (Proc. Zool. Soc., 1879, 222); *Triccus Sclateri*, Cabanis
and Heine (Mus. Hein., II, 51); *Xiphocolaptes Sclateri*, Ridgway (Proc.
U. S. Nat. Mus., XII, 6).

In conclusion, I quote the brief appreciations of Mr. Sclater written
by representative American naturalists whom I have invited to place
upon record their judgment as to the value of his services to science.

Dr. Clinton Hart Merriam, chief of the division of economic ornithology and mammalogy of the United States Department of Agricul-
ture, writes as follows:

The value of Sclater's contributions to American ornithology can hardly be over
estimated. What Nuttall and Wilson and Audubon and Baird have done for the
birds of North America, Sclater has done for those of Central and South America.
There is this difference in the method of treatment—that while the publications of
North American ornithologists have been chiefly faunal or geographic, Sclater's
have been for the most part systematic, dealing with assemblages of species rather
than with the ornithology of special areas, though he has made some important
faunal contributions also. In the field of zoological geography he early attained
distinction, and his primary regions, based on the distribution of birds. have been
widely accepted.

The excellent bibliography of his writings, prepared and published by the United
States National Museum, is not only a model for this kind of work, but is also a
most useful addition to the literature of systematic zoology.

For half a century Sclater has given practically the whole of his time to the
study of birds and mammals. For nearly forty years he has had charge of the
principal zoological publication of the world (the Proceedings of the Zoological
Society of London), and the greater part of the time has edited the leading ornithological journal (The Ibis), so that a large share of the literature of zoology has
passed directly under his eye. During the whole of this long period he has been
at the head of one of the best zoological gardens and the greatest zoological society ever established—the Zoological Society of London. Naturally his office came
to be the meeting ground of naturalists from all quarters of the globe, and speci
mens of new and rare animals continually poured into his hands. For these
reasons he has been in a position, more than any other man of his time, to keep

abreast of the progress of zoological science. That these opportunities have not been neglected is shown by the extraordinary array of titles, more than 1,200 in number, contained in his bibliography. The vast majority of these papers relate to the birds of tropical America, in which field the name of Sclater, like that of our own lamented Lawrence, will always occupy an exalted position.

Sclater is a good type of the industrious, systematic naturalist. His official position and personal energy brought him a wealth of new material. This he described in an endless series of papers on new species and new genera. Then, as additional specimens and additional species came in, he promptly published more comprehensive treatises in the form of synopses of genera or larger assemblages. And later, when still ampler material cast new light on the subject, he in numerous instances revised the same groups over again, correcting early errors, adding new species, and bringing the history of the groups down to date. These synopses and monographic revisions are the most important and useful of Sclater's contributions to science. Their number is amazing. Among the groups treated are the Orioles, Tanagers, Callistes, Pheasants, Cuckoos, Honey Creepers, Jacamars, Puff Birds, American Ant Birds (*Formicariidæ*), American Rails, and many others. In addition to all these, his Nomenclator Avium Neotropicalium and Argentine Ornithology have come to be indispensable to the student of South American birds. And finally, as a fitting climax to this remarkable series, he has lived to erect his own monument in the admirable volumes he has contributed to the British Museum's Catalogue of Birds.

But Sclater's contributions to zoological science are not limited to birds. In the field of mammals he has published many important papers, illustrated by colored plates of high merit. Among the more useful of these are articles on the Deer, Rhinoceroses, and African Monkeys. He is now publishing, under joint authorship with Mr. Oldfield Thomas, a superb illustrated work on the antelopes and their allies, "The Book of Antelopes," the second volume of which is already well advanced. That the period of his activities may be continued far into the future is the earnest hope of his American friends.

Prof. Joel Asaph Allen, of the American Museum of Natural History, New York City, writes:

It is particularly fitting that the series of bibliographies published by the United States National Museum should include the writings of Philip Lutley Sclater, who has been for many years the most eminent authority and one of the most prolific writers on the ornithology of Central and South America. While Mr. Sclater's writings cover a much wider field, including many papers relating to Old World birds and to general subjects in ornithology, and many valuable contributions to mammalogy as well, American birds early became his chosen specialty, and it has engaged his chief attention for over forty years, and it is to be hoped will continue to do so for many years to come.

The bibliography of his writings, from their extent and authoritative character, forms, as already said, a most welcome addition to the National Museum series of bibliographies, which already embraces those of Baird, Girard, Lea, and Lawrence. The utility of such compilations is beyond question; they are at once a monument of respect to the author so honored and a convenience to all working naturalists engaged in the same fields of research.

Mr. Robert Ridgway, Curator of Birds in the United States National Museum, writes as follows:

The name of Sclater is so much a part of Neotropical ornithology that any knowledge of the latter without equal familiarity with the former would be impossible. Certainly no other name occurs so frequently nor ranks more highly in the literature pertaining to the birds of tropical America.   Covering a period of more than forty years of unceasing activity, chiefly devoted to this, his favorite geographical field, the importance of Mr. Sclater's contributions to the ornithology of the Neotropical region can hardly be overestimated.   Other ornithologists, it is true, have rendered important services so far as portions of America are concerned, as Salvin for Mexico and Central America, and Lawrence for the same area and the West Indies, while the former has been associated with Sclater in the preparation of various monographic papers, the " Nomenclator Avium Neotropicalium " and other works; but only Sclater has covered impartially the Neotropical region as a whole.

The subject of the geographical distribution of animals, with special reference to the birds, may be said to have first received serious attention from Mr. Sclater, who nearly forty years ago published a zoo-geographical scheme, which may fairly be regarded as the most satisfactory, in some respects, of those which have been proposed by various authors.   Though not without its imperfections, the same may be said of all those proposed as improvements or substitutes, and none of the latter have received indorsement to the same extent as Mr. Sclater's.

Mr. Sclater's treatment of ornithological subjects is concise and conservative— more so, frequently, than some of us would wish it to be.   Some of us on this side of the Atlantic differ with him in nomenclatural matters and regarding the status and discrimination of subspecies or geographical races; but in these respects his methods are those of a particular school, which we are pleased to call the "old," and which few, if any, of his countrymen have forsaken.   We fondly hope, however, that the conservatism of our English brethren may sometime yield to the sound principles upon which the so-called "American" school have based their "innovations," and the complete harmony of methods between ornithologists of the two countries, so much to be desired, be thereby established.

Although Sclater's ornithological work has extended through so many years— far more than are allotted to most of us—neither his interest nor activity show sign of abatement, and it is sincerely hoped that a career so eminently useful may long be continued.

PHILIP LUTLEY SCLATER,

1844-1896.

PART I.

CHRONOLOGICAL CATALOGUE OF SEPARATE WORKS.

1

A Synopsis of the *Galbulidæ*. Pp. 1-10, 8 vo, 1853. [Reprinted, with additions, from the "Contributions to Ornithology" for 1852.]

A review of the genera and species of the family *Galbulidæ*. The genera treated of are: *Galbula, Jacamaralcyon, Jacamerops, Galbuloides,* and *Galbaleyrhynchus.* Seventeen species are enumerated.

(See papers Nos. 43, 45, 46, 69.)

2

Tanagrarum Catalogus Specificus. Pp. 1-16, 8vo, Basingstoke, 1854.

A catalogue of the known species of Tanagers, embracing 41 genera and 238 species. *Diva* is proposed for the name of a new genus, and the new species named are as follows: *Arremon axillaris, Ramphocelus dorsalis,* Bp. MS., *Buthraupis chloronota, Euphonia concinna,* and *Euphonia hirundinacea,* Bp. MS.

3

Synopsis of the Fissirostral Family *Bucconidæ,* accompanied by four coloured plates of hitherto unfigured species. Pp. 3-24, pls. i-iv, London, 1854. [Reprint, with additions, from the Ann. and Mag. Nat. Hist., ser. 2, 1854.]

A review of the species (33 in number) of the family *Bucconidæ.* The genera treated of are: *Bucco, Malacoptila, Monasa,* and *Chelidoptera.* The following species are figured: *Bucco ruficollis, B. bicinctus, B. lanceolatus,* and *Chelidoptera albipennis.*

(See paper No. 66.)

4

Synopsis Avium Tanagrinarum. A descriptive catalogue of the known species of Tanagers, 8vo, London, 1856. [Reprint, from Proc. Zool. Soc. London, 1856, pp. 64, 108, 230.]

(See papers Nos. 86, 86a, 86b.)

5

A Monograph of the Birds forming the Tanagrine Genus *Calliste;* illustrated by coloured plates of all the known species. Pp. i-xviii, 1-104, pls. i-xlv, 8vo, London, Van Voorst, 1857.

A monograph of the genus *Calliste,* which embraces the following 52 species: *C. tatao, C. cœlicolor, C. yeni, C. tricolor, C. fastuosa, C. festiva, C. cyaneiventris, C. thoracica, C. schranki, C. punctata, C. guttata, C. xanthogastra, C. graminea, C. rufigularis, C. aurulenta, C. sclateri, C. pulchra, C. arthusi, C. icterocephala, C. vitriolina, C. cayana, C. cyanolæma, C. cucullata, C. flava, C. pretiosa, C. melanonota, C. cyanoptera, C. gyrola, C. gyroloides, C. desmaresti, C. braziliensis, C. flavicentris, C. vieilloti, C. boliviana, C. atricærulea, C. ruficervix, C. atricapilla, C. argentea, C. nigriviridis, C. cyanescens, C. larvata, C.francescæ, C. nigricincta, C. cyaneicollis, C. labradorides, C. rufigenis, C. parzudakii, C. lunigera, C. chrysotis, C. xanthocephala, C. venusta,* and *C. inornata.* All the species are figured except *C. cyanolæma, C. vieilloti, C. nigriviridis,* and *C. francescæ.*

6

Guide to the Gardens of the Zoological Society of London, 47 editions, 8vo, London, 1859-93.

A popular illustrated guide to the Gardens of the Zoological Society of London, giving a concise account of the animals exhibited therein.

7

Zoological Sketches by Joseph Wolf. Made for the Zoological Society of London, from animals in their vivarium, in the Regent's Park. Edited, with notes, by P. L. Sclater. Vol. I, pls. i-l (1861); Vol. II, pls. i-l (1867), with letterpress to each plate, Folio, London, 1861-67.

The following species are figured and remarked upon: (Vol. I) *Troglodytes niger. Cercopithecus pluto (stangeri* on plate), *Felis leo, F. leopardus, F.*

picta, F. cyra, F. macroscelis, F. serval, F. chaus, F. caracal (2 plates), *F. canadensis, F. jubata, Bassaris astuta, Mephitis humboldtii, Canis azaræ, Ursus syriacus, Trichecus rosmarus, Cervus canadensis, C. leucurus, Orcas canna* (jr.), *Gazella subgutturosa, Oryx leucoryx, Ovis cycloceros (cignai* on plate), *Capra jemlaica, Auchenia pacos, Hippopotamus amphibius, Potamochœrus africanus, P. penicillatus, Myrmecophaga jubata, Thylacinus cynocephalus, Phascolomys wombat, Falco sacer, F. grœnlandicus, F. islandicus, Gypohierax angolensis, Phasianus torquatus, P. versicolor, Gallophasis horsfieldii, Tetraogallus caspius, Galloperdix lunulosa, Rhea americana, Casuarius bennettii, Apteryx mantelli, Otis tarda, Grus montignesia (japonensis* on plate), *Mycteria australis, Cygnus nigricollis, Chloephaga poliocephala (Bernicla magellanica* on plate), and *Xiphosoma caninum.* (Vol. 11) *Macacus ocreatus, Lemur nigrifrons, Chiromys madagascariensis, Canis cerdo, Felis yaguarundi, F. lynx, F. viverrina* (on plate *bengalensis*), *Viverricula malaccensis, Mellivora capensis, M. indica, Arctictis binturong, Otaria hookeri, Cervus maral* (on plate *C. walticidii*), *C. mantchuricus, C. taivanus, C. sika, C. rusa, C. swinhoii, C. humilis, Oryx leucoryx* (jr.), *Capra megaceros, Ovis tragelaphus, Sus andamanensis, Dicotyles torquatus, Elephas africanus, Bradypus tridactylus, Macropus rufus, Phascolomys latifrons (lasiorhinus* on plate), *Ptilonorhynchus holosericeus, Buceros bicornis, B. rhinoceros, Aquila nœvia, Phasianus sœmmerringii, P. reevesii, Euplocamus erythrophthalmus, E. prœlatus (Gallophasis horsfieldi* on plate), *E. vieilloti, E. swinhoii, E. lineatus, Ceriornis satyra, Talegalla lathami, Struthio camelus, Ocydromus australis, Ciconia senegalensis (Mycteria senegalensis* on plate), *Balæniceps rex, Rhinochetusjubatus, Tantalus ibis, T. leucocephalus, Chloephaga magellanica, Anas sentulata (Casarca leucoptera* on plate), and *Clotho nasicornis.*

8

Catalogue of a Collection of American Birds belonging to P. L. Sclater.

Pp. i–xvi, 1–368, pls. i–xx, 8vo, London, 1862.

A synonymic catalogue of the American species (2.170 in number, represented by 4,100 specimens) of the orders *Passeres, Fissirostres* and *Scansores,* in the collection of Mr. Sclater. The new genera *Hemidarnis, Hyetornis, Curæus, Morococcyx, Microchelidon* (changed to *Neochelidon*), *Oncostoma,* and *Pseudoleistes* are created; 6 new sectional names are founded, viz, *Microcerculus* (sect. of *Cyphorinus*), *Chlorura* (sect. of *Embernagra*), *Microrhopias* (sect. of *Formicivora*), *Potamopsar* (sect. of *Quiscalus*), *Tabara* (*= Taraba,* Less., sect. of *Thamnophilus*), and *Thryomanes* (sect. of *Thryothorus*); and the following MS. names are adopted: *Heterocercus* (Hartl.), *Ancistrops* (Scl.), *Omnatornis* (Scl.) (as a synonym of *Acropternis*), and *Thripadectes* (Scl.). Four new species are named, viz, *Glyphorhynchus major, Momotus swainsoni, Chelidoptera brasiliensis,* and *Chloronerpes malherbii,* and the following species, for which only MS. names had previously been employed by the author, are recognized as valid and the names adopted: *Tachyphonus cristatellus, Paroaria cervicalis, Chrysomitris uropygialis, Icterus xanthomus, Quiscalus æquatorialis, Q. assimilis, Thamnophilus strenuus, Pachyrhamphus cinereiventris, P. dorsalis, Buco napensis, Chœtura cinereiventris,* and *Conurus propinquus.* The specific names of *Thaumastura fanny* (Less.), *T. enicurus* (Vieill.), and *Synallaxis elegans* Scl. are emended to *francesiæ, henicura* and *elegantior,* respectively, and several other similar alterations are made. The species figured are: *Turdus pinicola, Cinclus leuconotus, Campylorhynchus jocosus, Thryothorus pleurostictus, Hylophilus ochraceiceps, Diglossa indigotica, Dacnis egregia,* ♂, ♀: *D. pulcherrima, Calliste cyanotis, Chlorospingus castaneicollis, Embernagra chrysoma, Sclerurus mexicanus, Synallaxis castanea, Anabazenops subalaris, Myrmotherula ornata,* ♂. ♀: *Formicivora boucardi,* ♂. ♀: *Platyrhynchus coronatus, Oncostoma cinereigulare, Todirostrum schistaceiceps, Mitius coronulatus,* and *Chiroxiphia regina.*

9

List of Vertebrated Animals living in the Gardens of the Zoological Society of London, 1862. Pp. i–vi, 1–100, 8vo, London, 1862.

The same. 2d ed., pp. i–vi, 1–120, 8vo, London, 1863.

The same. 1865. 3d ed., pp. i–viii, 1–148, 8vo, London, 1865.

The same. 1866. 4th ed., pp. i–viii, 1–204, 8vo, London, 1867.

Revised List of the Vertebrated Animals now or lately living in the Gardens of the Zoological Society of London. Pp. i–viii, 1–399, 8vo, London, 1872.

List of the Vertebrated Animals now or lately living in the Gardens of the Zoological Society of London. 6th ed., 1877, pp. i–x, 1–519, 8vo, London, 1877.

The same. 7th ed., 1879, pp. i–xii, 1–579, 8vo, London, 1879.

The same. 8th ed., 1883, pp. i–xvi, 1–682, 8vo, London, 1883.

Systematic catalogues of the species and of the individual specimens of vertebrated animals that have been exhibited in the Gardens of the Zoological Society of London prior to the year 1883.

10

List of the species of *Phasianidæ,* with remarks on their Geographical Distribution. Proc. Zool. Soc. London, 1863, 8vo, London, 1863. [Reprint, with additions, p. 113; pp. i–iii, 1–15; pls. 1–12.]

A list of the 56 known species of Pheasants, with remarks upon them and tables of their geographical distribution. The following species are figured: *Phasianus reevesii, P. sœmmerringii, Thaumalea amherstiæ, Crossoptilon tibetanum, C. auritum, Euplocamus prælatus, E. vieilloti, E. erythrophthalmus, E. lineatus, Ceriornis melanocephala, C. temminckii,* and *Polyplectron bicalcaratum.* The genera included are the following: *Lophophorus, Pucrasia, Phasianus, Thaumalea, Crossoptilon, Euplocamus, Gallus, Ceriornis, Pavo, Polyplectron, Argus, Meleagris, Numida, Phasidus* and *Agelastus.*

(See paper No. 285.)

11

Nitzsch's Pterylography, translated from the German. Edited by P. L. Sclater. Pp. i–xii, 1–181, pls. i–x, folio, London, 1867. [Published by the Ray Society.]

12

Exotic Ornithology, containing figures and descriptions of new or rare species of American Birds. By P. L. Sclater and O. Salvin. Pp. i–vi, 1–204, pls. i–c. London, 1869. [Issued in two sizes, small folio and large folio.]

Figures and descriptions of 104 species, belonging to 51 different genera, of birds of the Neotropical Region, with notes on their habits and distribution. One new genus—*Centropelma*—and one new species—*Porzana hauxwelli*—are described, and the species of each genus, illustrations of representatives of which are given, are enumerated and diagnosed. Figures are given of the following species: *Lipaugus unirufus, L. subalaris, L. rufescens,* ♂, ♀: *Furnarius torridus, Xipholena atropurpurea,* ♂. ♀: *Ptilogonys caudatus* ♂, ♀: *Vireolanius melitophrys, Vireolanius pulchellus,* ♂, ♀:

*Phlogopsis maclannani, Cinclocerthia ruficauda,
C. macrorhyncha, C. gutturalis, Accipiter ventralis, A. chionogaster, ♀; Rupicola sanguinolenta,
Porzana rubra, Accipiter erythrocnemis, A. castanilius, Cichlopsis leucogenys, Nyctibius bracteatus,
Oyphorhinus lawrencii, C. phaeocephalus, Troglodytes solstitialis, T. brunneicollis, Icterus pustulatus, ♂, ♀; Myiadestes obscurus, M. unicolor, M.
ralloides, ad. and young; M. elisabethae, Hylactes
castaneus, Œdicnemus superciliaris, Lanio aurantius, ♂, ♀; L. leucothorax, ♂, ♀; Tachyphonus
phoeniceus, ♂, ♀; T. delattrii, ♂, ♀; Xiphocolaptes emigrans, X. major, Accipiter chilensis, ♂,
♀; Leucopternis superciliaris, Geotrygon chiriquensis (ᴐ·albifacies), G. boucieri, Chlorophonia frontalis, C. longipennis, C. occipitalis, C. ; Melanotis hypoleucus, ad. and young; Tinamus robustus, Crypturus sallaei, ♂, ♀; C. boucardi, ♂, ♀;
C. meserythrus, Tigrisoma cabanisi, ad. and
young; Leucopternis palliata, Scops flammeola, S.
barbarus (in normal and abnormal plumages),
Chaetura semicollaris, Porzana hauxwelli (n. sp.),
P. melanophaea, P. albigularis ♂, ♀; P. leucopyrrha, Fulica ardesiaca, F. armillata, F. leucopyga, F. leucoptera, Leucopternis polionota,
Geotrygon chiriquensis, Cardinalis phoenicens ♂,
♀; Pyrgisoma rubricatum, P. leucotis, P. cabanisi,
P. kieneri, Oxyrhamphus frater, female ad. and
young; Thyrorhina schomburgki, Chlorophonia
callophrys, ♂, ♀; Accipiter bicolor, ♂ and ♀ jr.;
Turdus gigas, T. albicollis, T. leuconotus, T. crotopezus, T. albiventris, T. phaeopygus, ad. and jr.; T.
gymnophthalmus, Bucco striolatus, ♀; Porzana
castaneiceps, Attagis chimborazensis, Formicivora
strigilata, ♂, ♀; Conurus hoffmanni, Rallus antarcticus, Rallus semiplumbeus, Pitylus humeralis,
Accipiter guttatus, Ampelion arcuatus, ♂, ♀; Asturina nattereri, ♂ ad. and jr.; A. ruficauda, ad. and
jr.; A. pucherani, ad. and jr.; A. plagiata, ad. and
jr.; Botaurus pinnatus, Tigrisoma fasciatum,
imm.; Thripadectes flammulatus, Icterus abeillei,
♂, ♀; Centropelma (gen. nov.) micropterum, Centrites oreas, ♂, ♀; Gallinago imperialis, G. nobilis, Querquedula puna, and Merganetta turneri,
♂, ♀.*

13

Nomenclator Avium Neotropicalium
sive Avium quae in Regione Neotropica
hucusque repertae sunt nomina systematice disposita, adjecta sua cuique specei
patria: accedunt generum et specierum
novarum diagnoses. Auctoribus Philippo Lutley Sclater et Osberto Salvin.
Pp. i-viii, 1-163. Small folio, Londini,
1873.

A systematic list of the orders, families, genera
and species of the birds of the Neotropical
Region. Nine new genera, viz, *Uropelia, Phlogothraupis, Porphyrospiza, Clibanornis, Microbates,
Neocoleus, Gymnopelia, Nothoprocta*, and *Onlodromas*, and the following new species are described: *Basileuterus leucopygius, Hylophilus
muscicapinus, Cyclorhis albiventris, Chlorophanes
purpurascens, Euphonia chalcopasta, Chlorospingus semifuscus, Arremon wuchereri, Haplospiza
uniformis, Onipolegus pusillus, Euscarthmus
wuchereri, Serpophaga subflava, S. poecilocerca,
Phyllomyias platyrhyncha, Lipaugus immundus,
Casiornis fusca, Furnarius agnatus, Philydor
erythronotus, Margarornis stellata, Picolaptes
puncticeps, Thamnophilus tristis, Myrmotherula
pyrrhonota, Microbates torquatus, Cercomacra
carbonaria, Rhinocrypta fusca, Dendrocygna discolor, Querquedula andium, Leptoptila rufinucha,
Odontophorus hypospodius, Psophia napensis,
Tinamus ruficeps*, and *Nothoprocta curvirostris.*

14

**List of the Zoological Works and
Memoirs of P. L. Sclater, 1850-75.** Pp.
1-32, 8vo, London, 1876.

15

A Monograph of the Jacamars and Puffbirds, or families *Galbulidae* and *Buccon-*

ida. Pp. i-liv, 1-171, pls. i-lv, 4to, London, 1882.

A monograph of the *Galbulidae* and *Bucconidae*,
including general remarks on the families, their
structure, history, habits, classification and
geographical distribution, with descriptions and
synonyms of and notes on the genera and species.
Sixty-two species are enumerated, viz, *Urogalba
paradisea*, ♂; *U. amazonum, Galbula viridis*, ♂,
♀; *G. rufo-viridis*, ♂, ♀; *G. ruficauda*, ♂, ♀; *G.
melanogenia*, ♂, ♀; *G. tombacea*, ♂, ♀; *G. albirostris*, ♂, ♀; *G. cyanicollis*, ♂; *G. leucogastra*, ♂,
♀; *G. chalcothorax*, ♂; *Brachygalba lugubris*, ♂,
♀; *B. goeringi*, ♂; *B. salmoni, B. albigularis, B.
melanosterna*, ♂; *Jacamaralcyon tridactyla*, ♂;
Galbalcyrhynchus leucotis, ♂, ♀; *B. macrorhynchus
grandis*, ♂, ♀; *Bucco collaris*, ♂; *B. macrorhynchus
B. dysoni, B. hyperrhynchus, B. swainsoni, B. pectoralis, B. ordi, B. tectus, B. picatus, B. subtectus*, ♂;
B. macrodactylus, ♂; *B. ruficollis, B. bicinctus, B.
tamatia*, ♂; *B. pulmentum, B. maculatus, B. striatipectus, B. chacuru, B. striolatus*, ♀; *B. radiatus*, ♂,
♀; *Malacoptila fusca*, ♂; *M. rufa, M. torquata, M.
panamensis*, ♂, ♀; *M. inornata*, ♂, ♀; *M. fulvigularis, M. substriata, Micromonacha lanceolata, Nonnula rubecula, N. cineracea, N. ruficapilla, N. frontalis, N. brunnea, Hapaloptila castanea, Monacha
nigra, M. flavirostris, M. morphoeus, M. peruana, M.
grandior*, ♀; *M. pallescens, M. nigrifrons*, ♂; *Chelidoptera tenebrosa* (bird and egg), and *C.brasiliensis*.
All the above-named species are figured (in many
cases both sexes) except *Bucco picatus* and *Nonnula frontalis*. The genera treated of are *Urogalba, Galbula, Brachygalba, Jacamaralcyon, Galbalcyrhynchus, Jacamerops, Bucco, Malacoptila,
Micromonacha, Nonnula, Hapaloptila, Monacha*
and *Chelidoptera*.

16

**Forster's Catalogue of the Animals of
North America or Faunula Americana.**
[Reprint, by the Willughby Society.]
Edited by P. L. Sclater. Pp. i-iv, 1-
43, pl. 1, 8vo, London, 1882.

17

Forster's Animals of Hudson's Bay.
[Reprint, by the Willughby Society.]
Edited by P. L. Sclater. Pp. i-iv, 382-
433, 8vo, London, 1882.

18

**Wagler's Six Ornithological Memoirs
from the "Isis."** [Reprint, by the Willughby Society.] Edited by P. L. Sclater.
Pp. i-iv, 1-138, 8vo, London, 1884.

19

**Catalogue of the *Passeriformes*, or
Perching Birds, in the Collection of the
British Museum. *Fringilliformes.* Part
II, containing the families *Caerebidae*,
Tanagridae, and *Icteridae*.** Pp. i-xvii, 1-
431, pls. i-xviii, 8vo, London, 1886. (Cat.
Bds. Brit. Mus., Vol XI.)

A descriptive catalogue of the known species
(575 in number, referable to 100 genera, represented in the British Museum collection by 5,494
specimens) of the families *Caerebidae, Tanagridae*,
and *Icteridae*. Three new genera are proposed,
viz, *Pseudodacnis, Delothraupis*, and *Gymnostinops*, and the following new species are described:
*Dacnis salmoni, Thlypopsis amazonum, Arremon
nigrirostris*, and *Agelaeus forbesi*. Figures are
given of *Diglossa mystacalis, Conirostrum fraseri*,
♂; *Dacnis salmoni*, ♀; *D. cerebicolor*, ♂, ♀; *Chlorophanes purpurascens*, ♂; *Certhiola martinicana,
C. dominicana, Chlorophonia roraimae*, ♂; *C. flavirostris*, ♀; *Euphonia concinna*, ♂, ♀; *E. finschi*,
♂; *E. saturata*, ♂; *E. melanura*, ♂, ♀; *E. vittata*,
♂; *Phoenicothraupis gutturalis*, ♀; *Nemosia albigularis*, ♂, ♀; *Thlypopsis ornata*, ♂; *Chlorospingus
♂; Buarremon leucopis, B. comptus, B. tricolor,
Arremon wuchereri*, ♂, and *Icterus hauxwelli*.

20

Catalogue of the *Passeriformes*, or Perching Birds, in the Collection of the British Museum. *Oligomyodæ*, or the families *Tyrannidæ*, *Oxyrhamphidæ*, *Pipridæ*, *Cotingidæ*, *Phytotomidæ*, *Philepittidæ*, *Pittidæ*, *Xenicidæ*, and *Eurylæmidæ*. Pp. i-xix, 1–494, pls. i-xxvi, 8vo, London, 1888. (Cat. Bds. Brit. Mus., Vol. XIV.)

A descriptive catalogue of the known species of the above-mentioned families. The species enumerated are 665 in number, referred to 142 genera, and represented in the collection of the British Museum by 7,300 specimens, each one of which is catalogued with the locality whence it came. Three new genera are created, viz, *Ochthornis*, *Cænotriccus* and *Coracopitta*; the new term *Calopitta* is adopted for a section of *Pitta*; Bonaparte's MS. name *Lathriosoma* is published as a synonym of *Aulia*; Reichenbach's genus *Ilicura* is emended to *Helicura*, and the two species *Empidochanes salvini* and *Chloropipo holochlora* are described. The following species are figured: *Agriornis pollens*, *A. insolens*, *A. solitaria*, *Tænioptera holospodia*, *Ochthodiæta fusco-rufus*, *Ochthœca leucometopa*, *O. citrinifrons*, *O. pulchella*, *Platyrhynchus flavigularis*, *P. albigularis*, *Euscarthmus russatus*, *E. impiger*, *Leptopogon erythrops*, *Tyranniscus cinericeps*, *T. gracilipes*, *Elainea olivina*, *Rhynchocyclus fulvipectus*, *Sirystes albocinereus*, *Muscivora occidentalis*, ♂, ♀; *Onipodectes subbrunneus*, *Myiobius flavicans*, *M. roraimæ*, *Ceratopipra iracunda*, *Heteropelma wallacii*, *H. flavicapillum*, *H. igniceps*, *Heterocercus aurantiivertex*, *Hadrostomus homochrous*, ♂, ♀, *Pachyrhamphus spodiurus*, ♂, ♀, and *Iodopleura leucopygia*.

21

Argentine Ornithology. A descriptive catalogue of the Birds of the Argentine Republic. By P. L. Sclater, with notes on their habits by W. H. Hudson. Vol. I, pp. i-xxiv, 1–208, pls. i-x (1888); Vol. II, pp. i-xv, 1–251, pls. xi-xx (1889). Royal 8vo, London, 1888–89.

A history of the birds of the Argentine Republic, containing their descriptions, notes on their habits, and some of their synonyms. The total number of species assigned to the Argentine Avifauna is 434, of which the following are figured: *Mimus triurus*, *Cinclus schulzi*, *Cyclorhis ochrocephala*, *C. altirostris*, *Stephanophorus leucocephalus*, *Saltatricula multicolor*, *Molothrus badius*, *M. rufoaxillaris*, pull.; *Tænioptera rubetra*, *Phytotoma rutila*, ♂, ♀; *Homorus lophotes*, *Drymornis bridgesi*, *Chœtocercus burmeisteri*, *Hydropsalis furcifera*, *Coccyzus cinereus*, *Conurus molinæ*, *Bolborhynchus aymara*, *Buteo swainsoni*, *Ardetta involucris*, *Cygnus nigricollis*, *Rallus maculatus*, and *Nothura darwini*. Lists are appended of the principal authorities upon the Ornithology of the Argentine Republic, and the principal localities mentioned in the work where collections were made.

22

Catalogue of the *Passeriformes*, or Perching Birds, in the Collection of the British Museum. *Trachcophonæ*, or the families *Dendrocolaptidæ*, *Formicariidæ*, *Conopophagidæ*, and *Pteroptochidæ*. Pp. i-xvii, 1–371, pls. i-xx, 8vo, London, 1890. (Cat. Bds. Brit. Mus., Vol. XV.)

A descriptive catalogue of the known species of the above-mentioned families, embracing 531 species, referred to 92 genera, represented in the collection of the British Museum by 4,482 specimens. The genus *Thamnocharis* and the two species *Cercomacra hypomelæna* and *Liosccles erithacus* are described as new. The following species are figured: *Geositta crassirostris*, *Furnarius torridus*, *Synallaxis adusta*, *Siptornis suberistata* (*Synallaxis suberistata* on plate), *Phacelodomus ruppennis*, *Automolus holostictus*, *A. rubidus*, *Philydor erythronotus*, *P. consobrinus*, *Dendrornis polystictus*, *Thamnophilus æthiops*, ♂, ♀; *T. nigriceps*, *T. insignis*, ♂, ♀; *T. albinuchalis*, ♂. ♀; *Myrmotherula erythrura*, ♂. ♀; *Hypocnemis lepidonota*, ♂, ♀, *Grallaria haplonota*, *G. erythrotis*, *G. rufo-cinerea*, and *G. fulviventris*.

23

The Geographical Distribution of Birds; an address delivered before the Second International Ornithological Congress at Budapest, May, 1891. Pp. 1–45, 8vo, Budapest, 1891.

An address on the recent advances in our knowledge of the geographical distribution of birds, being a review of the principal additions made to the literature of geographical ornithology since 1875.

(See paper No. 1128.)

24

Catalogue of the Picariæ in the Collection of the British Museum. *Scansores* and *Coccyges*, containing the families *Rhamphastidæ*, *Galbulidæ*, and *Bucconidæ*. 8vo, London, 1891. (Cat. Bds. Brit. Mus., XIX, pp. 122–208, pls. vi-x.)

A descriptive catalogue of the known species of *Rhamphastidæ*, *Galbulidæ* and *Bucconidæ*, comprising 18 genera and 123 species, represented in the national collection by 1,335 specimens. Each specimen is catalogued with the locality where it was obtained. *Brachygalba fulviventris* is described as a new species, and the following species are figured: *Pteroglossus didymus*, *Aulacorhamphus erythrognathus*, *A. calorhynchus*, *A. whitelyanus*, and *A. cyanolæmus*.

25

A new List of Chilian Birds. Compiled by the late Harry Berkeley James, with a preface by P. L. Sclater. Pp. i-vii, 1–15, royal 8vo, London, 1892.

A list of 255 species and their native names, by the late H. B. James, with a preface containing an obituary notice of the author by Mr. Sclater.

26

The Book of Antelopes. By P. L. Sclater and Oldfield Thomas. Illustrated by Joseph Wolf and J. Smit. Part I, pp. 1–57, 4to, 1895.

An illustrated monograph of the antelopes, including their synonymy, characters, history, and habits. The species treated of are: *Bubalis busiaphus*, *B. major*, *B. tora*, *B. swaynei*, *B. cokei*, *B. caama*, *B. jacksoni*, *B. lichtensteini*, and *Damaliscus hunteri*. The following species are figured: *Bubalis busilaphus*, *B. swaynei*, *B. cokei*, *B. caama*, *B. lichtensteini*, and *Damaliscus hunteri*. Part I includes the genera *Bubalis* and *Damaliscus*.

(For list of publications subsequent to December, 1894, see APPENDIX.)

PART II.

A CHRONOLOGICAL CATALOGUE OF PAPERS PUBLISHED IN THE MEMOIRS, PROCEEDINGS AND JOURNALS OF LEARNED SOCIETIES, AND OTHER PERIODICALS.

27
Note on the Water Rail.

Zoologist, II, 1844, p. 669.

Note on the Water Rail (*Rallus aquaticus*) breeding near Odiham, in Hampshire.

28
Marten killed in Wales.

Zoologist, III, 1845, p. 1018.

Note on a specimen of the Marten Cat (*Martes foina*) taken in a trap near Odiham, Hampshire, with reference to a specimen killed in Wales by a pack of hounds.

29
Arrival of Summer Birds near Odiham in 1845.

Zoologist, III, 1845, p. 1067.

A list of 9 migratory birds, with dates of their arrival near Odiham in the summer of 1845.

30
Occurrence of Aquatic Birds near Odiham.

Zoologist, III, 1845, p. 1077.

Note on the occurrence near Odiham of *Oidemia nigra*, *Chenalopex ægyptiacus* and *Anas sponsa*.

31
Early appearance of the Tufted Duck.

Zoologist, IV, 1846, p. 1214.

Note on a specimen of the Tufted Duck (*Fuligula cristata*) shot on the Ichen, in Hampshire, on October 13, 1845.

32
Occurrence of Sabine's Snipe in Hampshire.

Zoologist, IV, 1846, p. 1300.

Note on the occurrence of a specimen of Sabine's Snipe (*Scolopax sabini*) near Basingstoke.

33
Description of an apparently new species of *Calliste*.

Contr. to Ornithology, 1850, p. 50.

Calliste chrysonota is described.

34
On some new species of *Calliste*.

Contr. to Ornithology, 1851. pp. 21-25, pl. lxix.

Calliste virescens (p. 22, pl. lxix, fig. 1), *C. xanthogastra* (p. 23) and *C. chrysophrys* (p. 24, pl. lxix, fig. 2) are described, and a description of *C. punctata* (Linn.) is also given.

35
Synopsis of the Tanagrine genus *Calliste*.

Contr. to Ornithology, 1851, pp. 49-69, pl. lxx.

Characters are given of 48 species of *Calliste*, of which the following are described as new: *Calliste castaneoventris*, *C. ruficapilla*, *C. lunigera*, *C. lamprotis*, *C. cœlicolor*, *C. leucotis* and *C. castanonota*. *C. icterocephala* and *C. lunigera* are figured.

36
Synopsis of the genus *Euphonia*, with descriptions of new species.

Contr. to Ornithology, 1851, pp. 81-92, pl. lxxv.

Twenty-three species of the genus *Euphonia* are characterized, of which the following are described as new: *Euphonia melanura*, *E. frontalis* (Bp. MS.), and *E. pyrrhophrys*. The last-named species and *E. nigricollis* are figured. Three other species of doubtful status are considered.

37
Remarks on the Prince of Canino's "Note sur les Tangaras."

Contr. to Ornithology, 1851, pp. 93-96.

Observations to correct what appear to be errors in the synonymy of the paper. The generic names *Euschemon* and *Euprepiste* are proposed, and *Chlorophonia* is emended to *Chloreuphonia*.

38
On the genus *Tanagrella*, Swainson.

Contr. to Ornithology, 1851, pp. 97, 98, pl. lxxiv.

Remarks on the three species, *T. velia*, *T. cyanomelas* and *T. calophrys*, of which *T. calophrys* is figured.

39
On the genus *Chlorochrysa*, Bp.

Contr. to Ornithology, 1851, pp. 99-101, pl. lxxiii.

C. calliparæa and *C. phœnicotis* are remarked upon and figured.

40
On the genus *Dacnis*, Cuvier, with description of a new species.

Contr. to Ornithology, 1851, pp. 105-110.

A synopsis of the genus *Dacnis*. Six species are enumerated, of which *D. cærebicolor* is described as new, and remarks are added upon other species of doubtful status.

41

On a new species of Manakin.

Contr. to Ornithology, 1851, p. 143.

Pipra flavicollis is described.

42

On two new species of Birds of the genus *Tænioptera*. .

Proc. Zool. Soc. London, 1851, pp. 193, 194, pls. xli, xlii.

Tænioptera erythropygia and *T. striaticollis* are described and figured.

(See *Proc. Zool. Soc. London*, 1855, p. 77.)

43

Synopsis of the genus *Galbula*.

Contr. to Ornithology, 1852, pp. 29–33.

A synopsis of the genus *Galbula* ; eleven species are enumerated, of which *G. maculicauda* and *G. inornata* are described as new.

(See also *Contr. to Ornithology*, 1852, pp. 61, 93, and paper No. 1.)

44

On a new species of the genus *Nigrita*.

Contr. to Ornithology, 1852, p. 34, pl. lxxxiii.

Nigrita bicolor is described and figured.

45

On a new species of *Galbula*.

Contr. to Ornithology, 1852, p. 61.

G. melanogenia is described.

(See also *Contr. to Ornithology*, 1852, pp. 29, 93, and paper No. 1.)

46

Further remarks on the *Galbulidæ*.

Contr. to Ornithology, 1852, pp. 93–95, pl. xc.

Notes on the genera of the family *Galbulidæ*. *Galbula melanogenia* is figured.

(See also *Contr. to Ornithology*, 1852, pp. 29, 61, and paper No. 1.)

47

On certain species of *Dacnis*.

Contr. to Ornithology, 1852, pp. 101, 102, pl. xciii.

Observations on *D. speciosa* (which is figured as *D. analis*) and *D. plumbea*. *D. cœrebicolor* is also figured.

48

List of a collection of Birds made by James Daubeny, esq., on the coasts of the Red Sea in 1851.

Contr. to Ornithology, 1852, pp. 123–126.

A catalogue of 76 species, with critical remarks upon some of them.

49

Description de six Oiseaux nouveaux appartenant à la collection du Muséum d'Histoire Naturelle de Paris.

Rev. et Mag. de Zool., 1852, pp. 8, 9.

Arremon mysticalis, *Pipilopsis flavigularis*, *Pipræidea albiventris*, *Pipra iridorei*, *P. flavicapilla* and *P. pyrocephala* are described.

50

Description d'une nouvelle espèce de *Cotinga* provenant de l'expédition de MM. Castelnau et Deville dans l'Amerique du Sud. Par E. Deville et P. L. Sclater.

Rev. et Mag. de Zool., 1852, pp. 226, 227.

Cotinga porphyrolæma is described.

51

Description of some new species of Birds from the Parisian collections.

Contr. to Ornithology, 1852, pp. 129–132, pls. xcvi-c.

Reprint of the two preceding papers. Figures are given of the following species: *Cotinga porphyrolæma*, *Arremon mysticalis*, *Pipilopsis flavigularis*, *Pipræidea albiventris*, *Pipra iridorei*, *P. flavicapilla* and *P. pyrocephala*.

52

List of a collection of Birds procured by Mr. C. T. Andersson in the Damara country in southwestern Africa, with notes. By H. E. Strickland and P. L. Sclater.

Contr. to Ornithology, 1852, pp. 141–160.

A list of 111 species, with remarks upon them. Fourteen new species are described by Strickland, and one by Sclater, viz., *Sphenœacus pycnopygius*.

53

On two new species of South American Birds.

Proc. Zool. Soc. London, 1852, p. 34, pls. xlvii, xlviii.

Culicivora boliviana and *Pipra flavo-tincta* are described and figured.

54

On a new species of *Dendrocolaptes*.

Proc. Zool. Soc. London, 1853, pp. 68, 69, pl. lii.

Dendrocolaptes eytoni is described and figured.

55

Descriptions of new species of *Bucconidæ*.

Proc. Zool. Soc. London, 1853, pp. 122–124, pls. l, li.

A new generic name, *Nonnula*, is proposed, and the following new species are described: *Bucco radiatus*, *B. striatipectus*, *Malacoptila fulvogularis*, *M. substriata* and *M. aspersa*. *Bucco radiatus* and *Malacoptila substriata* are figured.

56

Description de deux nouvelles espèces d'Oiseaux.

Rev. et Mag. de Zoologie, 1853. p. 480.

Dacnis pulcherrima and *Formicivora ornata* are described.

57

Note sur deux nouvelles espèces du genre Momot (*Momotus*).

Rev. et Mag. de Zoologie, 1853, pp. 489, 490.

Momotus semirufus and *M. subrufescens* are described.

58

Characters of some new or imperfectly described species of Tanagers.

Proc. Zool. Soc. London, 1854, pp. 95–98, pls. lxiv, lxv.

The following species are characterized: *Arremon axillaris*, *Ramphocelus dorsalis*, Bp. MS., *Buthraupis chloronota*, *Euphonia concinna* and *E. hirundinacea*, Bp. *Buthraupis chloronota*, *Euphonia concinna* and *E. hirundinacea* are figured.

59

List of a collection of birds received by Mr. Gould from the Province of Quijos, in the Republic of Ecuador.

Proc. Zool. Soc. London, 1854, pp. 109–115, pls. lxvi, lxvii.

A list of 69 species, with remarks upon them. The following species are described as new: *Gal-*

bula chalcothorax, Tyrannula phœnicura, and *Arremon spectabilis. Tyrannula phœnicura, T. ornata,* and *Arremon spectabilis* are figured.

60

Descriptions of two new Tanagers in the British Museum.

Proc. Zool. Soc. London, 1854, pp. 157, 158, pls. lxviii, lxix.

Chlorospingus melanotis and *Tachyphonus xanthopygius* are described and figured.

61

Description of a new Tanager of the genus *Calliste.*

Proc. Zool. Soc. London, 1854, p. 248.

Calliste venusta is described.

62

Description of a second species of the genus *Procnias.*

Proc. Zool. Soc. London, 1854, p. 249.

Procnias occidentalis is described.

63

On two new species of *Dacnis,* and on the general arrangement of the genus.

Proc. Zool. Soc. London, 1854, pp. 251, 252.

Dacnis hartlaubi and *D. egregia* are described, and a list of the species of *Dacnis* is given.

64

Descriptions of six new species of Birds of the subfamily *Formicariinæ.*

Proc. Zool. Soc. London, 1854, pp. 253-255, pls. lxx-lxxiv.

Myrmeciza leucaspis, M. margaritata, Hypocnemis melanolæma, H. melanosticta, Formicivora caudata and *Pithys erythrophrys* are described and figured.

65

On a new species of Tanager in the British Museum.

Ann. and Mag. Nat. Hist., ser. 2, XIII, pp. 24, 25 (1854).

Remarks on the three known species of *Phœnicothraupis,* of which *P. gutturalis* is described as new.

66

A synopsis of the Fissirostral family *Bucconidæ.*

Ann. and Mag. Nat. Hist., ser. 2, XIII, pp. 353-305, 474-484 (1854).

A review of the species of the family *Bucconidæ. Malacoptila frontalis* is described as new. The genera treated of are: *Bucco, Malacoptila, Monasa* and *Chelidoptera.*

(Also printed separately with plates added. See paper No. 3.)

67

List of Birds exposed for sale in the market at Rome in January, 1853.

Zoologist, 1854, pp. 4160-4164.

An annotated list of birds exposed for sale in the Piazza della Rotonda, Rome.

68

On the genus *Culicivora* of Swainson and its component species.

Proc. Zool. Soc. London, 1855, pp. 11, 12.

The generic term *Polioptila* is proposed in the place of *Culicivora,* and the four known species of the genus are characterized.

69

Remarks on the arrangement of the Jacamars (*Galbulidæ*), with descriptions of some new species.

Proc. Zool. Soc. London, 1855, pp. 13-16, pl. lxxvii.

Additional information concerning the arrangement of the *Galbulidæ* and descriptions of the following new species: *Galbula fuscicapilla, Urogalba amazonum,* and *Brachygalba melanosterna,* the first named of which is figured. A table showing the distribution of the 20 known species is appended.

(See *Contr. to Ornithology,* 1852, pp. 29, 61, 93, and paper No. 1.)

70

Characters of six new species of the genus *Thamnophilus.*

Proc. Zool. Soc. London, 1855, pp. 18, 19, pls. lxxix-lxxxii.

Thamnophilus transandeanus, T. leuchauchen, T. albinuchalis, T. melanonotus, T. nigrocinereus and *T. cæsius* are described. *T. leuchauchen, T. melanonotus, T. nigrocinereus* and *T. cæsius* are figured.

71

Note on the sixteen species of Texan Birds named by Mr. Giraud, of New York, in 1841.

Proc. Zool. Soc. London, 1855, pp. 65, 66.

Critical remarks on the species described in Mr. J. P. Giraud's work, "Descriptions of sixteen new species of North American birds, collected in Texas, 1838." New York, 1841. Folio.

72

On a new species of the genus *Todirostrum* of Lesson.

Proc. Zool. Soc. London, 1855, pp. 66, 67, pl. lxxxiv.

Todirostrum nigriceps is described and figured. *T. spiciferum,* Lafr., is also figured, and notes are added on other species of the genus.

73

On some new or little-known species of Birds in the Derby Museum at Liverpool.

Proc. Zool. Soc. London, 1855, pp. 74-77, pls. lxxxv-lxxxviii.

Remarks on the new and rare species in the Derby Museum. The following new species are described and figured: *Conirostrum ferrugineiventre, Synallaxis erythrothorax, Ramphocænus cinereiventris,* and *Cyphorinus albigularis.* A list of the known species of *Conirostrum* is given.

74

Descriptions of four new or little-known Tanagers.

Proc. Zool. Soc. London, 1855, pp. 83-85, pls. lxxxix-xcii.

Descriptions and figures are given of *Arremon erythrorhynchus* (n. sp.), *Tachyphonus xanthopygius, Tanagra notabilis,* and *Saltator arremonops.*

75

Descriptions of some new species of Ant Thrushes (*Formicariinæ*) from Santa Fé di Bogota.

Proc. Zool. Soc. London, 1855, pp. 88-90, pls. xciv-xcvii.

The generic name *Psilorhamphus* is proposed in the place of *Leptorhynchus,* Ménét. The following species are described: *Grallaria hypoleuca, G. modesta, Chamæza mollissima, Formicivora callinota, Dysithamnus semicinereus,* and *Pyriglena tyrannina.* All except *Grallaria hypoleuca* are figured.

76

Descriptions of some new species of Birds from Santa Fé di Bogota.

Proc. Zool. Soc. London, 1855, pp. 109, 110, pls. xcix–cii.

Descriptions and figures are given of the following species: *Nemosia albigularis*, *Pyriglena ellisiana*, *Anthus bogotensis*, and *Otocorys peregrina*.

77

On the Birds received in collections from Santa Fé di Bogota.

Proc. Zool. Soc. London, 1855, pp. 131–164, pls. ciii, civ.

A list of 435 species, with remarks upon some of them. The name *Heteroenemis* is proposed in the place of Strickland's genus *Holocnemis*, and the species *Heteroenemis marginata* and *Todirostrum gracilipes* are described as new. *Vireolanius icterophrys* and *Ampelion cinctus* are figured.

(See also *Proc. Zool. Soc. London*, 1856, p. 25; 1857, p. 15.)

78

Characters of some apparently new species of *Bucconidæ*, accompanied by a Geographical Table of the Family.

Proc. Zool. Soc. London, 1855, pp. 193–196, pls. cv, cvi.

The following species are characterized and remarked upon: *Bucco hyperrhynchus* (Bp.), *B. dysoni*, Gray, MS.; *B. pulmentum* (Bp. et Verr. MS.), *Monasa peruana*, Bp. et Verr. MS.; *Bucco picatus*, sp. nov., and *Malacoptila nigrifusca*, sp. nov. *B. hyperrhynchus* and *B. pulmentum* are figured. A geographical table of the *Bucconidæ* is added.

79

Note on the genus *Legriocinclus*, Lesson, and its synonyms.

Proc. Zool. Soc. London, 1855, pp. 212–214.

Remarks on the genus *Legriocinclus*, with a list of its synonyms, and adoption of the name *Cinclocerthia* in its stead.

80

Description of a newly discovered Tanager of the genus *Buarremon*.

Proc. Zool. Soc. London, 1855, p. 214, pl. cix.

Buarremon leucopterus (Jard.) is characterized and figured.

81

Characters of two new species of Tanagers.

Proc. Zool. Soc. London, 1855, pp. 227, 228, pl. cx.

Lesson's name *Iridosornis* is emended to *Iridornis*, and the species *Dubusia auricrissa* and *Iridornis porphyrocephala* are described; the latter is figured.

82

A draft arrangement of the genus *Thamnophilus*, Vieillot.

Edinburgh New Phil. Jour., n s., I, pp. 226–249 (1855).

Descriptions of and remarks upon 39 species of *Thamnophilus*, of which *T. ventralis* and *T. maculipennis* are described as new.

83

Note on the Zoological Appendix to the Report of the U. S. Naval Astronomical Expedition to the Southern Hemisphere, and on the Geographic Range and distribution of the Tanagrine Genera *Calliste* and *Euphonia*.

Proc. Zool. Soc. London, 1856, pp. 18, 19.

Note on the correct habitat of *Calliste cyaneicollis*, *C. gyroloides*, and *Euphonia rufiventris*, together with a table showing the geographical distribution of the genus *Calliste*.

84

On some additional species of Birds received in collections from Bogota.

Proc. Zool. Soc. London, 1856, pp. 25–31, pls. cxvi–cxix.

A list of, and remarks upon. 23 additional species from Bogota. The following new species are described: *Synallaxis elegans*, *S. mœsta*. *Anabates erythropterus*, *Margarornis brunnescens*, *Orthoëca fumicolor*, *Euscarthmus agilis*, *Pipra coracina*, Verr. MS.; *Conopophaga cucullata*, *Chlorospingus xanthophrys*, *C. lichtensteini*, *Gallinago nobilis*, and *Rallus semiplumbeus*. Figures are given of *Margarornis brunnescens*, *Orthoëca fumicolor*, *Euscarthmus agilis*, and *Conopophaga cucullata*.

(See also *Proc. Zool. Soc. London*, 1855, p. 131; 1857, p. 15.)

85

Note on *Psaltria flaviceps*, a third American species of the Parine genus *Psaltria*.

Proc. Zool. Soc. London, 1856, pp. 37, 38.

Ægithalus flaviceps of Sundevall is here referred to the genus *Psaltria*.

86

Synopsis Avium Tanagrinarum. A descriptive catalogue of the known species of Tanagers. Part I.

Proc. Zool. Soc. London, 1856, pp. 64–94.

Part I contains the following genera: *Pitylus*, *Orchesticus*, *Diucopis*, *Saltator*, *Psittospiza*, *Lamprospiza*, *Cissopsis*, *Oreothraupis*, *Arremon*, *Phœnicophilus*, *Buarremon* and *Chlorospingus*.

Two new generic names are proposed: *Oreothraupis* and *Carenochrous* (a new sectional name of *Buarremon*), and the following new species are described: *Arremon d'orbignii*, *A. devillii*, *Buarremon phæopleurus*, and *Chlorospingus flaviventris*.

86 a

Synopsis Avium Tanagrinarum. A descriptive catalogue of the known species of Tanagers. Part II.

Proc. Zool. Soc. London, 1856, pp. 108–132.

Part II contains the following genera: *Pyrrhocoma*, *Nemosia*, *Cypsnagra*, *Tachyphonus*, *Trichothraupis*, *Eucometis*, *Lanio*, *Phœnicothraupis*, *Lamprotes*, *Orthogonys*, *Pyranga* and *Ramphocelus*.

The generic name *Eucometis* is proposed, and the following new species are described: *Nemosia guirina*, *N. insignis*, *N. auricollis*, and *Ramphocelus unicolor*.

86 b

Synopsis Avium Tanagrinarum. A descriptive catalogue of the known species of Tanagers. Part III.

Proc. Zool. Soc. London, 1856, pp. 230–281.

Part III embraces the following genera: *Spindalis*, *Tanagra*, *Dubusia*, *Compsocoma*, *Buthraupis*, *Stephanophorus*, *Pœcilothraupis*, *Iridornis*, *Calliste*, *Diva*, *Pipridea*, *Chlorochrysa*, *Tanagrella*, *Glossiptila*, *Chlorophonia* and *Euphonia*.

The new generic term *Glossiptila* is proposed; Swainson's genus *Pipræidea* is emended to *Pipridea*, and the following new species are described: *Calliste vieilloti*, *C. cyanescens*, *Pipridea venezuelensis*, *Euphonia fulvicrissa*, and *E. crassirostris*. A table showing the geographical distribution of the *Tanagridæ* is subjoined. Altogether 272 species of Tanagers are treated in this and the two preceding papers.

(The Synopsis Avium Tanagrinarum as a whole was also printed separately. See paper No. 4.)

87

Note on *Buglodytes albicilius*.

Proc. Zool. Soc. London, 1856, p. 97.

Remarks on *Buglodytes albicilius*, Bp., and its synonyms.

88

On some new or imperfectly known species of *Synallaxis*.

Proc. Zool. Soc. London, 1856, pp. 97-99.

Synallaxis ruficapilla, Vieill.; *S. spixi*, and *S. caniceps*, spp. nn., are characterized and remarked upon.

89

List of Mammals and Birds collected by Mr. Bridges in the vicinity of the town of David, in the Province of Chiriqui, in the State of Panama.

Proc. Zool. Soc. London, 1856, pp. 138-143.

Five species of mammals and 46 species of birds are enumerated and remarks made upon them. Two new birds are described, viz. *Thamnophilus bridgesi* and *Geotrygon chiriquensis*. The name *Aglaia fanny*, Lafr. (*Calliste fanny*, Gray) is changed to *Calliste franciscæ*.

90

Note on some Birds from the Island of Ascension.

Proc. Zool. Soc. London, 1856, pp. 144, 145.

A list of six species with remarks upon them.

91

On the species of the American genus *Parra*.

Proc. Zool. Soc. London, 1856, pp. 282, 283.

The characters are given of five species of the genus *Parra*, two of which are new, viz. *P. intermedia* (Verr. MS.), and *P. melanopygia*.

92

Catalogue of the Birds collected by M. Auguste Sallé in southern Mexico, with descriptions of new species.

Proc. Zool. Soc. London, 1856, pp. 283-311, pls. cxx, cxxi.

A list of 233 species, with remarks upon them. The following species are described as new: *Certhiola mexicana*, *Anabates rubiginosus*, *A. cervinigularis*, *Anabazenops variegaticeps*, *Xenops mexicanus*, *Sclerurus mexicanus*, *Scytalopus prostheleucus*, *Parus meridionalis*, *Formicarius moniliger*, *Todirostrum cinereigulare*, *Muscivora mexicana*, *Tyrannula sulphureipyga*, *Elainea variegata*, *Pipra mentalis*, and *Myiadestes unicolor*. *Phæthornis adolphi* is adopted for Sallé's MS. name *Pygmornis adolphi*. *Granatellus sallæi* and *Pipra mentalis* are figured.

(See also *Proc. Zool. Soc. London*, 1857, pp. 81, 201, 226; 1858, p. 294.)

93

On a new Tanager of the genus *Calliste*.

Proc. Zool. Soc. London, 1856, p. 311.

Calliste rufigenis is described.

94

Descriptions of eight new species of Birds from South America.

Ann. and Mag. Nat. Hist., ser. 2, XVII, pp. 466-470 (1856).

The characters are given of a new genus (*Diglossopis*) and eight new species viz. *Synallaxis castanea*, *Diglossopis cærulescens*, *Diglossa indigotica*, Verr. MS.; *Anabates infuscatus*, *A. lineaticeps*, *Myiadestes venezuelensis*, *Pipreola melanolæma*, and *Chiroxiphia regina* (Natt. MS.).

95

Description of a new species of Tanager of the genus *Saltator*.

Proc. Acad. Nat. Sci. Phila., 1856, p. 261.

Saltator atripennis is described.

96

Characters of an apparently undescribed Bird belonging to the genus *Campylorhynchus*, of Spix, with remarks upon other species of the same group.

Proc. Acad. Nat. Sci. Phila., 1856, pp. 263-265.

Campylorhynchus humilis is described and a list of the species of the genus *Campylorhynchus* given.

97

The Palombière of Bagnères de Bigorre.

Zoologist, 1856, pp. 4943, 4944.

An account of the method of capturing pigeons at Bagnères de Bigorre in the Department of the Hautes-Pyrénées, France.

98

Notes on the Birds in the Museum of the Academy of Natural Sciences of Philadelphia and other collections in the United States of America.

Proc. Zool. Soc. London, 1857, pp. 1-8.

Notes on the specimens of birds observed during a visit to several museums in the United States. The new genus *Neocorys* is proposed for the reception of *Alauda spraguei* of Audubon, and *Glaucidium californicum* is suggested as the name of a new species of Owl. *Icterus wagleri* is described.

99

Further additions to the list of Birds received in collections from Bogota.

Proc. Zool. Soc. London, 1857, pp. 15-20.

An additional list of 52 species from Bogota, with remarks upon them. *Anabates striaticollis*, Lafr. MS., and *Sclerurus brunneus* are described as new.

(See also *Proc. Zool. Soc. London*, 1855, p. 131; 1856, p. 25.)

100

Characters of some apparently new species of American Ant Thrushes.

Proc. Zool. Soc. London, 1857, pp. 46-48.

The following new species are described: *Formicarius trivittatus*, *Conopophaga castaneiceps*, *Hypocnemis elegans*, *Myrmeciza hemimelæna*, and *Formicivora hæmatonota*.

101

Description of a new Tanager of the genus *Euphonia*.

Proc. Zool. Soc. London, 1857, p. 66, pl. cxxiv.

Euphonia gouldi is described and figured.

102

Review of the species of the South American subfamily *Tityrinæ*.

Proc. Zool. Soc. London, 1857, pp. 67-80.

A synopsis of the species (22 in number) of *Tityrinæ*, embracing the genera *Tityra* and *Pachyramphus*. *Pachyramphus albo-griseus* is described as new. A table showing the geographical distribution of the species is appended. The text is illustrated.

103

On *Parus meridionalis* and some other species mentioned in the Catalogue of

Birds collected by M. Sallé in southern Mexico.

Proc. Zool. Soc. London, 1857, pp. 81, 82.

Notes made on M. Sallé's collection from Mexico after comparison with other specimens from the same locality.

(See also *Proc. Zool. Soc. London*, 1856, p. 283.)

104

On three new species of the genus *Todirostrum*.

Proc. Zool. Soc. London, 1857, pp. 82–84, pl. cxxv.

Todirostrum calopterum, T. capitale, and *T. exile* are described and figured. A list of the known species of *Todirostrum* is given.

105

List of Birds collected by Mr. Thomas Bridges, corresponding member of the Society, in the Valley of San José, in the State of California.

Proc. Zool. Soc. London, 1857, pp. 125–127.

A list of 33 species, with remarks upon some of them. The name *Glaucidium californicum* is adopted for *G. infuscatum*, Cassin.

106

Note on the Upland Goose.

Proc. Zool. Soc. London, 1857, p. 128.

Note pointing out that *Chloephaga magellanica* is the correct name for the true "Upland Goose."

(See also *Proc. Zool. Soc. London*, 1858, p. 289.)

107

Descriptions of twelve new or little-known species of the South American Family *Formicariidæ*.

Proc. Zool. Soc. London, 1857, pp. 129–133, pl. cxxvi.

Characters are given of the following species: *Grallaria ferrugineipectus, G. loricata, Hypocnemis melanopogon, Formicivora melana, F. urosticta, F. hauxwelli, F. cinerascens, Herpsilochmus pectoralis*, and *Thamnophilus melanothorax* (nn. spp.), *Formicivora brevicauda*, Sw., *Dysithamnus xanthopterus*, Burm., and *Thamnophilus melanoceps*, Spix. *Formicivora urosticta* and *F. hauxwelli* are figured.

108

List of additional species of Mexican Birds obtained by M. Auguste Sallé from the environs of Jalapa and S. Andres Tuxtla.

Proc. Zool. Soc. London, 1857, pp. 201–207.

An additional list of 62 species obtained by M. Sallé in Mexico, with notes on many of them. *Camptostoma imberbe* (gen. et spec. nov.) is described. Figure in text.

(See also *Proc. Zool. Soc. London*, 1856, p. 283; 1857, pp. 81, 226; 1858, p. 294.)

109

On a collection of Birds made by Signor Matteo Botteri in the vicinity of Orizaba in Southern Mexico.

Proc. Zool. Soc. London, 1857, pp. 210–215.

A list of 38 species, with remarks upon them. *Neochloe brevipennis*, gen. et sp. nov., and *Zonotrichia botterii*, sp. nov., are described.

110

Notes on an unnamed Parrot from the Island of Santo Domingo, now living in

the Society's Gardens; and on some other species of the same family.

Proc. Zool. Soc. London, 1857, pp. 224–226, pl. cxxvii.

Chrysotis sallæi is proposed as the name for a new species of Parrot, and remarks are made on other species of *Psittaci*. The new genus *Polychlorus* is proposed for the reception of *Psittacus polychlorus*, Scopoli, and *Psittacodis westermanni*, Bp.

111

On a collection of Birds received by M. Sallé from southern Mexico.

Proc. Zool. Soc. London, 1857, pp. 226–230.

Remarks on a third list, consisting of 29 species, obtained by M. Sallé from Mexico. *Diplopterus excellens* is described as new.

(See also *Proc. Zool. Soc. London*, 1856, p. 283; 1857, pp. 81, 201; 1858, p. 294.)

112

Review of the species of the Fissirostral Family *Momotidæ*.

Proc. Zool. Soc. London, 1857, pp. 248–260, pl. cxxviii.

The family name *Momotidæ* is proposed instead of that of *Prionitidæ*, Illiger. A synopsis of the family is given, with descriptions of two new genera, viz, *Prionirhynchus* and *Eumomota*, and two new species, *Momotus microstephanus* and *M. nattereri*. A table of the geographical distribution of the family is added. *Prionirhynchus carinatus* is figured. The genera included are *Momotus, Hylomanes, Prionirhynchus* and *Eumomota*.

113

On a collection of Birds transmitted by Mr. H. W. Bates from the Upper Amazon.

Proc. Zool. Soc. London, 1857, pp. 261–268.

An annotated catalogue of 79 species, of which *Eubucco aurantiicollis* is described as new.

114

Descriptions of eleven new species of Birds from Tropical America.

Proc. Zool. Soc. London, 1857, pp. 271–277, pl. cxxx.

The genus *Melanoptila* (illustrated in text) and the following new species are characterized: *Campylorhynchus pardus, C. striaticollis, Anabazenops guttulatus, Synallaxis multo-striata, Turdus fulviventris* (Verr. MS.). *T. ignobilis, Cinclus leuconotus, Tyrannus atrifrons, Melanoptila glabrirostris, Lipaugus rufescens*, and *Tinamus castaneus. Anabazenops guttulatus* is figured.

115

Notes on Californian Birds. By Thomas Bridges, corresponding member. Communicated, with remarks by Philip Lutley Sclater.

Proc. Zool. Soc. London, 1858, pp. 1–3, pl. cxxxi.

Notes on 11 species. *Melanerpes rubrigularis* (described in *Ann. and Mag. Nat. Hist.*, ser. 3, I, p. 127, 1858) is figured.

(See paper No. 135.)

116

Notes on a collection of Birds received by M. Verreaux, of Paris, from the Rio Napo in the Republic of Ecuador.

Proc. Zool. Soc. London, 1858, pp. 59–77, pl. cxxxii.

A list of 174 species, with remarks upon them. Three new genera—*Agathopus; Creurgops*, Verr. MS.; *Euchætes*, Verr. MS.;—and the following new species are characterized: *Anabates melanopezus*, *A. pulvericolor* (Lafr. MS.), *Synallaxis brunneicaudalis* (Lafr. MS.), *S. albigularis* (Lafr. MS.), *Malacocichla maculata*, (Verr. MS.), *Thamnophilus æthiops*, *T. capitalis*, *Dysithamnus leucostictus*, *Pyriglena serva*, *Heterocnemis albigularis*, *Conopophaga torrida*, *Grallaria flavirostris*, *G. fulviventris*, *Todirostrum picatum*, *Cyclorhynchus œquinoctialis*, *Platyrhynchus coronatus*, Verr. MS.; *Elania luteiventris*, *Agathopus micropterus*, *Creurgops verticalis*, Verr. MS.; *Euchætes coccineus*, Verr. MS., and *Coleopicus verreauxi*, Malh. *Euchætes coccineus* and *Creurgops verticalis* are figured.

117

Notes on some Birds of southern Mexico.

Proc. Zool. Soc. London, 1858, pp. 95–99.

Notes on 14 species, with a résumé of the numbers of species of birds inhabiting southern Mexico.

118

On some new or little-known species of Accipitres in the collection of the Norwich Museum.

Proc. Zool. Soc. London, 1858, pp. 128–133.

Remarks on certain species of Accipitres in the Norwich Museum with descriptions of two new ones, viz, *Buteo zonocercus* and *Scops usta*. *Syrnium albitarse*, Gray, is also characterized.

(See *Trans. Zool. Soc. London*, IV, pp. 261–266, pls. 58–61.)

119

On some new or little-known species of Accipitres in the collection of the Norwich Museum.

Trans. Zool. Soc. London, IV, pp. 261–266, pls. 58–61.

Buteo zonocercus, *Syrnium albitarse*, Gray; *Scops usta*, and *Urubitinga schistacea* (Sund.), are described upon, and figured.

(Reprint from *Proc. Zool. Soc. London*, 1858, pp. 128–133, with plates added.)

120

Note on the variation of the form of the Upper Mandible in a Rapacious Bird.

Proc. Zool. Soc. London, 1858, p. 150.

Note on, with illustration of, an abnormal variation in the form of the upper mandible of *Urubitinga unicincta*.

121

Synopsis of the American Ant Birds (*Formicariidæ*). Part I, containing the *Thamnophilinæ*.

Proc. Zool. Soc. London, 1858, pp. 202–224, pls. cxxxix, cxl.

A review of the species of the subfamily *Thamnophilinæ*. A new genus—*Pygiptila*—is proposed, and *Thamnophilus amazonicus* is given as a new name for *T. ruficollis*, Spix, which had been applied to the female of the species. *T. amazonicus* and *Dysithamnus leucostictus* are figured. The genera treated of in this part are, *Cymbilanius*, *Batara*, *Thamnophilus*, *Pygiptila*, *Dysithamnus* and *Thamnomanes*.

122

Synopsis of the American Ant Birds (*Formicariidæ*). Part II, containing the *Formicivorinæ* or Ant Wrens.

Proc. Zool. Soc. London, 1858, pp. 232–254, pls. cxli, cxlii.

A review of the species of the subfamily *Formicivorinæ*, with descriptions of two new genera, *Myrmotherula* and *Cercomacra*, and five new species, *Myrmotherula multostriata*, *Formicivora erythrocerca*, *Cercomacra nigricans*, *Pyriglena maculicaudis* and *Hypocnemis schistacea*. Figures are given of *Myrmotherula surinamensis*, *M. multostriata*, and *Formicivora erythrocerca*. Part II includes the following genera: *Herpsilochmus*, *Myrmotherula*, *Formicivora*, *Pithorhamphus*, *Rhamphocænus*, *Cercomacra*, *Pyriglena*, *Heterocnemis*, *Myrmeciza* and *Hypocnemis*.

123

Synopsis of the American Ant Birds (*Formicariidæ*). Part III, containing the third subfamily, *Formicariinæ* or Ant Thrushes.

Proc. Zool. Soc. London, 1858, pp. 272–289, pl. cxliii.

A review of the species of the subfamily *Formicariinæ*. Four new genera are characterized, viz, *Gymnocichla*, *Myrmelastes*, *Grallaricula* (figure in text), and *Phlogopsis* (nom. emend. pro *Phlegopsis*, Reich.), and descriptions are given of *Myrmelastes plumbeus* and *M. nigerrinus*, nn. spp. *Myrmelastes plumbeus* is figured. The following genera are treated of in Part III: *Pithys*, *Gymnocichla*, *Myrmelastes*, *Rhopoterpe*, *Phlogopsis*, *Formicarius*, *Chamæza*, *Grallaria*, *Grallaricula*, *Conopophaga* and *Corythopis*.

124

Additional note on the Upland Goose (*Chloephaga magellanica*.)

Proc. Zool. Soc. London, 1858, pp. 290, 291.

An additional note on the Upland Goose, stating the difference in the colour of the legs of both sexes; also a note pointing out that the Ashyheaded Goose should bear the name of *Chloephaga poliocephala*.

(See also *Proc. Zool. Soc. London*, 1857, p. 128.)

125

On some new or little-known species of Tanagers from the collection of M. Verreaux, of Paris.

Proc. Zool. Soc. London, 1858, pp. 293, 294.

Descriptions of *Chlorospingus castaneicollis* and *Calliste cyanotis*, nn. spp., and remarks on *Buarremon ruficuchus*, *Chlorospingus albitemporalis*, and *Calliste xanthocephala*.

126

On a collection of Birds received by M. Auguste Sallé from Oaxaca in southern Mexico.

Proc. Zool. Soc. London, 1858, pp. 294–305.

A list of 86 species, with remarks upon them. A new genus (*Chamæospiza*) and the following new species are described: *Troglodytes brunneicollis*, *Formicivora boucardi*, *Empidonax bairdi*, *Pipilo albicollis*, and *Petrochelidon swainsoni* (new name for *Hirundo melanogaster*, Sw.).

(See also *Proc. Zool. Soc. London*, 1856, p. 283; 1857, pp. 81, 201, 226.)

127

Description of a new species of the genus *Buteo* from Mexico.

Proc. Zool. Soc. London, 1858, p. 356.

Buteo fuliginosus is described.

(See *Trans. Zool. Soc. London*, IV, p. 267, pl. 62.)

128

Description of a new species of the genus *Buteo* from Mexico.

Trans. Zool. Soc. London, IV, p. 267, pl. 62.

Buteo fuliginosus is described and figured.

(Reprint from *Proc. Zool. Soc. London*, 1858, p. 356.)

129

List of Birds collected by Geo. Cavendish Taylor, esq., in the Republic of Honduras.

Proc. Zool. Soc. London, 1858, pp. 356-360.

A list of 39 species, with remarks upon them.

130

Characters of five new species of American Birds.

Proc. Zool. Soc. London, 1858, pp. 446-440.

The following species are characterized: *Euchlornis frontalis, Turdus leucauchen, Geothlypis speciosa, Cyclorhis flavipectus*, and *Cinclodes bifasciatus*.

131

List of Birds collected by Mr. Louis Fraser at Cuenca, Gualaquiza and Zamora, in the Republic of Ecuador.

Proc. Zool. Soc. London, 1858, pp. 449-461, pl. cxlv.

A list of 88 species, with remarks upon them. The following new species are described: *Conirostrum fraseri, Phrygilus ocularis, Synallaxis antisiensis*, and *Tyrannulus chrysops. Phrygilus ocularis* is figured.

132

On two species of Ant Birds in the collection of the Derby Museum at Liverpool.

Proc. Zool. Soc. London, 1858, pp. 540, 541.

Remarks on *Myrmeciza exsul*, sp. nov., and *Dysithamnus olivaceus*.

133

Note on the genus *Cichlopsis* of Cabanis.

Proc. Zool. Soc. London, 1858, pp. 541-543.

Note on the genus *Cichlopsis*, with the description and synonyms of *C. leucogonys*. The new genus *Phainopepla* is proposed for the reception of Swainson's *Ptilogonys nitens*.

134

On the Birds collected by Mr. Fraser in the vicinity of Riobamba, in the Republic of Ecuador.

Proc. Zool. Soc. London, 1858, pp. 549-556, pl. cxlvi.

A list of 59 species, with remarks upon them, and descriptions of the following new species: *Troglodytes solstitialis, Catamenia homochroa, Agriornis solitaria. Elainia griseigularis*, and *E. stictoptera. Elainia griseigularis* and *E. stictoptera* are figured.

135

Description of a new species of Woodpecker discovered by Mr. Thomas Bridges in northern California.

Ann. and. Mag. Nat. Hist., ser. 3, I, p. 127 (1858).

Melanerpes rubrigularis is described.

(A figure of this bird is given in *Proc. Zool. Soc. London*, 1858, pl. cxxxi.)

136

Description of a new species of Bird from Palestine.

Ann. and Mag. Nat. Hist., ser. 3, II, pp. 465, 466 (1858).

Amydrus tristramii is described.

137

On the general Geographical Distribution of the members of the class Aves.

Journ. of Proc. Linn. Soc. London (Zool.), II, pp. 130-145 (1858).

A scheme for dividing the earth's surface into six zoologic-geographical regions from an ornithological point of view, with lists of the characteristic forms belonging to each region.

138

On the Zoology of New Guinea.

Journ. of Proc. Linn. Soc. London (Zool.), II, pp. 149-170 (1858).

General remarks on the zoology of New Guinea, with a list of 10 species of mammals and 170 species of birds; also a note on the correct zoogeographical position of New Guinea. *Melanocharis* is proposed as a new genus for the reception of *Dicæum nigrum*, Less., and Pucheran's generic name *Trugon* is emended to *Eutrygon. Cracticus personatus*, Temm. MS., is described.

139

Descriptions of new species of the American family *Tyrannidæ*.

Proc. Zool. Soc. London, 1859, pp. 40-46.

The new generic names *Mitrephorus* and *Legatus* are proposed; Bonaparte's genus *Miozeta* is emended to *Myiozetetes*, and the following species are characterized: *Attila citriniventris, Myiodynastes nobilis, Contopus mesoleucus. C. sordidulus, Mitrephorus phæocercus, Pyrocephalus mexicanus, Elainea placens, Mionectes assimilis*, nn. spp., and *Myiodynastes luteiventris*, Bp. The known species of the genera *Attila, Myiodynastes* and *Contopus*, are enumerated.

140

Description of a new species of Owl of the genus *Ciccaba*.

Proc. Zool. Soc. London, 1859, p. 131.

Ciccaba nigrolineata is described.

(See *Trans. Zool. Soc. London*, IV, p. 268, pl. 63.)

141

Description of a new species of Owl of the genus *Ciccaba*.

Trans. Zool. Soc. London, IV, p. 268, pl. 63.

Ciccaba nigrolineata is described and figured.

(Reprint from *Proc. Zool. Soc. London*, 1859, p. 131, with plate added.)

142

Note on the Spur-winged Geese (*Plectropterus*) now living in the Society's Gardens.

Proc. Zool. Soc. London, 1859, pp. 131, 132, pl. cliii.

Plectropterus rüppellii is proposed for the name of a new species, and the points in which it differs from *P. gambensis* are given. Both species are figured.

(See also *Proc. Zool. Soc. London*, 1860, p. 38.)

143

List of the first collection of Birds made by Mr. Louis Fraser at Pallatanga, Ecuador, with notes and descriptions of new species.

Proc. Zool. Soc. London, 1859, pp. 135, 147, pl. cliv.

A list of 102 species, with remarks upon them. The following new species are characterized: *Vireo josephæ, Nemosia ornata, Anabates subalaris, A. temporalis, Dysithamnus unicolor, Formicivora caloptera, Pachyramphus homochrous*, and *Cephalopterus penduliger* (named and figured in the "Ibis," 1859, p. 114, pl. iii). *Vireo josephæ* is figured.

(See also *Proc. Zool. Soc. London*, 1860, p. 63.)

144

On some new species of *Synallaxis*, and on the Geographical Distribution of the genus.

Proc. Zool. Soc. London, 1859, pp. 191-197.

Synallaxis pudica, S. stictothorax and *S. scutata* are described as new, and the 41 known species (including *S. lamnosticta*, n. sp.) of the genus are enumerated. A table showing the distribution of *Synallaxis* is given.

145

[Exhibition of two rare species of Arctic Birds, *Colymbus adamsi* and *Eurinorhynchus pygmaeus*.]

Proc. Zool. Soc. London, 1859, p. 201.

146

A record of the number of days of incubation of Birds which breed in the Society's Gardens.

Proc. Zool. Soc. London, 1859, pp. 205, 206.

A table giving the period of incubation of 18 species of birds which breed in the Zoological Society's Gardens.

147

Remarks on exhibiting specimens of two species of Divers (*Colymbus*) from Mr. Gurney's collection.

Proc. Zool. Soc. London, 1859, pp. 206, 207.

Remarks on *Colymbus adamsi*, G. R. Gray, and *C. pacificus*, Lawrence, and observations as to their deserving specific rank.

148

On a collection of Birds from Vancouver's Island.

Proc. Zool. Soc. London, 1859, pp. 235-237.

A list of 35 species, with remarks upon them.

149

A synopsis of the Thrushes (*Turdidæ*) of the New World.

Proc. Zool. Soc. London, 1859, pp. 321-347.

A synopsis of the *Turdidæ* of America. The generic name *Margarops* is proposed in the place of *Cichlalopia*, Bp.; *Seminerula* and *Mimocichla* are proposed for new sections of *Turdus* and *Galeoscoptes*, respectively, and *Turdus pinicola* and *Catharus occidentalis* are described as new species. A table showing the geographical distribution of the Thrushes in America is added. The genera treated of are: *Catharus, Turdus, Cichlerminia, Margarops, Galeoscoptes, Melanoptila, Melanotis, Rhamphocinclus, Cinclocerthia, Harporhynchus, Oreoscoptes* and *Mimus*.

150

[Exhibition of an Egg laid by the Apteryx (*A. mantelli*), which had been living in the Gardens since 1852.]

Proc. Zool. Soc. London, 1859, p. 350.

(See also *Proc. Zool. Soc. London*, 1860, p. 194.)

151

[Exhibition of Eggs of *Grus montignesia, G. virgo* and *G. cinerea*; also of an Egg of *Balæniceps rex*.]

Proc. Zool. Soc. London, 1859, p. 353.

152

On a series of Birds collected in the vicinity of Jalapa, in Southern Mexico.

Proc. Zool. Soc. London, 1859, pp. 362-369.

A list of 226 species, with observations on the more remarkable ones. Three new species are described, viz, *Cotyle fulvipennis, Dendrornis erythropygia*, and *Piaya thermophila*.

153

List of Birds collected by M. A. Boucard, in the State of Oaxaca, in southwestern Mexico, with descriptions of new species.

Proc. Zool. Soc. London, 1859, pp. 369-393.

A list of 238 species, with remarks upon them. *Dendromanes* is proposed as a new generic name, and the following new species are described: *Campylorhynchus jocosus, Thryothorus felix, Cyphorinus pusillus. Hylophilus ochraceiceps, Cæreba carnipes?, Oryzoborus funereus, Spermophila corvina, Dendromanes homochrous, Lipaugus unirufus, Columba nigrirostris, Tinamus boucardi*, Sallé MS., and *T. meserythrus*.

154

On some new or little-known Birds from the Rio Napo.

Proc. Zool. Soc. London, 1859, pp. 440, 441.

Buarremon castaneiceps and *Grallaria nuchalis* are described as new, and remarks made upon seven other little-known species.

155

On some Hybrid Ducks bred in the Society's Gardens.

Proc. Zool. Soc. London, 1859, p. 442, pl. clviii.

Remarks on a hybrid between *Tadorna vulpanser*, ♂, and *Casarca cana*, ♀, and on other cases of hybridisation in the Zoological Society's Gardens. A figure of *Tadorna vulpanser* × *Casarca cana* is given.

155

On the Ornithology of Central America. By Philip Lutley Sclater and Osbert Salvin.

Ibis, 1859, pp. 1-22.

Part I opens with a summary of the present knowledge of Central American Ornithology. Fourteen families are covered in this installment, containing 121 species, of which *Cistothorus elegans, Vireolanius pulchellus* and *Cæreba lucida* are described as new.

155 a

On the Ornithology of Central America. By Philip Lutley Sclater and Osbert Salvin.

Ibis, 1859, pp. 117-138, pls. iv, v.

Part II. This part embraces fifteen families, with 129 species, of which *Xiphocolaptes emigrans, Sayornis aquatica, Empidonax albigularis*, and *Elainia vilissima* are described as new, and the last, with *E. placens*, is figured. Eggs of the following species are also figured: *Tanagra vicaria, Pyrgisona biarcuatum, Pitangus derbianus, Tyrannus melancholicus, Myiozetetes texensis, Cyanocitta melanocyanea*, and *Turdus grayii*.

155 b

On the Ornithology of Central America. By Philip Lutley Sclater and Osbert Salvin.

Ibis, 1859, pp. 213-234.

Part III. Twenty-five families are treated of in this part, embracing 132 species. *Lophostrix stricklandi* is described as new.

The three installments composing the paper "On the Ornithology of Central America," enumerate 382 species occurring in that country, eight of which are here described for the first time.

157

Characters of an undescribed species of Hawk from New Caledonia.

Ibis, 1859, pp. 275, 276, pl. viii.

Accipiter haplochrous is described and figured.

158

[Recent Ornithological Publications.]

Ibis, 1859, pp. 318–329.

A record of Ornithological literature, with an abstract of the contents of each work mentioned. The new genus *Phœornis* is proposed for the reception of Cassin's *Tœnioptera obscura*.

159

A list of the Tyrant Birds of Mexico, with descriptions of some new species.

Ibis, 1859, pp. 436–445, pl. XIV.

A list of 43 species of *Tyrannidæ* from Mexico with remarks upon them. *Empidonax brachytarsus*, *Cyclorhynchus cinereiceps*, and *Todirostrum schistaceiceps* are described as new, and *Camptostoma imberbe* and *Mitrephorus phæocercus* are figured.

160

[Recent Ornithological Publications.]

Ibis, 1859, pp. 454–461.

A list of Ornithological works, with short abstracts of their contents. A new genus, *Nesopsar*, is described.

161

Descriptions of two new species of American Parrots.

Ann. and Mag. Nat. Hist., ser. 3, IV, pp. 224–226 (1859).

Conurus holochlorus and *C. xantholæmus* are described, and lists given of the Parrots inhabiting Mexico and certain islands in the West Indies.

162

Further evidence of the distinctness of the Gambian and Rüppell's Spur-winged Geese (*Plectropterus gambensis* and *P. rüppellii*).

Proc. Zool. Soc. London, 1860, pp. 38–42.

Further remarks on the distinctness of *Plectropterus gambensis* and *P. rüppellii* on comparison of their internal structures, with tables of their correct synonymy. Figures of the skulls and tracheæ of the two species are given in the text.

(See also *Proc. Zool. Soc. London*, 1859, p. 131.)

163

List of additional species of Birds collected by Mr. Louis Fraser at Pallatanga, Ecuador, with notes and descriptions of new species.

Proc. Zool. Soc. London, 1860, pp. 63–73.

Remarks on a second collection obtained by Mr. Fraser at Pallatanga, consisting of 64 species, including 19 from Chillanes. The term *Eupsilostoma* is proposed as a new generic name, and the following new species are described: *Thryothorus mystacalis*, *Synallaxis erythrops*, *Grallaria regulus*, *Myiarchus nigriceps*, *Platyrhynchus albogularis*, *Eupsilostoma pusillum*, *Tyrannulus flavidifrons* and *T. cinereiceps*.

(See also *Proc. Zool. Soc. London*, 1859, p. 135.)

164

List of Birds collected by Mr. Fraser in the vicinity of Quito and during excursions to Pichincha and Chimborazo, with notes and descriptions of new species.

Proc. Zool. Soc. London, 1860, pp. 73–83, pl. clix.

A list of 52 species, with remarks upon them. A new genus, *Oreomanes*, is made (figure in text), and the following new species are described: *Thryothorus euophrys*, *Oreomanes fraseri*, *Cinclo-des excelsior*, *C. albidiventris*, *Agriornis andicola* and *Attagis chimborazensis*. *Oreomanes fraseri* is figured.

165

List of Birds collected by Mr. Fraser in Ecuador, at Nanegal, Calacali, Perucho, and Puellaro, with notes and descriptions of new species.

Proc. Zool. Soc. London, 1860, pp. 83–97, pl. clx.

An annotated list of 130 species, of which the following are described as new: *Thryothorus nigricapillus*, *Basileuterus semicervinus*, *Oryzoborus æthiops*, *Pipreola jucunda*, *Pipra deliciosa* (figure in text), *Masius coronulatus*, *Cyclorhynchus fulvipectus* and *Myiobius villosus*. *Pipreola jucunda* is figured (called *Euchlornis jucunda* on plate).

166

[Exhibition of a large Horned Owl (*Bubo maximus*, var.) from Pångkông Lake, Thibet.]

Proc. Zool. Soc. London, 1860, p. 90.

167

Note on the Punjab Sheep living in the Society's Gardens.

Proc. Zool. Soc. London, 1860, pp. 126–130, pls. lxxix, lxxx.

Notes on the differences between *Ovis vignii* and *O. cycloceros* (both of which are figured), and observations on the distinguishing characters of the other two Indian species of wild sheep, *O. hodgsoni* and *O. nahoor*.

(Cuts of skulls of first two mentioned species in text.)

168

[Additions to the Menagerie during the months of January and February.]

Proc. Zool. Soc. London, 1860, p. 183.

169

[Exhibition of *Oreophasis derbianus*; and announcement of the addition of *Sieboldia maxima* and *Balæniceps rex* to the Society's Menagerie.]

Proc. Zool. Soc. London, 1860, p. 184.

170

[Exhibition of the Egg of the King Vulture (*Gyparchus papa*).]

Proc. Zool. Soc. London, 1860, pp. 193, 194.

Believed to be the first well-authenticated egg of this species known.

171

[Exhibition of a second specimen of the Egg of the Apteryx (*A. mantelli*).]

Proc. Zool. Soc. London, 1860, p. 194.

(See also *Proc. Zool. Soc. London*, 1859, p. 350.)

172

On the Rheas in the Society's Menagerie, with remarks on the known species of Struthious Birds.

Proc. Zool. Soc. London, 1860, pp. 207–211.

Remarks on *Rhea americana* and *R. darwinii*, and description of a new species, *R. macrorhyncha*, with a summary of the state of knowledge of the Struthious Birds. Figures are given in text of the heads of the three species of *Rhea*.

(See papers Nos. 177, 276.)

173

On the Black-shouldered Peacock of Latham (*Pavo nigripennis*).

Proc. Zool. Soc. London, 1860, pp. 221, 222.

Remarks pointing out that the Black-shouldered Peacock of Latham differs from the two other species of *Pavo*, and must therefore bear a different specific name. *Pavo nigripennis* is proposed.

174

On the species of the genus *Prioniturus*, and on the Geographical Distribution of the *Psittacidæ* in the Eastern Archipelago.

Proc. Zool. Soc. London, 1860, pp. 223-228.

Remarks on the three known species of *Prioniturus* and their synonymy, and a list of the *Psittacidæ* inhabiting the Eastern Archipelago, and their Geographical Distribution. A new generic name, *Opopsitta*, is adopted.

175

[Additions to the menagerie during the months of March and April.]

Proc. Zool. Soc. London, 1860, pp. 242, 243.

176

List of mammalia collected by Mr. J. Monteiro in Angola.

Proc. Zool. Soc. London, 1860, pp. 245-247.

A list of nine species, with remarks upon them. *Colobus angolensis* is described as new, and the five known species of *Colobus* are enumerated.

177

Notes on two Struthious Birds now living in the Society's Gardens.

Proc. Zool. Soc. London, 1860, pp. 247-250.

Notes on *Dromæus irroratus*, Bartl., and *Casuarius bicarunculatus*, n. sp. Cuts of the throat-wattles of both species are given in the text.

(See also *Rep. Brit. Assoc. Adv. Sci.*, 1861, Pt. I, pp. 176-178; Pt. II, pp. 158,159; *Trans. Zool. Soc. London*, IV, p. 353, 1862).

(See also paper No. 172.)

178

Notes on a collection of Birds from the vicinity of Orizaba and neighbouring parts of southern Mexico.

Proc. Zool. Soc. London, 1860, pp. 250-254, pl. clxiii.

A list of 44 species, with notes on them. *Coccothraustes maculipennis* is described, and *Basileuterus mesochrysus*, *Thamnophilus melanocristus*, and *Tinamus robustus* are named. *Coccothraustes maculipennis* is figured.

179

[Exhibition of a specimen of a new form of Dormouse (*Platacanthomys lasiurus* Blyth.).]

Proc. Zool. Soc. London, 1860, p. 260.

180

List of Birds collected by Mr. Fraser at Babahoyo, in Ecuador, with descriptions of new species.

Proc. Zool. Soc. London, 1860, pp. 272-290, pl. clxiv.

A list of 134 species, with remarks upon them, and descriptions of the following new species: *Geothlypis semiflava*, *Cyclorhis viridiceps*, *Saltator flavidicollis*, *Embernagra chrysoma*, *Spermophila ophthalmica*, *Oryzoborus occidentalis*, *Cassiculus flaviceps*, *Xiphorhynchus thoracicus*, *Formicivora consobrina*, *Cercomacra maculosa*, *Pachyrhamphus spodiurus*, *Attila torridus*, *Fluvicola atripennis*, *Megarhynchus chrysogaster*, *Tyrannus nivigularis*, *Myiarchus phæocephalus*, *Cyclorhynchus subbrunneus*, *Muscivora occidentalis*, *Bucco leucocrissus*, *Piaya nigricrissa* and *Dryocopus fuscipennis*. *Cyclorhis viridiceps* is figured, and

Xiphorhynchus pusillus, from New Granada, is described in a footnote on page 278.

181

A list of Birds collected by Mr. Fraser at Esmeraldas, Ecuador, with descriptions of new species.

Proc. Zool. Soc. London, 1860, pp. 291-298.

An annotated list of 94 species, of which *Cyphorinus phæocephalus* and *Bucco subtectus* are described as new.

182

Characters of eleven new species of Birds discovered by Osbert Salvin in Guatemala. By Philip Lutley Sclater, M. A., Secretary to the Society, and Osbert Salvin, M. A., F. Z. S.

Proc. Zool. Soc. London, 1860, pp. 298-301.

The genus *Thamnistes* and the following species are characterized: *Polioptila albiloris*, *Dendroeca chrysoparia*, *Hylophilus cinereiceps*, *Glyphorhynchus pectoralis*, *Thamnistes anabatinus*, *Platyrhynchus cancrominus*, *Tyrannulus semiflavus*, *Heteropelma veræ-pacis*, *Lipaugus holerythrus*, *Pionus hæmatotis* and *Corethrura rubra*.

183

Note on the Skull of the Red River-hog (*Potamochœrus penicillatus*).

Proc. Zool. Soc. London, 1860, pp. 301, 302.

Note on the generic differences of *Potamochœrus* and *Sus*, as observed on comparing the skull of *Potamochœrus penicillatus* with that of *Sus indicus*. An illustration of the skull of the former species is given in the text.

184

Description of a new species of Manakin from northern Brazil.

Proc. Zool. Soc. London, 1860, pp. 312, 313.

Pipra heterocerca is described.

185

Description of a new Tyrant-bird of the genus *Elainea*, from the Island of Saint Thomas, West Indies.

Proc. Zool. Soc. London, 1860, pp. 313, 314.

Elainea riisii is described.

186

[Exhibition of a drawing of a species of Rock Kangaroo just received by the Society from Australia.]

Proc. Zool. Soc. London, 1860, p. 323.

Exhibition to the Zoological Society of London of a drawing of *Petrogale xanthopus*. and list of 11 species of *Macropodidæ* living in the Society's Gardens.

187

[Additions to the Menagerie during the months of May and June.]

Proc. Zool. Soc. London, 1860, pp. 371, 372.

188

Note on the Japanese Deer living in the Society's Menagerie.

Proc. Zool. Soc. London, 1860, pp. 375-377.

Notes on *Cervus sika* and its synonyms.

189

Catalogue of the Birds of the Falkland Islands.

Proc. Zool. Soc. London, 1860, pp. 382-391, pl. clxxiii.

A list of 57 species, with remarks upon them. *Chloephaga rubidiceps* is described as new, and figured, and *Sterna meridionalis*, Cassin, is renamed *S. cassini.*

(See also *Proc. Zool. Soc. London*, 1861, p. 45; 1864, p. 73.)

190

[Additions to the Menagerie during the months of July, August, September, and October.]

Proc. Zool. Soc. London, 1860, pp. 415–417.

191

[Exhibition of Bird Skins from Port Churchill, Hudson's Bay.]

Proc. Zool. Soc. London, 1860, p. 418.

192

Notice of some rare species of Quadrumana now living in the Society's Menagerie.

Proc. Zool. Soc. London, 1860, pp. 419–422, pl. lxxxii.

Remarks on *Macacus ocreatus*, *M. maurus*, *Cercopithecus rufo-viridis* and *Cynocephalus anubis*, with a catalogue of the quadrumana living in the Zoological Society's Gardens, and a list of those that have bred there.

193

[Additions to the Menagerie during the month of November.]

Proc. Zool. Soc. London, 1860, p. 442.

194

[On the Babirussa and other *Suidæ* living in the Zoological Society's Gardens.]

Proc. Zool. Soc. London, 1860, p. 443, pl. lxxxiii.

Note on and figure of *Babirussa alfurus*, and a list of the *Suidæ* living in the Zoological Society's Gardens.

195

Note on *Ovis polii* of Blyth.

Proc. Zool. Soc. London, 1860, pp. 443, 444.

Note on a pair of horns of *Ovis polii* and their dimensions, with illustration of same in text.

196

Report on the Indian Pheasants bred in the Society's Menagerie during the years 1858, 1859, and 1860.

Proc. Zool. Soc. London, 1860, pp. 444, 445.

Remarks on the breeding of the five species of Himalayan Pheasants in the Zoological Society's Gardens, with a tabular list showing the results of the breeding seasons of 1858, 1859 and 1860.

197

Characters of ten new species of American Birds.

Proc. Zool. Soc. London, 1860, pp. 461–467.

The name *Neopelma* is proposed for a new section of *Heteropelma*. The species characterized are the following: *Campylorhynchus nigriceps*, *C. gularis*, *Vireo modestus*, *Vireosylvia cobanensis*, *Myiobius flavicans*, *M. pulcher*, *M. crypterythrus*, *M. cryptoxanthus*, *Heteropelma amazonum* and *H. flavicapillum*. The known species of the genera *Myiobius* and *Heteropelma* are enumerated.

198

On the Eggs of two Raptorial Birds from the Falkland Islands.

Ibis, 1860, pp. 24–26, pl. 1.

Remarks on and figures of the eggs of *Buteo erythronotus* and *Milvago australis.*

(See *Ibis*, 1860, p. 432.)

199

Note on Wallace's Standard-wing, *Semioptera wallacii.*

Ibis, 1860, pp. 20–28, pl. ii.

Remarks on and figure of *Semioptera wallacii*, discovered by Mr. Wallace in the Island of Batchian.

200

Contributions to the Ornithology of Guatemala. By Osbert Salvin and Philip Lutley Sclater. Part I.

Ibis, 1860, pp. 28–45, pl. iii.

Part I contains notes on 80 species collected in Guatemala by Mr. Salvin, of which *Thryothorus pleurostictus*, *Elainia subpagana*, *Malacoptila veræpacis*, and *Chrysotis guatemalæ*. Hartl. MS., are described as new. *Chætura rutila* is figured.

200 a

Contributions to the Ornithology of Guatemala. By Osbert Salvin and Philip Lutley Sclater. Part II.

Ibis, 1860, pp. 272–278.

Part II contains a list of 39 species not previously known from this country, with notes upon them.

200 b

Contributions to the Ornithology of Guatemala. By Osbert Salvin and Philip Lutley Sclater. Part III.

Ibis, 1860, pp. 396–402, pl. xiii.

Part III contains a list, with notes, of 52 species additional to those already recorded from Guatemala. *Pionus hæmatotis* is figured. Five hundred and three species are known to occur in this country, of which number 171 are treated in this and the two preceding parts.

201

On an undescribed species of Hawk from New Granada.

Ibis, 1860, pp. 147–149, pl. vi.

Accipiter collaris (Kaup MS.) is described and figured.

202

Note on the Egg and Nestling of the Californian Vulture.

Ibis, 1860, p. 278, pls. viii, ix.

Remarks on and figures of the egg and nestling of *Cathartes californianus.*

203

Note on the Birds of Prey of New Guinea.

Ibis, 1860, pp. 322, 323, pl. x.

Note on the raptorial birds inhabiting New Guinea; the eight known species are enumerated, of which *Accipiter poliocephalus* is figured.

204

[Announcement of the transfer by Her Majesty the Queen of a specimen of *Phacochærus æliani* to the care of the Society.]

Proc. Zool. Soc. London, 1861, p. 30.

205

[Exhibition of a specimen of the American Meadow Starling (*Sturnella ludoviciana*).]

Proc. Zool. Soc. London, 1861, p. 30.

205

[Exhibition of a specimen of a Caprimulgine Bird, closely allied to *Cosmetornis vexillaria*, from the collection of E. Gabriel, esq.]

Proc. Zool. Soc. London, 1861, p. 44.

207

[Exhibition of the hoof of a Bull (*Bos taurus*, var. *domesticus*) from the Falkland Islands, belonging to Captain Abbott.]

Proc. Zool. Soc. London, 1861, p. 44.

208

Additions and corrections to the list of the Birds of the Falkland Islands.

Proc. Zool. Soc. London, 1861, pp. 45–47.

Corrections are made of the "Catalogue of the Birds of the Falkland Islands" (*Proc. Zool. Soc. London*, 1860, p. 382) and 10 additional species enumerated. A list of the Penguins inhabiting the Falkland Islands is also given.

(See also *Proc. Zool. Soc. London*, 1864, p. 73.)

209

[Additions to the Menagerie during the month of December, 1860.]

Proc. Zool. Soc. London, 1861, p. 59.

210

[Exhibition of a living specimen of a Water Tortoise (*Chelodina longicollis*) from South Australia.]

Proc. Zool. Soc. London, 1861, p. 50.

211

Note on the reproduction of the Red River-hog (*Potamochœrus penicillatus*) in the Society's Menagerie.

Proc. Zool. Soc. London, 1861, pp. 62, 63, pl. xii.

Report on the breeding of *Potamochœrus penicillatus* in the Zoological Society's Gardens. The female and young are figured.

212

List of a collection of Birds made by the late Mr. W. Osburn in Jamaica, with notes.

Proc. Zool. Soc. London, 1861, pp. 69–82, pl. xiv.

An annotated list of 92 species. *Laletes* and *Siphonorhis* (woodcut in text) (nn. gg.), and *Laletes osburni* and *Elainea fallax* (nn. spp.), are described. *Vireo modestus* and *Laletes osburni* are figured. The head of *Nesopsar nigerrimus* is figured in text.

213

[Exhibition of an example of *Pentacrinus caput-medusæ*.]

Proc. Zool. Soc. London, 1861, p. 87.

214

[Additions to the Menagerie during the months of January and February, 1861.]

Proc. Zool. Soc. London, 1861, p. 101.

215

Characters of some new species of American Passeres.

Proc. Zool. Soc. London, 1861, pp. 127–131.

The following species are characterized: *Poospiza buffoni*, *Troglodytes hypædon*, *Basileuterus* *uropygialis*, *Hylophilus insularis*, *Chlorophanes guatemalensis*, *Chlorophonia flavirostris*, *Euphonia vittata*, *Tanagra subcinerea*, *Ramphocelus ephippialis* and *Saltator isthmicus*.

216

On a new species of the genus *Copsychus* from Borneo.

Proc. Zool. Soc. London, 1861, pp. 185–187.

Copsychus suavis is described, and a list of the 10 known species of *Copsychus* is given.

217

[On the addition to the Menagerie of some Three-toed Sand-grouse and some rare Australian Finches.]

Proc. Zool. Soc. London, 1861, pp. 196, 197.

218

[List of Animals presented to the Society by H. E. Sir George Grey, K. C. B., F. Z. S.]

Proc. Zool. Soc. London, 1861, pp. 208, 209.

This collection comprised specimens of 10 species of mammals, 3 species of birds (one of which is named *Gallinula nesiotis*, n. sp.), and 10 species of reptiles.

(See also *Proc. Zool. Soc. London*, 1861, p. 307.)

219

On a new Bird of the genus *Lipaugus* of Boié.

Proc. Zool. Soc. London, 1861, pp. 209–212.

Lipaugus subalaris is described, and the nine known species of the genus *Lipaugus* are enumerated.

220

[Additions to the Menagerie during the months of March and April, 1861.]

Proc. Zool. Soc. London, 1861, pp. 233, 234.

221

On the Island-hen of Tristan d'Acunha.

Proc. Zool. Soc. London, 1861, pp. 260–263, pl. xxx.

Gallinula nesiotis is characterized and figured.

222

[Additions to the Menagerie during the month of May, 1861.]

Proc. Zool. Soc. London, 1861, pp. 264, 265.

223

[Report on some specimens of animals forwarded by Captain Speke.]

Proc. Zool. Soc. London, 1861, p. 208.

224

[Exhibition of a cast of the skull of the Aye-Aye (*Chiromys madagascariensis*).]

Proc. Zool. Soc. London, 1861, p. 306.

225

[Report of the return of Mr. Benstead from the Cape with a second collection of animals, presented to the Society by Sir George Grey.]

Proc. Zool. Soc. London, 1861, p. 307.

This collection consisted of specimens of four species of mammals and three species of birds.

(See also *Proc. Zool. Soc. London*, 1861, p. 208.)

225

[Additions to the Menagerie during June, July, August, September, and October, 1861.]

Proc. Zool. Soc. London, 1861, pp. 365-368.

227

[Exhibition of original drawings by Mr. Vigne of *Ovis cycloceros* and *O. rignii*.]

Proc. Zool. Soc. London, 1861, pp. 368, 369.

228

On a new species of Finch, of the genus *Sycalis*, from Mexico.

Proc. Zool. Soc. London, 1861, pp. 376, 377.

Sycalis chrysops is described.

229

Descriptions of twelve new species of American Birds of the families *Dendrocolaptidæ*, *Formicariidæ*, and *Tyrannidæ*.

Proc. Zool. Soc. London, 1861, pp. 377, 383, pl. xxxvi.

A new genus—*Sphenopsis*—and the following new species are described: *Leptasthenura paraensis*, *Philydor subfulvus*, *Xenops littoralis*, *Sphenopsis ignobilis*, *Thamnistes æquatorialis*, *Ramphocænus sanctæ marthæ*, *Grallaria mexicana*, *Copurus fuscicapillus*, *Platyrhynchus flavigularis*, *Phyllomyias griseocapilla* (Lafr. MS.), *P. semifusca*, and *Tyrannus inca*, Licht. MS. *Phyllomyias griseocapilla*, and *P. semifusca* are figured. The known species of the genera *Philydor*, *Copurus* and *Grallaria*, are enumerated.

230

[Exhibition of the skins of an Otter from Amoy and a Hare from the Island of Formosa, forwarded by Mr. Swinhoe.]

Proc. Zool. Soc. London, 1861, pp. 389, 390.

231

[Report on a collection of Skins shipped by Mr. Swinhoe on board the *Harkaway*.]

Proc. Zool. Soc. London, 1861, pp. 390, 391.

This collection contained specimens of mammals, reptiles, and fishes; one of the last is described as new by Dr. Günther, under the name of *Tropidonotus orientalis*, and a figure is given of it.

232

Note on the Ocellated Turkey of Honduras.

Proc. Zool. Soc. London, 1861, pp. 402, 403, pl. xl.

Meleagris ocellata is remarked upon and the heads of the two sexes are figured.

233

Index generis *Elaineæ* ex familia *Tyrannidarum* additis novarum specierum diagnosibus.

Proc. Zool. Soc. London, 1861, pp. 406-408, pl. xli.

The 17 known species of *Elainea* are enumerated, of which *E. semipagana*, *E. pallatangæ*, *E. subplacens* and *E. implacens* are described as new. *E. pallatangæ* is figured.

234

Note on *Milvago carunculatus* and its allied species.

Ibis, 1861, pp. 19-23, pl. i.

The description, synonymy and figure of *Milvago carunculatus* (Des Murs), and a list of its allied species.

235

Notice of the occurrence of the American Meadow Starling (*Sturnella ludoviciana*) in England.

Ibis, 1861, pp. 176-180.

Note on the occurrence of *Sturnella ludoviciana* in England, and a summary notice of the geographical distribution of it and its allies.

236

On the American Barbets (*Capitonidæ*).

Ibis, 1861, pp. 183-190, pl. vi.

A synopsis of the American *Capitonidæ* (genera *Tetragonops* and *Capito*). *Capito tschudii* and *C. melanotis*, Hartl. MS., are characterized, and *Tetragonops ramphastinus* is figured.

237

Remarks on the Geographical Distribution of the genus *Turdus*.

Ibis, 1861, pp. 277-282, pl. viii.

Remarks on the geographical distribution of the Thrushes of the genus *Turdus*. *Turdus fulviventris* is figured.

238

On a rare species of Hawk, of the genus *Accipiter*, from South America.

Ibis, 1861, pp. 313, 314, pl. x.

Accipiter pectoralis (Cuv. MS.) is characterized and figured.

239

Note on the *Hypotriorchis castanonotus* of Dr. Heuglin.

Ibis, 1861, pp. 346, 347, pl. xii.

Hypotriorchis castanonotus, Heuglin. is remarked upon and figured.

240

Characters of eight new species of American Birds.

Ann. and Mag. Nat. Hist., ser. 3, VII, p. 327-330 (1861).

Reprint of a portion of the paper entitled "Characters of ten new species of American birds," published in *Proc. Zool. Soc. London*, 1860, p. 461.

241

On two new species of *Heteropelma*.

Ann. and Mag. Nat. Hist., ser. 3, VII, p. 487 (1861).

Reprint of a portion of the paper mentioned in the description of the preceding title.

242

Habits and Nest of the Pichincha Humming Bird.

Zoologist, 1861, pp. 7313, 7314.

Remarks on the habits and description of the nest of the Pichincha Humming bird. A figure of the nest is given in the text.

243

Note upon the northern limit of the Quadrumana in the New World.

Nat. Hist. Review, 1861, pp. 507-510.

Remarks on the errors in the geographical limits of the range of the Quadrumana in America, as laid down in Johnston's and other physical atlases.

244

Report on the present state of our knowledge of the birds of the genus *Ap-*

teryx living in New Zealand. By Philip Lutley Sclater and Ferdinand von Hochstetter.

Rep. Brit. Assoc. Adv. Sci., 1861, pt. 1, pp. 176–178.

Remarks upon the four known species of the genus *Apteryx* inhabiting New Zealand.

(See also Proc. Zool. Soc. London, 1860, p. 247; Rep. Brit. Assoc. Adv. Sci., 1861, Pt. II, p. 158; Trans. Zool. Soc. London, IV, p. 353, 1862.)

245

Remarks on the late increase of our knowledge of the Struthious Birds.

Rep. Brit. Assoc. Adv. Sci., 1861, pt. 2, pp. 158, 159.

Additional information on the Struthious birds, with a list of the known species.

(See also Proc. Zool. Soc. London, 1860, p. 247; Rep. Brit. Assoc. Adv. Sci., 1861, Pt. I, p. 176; Trans. Zool. Soc. London, IV, p. 353, 1862.)

246

A Naturalist's Impressions of Spain.

Galton's Vacation Tourists in 1861.

247

[Exhibition of a tracing of the outline of a skull of the adult male *Rhinoceros sumatranus*, on behalf of Mr. E. Blyth, corr. memb.]

Proc. Zool. Soc. London, 1862, p. 1.

248

[Remarks on some specimens forwarded by Captain Speke.]

Proc. Zool. Soc. London, 1862, pp. 12, 13.

This collection consisted of six specimens of mammals, four skins of birds, and two skins of fishes, forwarded by Capt. J. H. Speke from Dukhumi, East Africa.

249

On some Birds recently collected by M. Boucard in southern Mexico.

Proc. Zool. Soc. London, 1862, pp. 18–20, pl. iii.

A list of 16 species, with remarks upon them. *Harporhynchus ocellatus* is described and figured.

250

[Additions to the Menagerie in November and December, 1861.]

Proc. Zool. Soc. London, 1862, p. 22.

251

[Remarks on some Snakes received from Bahia.]

Proc. Zool. Soc. London, 1862, p. 23.

A list of five species of snakes received from Dr. Wucherer, of Bahia.

252

[Extracts from Dr. G. Bennett's letter respecting the Kagus intended to be sent by him to the Society, etc.]

Proc. Zool. Soc. London, 1862, pp. 84–86.

253

On a new species of *Malacoptila* from western Ecuador.

Proc. Zool. Soc. London, 1862, pp. 86, 87, pl. viii.

Malacoptila poliopis is described and figured.

254

[Extracts from a letter from Dr. G. Bennett, F. Z. S., announcing the shipment of a living Kagu for the Society, etc.]

Proc. Zool. Soc. London, 1862, p. 107.

255

Characters of nine new species of Birds received in collections from Bogota.

Proc. Zool. Soc. London, 1862, pp. 109–112, pl. xi.

The genus *Empidochanes* and the following new species are described: *Turdus ephippialis, Hylophilus ferrugineifrons, Chloronpangus olagineus, Philydor panerythrus, Leptopogon erythrops, L. pœcilotis, Myiobius bellus, Empidochanes pœcilurus* and *Urochroma stictoptera. Urochroma stictoptera* is figured.

256

On two new species of Tyrant Birds from Ecuador.

Proc. Zool. Soc. London, 1862, p. 113.

Mecocerculus is proposed as a new genus, and the new species *Ochthoëca citrinifrons* and *Mecocerculus gratiosus* are described.

257

[Announcement of the arrival of two living Paradise Birds (*Paradisea papuana*) purchased for the Society by Mr. A. R. Wallace.]

Proc. Zool. Soc. London, 1862, p. 123.

258

[Additions to the Menagerie during the months of January, February, and March, 1862.]

Proc. Zool. Soc. London, 1862, pp. 139, 140.

259

[Report on the arrival of a living Kagu, presented to the Society by Dr. George Bennett, F. Z. S., of Sydney, and of several other specimens of living animals.]

Proc. Zool. Soc. London, 1862, p. 141, pl. xiv.

Cacatua ducorpsii is figured.

260

Note on the Deer of Formosa.

Proc. Zool. Soc. London, 1862, pp. 150–152, pls. xvi, xvii.

The four species of deer inhabiting the coasts of China and Japan are enumerated. *Cervus swinhoei* is described as a new species, and the differences between *C. sika* and *C. taëvanus* are pointed out. *C. swinhoei* and *C. taëvanus* are figured.

261

[Exhibition on behalf of Capt. J. W. P. Orde, F. Z. S., of a specimen of a black variety of the Water-Vole (*Arvicola amphibius?*) and of a Red-crested Duck (*Branta rufina*).]

Proc. Zool. Soc. London, 1862, p. 163.

262

[Exhibition of Drawings representing the four known species of Wild Asses.]

Proc. Zool. Soc. London, 1862, pp. 163, 164.

Exhibition to a meeting of the Zoological Society of London of drawings of *Asinus hemionus, A. indicus, A. hemippus* and *A. tæniopus*, with remarks on their geographical distribution and distinctive characters.

263

[Additions to the Menagerie during the months of April and May, 1862.]

Proc. Zool. Soc. London, 1862, pp. 184–186.

264

[On some interesting additions to the Menagerie.]

Proc. Zool. Soc. London, 1862, pp. 186, 187.

Remarks on two Spider Monkeys, *Ateles frontalus* and *A. hybridus*, and two young bears from Japan, for which the name *Ursus japonicus* is suggested.

(See also *Proc. Zool. Soc. London*, 1862, p. 261.)

265

[Extracts from a letter from Dr. Lamprey, dated Shanghai, July 31, 1862.]

Proc. Zool. Soc. London, 1862, pp. 220, 221.

Notes on some species of Pheasants, Partridges and Quails of China.

266

[Notice of a living Aye-Aye (*Chiromys madagascariensis*) in the Society's Menagerie.]

Proc. Zool. Soc. London, 1862, p. 222.

267

[Extracts from letters from Dr. G. Bennett, F. Z. S.]

Proc. Zool. Soc. London, 1862, pp. 246–250.

268

[Letter from Sir Robert Schomburgk, H. M. consul for Siam, respecting a *Diardigallus crawfurdi*.]

Proc. Zool. Soc. London, 1862, pp. 250, 251.

269

Note on the Japanese Bear.

Proc. Zool. Soc. London, 1862, p. 261, pl. xxxii.

Additional observations on and figure of *Ursus japonicus*.

(See also *Proc. Zool. Soc. London*, 1862, p. 186.)

270

[Additions to the Menagerie during the months of June, July, August, September, and October, 1862.]

Proc. Zool. Soc. London, 1862, pp. 321–325.

271

Notes on the Incubation of *Python sebœ*, as observed in the Society's Gardens.

Proc. Zool. Soc. London, 1862, pp. 365–368.

Notes on the incubation of the West African Python, and observations on the difference in its temperature during that period and in the normal state.

(See also *Ann. and Mag. Nat. Hist.*, ser. 3, IX, p. 310, 1862.)

272

On some Birds to be added to the Avifauna of Mexico.

Proc. Zool. Soc. London, 1862, pp. 368, 369, pl. xlvi.

A list of eight species, not before known, from Mexico. *Vireo hypochryseus* is described as new and figured.

273

[Additions to the Menagerie during the month of November, 1862.]

Proc. Zool. Soc. London, 1862, p. 376.

274

Additional notes on the American Barbets.

Ibis, 1862, pp. 1, 2, pl. i.

Additional notes on the *Capitonidœ*, with description and figure of *Capito maculicoronatus*, Lawr.

(See also *Ibis*, 1861, p. 182.)

275

Note on *Falco circumcinctus*, a rare Bird of Prey from South America.

Ibis, 1862, pp. 23–25, pl. ii.

Falco circumcinctus (Kaup) is figured and remarked upon.

276

On the Struthious Birds living in the Society's Menagerie.

Trans. Zool. Soc. London, IV, pp. 353–364, pls. lxviia–lxxvi (1862).

A general account of the Struthious birds living in the Zoological Society's Gardens, and an enumeration of the existing *Struthiones*. The following species are figured: *Struthio camelus*, *Rhea americana*, *R. macrorhyncha*, *R. darwinii*, *Casuarius galeatus*, *C. bicarunculatus*, *C. uniappendiculatus*, *C. bennettii*, *Dromœus novœ-hollandiœ*, and *D. irroratus*.

(See also *Proc. Zool. Soc. London*, 1860, pp. 207, 247; *Rep. Brit. Assoc. Adv. Sci.*, 1861, Pt. I, p. 176; Pt. II, p. 158.)

277

Note on the Temperature of the female *Python sebœ* during incubation.

Ann. and Mag. Nat. Hist., ser. 3, IX, pp. 310, 311 (1862).

A table of temperatures taken during the incubation of the West African Python in the Zoological Society's Gardens.

(See also *Proc. Zool. Soc. London*, 1862, p. 365.)

278

[On two rare Fruit Pigeons living in the Society's Menagerie.]

Proc. Zool. Soc. London, 1863, p. 1.

Remarks on *Carpophaga microcera* and *Ptilopus fasciatus*.

279

[Additions to the Menagerie during the month of December, 1862.]

Proc. Zool. Soc. London, 1863, p. 47.

280

[Exhibition of a collection of insects and fresh-water shells from Madagascar, transmitted by Mr. J. Caldwell, and notes respecting them communicated by Mr. Caldwell.]

Proc. Zool. Soc. London, 1863, pp. 48, 49.

281

On a new species of the genus *Pipra* from New Granada.

Proc. Zool. Soc. London, 1863, pp. 63, 64, pl. x.

Pipra leucorrhoa is described and figured

282

[Exhibition of a skin of the female of *Diardigallus prœlatus*, transmitted by Sir R. Schomburgk.]

Proc. Zool. Soc. London, 1863, pp. 76, 77.

283

On the American Spine-tailed Swifts of the genus *Chætura*.

Proc. Zool. Soc. London, 1863, pp. 98–102, pl. xiv, fig 1.

A synopsis of the American species of the genus *Chætura*. *C. cinereiventris* is figured.

284

[Announcement of the arrival of a collection of Indian Pheasants.]

Proc. Zool. Soc. London, 1863, p. 104.

This collection consisted of specimens of seven species of Pheasants and one species of Hornbill.

285

List of the species of *Phasianidæ*, with remarks on their Geographical Distribution.

Proc. Zool. Soc. London, 1863, pp. 113–127, pl. xvi.

A list of the 56 known species of Pheasants, with remarks on them and tables of their geographical distribution. *Euplocamus nobilis* is described as new and figured.

(Also separately published with additional plates. See paper No. 10.)

286

On the Mammals and Birds collected in Madagascar by Dr. Charles Moller.

Proc. Zool. Soc. London, 1863, pp. 160–165.

Two species of mammals and 40 species of birds are enumerated and remarked upon.

287

On a new Spine-tailed Swift from western Africa.

Proc. Zool. Soc. London, 1863, p. 205, pl. xiv, fig. 2.

Chætura cassini is described and figured, and the characters in which it differs from *C. sabini* are pointed out.

288

Observations on the Birds of southeastern Borneo, by the late James Mottley, esq., of Banjermassing, with notes by P. L. Sclater.

Proc. Zool. Soc. London, 1863, pp. 206–224.

A list of 134 species, with notes upon them.

289

[Observations on some of the Animals in the Zoological Gardens of Amsterdam, Rotterdam, and Antwerp.]

Proc. Zool. Soc. London, 1863, pp. 224, 225.

Notes on some of the interesting species of animals seen during a visit to the above-mentioned gardens.

290

Record of the period of gestation of certain Ruminants which breed in the Society's Gardens.

Proc. Zool. Soc. London, 1863, pp. 230, 231.

A list of the ruminants which breed in the Zoological Society's Gardens, with their periods of gestation.

291

Notes on the method of Incubation among the Birds in the order *Struthiones*.

Proc. Zool. Soc. London, 1863, pp. 233–235.

Notes on the different manners in which certain birds of the families *Struthionidæ* and *Apterygidæ* hatch their eggs and the periods taken by each of them.

292

Note on the occurrence of the European Sea Eagle in North America.

Proc. Zool. Soc. London, 1863, pp. 251–253.

Note on the supposed occurrence of *Haliaëtus albicilla* in Nova Scotia and Newfoundland.

(See also *Proc. Zool. Soc. London*, 1865, p. 731.)

293

[Announcement of Mr. James Thompson's departure for India to bring home collections of living animals which had been offered to the Society.]

Proc. Zool. Soc. London, 1863, pp. 370, 371.

294

On some new and interesting Animals recently acquired for the Society's Menagerie.

Proc. Zool. Soc. London, 1863, pp. 374–378, pls. xxxi–xxxiv.

Remarks on *Lagothrix humboldtii, Galago alleni, Nycticebus tardigradus, Bubo fasciolatus, Phlogœnas bartletti* (sp. nov.), *Chauna chavaria* and *Tropidonotus feroz*. *Lagothrix humboldtii, Galago alleni, Bubo fasciolatus* and *Phlogœnas bartletti* are figured.

295

[Exhibition of some variegated wool from Ohio.]

Proc. Zool. Soc. London, 1863, p. 438.

296

Note on the breeding of Bennett's Cassowary in the Society's Gardens.

Proc. Zool. Soc. London, 1863, pp. 518, 519, pl. xlii.

Remarks on the breeding of *Casuarius bennetti* in the Zoological Society's Gardens, with a figure of the young bird.

(See also *Proc. Zool. Soc. London*, 1864, p. 271.)

297

Note on the Harrier of Bourbon (*Circus maillardi*, Verreaux).

Ibis, 1863, pp. 163–165, pl. iv.

Circus maillardi is remarked upon and figured.

298

Note on the Eastern-Asiatic Thrushes of the genus *Turdus*.

Ibis, 1863, pp. 195–198.

Turdus hortulorum is described as new, and a table of the geographical distribution of the thrushes of the genus *Turdus* in eastern Asia is given.

299

Synopsis of the known species of *Dacnis*.

Ibis, 1863, pp. 311–317, pl. vii.

A synopsis of the 12 known species of *Dacnis*, of which *Dacnis venusta* is figured.

300

List of recent additions to the genus *Calliste*.

Ibis, 1863, pp. 450–452, pl. xii.

A list of, with remarks upon, five additional species of *Calliste* described since the publication of the "Monograph of the birds forming the Tanagrine genus *Calliste*." *C. dowii* is figured.

301

Note on the Wombats living in the Gardens of the Zoological Society.

Ann. and Mag. Nat. Hist., ser. 3, XII, p. 78 (1863).

Note on the distinctness of certain species of *Phascolomys*.

302

Note on Pallas's Sand Grouse.

Zoologist, 1863, p. 8721.

Note on the occurrence of Pallas's Sand Grouse (*Syrrhaptes paradoxus*) in England in 1859.

303

List of a collection of Birds from Huaheine, Society Islands.

Proc. Zool. Soc. London, 1864, pp. 8, 9.

A list of 10 species, with remarks upon them.

304

On some additions to the list of the Birds of the Falkland Islands.

Proc. Zool. Soc. London, 1864, p. 73.

The occurrence of *Egretta leuce* and *Prion turtur* in the Falkland Islands is recorded.

(See also *Proc. Zool. Soc. London*, 1860, p. 382; 1861, p. 45.)

305

On the species of the genus *Chauna*.

Proc. Zool. Soc. London, 1864, pp. 74–76, pl. xi.

The diagnoses of the three species *Chauna chavaria, C. derbiana* and *C. nigricollis* are given, of which the last is described as a new species and figured.

(See paper No. 389.)

306

On the Mammals collected and observed by Capt. J. H. Speke during the East-African expedition. With notes by Capt. J. H. Speke.

Proc. Zool. Soc. London, 1864, pp. 98–100, pls. xii, xiii.

A list of 39 species, with Captain Speke's field notes. *Tragelaphus spekii* and *Oreas livingstonii* are described as new species, of which the former and *Golunda pulchella* are figured.

307

On the Birds collected by Capt. J. H. Speke during the East-African expedition. With notes by Capt. J. H. Speke.

Proc. Zool. Soc. London, 1864, pp. 106–115, pl. xiv.

A list of 62 species, with remarks upon them. *Psalidoprocne albiceps* is described and figured.

308

On the species of the American genus *Coccyzus*.

Proc. Zool. Soc. London, 1864, pp. 119–122.

The eight known species of *Coccyzus* are enumerated, and their synonomy and geographical ranges given. *C. bairdi* is described as a new species.

(See also *Proc. Zool. Soc. London*, 1870, p. 165.)

309

[On some important additions to the Menagerie.]

Proc. Zool. Soc. London, 1864, pp. 138, 139.

310

[Announcement of the arrival of a living *Didunculus* and of other additions to the Society's Menagerie.]

Proc. Zool. Soc. London, 1864, p. 158.

311

On two new species of Birds from New Granada.

Proc. Zool. Soc. London, 1864, pp. 166, 167.

Basileuterus cinereicollis and *Thripophaga guttuligera* are described.

312

[Announcement of Mr. James Thompson's (the Society's head keeper) safe arrival at Calcutta.]

Proc. Zool. Soc. London, 1864, p. 168.

313

[Exhibition of a series of bird skins collected by the Rev. H. B. Tristram's expedition in Palestine.]

Proc. Zool. Soc. London, 1864, pp. 169, 170.

Exhibition to the Zoological Society of London of a series of bird skins from Palestine, of which *Passer moabiticus* and *Caprimulgus tamaricis* are characterized.

314

List of a collection of Birds procured by Mr. George H. White in the vicinity of the City of Mexico.

Proc. Zool. Soc. London, 1864, pp. 172–179.

An annotated list of 156 species.

315

On a new species of White Cockatoo living in the Society's Gardens.

Proc. Zool. Soc. London, 1864, pp. 187, 189, pl. xvii.

Cacatua ophthalmica is described, and a list of the species of *Cacatua*, with their diagnoses, given. *Cacatua ducorpsii* is figured. *C. ophthalmica* was figured as *C. ducorpsii* (*Proc. Zool. Soc. London*, 1862, pl. xiv).

316

Notes on the species of *Tadorna* in the Society's Menagerie.

Proc. Zool. Soc. London, 1864, p. 189, pls. xviii, xix.

A diagnosis of the six species of *Tadorna*, with remarks upon their habits, variation in the colouring of the sexes, and geographical distribution. *Tadorna tadornoides* and *T. variegata* are figured.

(See also *Proc. Zool. Soc. London*, 1864, p. 299; 1866, p. 148.)

317

Characters of a new species of *Falco* discovered by the late Dr. Dickinson, of the Central African Mission, on the River Shiré.

Proc. Zool. Soc. London, 1864, p. 248.

Falco dickinsoni is described, and the new subgenus *Dissodectes* is proposed, to include this species, together with *Falco ardesiacus* and *F. zoniventris*.

318

Note on the species of Cuckoos of the genus *Neomorphus*.

Proc. Zool. Soc. London, 1864, pp. 249, 250.

Neomorphus geoffroyii and *N. rufipennis* are characterized.

(See also *Proc. Zool. Soc. London*, 1866, p. 59.)

319

[Remarks on the Breeding of Bennett's Cassowary in the Society's Gardens.]

Proc. Zool. Soc. London, 1864, p. 271.

Remarks on Bennett's Cassowary (*Casuarius bennettii*) breeding in the Zoological Society's Gardens, and exhibition of the skeleton of the original typical example of this species.

(See also *Proc. Zool. Soc. London*, 1863, p. 518.)

320

Characters of three new American Parrots.

Proc. Zool. Soc. London, 1864, pp. 297, 298, pl. xxiv.

Conurus rhodogaster, Natt. MS., *Brotogerys chrysosema*, Natt. MS., and *Chrysotis finschi* are described. *Conurus rhodogaster* is figured.

321

Note on the Geographical Distribution of the Ducks of the genus *Dendrocygna*.

Proc. Zool. Soc. London, 1864, pp. 209–301.

The geographical distribution of the species of the genus *Dendrocygna* is given, and remarks made upon them.

(See also *Proc. Zool. Soc. London*, 1864, p. 189; 1866, p. 148.)

322

Notes on a collection of Birds from the Isthmus of Panama. By P. L. Sclater and Osbert Salvin.

Proc. Zool. Soc. London, 1864, pp. 342–373, pl. xxx.

An annotated list of 272 species collected by Mr. James M'Leannan on the Isthmus of Panama. The following species are described as new : *Cassiculus microrhynchus*, *Myrmeciza immaculata*, *Camptostoma flaviventre* and *Conurus ocularis*. *Eucometis cassinii* is figured.

323

[Announcement of Mr. James Thompson's return from Calcutta with a valuable collection of animals.]

Proc. Zool. Soc. London, 1864, pp. 373, 374.

324

[Notice of additions to the Menagerie.]

Proc. Zool. Soc. London, 1864, pp. 374, 375.

325

[Exhibition of a series of specimens of birds' eggs collected in the vicinity of Barrackpore and presented to the Society by Lieut. R. C. Beavan, with notes on their nesting habits.]

Proc. Zool. Soc. London, 1864, p. 375.

A list of 24 species is given, with notes by Lieutenant Beavan on their nesting habits.

326

Description of a new species of Duck from Madagascar.

Proc. Zool. Soc. London, 1864, pp. 487, 488, pl. xxxiv.

Anas melleri is described and figured.

327

[On some additions to the Menagerie.]

Proc. Zool. Soc. London, 1864, p. 587.

328

Descriptions of seven new species of Birds discovered by the late Dr. John Natterer in Brazil.

Proc. Zool. Soc. London, 1864, pp. 605–611, pls. xxxvii–xxxix.

The new genus *Liosceles* (figured in text) is proposed and the following species are described : *Granatellus pelzelni*, *Tanagra olivina*, Natt. MS., *Spermophila pileata* (Natt. MS.), *Poospiza oxyrhyncha* (Natt. MS.), *Hypocnemis flavescens* (Natt. MS.), *Pteroptochus thoracicus* and *Pipra nattereri*. The three known species of *Granatellus* are diagnosed, and figures are given of *Granatellus pelzelni*, *G. venustus*, *Pteroptochus thoracicus* and *Pipra nattereri*.

329

Note on the Quadrumana living in the Society's Menagerie.

Proc. Zool. Soc. London, 1864, pp. 709–712, pls. xl, xli.

A systematic list of the species of Quadrumana living in the Zoological Society's Menagerie, with notes upon the following : *Macacus speciosus*, *M. cyclopis*, *Galago garnetti* and *G. crassicaudata*. *Galago garnetti* and *Pithecia satanas* are figured.

330

Note on the Caprimulgine genus *Cosmetornis*.

Ibis, 1864, pp. 114, 115, pl. ii.

Notes on *Cosmetornis vexillarius* and *C. burtoni*, of which the former is figured.

331

On the Birds of the Comoro Islands.

Ibis, 1864, pp. 292–301, pl. vii.

General remarks on the Comoro Islands and an annotated list of 23 species of birds. *Accipiter francesi* is figured.

332

On the Rapacious Birds collected by the late Dr. Dickinson in the Zambesi Region.

Ibis, 1864, pp. 301–307, pl. viii.

A list of 22 species, with remarks upon them. *Falco dickinsoni* is figured.

333

On a new species of *Tetragonops*.

Ibis, 1864, pp. 371, 372, pl. x.

Tetragonops frantzii is described and figured.

334

Note on the Great Auk.

Ann. and Mag. Nat. Hist., ser. 3, XIV, p. 320 (1864).

Note calling attention to the existence of specimens of the skins and eggs of the great auk omitted from Mr. Champley's list. (*Ann. and Mag. Nat. Hist.*, ser. 3, XIV, p. 235.)

335

The Mammals of Madagascar.

Quart. Journ. Sci., London, I, pp. 213–219, pl. ii (1864).

A summary view of the mammal fauna of Madagascar and arguments, from the evidence thus adduced, as to the former connection of this island with the continents of Africa, Asia and America, and its present position in zoological geography. The name Lemuria is proposed for this supposed submerged continent. A plate of the typical mammals of Madagascar is subjoined.

336

[Notice of a Mantchurian Deer received from Mr. Swinhoe.]

Proc. Zool. Soc. London, 1865, pp. 1, 2.

Note on the Mantchurian Deer which had been sent to the Gardens of the Zoological Society of London by Mr. Swinhoe.

337

[Notice of a Prong-horned Antelope added to the Society's Menagerie.]

Proc. Zool. Soc. London, 1865, p. 60, pl. iii.

Note, accompanied by a figure, on the acquisition, by the Zoological Society of London, of a young male specimen of *Antilocapra americana*.

338

[Remarks upon a stuffed specimen of a Water-Pipit (*Anthus spinoletta*) from the collection of the Bishop of Oxford.]

Proc. Zool. Soc. London, 1865, p. 60.

Remarks upon, and exhibition to a meeting of the Zoological Society of London, of a stuffed specimen of *Anthus spinoletta* (Linn.), which had been shot near Brighton.

339

[Exhibition of the type specimen of *Galago monteiri* and remarks on *Galago crassicaudata* and *G. crassicaudata* var. *kirkii*.]

Proc. Zool. Soc. London, 1865, pp. 60, 61.

Exhibition to a meeting of the Zoological Society of London of the type specimen of *Galago monteiri*, and remarks pointing out the differential characters of the species, *G. crassicaudata* and *G. crassicaudata* var. *kirkii*.

340

Note on the Breeding of a Ground-Pigeon in the Society's Menagerie.

Proc. Zool. Soc. London, 1865, pp. 238-240.

Note on *Phlogœnas crinigera* breeding in the Zoological Society's Gardens, and remarks on the separation, by Bonaparte, of the Ground Pigeons of America from those of the Old World.

341

On a new species of the genus *Basileuterus* of Cabanis, with a synopsis of the known species of the genus.

Proc. Zool. Soc. London, 1865, pp. 282-286, pls. ix, x.

Basileuterus mesoleucus is described as new, and a synopsis of the 15 known species of the genus *Basileuterus* is given. The following species are figured: *B. mesoleucus*, *B. cinereicollis*, *B. semicervinus* and *B. uropygialis*.

342

[Notice of several additions to the Society's Menagerie.]

Proc. Zool. Soc. London, 1865, p. 318.

343

Description of a new species of Passerine Bird from Madagascar.

Proc. Zool. Soc. London, 1865, pp. 326, 327, pl. xiii.

Hylophorba ruticilla (gen. et sp. nov.) is described and figured.

344

Description of a new species of Indian Porcupine.

Proc. Zool. Soc. London, 1865, pp. 352-356, pl. xvi.

Hystrix malabarica, Day, is described and figured, and a list of the known species of *Hystrix* and their localities added.

345

[Remarks upon a collection of Bird Skins formed by the Society's corresponding member, M. Adolphe Boucard, in the vicinity of Vera Cruz, Mexico.]

Proc. Zool. Soc. London, 1865, p. 397.

Exhibition of, to a meeting of the Zoological Society of London, and notes upon, a collection of bird skins obtained near Vera Cruz, Mexico, by M. A. Boucard.

346

Description of a new Accipitrine Bird from Costa Rica.

Proc. Zool. Soc. London, 1865, pp. 429, 430, pl. xxiv.

Leucopternis princeps is described and figured.

347

[Remarks on a rare Parrot from Dominica.]

Proc. Zool. Soc. London, 1865, pp. 437, 438.

Remarks on a young specimen of *Chrysotis augusta* which had been sent by Mr. Bernard from Dominica, West Indies, to the Gardens of the Zoological Society of London.

348

[Exhibition of a photograph of a pair of Gayals intended for the Menagerie.]

Proc. Zool. Soc. London, 1865, p. 465.

349

[Exhibition of a drawing of *Paradisea calva*, lately discovered in the Island of Waigiou.]

Proc. Zool. Soc. London, 1865, p. 465.

350

[Notice of recent additions to the Menagerie.]

Proc. Zool. Soc. London, 1865, p. 466.

351

[Exhibition of specimens of *Heliomaster angelæ*, and notes thereupon by Professor Burmeister, For. Memb.]

Proc. Zool. Soc. London, 1865, pp. 466, 467.

352

Report on a collection of Animals from Madagascar, transmitted to the Society by Mr. J. Caldwell.

Proc. Zool. Soc. London, 1865, pp. 467-470, pl. xxvii.

This collection consisted of two species of mammals (*Nyctinomus* (*Mormopterus* n. subg.) *jugularis*, n. sp., and *Mus*, sp.?) determined by Dr. W. Peters, five species of reptiles determined by Dr. Günther, and one crayfish (*Astacus caldwelli* n. sp.) determined by Mr. Spence Bate. The crayfish is figured.

353

[Announcement of the arrival of a young male African Elephant in the Society's Gardens.]

Proc. Zool. Soc. London, 1865, p. 510.

354

Notes on the genera and species of *Cypselidæ*.

Proc. Zool. Soc. London, 1865, pp. 593-617, pls. xxxiii, xxxiv.

Observations on the correct position in the natural system of the *Cypselidæ*, as evidenced by the form of the sternum and the number of the phalanges of the toes, together with a synopsis of the family. *Hirundinapus* and *Nephœcetes* are revised from *Hirundapus* and *Nephocætes* as sectional names of *Chætura* and *Cypseloides*, respectively, *Cypselus infumatus* and *Chætura biscutata* are described as new species, and *Cypselus squamatus* and *Chætura biscutata* are figured. The genera treated of are: *Cypselus*, *Panyptila*, *Chætura*, *Cypseloides*, *Collocalia* and *Dendrochelidon*.

355

[Exhibition of bird skins collected by Mr. Henry Whitely in Japan.]

Proc. Zool. Soc. London, 1865, p. 618.

356

On a new Parrot of the genus *Nasiterna*.

Proc. Zool. Soc. London, 1865, pp. 620–622, pl. xxxv.

Nasiterna pusio is described and figured.

357

[On recent additions to the Menagerie, with notes.]

Proc. Zool. Soc. London, 1865, pp. 675, 676.

358

[Notices of Animals observed in several Continental Zoological Gardens.]

Proc. Zool. Soc. London, 1865, pp. 676, 677.

Remarks on the animals observed during a visit to the Zoological Gardens of Hamburg, Rotterdam and Amsterdam.

359

On the structure of *Leptosoma discolor*.

Proc. Zool. Soc. London, 1865, pp. 682–689.

Remarks on some peculiar points in the structure of *Leptosoma discolor*, and a suggestion that this species should form the type of a new family, near the *Coraciidæ* in the natural system. Illustrations in text.

360

[Correction of some previous remarks on the supposed occurrence of *Haliaëtus albicilla* in America.]

Proc. Zool. Soc. London, 1865, p. 731.

The supposed occurrence of *Haliaëtus albicilla* in America is stated to be an error, and the two specimens captured in Nova Scotia and Newfoundland (*Proc. Zool. Soc. London*, 1863, p. 251) are here referred to *H. leucocephalus*.

361

Note on two rare species of the American genus *Dendrœca*.

Ibis, 1865, pp. 87–89.

Note on *Dendrœca chrysoparia* and *D. occidentalis*, with diagnosis of the four closely allied species, *D. virens*, *D. occidentalis*, *D. townsendi* and *D. chrysoparia*.

362

Notes on Krüper's Nuthatch and on the other known species of the genus *Sitta*.

Ibis, 1865, pp. 306–311, pl. vii.

A description and figure of *Sitta krueperi*, Pelz. and remarks upon the twelve other known species of the genus *Sitta*.

363

Description of a new species of Tanager of the genus *Iridornis*.

Ibis, 1865, pp. 495, 496.

Iridornis reinhardti is described and figured.

364

Note on the so-called "Japanese" Pig (*Centuriosus pliciceps*, Gray; *Ptychochœrus plicifrons*, Fitzinger).

Ann. and Mag. Nat. Hist., ser. 3, XV, pp. 154, 155 (1865).

Note pointing out that the so-called "Japanese" pig is probably only a domesticated variety, and that its true home is China.

365

On the birth of a young Hippopotamus in the Zoological Society's Gardens at Amsterdam.

Rep. Brit. Assoc. Adv. Sci., 1865, pt. 2, p. 93.

Note on the birth of a young hippopotamus in the Zoological Society's Gardens at Amsterdam, which was believed to be the first successful instance of the reproduction of this animal in Europe.

366

The Mammals of Australia.

Quart. Journ. Sci., London, II, pp. 13–19 (1865). With a plate.

A summary view of the mammal-fauna of Australia, which serves to show that this fauna differs in a most marked degree from that of every other part of the world. A plate of the typical mammals of Australia is given.

367

The Mammals of South America.

Quart. Journ. Sci., London, II, pp. 605–621 (1865). With a plate.

A general outline of the mammal-fauna of South America, and a summary of its principal characteristics, which distinguish this region from the other regions of the world's surface. A plate of the typical mammals of South America is given.

368

[Notice of the addition of a Gayal (*Bos frontalis*) to the Society's Menagerie.]

Proc. Zool. Soc. London, 1866, p. 1, pl. i.

Notice of the addition of a young male Gayal to the Zoological Society's Gardens, which had been presented to the Society by Babu Rajendra Mullick. A figure of the animal is given.

369

[Remarks on *Lemur leucomystax*, Bartlett.]

Proc. Zool. Soc. London, 1866, pp. 1, 2.

Note pointing out that *Lemur leucomystax*, Bartlett, is probably only the female of *Lemur macaco*, Gm.

370

Report on Birds collected at Windvogelberg, South Africa, by Captain G. E. Bulger, C. M. Z. S.

Proc. Zool. Soc. London, 1866, pp. 21–23.

A list of 44 species, determined by Dr. Hartlaub, of which *Hemipteryx immaculata* is described as new.

371

[Remarks on the American Lepidosiren (*Lepidosiren paradoxa*).]

Proc. Zool. Soc. London, 1866, pp. 34, 35.

Remarks on the American Lepidosiren and the scarcity of specimens in European collections.

372

On a new American Cuckoo of the genus *Neomorphus*.

Proc. Zool. Soc. London, 1866, pp. 59, 60, pl. v.

Neomorphus salvini is described and figured, and a synopsis of the species of the genus *Neomorphus* given.

(See also *Proc. Zool. Soc. London*, 1864, p. 249.)

373

[Remarks on some Monkeys received from St. Kitts, West Indies.]

Proc. Zool. Soc. London, 1866, pp. 79, 80.

Remarks on the monkeys that inhabited St. Kitts, West Indies, which were undoubtedly referable to the common green monkey (*Cercopithecus callitrichus*, Geoffr.) of West Africa, and had probably been introduced.

(See also *Nature*, XXI, p. 153, 1879; XLI, p. 368, 1890.)

374

[Notice of recent additions to the Society's Menagerie.]

Proc. Zool. Soc. London, 1866, p. 80.

375

[Exhibition of a collection of Mammals and Birds from Japan.]

Proc. Zool. Soc. London, 1866, pp. 80, 81.

376

On the Birds of the vicinity of Lima, Peru. With notes on their habits by Prof. W. Nation, of Lima, C. M. Z. S. Part I. *

Proc. Zool. Soc. London, 1866, pp. 96–100, pl. xi.

An annotated list of 23 species, of which *Geositta crassirostris* and *Myiobius nationi* are described as new. *Myiobius nationi* and *M. pulcher* (from Ecuador) are figured.

*(For Part II see *Proc. Zool. Soc. London*, 1867, p. 340; Pt. III, 1869, p. 146; Pt. IV, 1871, p. 496; Pt. V, 1881, p. 484.)

377

[Notice of a Pudu Deer recently added to the Society's Menagerie.]

Proc. Zool. Soc. London, 1866, pp. 104, 105.

Notice of the addition to the Zoological Society's Menagerie of a specimen of *Cervus pudu* which had been presented by Mr. Charles Bath. The head of the animal is figured in the text.

378

Notes upon the American *Caprimulgidæ*.

Proc. Zool. Soc. London, 1866, pp. 123–145, pls. xlii, xiv.

General observations on the *Caprimulgidæ*, with a synopsis of the American species of the family, of which 42 are enumerated. Gray's genus *Eleothreptus* is emended to *Heleothreptus* and three new subgenera are created, viz, *Podochœtes*, *Diplopsalis* and *Macropsalis*. *Stenopsis ruficervix* is described as a new species. A table showing the distribution of the species in America is appended. Figures are given of *Stenopsis ruficervix* and *Antrostomus parvulus*. Illustrations are given in the text. The genera treated of are: *Nyctibius*, *Steatornis*, *Podager*, *Lurocalis*, *Chordeiles*, *Antrostomus*, *Stenopsis*, *Hydropsalis*, *Heleothreptus*, *Nyctidromus* and *Siphonornis*.

(See also *Proc. Zool. Soc. London*, 1866, p. 581.)

379

Additional notes on the *Anatidæ* of the genera *Dendrocygna* and *Tadorna*.

Proc. Zool. Soc. London, 1866, pp. 148–150.

Additional notes to previous communications on the genera *Dendrocygna* and *Tadorna* (cf. *Proc. Zool. Soc. London*, 1864, pp. 189, 200).

380

Catalogue of Birds collected by Mr. E. Bartlett on the River Ucayali, eastern Peru, with notes and descriptions of new species. By P. L. Sclater and Osbert Salvin.

Proc. Zool. Soc. London, 1866, pp. 175–201, pl. xviii.

An annotated catalogue of 253 species. Two new genera, viz, *Stigmatura* and *Metopothrix*, and the following new species are described: *Spermophila ocellata*, *Furnarius torridus*, *Synallaxis tericolor*, *S. vulpecula*, *Hypocnemis melanura*, *H. hemileuca*, *Muscisaxicola fluviatilis*, *Serpophaga hypoleuca*, *Metopothrix aurantiacus*, *Leucippus chlorocercus*, Gould MS., and *Thaumantias bartletti*, Gould MS. *Metopothrix aurantiacus* is figured.

(See also *Proc. Zool. Soc. London*, 1866, p. 566.)

381

[Notice of additions to the Society's Menagerie, and of the transmission of a Manatee to the Society by Mr. G. W. Latimer, of Puerto Rico.]

Proc. Zool. Soc. London, 1866, p. 201.

382

[Remarks on recent additions to the Society's Menagerie.]

Proc. Zool. Soc. London, 1866, p. 203.

383

Note on the genus *Geobates* of Swainson.

Proc. Zool. Soc. London, 1866, pp. 204, 205, pl. xxi.

Remarks on *Geobates brevicauda* of Swainson, which species is shown to have been described eight years previously by Maximilian, under the name of *Anthus pœcilopterus*. The name *Geobates pœcilopterus* must therefore be adopted. A description, list of synonyms, and a plate of the bird, are given.

384

[Notice of several interesting species of Mammals and Birds living in the Gardens of the Société Zoologique d'Acclimatation of Paris.]

Proc. Zool. Soc. London, 1866, p. 210.

385

On a new species of the genus *Accipiter* from New Granada.

Proc. Zool. Soc. London, 1866, pp. 302–304.

Accipiter ventralis is described, and a synopsis of the nine known American species of *Accipiter* is added.

386

[Notice of a rare American Monkey (*Pithecia leucocephala*) lately added to the Society's Menagerie.]

Proc. Zool. Soc. London, 1866, p. 305.

Note on a specimen of *Pithecia leucocephala*, which had been obtained in Demerara, and presented to the Zoological Society by Mr. W. H. Barton.

387

Descriptions of six new species of American Oscines.

Proc. Zool. Soc. London, 1866, pp. 320–324.

The genus *Spodiornis* (illustrated in text) and the following new species are described: *Turdus subcinereus*, *Cinclocerthia macrorhyncha*, *Thryothorus martinicensis*, *Hylophilus pectoralis*, *H. brunneiceps* and *Spodiornis jardini*.

388

[Notice of a specimen of the Californian Vulture (*Cathartes californianus*) recently added to the Society's collection.]

Proc. Zool. Soc. London, 1866, p. 366.

Note on, and illustration of, a specimen of *Cathartes californianus* presented to the Zoological Society's Menagerie by Dr. Colbert A. Canfield.

389

Note on *Chauna nigricollis*.

Proc. Zool. Soc. London, 1866, pp. 369, 370.

Note pointing out that *Chauna derbiana*, Gray, and *Chauna nigricollis*, Sclater, are identical.

(See paper No. 305.)

390

[Exhibition of a young specimen of *Chauna derbiana*, forwarded by Dr. W. Huggins, of San Fernando, Trinidad, C. M. Z. S.]

Proc. Zool. Soc. London, 1866, p. 417.

391

On some additions to the Catalogue of Birds collected by Mr. E. Bartlett on the River Ucayali. By P. L. Sclater and Osbert Salvin.

Proc. Zool. Soc. London, 1866, pp. 566, 567.

A list of, with remarks upon, 20 additional species to Mr. Bartlett's former list.

(See also *Proc. Zool. Soc. London*, 1866, p. 175.)

392

Additional notes on the *Caprimulgidæ*.

Proc. Zool. Soc. London, 1866, pp. 581–590, pls. xiv, xlvi.

Anatomical observations on the genus *Podargus*, and additional notes on various species of American *Caprimulgidæ*.* *Antrostomus ornatus* is described as new and figured. *Antrostomus maculicaudus* is also figured. Illustrations are given in the text.

*(For former paper, cf. *Proc. Zool. Soc. London*, 1866, p. 123.)

393

Note on the species of the genus *Muscisaxicola*.

Ibis, 1866, pp. 56–59.

Notes on the species of *Muscisaxicola* mentioned in Messrs. Philippi and Landbeck's article on this genus (*Wiegmann's Archiv*, 1865, p. 75), and an arrangement of the nine known species.

394

Note on "*Kittacincla auricularis*," Swinhoe.

Ibis, 1866, pp. 109, 110, pl. iv.

It is here pointed out that the generic term *Kittacincla*, as applied by Mr. Swinhoe to his new species *auricularis*, is incorrect, and that the species should be referred to the genus *Sibia*. *Sibia auricularis* is figured.

395

Note on the Distribution of the species of *Chasmorhynchus*.

Ibis, 1866, pp. 406, 407.

Remarks on the range of the four known species of *Chasmorhynchus*, and observations on the note of *C. nudicollis*.

396

Report on the Extinct Birds of the Mascarene Islands. By a committee consisting of Prof. A. Newton, Rev. H. B. Tristram, and Dr. Sclater.

Rep. Brit. Assoc. Adv. Sci., 1866, pt. 1, pp. 401, 402.

Report on the collections of extinct birds' bones which had been sent home from Mauritius by Mr. George Clark, and from Rodriguez by Mr. George Jenner.

397

On the Systematic Position of the Pronghorn (*Antilocapra americana*).

Rep. Brit. Assoc. Adv. Sci., 1866, pt. 2, pp. 77, 78; *Ann. and Mag. Nat. Hist.*, ser. 3, XVIII, pp. 401–404 (1866).

Note on the systematic position of *Antilocapra americana*, which, on account of its peculiarities in structure, is proposed to form the type of a new family, viz, *Antilocapridæ*, to be placed between *Camelopardalidæ* and *Bovidæ* in the natural system. A table of the distribution of the Ruminants is appended.

398

[Exhibition of Mexican Birds and characters of a new species.]

Proc. Zool. Soc. London, 1867, pp. 1, 2, pl. i.

Exhibition, to a meeting of the Zoological Society of London, of some specimens of birds collected in Mexico by M. A. Boucard, and description and figure of a new species, *Zonotrichia boucardi*.

399

[Extracts from letters received from Mr. E. Bartlett, from Xeberos, Peru.]

Proc. Zool. Soc. London, 1867, p. 2.

400

[Notice of a new species of Ratel (*Mellivora leuconota*).]

Proc. Zool. Soc London, 1867, p. 98, pl. viii.

Mellivora leuconota is described and figured.

401

[Notices of additions to the Menagerie.]

Proc. Zool. Soc. London, 1867, p. 179.

402

Notes upon some Parrots living in the Society's Menagerie.

Proc. Zool. Soc. London, 1867, pp. 183–185, pl. xvi.

Notes on various species of parrots living in the Zoological Society's Menagerie. *Ara ambigua* and *A. militaris* are diagnosed, the differences between *Cacatua ducorpsii* and *C. ophthalmica* are pointed out, and a figure is given of *Lorius chlorocercus*.

403

[Notices of additions to the Society's Menagerie and remarks upon *Saiga tatarica*.]

Proc. Zool. Soc. London, 1867, p. 240, pl. xvii.

Remarks on *Sus taivanus* and *Saiga tatarica*, specimens of which had recently been added to the Zoological Society's Menagerie. *Saiga tatarica* is figured.

404

List of Birds collected on the Blewfields River, Mosquito Coast, by Mr. Henry Wickham. By P. L. Sclater and Osbert Salvin.

Proc. Zool. Soc. London, 1867, pp. 278–280.

A list of 39 species, with remarks upon them.

405

[Remarks on specimens of Snakes (*Boidæ*) in the Society's Menagerie.]

Proc. Zool. Soc. London, 1867. p. 315.

Notice of the addition to the Zoological Society's collection of specimens of *Morelia variegata* and *Boa eques*.

406

[Remarks on Gulls (*Laridæ*) living in the Society's Menagerie.]

Proc. Zool. Soc. London, 1867, pp. 315, 316.

Note pointing out the differences of the three species *Larus argentatus*, *L. fuscescens*, and *L. fuscus*.

407

Notes on the Birds of Chili.

Proc. Zool. Soc. London, 1867, pp. 319–340.

A résumé of the birds of Chili, of which 209 species are enumerated.

408

On the Birds of the vicinity of Lima, Peru. With notes on their habits by Prof. W. Nation. Part II.*

Proc. Zool. Soc. London, 1867, pp. 340–344, pls. xx, xxi.

A list of 12 species, with remarks upon them. *Poospiza bonapartii* and *Porzana erythrops*, nn. spp., are described and figured.

*(For part I, see *Proc. Zool. Soc. London*, 1866, p. 96; Pt. III, 1869, p. 146; Pt. IV, 1871, p. 406; Pt. V, 1881, p. 484.)

409

[Announcement of the arrival of a Lyre-Bird (*Menura superba*) in the Society's Gardens.]

Proc. Zool. Soc. London, 1867, p. 391.

410

[Report of the birth of a young male Giraffe, and list of Giraffes that have lived in the Society's Gardens.]

Proc. Zool. Soc. London, 1867, pp. 391, 392.

411

[Notices of additions to the Society's Menagerie.]

Proc. Zool. Soc. London, 1867, p. 473.

412

[Exhibition of a skull of *Tapirus bairdi* from Nicaragua.]

Proc. Zool. Soc. London, 1867, p. 473.

413

List of Birds collected by Mr. Wallace on the Lower Amazons and Rio Negro. By P. L. Sclater and Osbert Salvin.

Proc. Zool. Soc. London, 1867, pp. 566–596, pls. xxix, xxx.

An annotated catalogue of 282 species, from the examination of which conclusions are drawn as to the general character and derivation of the avifauna of the Para District. The three species, *Hylophilus rubrifrons*, *H. semicinereus* and *Heteropelma wallacii*, are described as new. Figures are given of *Hylophilus semicinereus*, *H. rubrifrons*, and *Turdus phæopygus* (jr.). Gould's MS. name *Polytmus leucorrhous*, is here published for the first time.

414

[Notices of additions to the Society's Menagerie.]

Proc. Zool. Soc. London, 1867, pp. 686, 687.

415

[Exhibition of a rare Snake (*Siphlopis fitzingeri*).]

Proc. Zool. Soc. London, 1867, p. 687.

416

[Exhibition of the Nest and Eggs of the Nutcracker (*Nucifraga caryocatactes*).]

Proc. Zool. Soc. London, 1867, p. 687.

417

Catalogue of Birds collected by Mr. E. Bartlett on the River Huallaga, eastern Peru, with notes and descriptions of new species. By P. L. Sclater and Osbert Salvin.

Proc. Zool. Soc. London, 1867, pp. 748, 749, pl. xxxiv.

A tabular list of 205 species, showing the localities whence they were obtained, with notes on the more remarkable ones and descriptions of the following: *Dendrocolaptes radiolatus*, Scl. MS.; *Thamnophilus murinus*, Natt. MS.; *Dysithamnus ardesiacus*, *Myrmotherula cinereiventris*, Scl. MS.; *Leptopogon peruvianus*, *Chætura brachycerca*, and *Celeus citreopygius*, Bp. MS. *Chætura brachycerca* is figured.

418

[Notices of additions to the Society's Menagerie.]

Proc. Zool. Soc. London, 1867, pp. 815–820, pls. xxxvi, xxxvii.

Attention is called to the more noticeable additions to the Zoological Society's Menagerie, of which *Felis aurata* and *Gazella sœmmerringi* are figured. *Tribonyx mortieri* and *Ursus piscator* are figured in text.

419

[Notice of the arrival of a collection of Animals from Calcutta.]

Proc. Zool. Soc. London, 1867, pp. 820, 821.

420

[Notices of additions to the Menagerie.]

Proc. Zool. Soc. London, 1867, pp. 890, 891.

421

[Notice of the Exhibition of a skin of *Chionis minor*.]

Proc. Zool. Soc. London, 1867, p. 891.

422

[Remarks on the breeding of the Eland in captivity.]

Proc. Zool. Soc. London, 1867, pp. 953, 954.

An extract of a letter from Lord Hill, giving an account of the Elands which had bred while in his possession at Hawkstone, Shropshire.

423

List of Birds collected at Pebas, Upper Amazons, by Mr. John Hauxwell, with notes and descriptions of new species. By P. L. Sclater and Osbert Salvin.

Proc. Zool. Soc. London, 1867, pp. 977–981, pl. xlv.

An annotated catalogue of 135 species and descriptions of the following new species: *Oryzoborus melas*, *Perenostola fortis*, *Tyranniscus gracilipes*, Scl. MS., and *Porzana fasciata*. *Perenostola funebris* is figured.

424

On Peruvian Birds collected by Mr. H. Whitely. By P. L. Sclater and Osbert Salvin. Part I.*

Proc. Zool. Soc. London, 1867, pp. 982-991, pl. xlvi.

A list of 58 species, with remarks upon them. *Muscisaxicola rubricapilla* is figured.

*(For Part II see *Proc. Zool. Soc. London*, 1868, p. 173; Pt. III, 1868, p. 568; Pt. IV, 1869, p. 151; Pt. V, 1869, p. 590; Pt. VI, 1873, p. 184; Pt. VII, 1873, p. 779; Pt. VIII, 1874, p. 677; Pt. IX, 1876, p. 15.)

425

Remarks on Dr. Léotaud's "Birds of Trinidad."

Ibis, 1867, pp. 104-108.

A commentary on Dr. A. Léotaud's "Oiseaux de l'île de la Trinidad (Antilles)." Royal 8vo, Port d'Espagne, 1866.

426

On the *Antilocapridæ*.

Ann. and Mag. Nat. Hist., ser. 3, XIX, p. 58 (1867).

A rejoinder to Dr. J. E. Gray's criticism* of a former paper on the *Antilocapridæ*.†

Ann. and Mag. Nat. Hist., ser. 3, XVIII, p. 408 (1866).
† *Rep. Brit. Assoc. Adv. Sci.*, 1866, pt. 2, p. 77.

427

Note on the species of the genus *Tribonyx*.

Ann. and Mag. Nat. Hist., ser. 3, XX, pp. 122, 123 (1867).

A diagnosis of the three species *Tribonyx mortieri*, *T. gouldi* and *T. ventralis*, of which *T. gouldi* is described as new.

428

The Bellbirds of America.

Intellectual Observer, X, pp. 401-408 (1867).

Remarks upon the four known species of the genus *Chasmorhynchus*, and their distribution in America. *Chasmorhynchus nudicollis* is figured.

429

Barbets, and their Distribution.

The Intellectual Observer, XII, pp. 241-246 (1867).

Notes on the species of the family *Capitonidæ*, and their geographic range. *Megalaima asiatica* is figured.

430

Exhibition of a drawing of a new species of Impeyan (*Lophophorus l'huysi*).]

Proc. Zool. Soc. London, 1868, p. 1, pl. i.

Exhibition to a meeting of the Zoological Society of London of a drawing of *Lophophorus l'huysi*. *L. refulgens* and *L. l'huysi* are diagnosed. The latter is figured.

431

Descriptions of new species of Birds of the families *Dendrocolaptidæ*, *Strigidæ*, and *Columbidæ*. By P. L. Sclater and Osbert Salvin.

Proc. Zool. Soc. London, 1868, pp. 53-60, pl. v.

Dendrocincla rufeceps, *Dendrocolaptes puncticollis*, *Neops barbarus*, *Syrnium fulvescens*, *Leptoptila plumbeiceps* and *L. cerviniventris* are described, and the American species of each genus enumerated. *Dendrocolaptes puncticollis* is figured. The text is illustrated.

432

[Remarks upon a Bear recently added to the Society's Menagerie.]

Proc. Zool. Soc. London, 1868, pp. 71-73, pl. viii.

Remarks upon, and figure of, an apparently new species of bear recently added to the Zoological Society's Menagerie, to which the name *Ursus nasutus* is applied. A list of the living species of bears in the society's collection is given.

433

[Exhibition of an Egg of the Guacharo (*Steatornis caripensis*).]

Proc. Zool. Soc. London, 1868, pp. 73, 74.

Exhibition to the Zoological Society of an egg of *Steatornis caripensis* which had been taken from a cave in the Island of Trinidad. A figure of the egg is given in the text.

434

List of Birds collected at Conchitas, Argentine Republic, by Mr. William H. Hudson. By P. L. Sclater and Osbert Salvin.

Proc. Zool. Soc. London, 1868, pp. 137-146.

A list of 96 species, with notes on them. The generic name *Phacellodomus* is emended to *Phacellodomus*.

(See also *Proc. Zool. Soc. London*, 1869, pp. 158, 631.)

435

On Venezuelan Birds collected by Mr. A. Goering. By P. L. Sclater and Osbert Salvin. Part I.*

Proc. Zool. Soc. London, 1868, pp. 165-173, pl. xiii.

A tabular list of 126 species, showing the localities in which they were collected, with notes upon the more remarkable ones. A new genus, *Sublegatus*, is characterized; Baird's preoccupied generic name *Heterorhina* is altered to *Henicorhina*, and the following new species are described: *Basileuterus griseiceps*, *Eusearthmus impiger* and *Sublegatus glaber*, the last two of which are figured. Illustrations are given in the text.

*(For Part II see *Proc. Zool. Soc. London*, 1868, p. 626; Pt. III, 1869, p. 250; Pt. IV, 1870, p. 779; Pt. V, 1875, p. 234.)

436

On Peruvian Birds collected by Mr. H. Whitely. By P. L. Sclater and Osbert Salvin. Part II.*

Proc. Zool. Soc. London, 1868, pp. 173-178.

A list of 28 species, with remarks upon them. The text is illustrated.

*(For Part I see *Proc. Zool. Soc. London*, 1867, p. 982; Pt. III, 1868, p. 568; Pt. IV, 1869, p. 151; Pt. V, 1869, p. 590; Pt. VI, 1873, p. 184; Pt. VII, 1873, p. 779; Pt. VIII, 1874, p. 677; Pt. IX, 1876, p. 15.)

437

[Exhibition of a stuffed specimen of a Monkey (*Cercocebus albigena*) from Cabinda, north of the River Congo.]

Proc. Zool. Soc. London, 1868, p. 183.

Exhibition to a meeting of the Zoological Society of London of a stuffed specimen of *Cercocebus albigena*, which had been procured by Mr. J. J. Monteiro from Cabinda.

438

On the Seals of the Falkland Islands. By Capt. C. C. Abbott. Communicated, with notes, by P. L. Sclater.

Proc. Zool. Soc. London, 1868, pp. 189-192.

Remarks on *Morunga elephantina*, *Otaria jubata*, *O. falklandica* and *Stenorhynchus leptonyx*.

439

Notes on Baker's Antelope (*Hippotragus bakeri*).

Proc. Zool. Soc. London, 1868, pp. 214–218, pl. xvi.

Description of and notes on the adult and young of *Hippotragus bakeri*. The three known species of *Hippotragus* are enumerated. A young male is figured. Illustrations are given in the text.

440

[Remarks upon recent additions to the Society's Menagerie.]

Proc. Zool. Soc. London, 1868, pp. 261, 262.

441

Notes on the Pelicans living in the Society's Gardens.

Proc. Zool. Soc. London, 1868, pp. 264–260, pls. xxv, xxvi.

Notes on the 10 known species of *Pelecanus*, of which the following were represented in the Zoological Society's collection: *Pelecanus onocrotalus*, *P. mitratus*, *P. crispus*, *P. rufescens*, *P. conspicillatus* and *P. fuscus*. *P. rufescens* and *P. fuscus* are figured. The text is illustrated.

(See also *Proc. Zool. Soc. London*, 1871, p. 631.)

442

[Notice of the shipment from Australia of two living examples of Owen's Apteryx.]

Proc. Zool. Soc. London, 1868, p. 319.

443

Descriptions of new or little-known American Birds of the families *Fringillidæ*, *Oxyrhamphidæ*, *Bucconidæ*, and *Strigidæ*. By P. L. Sclater and Osbert Salvin.

Proc. Zool. Soc. London, 1868, pp. 322–329, pl. xxix.

The following species are described: *Peucæa notosticta*, n. sp., *Zonotrichia quinquestriata*, n. sp., *Pyrgisoma cabanisi*, n. sp, *P. kieneri*, Bp., *Oxyrhamphus frater*, n. sp, *Monasa grandior*, n. sp, and *Gymnoglaux lawrencii*, n. sp. The known species of the genera *Peucæa*, *Pyrgisoma* and *Gymnoglaux* are enumerated. *Gymnoglaux lawrencii* is figured. Illustrations are given in the text.

444

[Exhibition of and remarks upon a skin of the Australian Cassowary.]

Proc. Zool. Soc. London, 1868, pp. 376, 377.

Exhibition of, to a meeting of the Zoological Society of London, and remarks upon a skin of *Casuarius australis*. The points in which it differs from *C. galeatus* are shown.

445

Descriptions of four new species of Birds from Veragua. By P. L. Sclater and Osbert Salvin.

Proc. Zool. Soc. London, 1868, pp. 388–390.

The following species are described: *Pyranga testacea*, *Chlorospingus hypophæus*, *Leptotriccus superciliaris* and *Eupherusa egregia*.

446

[Exhibition of Heads of the Spanish Ibex (*Capra pyrenaica*).

Proc. Zool. Soc. London, 1868, pp. 403, 404.

447

[Notices of recent additions to the Society's Menagerie.]

Proc. Zool. Soc. London, 1868, p. 404.

448

Synopsis of the American Rails (*Rallidæ*). By P. L. Sclater and Osbert Salvin.

Proc. Zool. Soc. London, 1868, pp. 442–470, pl. xxxv.

A synopsis of the American rails, of which 48 species, belonging to 10 genera, are enumerated. The genus *Thyrorhina* and the subgenus *Neocrex* are created, and the species *Porzana levraudi* and *P. castaneiceps* described as new, the former being figured. A table showing the distribution of the *Rallidæ* in America is added. Illustrations are given in the text. The following are the genera treated of: *Rallus*, *Aramides*, *Porzana*, *Orex*, *Thyrorhina*, *Porphyrio*, *Porphyriops*, *Gallinula*, *Fulica* and *Heliornis*.

449

[On additions to the Society's Menagerie, and Report on Lecomte's Expedition to the Falkland Islands.]

Proc. Zool. Soc. London, 1868, pp. 526–530.

Remarks on the additions to the Zoological Society's Menagerie, with a figure of *Rhinoceros bicornis*; and report on Lecomte's Expedition to the Falkland Islands.

450

[Announcement of the arrival of a skin and skeleton of *Elaphurus davidianus*.]

Proc. Zool. Soc. London, 1868, p. 531.

451

[On additions to the Society's Menagerie.]

Proc. Zool. Soc. London, 1868, pp. 566, 567.

452

[Remarks on the Breeding of the Eleonora Falcon near Mogador.]

Proc. Zool. Soc. London, 1868, p. 567.

An account of that portion of the Island of Mogador where *Falco eleonoræ* was found breeding.

453

On Peruvian Birds collected by Mr. Whitely. By P. L. Sclater and Osbert Salvin. Part III.*

Proc. Zool. Soc. London, 1868, pp. 568–570.

Remarks upon 11 species, with a list of the 83 species obtained by Mr. Whitely in western Peru.

*(For Part I see *Proc. Zool. Soc. London*, 1867, p. 982; Pt. II, 1868, p. 173; Pt. IV, 1869, p. 151; Pt. V, 1869, p. 596; Pt. VI, 1873, p. 184; Pt. VII, 1873, p. 779; Pt. VIII, 1874, p. 677; Pt. IX, 1876, p. 15.)

454

Descriptions of some new or little-known species of Formicarians.

Proc. Zool. Soc. London, 1868, pp. 571–575, pl. xliii.

The new genus *Neoctantes* is created for the reception of *Xenops niger*, Natt. MS., Pelz., and the following species are described: *Thamnophilus nigriceps*, *Cercomacra napensis*, *Hypocnemis hypoxantha*, *Heteroenemis simplex*, and *Conopophaga gutturalis*, of which *Hypocnemis hypoxantha* is figured. A list of the new species of *Formicariidæ* described since the publication of the "Catalogue of American Birds" in 1862 is appended. The genus *Neoctantes* is illustrated in the text.

455

[On additions to the Society's Menagerie.]

Proc. Zool. Soc. London, 1868, p. 622.

456

[Exhibition of and remarks upon two specimens of *Ampeliceps coronatus*.]

Proc. Zool. Soc. London, 1868, pp. 622, 623.

Exhibition of, to a meeting of the Zoological Society of London, and remarks upon two specimens of *Ampeliceps coronatus* from the northern part of Cochin-China.

457

[Exhibition of and remarks upon the skin of a male Kaleege.]

Proc. Zool. Soc. London, 1868, p. 623.

Exhibition of, to a meeting of the Zoological Society of London, and remarks upon a male *Euplocamus cuvieri* which had been received from Arracan.

458

On the breeding of Mammals in the Gardens of the Zoological Society of London during the past twenty years.

Proc. Zool. Soc. London, 1868, pp. 623–626.

Two tables, the first giving a list of the different mammals that have bred in the Zoological Society's Gardens from 1848 to the end of 1867, and the number of instances of the breeding of each species; the second table giving comparative lists of the numbers of species of mammals that have lived in the Gardens during that period, and of those that have bred, thus showing the proportion of breeding species to the total number of species exhibited.

459

On Venezuelan Birds collected by Mr. A. Goering. By P. L. Sclater and Osbert Salvin. Part II.*

Proc. Zool. Soc. London, 1868, pp. 626–632.

A tabular list of 99 species, showing the localities where they were collected, with notes on the more remarkable ones. *Myiarchus erythrocercus*, Scl. MS., and *Heteropelma stenorhynchum* are described.

* (For Part I see *Proc. Zool. Soc. London*, 1868, p. 165; Pt. III, 1869, p. 250; Pt. IV, 1870, p. 779; Pt. V, 1875, p. 234.)

460

On a recently discovered Tanager of the genus *Calliste*.

Ibis, 1868, pp. 71, 72, pl. iii.

The characters and figure of *Calliste cabanisi*, originally described as *C. sclateri* (Cab. *Journ. f. Ornithol.*, 1866, p. 163), are given.

461

List* of Birds collected in the Straits of Magellan by Dr. Cunningham, with remarks on the Patagonian Avifauna. By P. L. Sclater and Osbert Salvin.

Ibis, 1868, pp. 183–189.

Remarks on the general character and origin (as attested by a tabular list of the Passeres) of the Patagonian avifauna, and a list of 44 species collected in the Straits of Magellan by Dr. Cunningham, with notes upon them.

*(For second list see *Ibis*, 1869, p. 283; third list, 1870, p. 499.)

462

[Exhibition of a Skin of *Spizaëtus nipalensis* from Japan.]

Proc. Zool. Soc. London, 1869, p. 1.

463

[Exhibition of and remarks upon some specimens of the Potto (*Perodicticus potto*).]

Proc. Zool. Soc. London, 1869, pp. 1, 2.

464

On a collection of Birds from the Solomon Islands.

Proc. Zool. Soc. London, 1869, pp. 118–120, pls. ix, x.

A list of 21 species, with notes on them. *Graccula kreffti*, *Eurystomus crassirostris*, and *Rallus intactus* are described as new, the first and last of which are figured. The previous works on the Solomon Islands birds are enumerated and remarked upon. A list of the known species of birds of the Solomon Islands and their distribution are given, and observations made with regard to the zoo-geographical position of the Solomon group.

465

Notes on the species of the genus *Asturina*. By P. L. Sclater and Osbert Salvin.

Proc. Zool. Soc. London, 1869, pp. 129–134.

A review of the genus *Asturina*. Seven species are enumerated, of which *A. ruficauda* is described as new.

466

[Exhibition of some Reptiles transmitted to the Society by Mr. G. Wilks, of Buenos Ayres, C. M. Z. S.]

Proc. Zool. Soc. London, 1869, p. 135.

467

On the Birds of the vicinity of Lima, Peru. With notes on their habits by Prof. W. Nation, of Lima, C. M. Z. S. Part III.*

Proc. Zool. Soc. London, 1869, pp. 146–148, pl. xii.

A list of 13 species, with notes. *Neorhynchus* is proposed to take the place of Lesson's preoccupied generic term *Callirhynchus*. *Neorhynchus nasesus* (on the plate *nasesus*) is figured.

*(For Part I see *Proc. Zool. Soc. London*, 1866, p. 96; Pt. II, 1867, p. 340; Pt. IV, 1871, p. 496; Pt. V, 1881, p. 484.)

468

[Exhibition of some new Australian Birds lately described by Mr. E. P. Ramsay.]

Proc. Zool. Soc. London, 1869, p. 149.

469

[Notices of additions to the Society's Menagerie during the months of January and February, 1869.]

Proc. Zool. Soc. London, 1869, p. 149.

470

[Exhibition of a Hybrid Pheasant.]

Proc. Zool. Soc. London, 1869, p. 149.

A hybrid between *Euplocamus nycthemerus* and *Thaumalia picta*.

471

On Peruvian Birds collected by Mr. Whitely. By P. L. Sclater and Osbert Salvin. Part IV.*

Proc. Zool. Soc. London, 1869, pp. 151–158, pl. xiii.

An annotated list of 47 species, of which *Saltator latielavius*, *Poospiza cæsar*, *Agriornis insolens*, and *Centrites oreas* are described as new. *Agrior-*

nis andicola (Scl., *P. Z. S.*, 1860, p. 78) is renamed *A. pollens*, the former name having been already used by Lafresnaye and D'Orbigny. *Poospiza cæsar* is figured.

*(For Part I see *Proc. Zool. Soc. London*, 1867, p. 982; Pt. II, 1868, p. 173; Pt. III, 1868, p. 568; Pt. V, 1869, p. 596; Pt. VI, 1873, p. 184; Pt. VII, 1873, p. 779; Pt. VIII, 1874, p. 677; Pt. IX, 1876, p. 15.)

472

Second list of Birds collected at Conchitas, Argentine Republic, by Mr. William H. Hudson, together with some notes upon another collection from the same locality. By P. L. Sclater and Osbert Salvin.

Proc. Zool. Soc. London, 1869, pp. 158–162.*

A list of 14 species not represented in Mr. Hudson's former collection, with remarks upon them; also a list, with notes, of 10 species collected by Mr. Haslehust, not represented in either of Mr. Hudson's collections.

*(See also *Proc. Zool. Soc. London*, 1868, p. 137; 1869, p. 631.)

473

On Venezuelan Birds collected by Mr. A. Goering. By P. L. Sclater and Osbert Salvin. Part III.*

Proc. Zool. Soc. London, 1869, pp. 250–254, pl. xviii.

A list of 50 species, with the localities in which they were collected and notes upon the more remarkable ones. *Brachygalba goeringi* is described and figured.

*(For Part I see *Proc. Zool. Soc. London*, 1868, p. 165; Pt. II, 1868, p. 626; Pt. IV, 1870, p, 779; Pt. V, 1875, p. 234.)

474

[Notice of additions to the Society's Menagerie.]

Proc. Zool. Soc. London, 1869, pp. 276, 277, pl. xx.

A list of the more noticeable additions to the Zoological Society's collection, of which *Phacochœrus æliani* is figured. Illustrations are given in the text.

475

[Exhibition of drawings illustrative of Wart Hogs.]

Proc. Zool. Soc. London, 1869, p. 277.

Exhibition, to a meeting of the Zoological Society of London, of drawings which showed the differences between *Phacochœrus æliani* and *P. æthiopicus*.

(See also *Ann. and Mag. Nat. Hist.*, ser. 4, VI, p. 404, 1870.)

476

On a collection of Birds made by Mr. H. S. le Strange near the city of Mexico. By P. L. Sclater and Osbert Salvin.

Proc. Zool. Soc. London, 1869, pp. 361–364.

Remarks on the rarer species (15 in number) contained in Mr. le Strange's collection of 262 species.

477

Notes on the species of the genus *Micrastur*. By P. L. Sclater and Osbert Salvin.

Proc. Zool. Soc. London, 1869, pp. 364–369.

A review of the genus *Micrastur*, of which seven species are enumerated.

478

[Notices of recent additions to the Menagerie.]

Proc. Zool. Soc. London, 1869, pp. 407, 408.

Ailurus fulgens is figured in the text.

479

Descriptions of six new species of American Birds of the families *Tanagridæ*, *Dendrocolaptidæ*, *Formicariidæ*, *Tyrannidæ*, and *Scolopacidæ*. By P. L. Sclater and Osbert Salvin.

Proc. Zool. Soc. London, 1869, pp. 416–420, pl. xxviii.

The following species are described: *Calliste florida*, *Synallaxis arequipæ*, *Gymnocichla chiroleuca*, *Grallaria princeps*, *Contopus ochraceus*, and *Gallinago imperialis*. *Calliste florida* is figured.

480

[Notices of recent additions to the Menagerie.]

Proc. Zool. Soc. London, 1869, pp. 430–432.

Orycteropus capensis is figured in the text.

481

[Exhibition of Snakes from Buenos Ayres.]

Proc. Zool. Soc. London, 1869, p. 432.

482

[Exhibition of some drawings of *Hippocampi* (*Hippocampus annulosus* and *H. brevirostris*).]

Proc. Zool. Soc. London, 1869, p. 432.

483

On two new Birds collected by Mr. E. Bartlett in eastern Peru. By P. L. Sclater and Osbert Salvin.

Proc. Zool. Soc. London, 1869, pp. 437–439, pl. xxx.

Neopipo rubicunda, gen. et. sp. nov., and *Euphonia chrysopasta*, sp. nov., are described and figured.

484

Descriptions of three new species of Tanagers from Veragua. By P. L. Sclater and Osbert Salvin.

Proc. Zool. Soc. London, 1869, pp. 439, 440, pls. xxxi, xxxii.

Buthraupis arcœi, *Tachyphonus chrysomelas* and *Chlorospingus punctulatus* are described. *Buthraupis arcœi* and *Tachyphonus chrysomelas* (both sexes) are figured.

485

[Notices of recent additions to the Menagerie.]

Proc. Zool. Soc. London, 1869, pp. 467, 469.

Macacus andamanensis and *Perodicticus potto* are figured in the text.

486

[Characters of a new species of *Ocydromus*.]

Proc. Zool. Soc. London, 1869, pp. 472, 473, pl. xxxv.

Ocydromus sylvestris is described and figured.

487

[Remarks on Animals observed in various zoological gardens on the Continent.]

Proc. Zool. Soc. London, 1869, pp. 527, 528.

Remarks on the more interesting animals observed during a visit to the gardens of Rotterdam, Amsterdam, Hamburg, Berlin, Cologne and Antwerp.

488

[Exhibition of and remarks upon the Egg of a species of Megapode.]

Proc. Zool. Soc. London, 1869, pp. 528, 529.

Exhibition, to a meeting of the Zoological Society of London, of the egg of an unknown species of Megapode, for which the name *Megapodius brazieri* was suggested.

489

Description of a new species of Mexican Wren.

Proc. Zool. Soc. London, 1869, pp. 591, 592, pl. xlv.

Thryothorus nisorius is described and figured.

490

Remarks on two species of Mammals described from specimens recently living in the Society's Gardens.

Proc. Zool. Soc. London, 1869, pp. 592–596, pl. xlvi.

Remarks on Dr. Gray's recently described species, *Mico sericeus* and *Cephalophus breviceps,* the former of which is pointed out to be referable to *Hapale chrysoleucos,* the latter to be a young example of *Cephalophus dorsalis* sive *badius.* *Cephalophus dorsalis* is figured.

491

On Peruvian Birds collected by Mr. Whitely. By P. L. Sclater and Osbert Salvin. Part V.*

Proc. Zool. Soc. London, 1869, pp. 596–601.

Two collections, one from Cosnipata, the other from Tinto, the former consisting of 42 species, of which a list is given, and 4 species are remarked upon; the latter collection containing 57 species, of which notes are made on 13 of the more remarkable ones, and *Ochthoeca polionota* and *Merganetta turneri* are described as new.

*(For Part I see *Proc. Zool. Soc. London,* 1867, p. 982; Pt. II, 1868, p. 173; Pt. III, 1868, p. 568; Pt. IV, 1869, p. 151; Pt. VI, 1873, p. 184; Pt. VII, 1873, p. 779; Pt. VIII, 1874, p. 677; Pt. IX, 1876, p. 15.)

492

[Remarks on the recent additions to the Society's Menagerie.]

Proc. Zool. Soc. London, 1869, pp. 602, 603.

493

On the breeding of Birds in the Gardens of the Zoological Society of London during the past twenty years.

Proc. Zool. Soc. London, 1869, pp. 626–629.

Two tables, the first giving a list of the different birds that have bred in the Zoological Society's Gardens from January, 1848, to December, 1868, and the number of instances of the breeding of each species; the second giving comparative lists of the numbers of species of birds that have lived in the Gardens during that period, and of those that have bred, thus showing the proportion of breeding species to the total number of species.

494

Third list of Birds collected at Conchitas, Argentine Republic, by Mr. William H. Hudson. By P. L. Sclater and Osbert Salvin.

Proc. Zool. Soc. London, 1869, pp. 631–636.*

This collection contained examples of 92 species. A list of those not included in Mr. Hudson's former collection, or which require further remarks, is given. Salvadori's MS. name *Leptoptila chalcauchenia* is adopted.

*(See *Proc. Zool. Soc. London,* 1868, p. 137; 1869, p. 158.)

495

On two new species of *Synallaxinæ.*

Proc. Zool. Soc. London, 1869, pp. 636, 637, pl. xlix.

Synallaxis curtata and *Leptasthenura andicola* are described and figured.

496

Note on the species of the genus *Hirundinea,* belonging to the family *Tyrannidæ.*

Ibis, 1869, pp. 195–198, pl. v.

Remarks on the three species, *Hirundinea bellicosa, H. ferruginea* and *H. rupestris,* which are diagnosed and figured.

(See also *Ibis,* 1882, p. 162.)

497

Second * list of Birds collected, during the survey of the Straits of Magellan, by Dr. Cunningham. By P. L. Sclater and Osbert Salvin.

Ibis, 1869, pp. 283–286.

A list of 33 species, with their localities and dates of capture. *Zonotrichia canicapilla* and *Phrygilus gayi* are remarked upon, and the synonyms given of the latter species and *P. aldunati.*

*(For first list see *Ibis,* 1868, p. 183; third list, 1870, p. 409.)

498

Touracoes and their distribution.

The Student and Intellectual Observer, II, pp. 1–6 (1869).

Notes on the species of the family *Musophagidæ,* with a table showing the distribution of the 18 known species. *Corythaix leucolopha* is figured.

499

[Notices of recent additions to the Menagerie.]

Proc. Zool. Soc. London, 1870, pp. 1, 2.

500

[Remarks on the Hairy Tapir (*Tapirus roulini*) of the Colombian Andes.]

Proc. Zool. Soc. London, 1870, pp. 51, 52.

501

On some new or little-known Birds from the Rio Paraná.

Proc. Zool. Soc. London, 1870, pp. 57, 58, pl. iii.

Notes on a small collection of birds obtained during the second American expedition to the Rio Paraná, under the command of Capt. T. J. Page, in 1859–60. *Cnipolegus cinereus* is described as new and illustrated in text. *Coryphistera alaudina* is figured.

502

[On additions to the Menagerie in January, 1870.]

Proc. Zool. Soc. London, 1870, p. 86, pl. v.

Remarks on the more noticeable additions to the Zoological Society's Menagerie, with figures of *Hylobates lar* and *H. hoolock.*

503

[Exhibition of a specimen of a newly described Lemur (*Propithecus damanus*).]

Proc. Zool. Soc. London, 1870, p. 112.

504

[Notice of a memoir on the Deer of the Old World.]

Proc. Zool. Soc. London, 1870, p. 114.

505

[Remarks on the Arrangement and Distribution of the *Cervidæ*.]

Proc. Zool. Soc. London, 1870, pp. 114–116.

A diagnosis and arrangement of the genera of the family *Cervidæ*, with a list of the 40 known species of the genus *Cervus* and their geographical distribution.

506

[On additions to the Menagerie in February, 1870.]

Proc. Zool. Soc. London, 1870, pp. 125–128, pl. x.

Notes on the more remarkable additions to the Zoological Society's collection, of which a Kangaroo (*Macropus erubescens*) is described as new and figured. The head of *M. erubescens* and the adult and young of *Cynonycteris collaris* are figured in the text.

507

[Further remarks on the locality of Amherst's Pheasant.]

Proc. Zool. Soc. London, 1870, pp. 128, 129.

Note on the locality of *Thaumalea amherstiæ.**

*(See also Swinhoe, *Proc. Zool. Soc. London*, 1870, p. 111.)

508

[Exhibition of a coloured drawing of a remarkable Pigeon (*Otidiphaps nobilis*).]

Proc. Zool. Soc. London, 1870, pp. 157, 158.

509

Notice of the arrival in the Society's Gardens of living specimens of two newly described species of *Phasianidæ*.

Proc. Zool. Soc. London, 1870, pp. 162–164, pls. xiv, xv.

Lophophorus sclateri and *Ceriornis blythii* are characterized and figured. The five known species of *Ceriornis* are enumerated.

510

Further notes on the Cuckoos of the genus *Coccyzus*.

Proc. Zool. Soc. London, 1870, pp. 165–170.

An amended synopsis of the genus *Coccyzus*. The eight known species are remarked upon.

(For former paper see *Proc. Zool. Soc. London*, 1864, p. 119.)

511

[On additions to the Society's Menagerie in March, 1870.]

Proc. Zool. Soc. London, 1870, pp. 219, 220.

512

[On additions to the Society's Menagerie in April, 1870, and description of *Canis lateralis*.]

Proc. Zool. Soc. London, 1870, pp. 279, 280, pl. xxiii.

Notes on the principal additions to the Zoological Society's Menagerie, and description and figure of *Canis lateralis*.

513

Characters of new species of Birds collected by Dr. Habel in the Galapagos Islands. By P. L. Sclater and Osbert Salvin.

Proc. Zool. Soc. London, 1870, pp. 322–327.

A tabular list of 37 species, giving the locality where each species was collected and the number of specimens obtained in each locality. The following new species are described: *Certhidea fusca, Camarhynchus variegatus, C. habeli, C. prosthemelas, Cactornis abingdoni, C. pallida,* and *Nyeticorax pauper.* The text is illustrated.

514

Notices of some new or little-known species of South American Birds.

Proc. Zool. Soc. London, 1870, pp. 328–330.

Thryothorus rufiventris, Natt. MS.; *Phlydor consobrinus* and *Melanerpes pulcher* are described. *Chætura brachycerca,* Scl. et Salv., is referred to *C. poliura,* and its synonyms and those of *C. cinereicauda* are given.

515

[Report on the additions to the Society's Menagerie during the month of May, 1870, and description of *Cervus alfredi*.]

Proc. Zool. Soc. London, 1870, pp. 380–383, pl. xxviii.

Cervus alfredi is described and figured. The heads of *Ibis bernieri* and *I. æthiopica* are illustrated in the text.

516

Synopsis of the *Cracidæ*. By P. L. Sclater and Osbert Salvin.

Proc. Zool. Soc. London, 1870, pp. 504–544.

A review of the family *Cracidæ*, embracing general observations on the *Cracidæ*, a chronological account of the writings of the principal authorities on the group, a synopsis of the species, and their geographical distribution. Fifty-two species are enumerated, one of which—*Ortalida ruficrissa*—is described as new. The genus *Stegnolæma* is created for the reception of *Ortalida montagnii,* Bp. The following genera are treated of: *Orax, Nothocrax, Pauxi, Mitua, Stegnolæma, Penelope, Penelopina, Pipile, Aburria, Chamæpetes, Ortalida* and *Oreophasis.*

517

On some recent additions to the Avifauna of Mexico. By P. L. Sclater and Osbert Salvin.

Proc. Zool. Soc. London, 1870, pp. 550, 551.

Remarks on five species not represented in previous collections from Mexico.

518

[Reports on additions to the Society's Menagerie in June, July, August, and September, 1870, and description of *Buceros subcylindricus*.]

Proc. Zool. Soc. London, 1870, pp. 663–671, pls. xxxv–xxxix.

Report on the additions to the Zoological Society's Menagerie (which include a large collection of Chilian animals sent from the Zoological Gardens of Santiago), with notes on the more remarkable specimens. *Buceros subcylindricus* is described as new and figured; figures are also given of *Macacus leoninus, Chunga burmeisteri, Metopiana peposaca,* and *Dafila spinicauda. Orycteropus æthiopicus* is figured in the text.

519

[Exhibition of a specimen of *Ceratodus forsteri*.]

Proc. Zool. Soc. London, 1870, p. 747.

520

On Venezuelan Birds collected by Mr. A. Goering. By P. L. Sclater and Osbert Salvin. Part IV.*

Proc. Zool. Soc. London, 1870, pp. 779–788, pls. xlvi, xlvii.

A list of 106 species, with remarks upon them and the localities where they were collected. The following 9 species are described as new: *Setophaga albifrons*, *Diglossa gloriosa*, *Chlorospingus goeringi*, *Buarremon merulae*, *Grallaria griseonucha*, *Ochthoëca superciliosa*, *O. nigrita*, *Conurus rhodocephalus* and *Urochroma dilectissima*. *Urochroma dilectissima*, *Chlorospingus goeringi* and *Diglossa gloriosa* are figured.

*(For Part I see *Proc. Zool. Soc. London*, 1868, p. 165; Pt. II, 1868, p. 626; Pt. III, 1869, p. 250; Pt. V, 1875, p. 234.)

521

[Reports on the additions to the Society's Menagerie in October and November, 1870.]

Proc. Zool. Soc. London, 1870, pp. 796–798.

522

Descriptions of three apparently new species of Tyrant Birds of the genus *Elainea*, with remarks on other known species.

Proc. Zool. Soc. London, 1870, pp. 831–835.

Elainea gigas, *E. fallax* and *E. pudica* are described, and a list is given of, and remarks made upon, the species of *Elainea* (16 in number) represented in Mr. Sclater's collection. The three species described are illustrated in the text.

523

On Birds collected by Mr. George M. Whitely on the coast of Honduras. By P. L. Sclater and Osbert Salvin.

Proc. Zool. Soc. London, 1870, pp. 835–839.

A nominal list of 135 species, with notes on the more interesting species.

524

Descriptions of five [six] new species of Birds from the United States of Colombia. By P. L. Sclater and Osbert Salvin.

Proc. Zool. Soc. London, 1870, pp. 840–844, pl. liii.

The following species are described: *Pheucticus uropygialis*, *Synallaxis wyatti*, *Tyranniscus leucogonys*, *T. improbus*, *T. griseiceps*, and *Trogon chionurus*. The known species of the genera *Pheucticus* and *Tyranniscus* are enumerated. Figures are given of *Tyranniscus leucogonys*, *T. cinereiceps* and *T. improbus*.

525

Note on the Systematic Position of *Indicator*.

Ibis, 1870, pp. 176–180.

From the evidence derived from an examination of the internal structure of the bird, it is here suggested that *Indicator* should form the type of a new family, *Indicatoridæ*, and be placed in the natural system in the *Coccygomorphæ*, next to the *Capitonidæ*. The text is illustrated.

526

Third* list of Birds collected, during the survey of the Straits of Magellan, by Dr. Cunningham. By P. L. Sclater and Osbert Salvin. With additional notes by the editor (A. Newton).

Ibis, 1870, pp. 499–504.

A list of 33 species, with the localities and dates of their collection. *Phalacrocorax carunculatus*, *Chlorophaga magellanica* and *Nectris amaurosoma* are remarked upon. A list of Dr. Cunningham's nests and eggs is given, and notes made on them by Prof. A. Newton.

*(For first list see *Ibis*, 1868, p. 183; second list, 1869, p. 283.)

527

Note on Ælian's Wart Hog.

Ann. and Mag. Nat. Hist., ser. 4, VI, pp. 404, 405 (1870).

Notes on Dr. Gray's supposed new species, *Phacochœrus sclateri*, which is shown to be only the female of *P. æliani*, and on the differences between *P. æliani* and *P. æthiopicus*.

(See also *Proc. Zool. Soc. London*, 1869, p. 277.)

528

Remarks on the Animals lately described by Dr. Gray as *Testudo chilensis* and *Ateles bartletti*.

Ann. and Mag. Nat. Hist., ser. 4, VI, p. 470 (1870). *

Remarks showing that the animals described as new by Dr. Gray under the names of *Testudo chilensis* and *Ateles bartletti* are not new. The former had been incorrectly determined by D'Orbigny and referred to *Testudo sulcata*, and the latter is pointed out to be referable to *Ateles variegatus*. It is proposed to change the name of *Testudo chilensis* to *Testudo argentina*.†

*(See also *Ann. and Mag. Nat. Hist.*, ser. 4, VII, p. 161, 1871.)

†(See also *Proc. Zool. Soc. London*, 1871, p. 743.)

529

The new Australian Mud-fish.

Nature, II, pp. 106, 107 (1870).

Remarks on and figure of *Ceratodus forsteri*.

530

On certain principles to be observed in the establishment of a National Museum of Natural History.

Rep. Brit. Assoc. Adv. Sci., 1870, Pt. II, pp. 123–128; *Nature*, II, pp. 455–458 (1870).

Propositions for the establishment, management and arrangement of a national museum of natural history, being remarks called forth by the occasion of the proposed removal of the natural-history objects in the British Museum at Bloomsbury, to a new institution at South Kensington.

531

African Rhinoceroses.

Student and Intellectual Observer, IV, pp. 321–326, pl. xi (1870).

Notes on the different species of African rhinoceroses, with the history and figure of the individual living in the Zoological Society's Gardens. The text is illustrated.

532

[Extracts from correspondence with Mr. G. W. des Vœux concerning the Rattailed Serpent of Santa Lucia (*Trigonocephalus lanceolatus*).]

Proc. Zool. Soc. London, 1871, pp. 2–4.

533

[Exhibition of and remarks on a horn of the male Indian Rhinoceros (*Rhinoceros unicornis*).]

Proc. Zool. Soc. London, 1871, pp. 8-11.

Exhibition to a meeting of the Zoological Society of London of a horn of a rhinoceros which had been torn off while in the Society's Gardens, with remarks on the liability under such circumstances of abnormal development in the reproduced horn. Illustrations are given in the text.

534

[Report on the additions to the Society's Menagerie in December, 1870, and observations on the register of "arrivals and departures" kept at the superintendent's office.]

Proc. Zool. Soc. London, 1871, pp. 36, 37.

535

[Exhibition of a specimen of *Ateles variegatus*.]

Proc. Zool. Soc. London, 1871, p. 39.

536

[Remarks on the so-called Axolotls in the Society's Gardens.]

Proc. Zool. Soc. London, 1871, pp. 41, 42.

Note on *Siredon mexicanus* and the supposed metamorphosis of the axolotl.

537

Notes on the types of *Tyrannula mexicana* of Kaup, and *Tyrannula barbirostris* of Swainson.

Proc. Zool. Soc. London, 1871, pp. 84, 85.

Notes pointing out that *Tyrannula mexicana*, Kaup, and *T. barbirostris*, Swainson, are referable to *Myiarchus cooperi*, Baird, and *Blacicus tristis* (Gosse), respectively.

538

Remarks on some species of *Dendrocolaptidæ* in the collection of the Smithsonian Institution.

Proc. Zool. Soc. London, 1871, pp. 85, 86.

Remarks on *Synallaxis candæi*, *Anabates ochrolæmus*, *A. montanus* and *Dendrocolaptes chuncotambo*.

539

[Report on additions to the Society's Menagerie in January, 1871.]

Proc. Zool. Soc. London, 1871, pp. 101, 102.

540

[Announcement of the birth of a Hippopotamus in the Society's Gardens.]

Proc. Zool. Soc. London, 1871, p. 145.

541

[Exhibition of and remarks upon a pair of corroded Tusks of the Indian Elephant.]

Proc. Zool. Soc. London, 1871, pp. 145, 146.

These tusks had been eaten away at their bases by a parasite.

542

Notes on the Monkeys of eastern Peru. By Edward Bartlett. (Communicated, with notes, by P. L. Sclater.)

Proc. Zool. Soc. London, 1871, pp. 217-220, pl. xiii.

Ten species of monkeys are enumerated and remarked upon. *Midas devillii* is figured.

543

Notes on rare or little-known Animals now or lately living in the Society's Gardens. Part I, Mammalia.*

Proc. Zool. Soc. London, 1871, pp. 221-240, pls. xiv-xvii.

Notes on 25 species of little-known animals exhibited in the Zoological Society's Menagerie. Figures are given of *Ateles cucullatus*, *A. melanochir*, *Lemur mongoz*, and *Cervus pudu*. The text is illustrated.

*(For Part II, Birds, see *Proc. Zool. Soc. London*, 1871, p. 489; Pt. III, Reptiles, 1871, p. 743.)

544

[Report on the additions to the Society's Menagerie in February, 1871.]

Proc. Zool. Soc. London, 1871, p. 258.

545

[Exhibition of the skin of a species of *Prinia* from Ceylon.]

Proc. Zool. Soc. London, 1871, p. 258.

The skin of *Prinia socialis* was exhibited to a meeting of the Zoological Society of London.

546

On the Birds of the Island of Santa Lucia, West Indies.

Proc. Zool. Soc. London, 1871, pp. 263-273, pl. xxi.

General notes on the zoological-geographical position of the West Indian Islands, and a summary of the previous works on the ornithology of the group. A list of 25 species from the Island of Santa Lucia is given and remarks made upon them. *Icterus laudabilis* is described and figured.

(See also *Proc. Zool. Soc. London*, 1872, p. 647; 1876, p. 13.)

547

[Report on the additions to the Society's Menagerie in March, 1871.]

Proc. Zool. Soc. London, 1871, pp. 298, 299, pl. xxix.

Viverra civetta is figured.

548

[Exhibition of and remarks upon the shell of a River Tortoise of the genus *Pelomedusa*.]

Proc. Zool. Soc. London, 1871, pp. 325, 326.

The sternum of *Pelomedusa* is figured in the text.

549

[Report on the additions to the Society's Menagerie in April, 1871.]

Proc. Zool. Soc. London, 1871, pp. 478-480, pl. xxxviii.

Remarks on the more noticeable additions to the Zoological Society's Menagerie, of which *Midas geoffroii* is figured.

550

Notes on rare or little-known Animals now or lately living in the Society's Gardens. Part II, Birds.*

Proc. Zool. Soc. London, 1871, pp. 480-496.

Twelve species of birds are remarked upon, of which *Cacatua gymnopis* is described as new. The text is illustrated.

*(For Part I, Mammals, see *Proc. Zool. Soc. London*, 1871, p. 221; Pt. III, Reptiles, 1871, p. 743.)

551

On the Birds of the vicinity of Lima, Peru. With notes on their habits by Prof. W. Nation, of Lima, C. M. Z. S. Part. IV.*

Proc. Zool. Soc. London, 1871, pp. 496–498.

Notes on five species, of which *Euscarthmus fulviceps* is described as new and illustrated in the text.

*(For Part I see *Proc. Zool. Soc. London*, 1866, p. 96; Pt. II, 1867, p. 340; Pt. III, 1869, p. 146; Pt. V, 1881, p. 484.)

552

On two new or little-known Parrots living in the Society's Gardens.

Proc. Zool. Soc. London, 1871, pp. 499, 500, pls. xl, xli.

Description of *Lorius tibialis*, n. sp., and remarks on *Trichoglossus mitchelli*. Both species are figured.

553

[Report on additions to the Society's Menagerie in May, 1871.]

Proc. Zool. Soc. London, 1871, pp. 543–546, pl. xliii.

Notes on the more remarkable animals added to the Zoological Society's Menagerie (including a second collection from the Santiago Zoological Gardens), with figure of *Tamandua tetradactyla*.

554

A revised list of the Neotropical *Laridæ*. By P. L. Sclater and Osbert Salvin.

Proc. Zool. Soc. London, 1871, pp. 564–580.

A synopsis of the Neotropical *Laridæ*, of which 32 species are enumerated. The name usually written *Chroicocephalus* for the hooded gulls is emended to *Chroocephalus*. Illustrations are given in the text. The following are the genera treated of: *Rhynchops, Anous, Nœnia, Phaethusa, Sterna, Gelochelidon, Onychoprion, Hydrochelidon, Larus, Leucophœus* and *Lestris*.

555

[Reports on additions to the Society's Menagerie for June, July, August, and September, 1871.]

Proc. Zool. Soc. London, 1871, pp. 623–627, pl. l.

Reports on the additions to the Zoological Society's Menagerie, with remarks on the more noticeable specimens. *Turtur aldabranus* * is proposed as a temporary name for a supposed new dove, and the young of *Tapirus bairdi* is figured.

*(See also *Proc. Zool. Soc. London*, 1871, p. 692.)

556

[Notice of the existence in Queensland of an undescribed species of Mammal.]

Proc. Zool. Soc. London, 1871, pp. 629, 630.

Extract of a letter containing the description of a supposed new species of mammal.

557

Additional remarks on certain species of Pelicans.

Proc. Zool. Soc. London, 1871, pp. 631–634,* pl. li.

Remarks on *Pelecanus onocrotalus, P. mitratus sive minor, P. rufescens, P. philippensis*, and *P. sharpii*, with a list of the known species (10 in number) of the genus *Pelecanus*. *P. sharpii* is figured. Illustrations are given in the text.

*(For former paper see *Proc. Zool. Soc. London*, 1868, p. 264.)

558

[Exhibition of and remarks on a skin of *Ateles variegatus*.]

Proc. Zool. Soc. London, 1871, pp. 651, 652.

559

Description of a new species of Dove from the coral reef of Aldabra.

Proc. Zool. Soc. London, 1871, pp. 692, 693, pl. lxxiii.

The temporary name *Turtur aldabranus*, applied to a supposed new dove (*Proc. Zool. Soc. London*, 1871, p. 623), is adopted, and the species described and figured.

560

[Report on the additions to the Society's Menagerie in October and November, 1871.]

Proc. Zool. Soc. London, 1871, pp. 699–701.

Remarks on the more noticeable additions to the Zoological Society's Menagerie (which include a third collection of animals from Chili), and notice of the changing of the name of the Pampas Cat from *Felis pajeros* to *Felis passerum*.

561

[Exhibition of and remarks upon a skin of the Water Opossum (*Chironectes variegatus*).]

Proc. Zool. Soc. London, 1871, p. 702.

562

Notes on rare or little-known Animals now or lately living in the Society's Gardens. Part III, Reptiles.*

Proc. Zool. Soc. London, 1871, pp. 743–749.

Notes on five species of the *Testudinata*, with special reference to the genus *Podocnemis*. *Testudo argentina*, suggested for the name of a new species (Ann. and Mag. Nat. Hist., ser. 4, VI, p. 471), is adopted. The text is illustrated.

*(For Part I, Mammals, see *Proc. Zool. Soc. London*, 1871, p. 221; Pt. II, Birds, 1871, p. 489.)

563

Remarks on a collection of Birds from Oyapok.

Proc. Zool. Soc. London, 1871, pp. 749, 750.

Ochthœca murina and *Heteropelma igniceps* are described as new, and a list of the known species of *Ochthœca* added.

564

Remarks on the species of the genera *Myiozetetes* and *Conopias*, belonging to the family *Tyrannidæ*.

Proc. Zool. Soc. London, 1871, pp. 751–756.

An arrangement of and remarks upon the species of the genera *Myiozetetes* and *Conopias*: eight species of the former genus and three of the latter are enumerated. An amended description of *Myiozetetes luteiventris* (*Elainea luteiventris*, Scl., *Proc. Zool. Soc. London*, 1858, p. 71) is given.

565

A revision of the species of the Fringilline genus *Spermophila*.

Ibis, 1871, pp. 1–23, pls. i, ii.

A revision of the species (24 in number) of the genus *Spermophila*, with remarks on their distribution. A list of 11 species unknown to the author is also given. The following species are figured: *Spermophila nigro-rufa* (♂, ♀), *S. pileata* (♂), *S. aurita* (♂), and *S. ocellata* (♀).

566

On the Land Birds of Juan Fernandez.

Ibis, 1871, pp. 178-183, pl. vii.

General remarks on the Juan Fernandez group of islands, with notes on six species of birds, of which *Anæretes fernandezianus* and *Oxyurus masafueræ* are figured.

567

Remarks on the Avifauna of the Sandwich Islands.

Ibis, 1871, pp. 356-362.

A summary of the avifauna of the Sandwich Islands, with critical remarks on Mr. S. B. Dole's "Synopsis of the Birds hitherto described from the Hawaiian Islands." (*Proc. Bost. Soc. Nat. Hist.*, XII, p. 294.) The new generic name *Chætoptila* is proposed.

568

Index of the Ornithological Literature of 1870. By Osbert Salvin and P. L. Sclater.

Ibis, 1871, pp. 417-484.

An alphabetical list of the ornithological publications in 1870, with a précis of their contents.

569

On certain species of Deer now or lately living in the Society's Menagerie.

Trans. Zool. Soc. London, VII, pp. 333-352, pls. xxviii-xxxix (1871).

A history of the introduction into the Zoological Society's Gardens of the following species of the genus *Cervus*, with their synonyms, distribution and figures: *C. davidianus, C. maral, C. cashmeerianus, C. mantchuricus, C. taëvanus, C. sika, C. duvaucelli, C. eldi*, and *C. swinhoii*. The distribution of the Elaphine deer (species allied to *Cervus elaphus*) is also given. The text is illustrated.

570

Reply to Dr. Gray on *Testudo chilensis*, etc.

Ann. and Mag. Nat. Hist., ser. 4, VII, pp. 161-163 (1871).

A reply to Dr. Gray's commentary of Mr. Sclater's criticisms on the species described by the former as *Ateles bartletti* and *Testudo chilensis*, and reference to the record of "occurrences" kept in the Zoological Society's Gardens.

(See *Ann. and Mag. Nat. Hist.*, ser. 4, VI, p. 470, 1870.)

571

Eared Seals and their Habits.

Nature, III, pp. 148, 149 (1871).

A short sketch of the characteristics and habits of the eared seals, being a review of Messrs. J. A. Allen and C. Bryant's memoir on the *Otariadæ*. (*Bull. Mus. Comp. Zool., Harvard Coll.*, II, 1870.)

572

On New Zealand Animals at the Zoological Gardens.

Nature, III, pp. 190-192 (1871).

An account of the chief peculiarities of the fauna of New Zealand, with illustrations.

573

Captain Sladen's Expedition.

Nature, IV, p. 405 (1871).

Letter on the publication of the notes relating to Captain Sladen's expedition to Yunan, and on the death of Dr. Thomas Anderson.

574

The Birds of the Lesser Antilles.

Nature, IV, pp. 473-475 (1871).

A review of the state of knowledge of the ornithology of the lesser West Indian Islands.

575

Remarks on a favourable occasion for the establishment of zoological observatories.

Rep. Brit. Assoc. Adv. Sci., 1871, Pt. II, p. 134.

On the establishment of zoological observatories on the occasion of the transit of Venus in 1874.

576

A Naturalist's Excursion in Wisconsin. Edited by H. W. Bates.

Illustrated Travels, III, pp. 1-8 (1871 ?).

An illustrated account of an excursion in Wisconsin, with descriptions of some of the places visited and observations on natural history of the country.

577

On the Quadrumana found in America north of Panama.

Proc. Zool. Soc. London, 1872, pp 2-9, pls. i, ii.

Ten species of monkeys are enumerated and remarks made upon them. Two tables are subjoined. The first shows which of the genera of South American monkeys are found in Central America, and how far they extend north; the second shows the range of the 10 species mentioned in the paper. *Nyctipithecus rufipes* is described as a new species and figured. *Ateles vellerosus* is also figured. The heads of *Mycetes caraya* and *M. villosus* are figured in the text.

578

[Report on the additions to the Society's Menagerie in December, 1871.]

Proc. Zool. Soc. London, 1872, pp. 23, 24.

579

On Kaup's Cassowary (*Casuarius kaupi*) and on the other known species of the genus.

Proc. Zool. Soc. London, 1872, pp. 147-150, pl. ix.

Remarks on *Casuarius kaupi*, with its synonyms and figure. A list of the known species of *Casuarius*, with their localities, is added. The text is illustrated.

(See also. *Proc. Zool. Soc. London*, 1874, p. 247; 1875, p. 84.)

580

[Report on the additions to the Society's Menagerie in January, 1870.]

Proc. Zool. Soc. London, 1872, pp. 183-185.

Notes on the more remarkable animals added to the Zoological Society's collection, with a list of the specimens of giraffes that have lived in the gardens.

581

[Announcement of the addition to the Society's collection of a female Sumatran Rhinoceros.]

Proc. Zool. Soc. London, 1872, p. 185.

582

[Report on the additions to the Society's Menagerie in February, 1872.]

Proc. Zool. Soc. London, 1872, pp. 493-496, pls. xxiii-xxvi.

Report on the additions to the Zoological Society's Menagerie, with notes on the more remarkable specimens. *Macacus rhesu-similis* is proposed as a temporary name for a new monkey, and a description given of the capture near Chittagong of a Sumatran rhinoceros. The following species are figured: *Rhinoceros lasiotis, Macacus rufescens, M. rhesu-similis*, and *Casuarius bicarunculatus*.

583

[Exhibition of a skin of the Yellow-billed Cuckoo (*Coccyzus americanus*) from Buenos Ayres.]

Proc. Zool. Soc. London, 1872, p. 406.

584

On the Birds of the Rio Negro of Patagonia. By W. H. Hudson, C. M. Z. S. With notes by P. L. Sclater.

Proc. Zool. Soc. London, 1872, pp. 534-550, pl. xxxi.

Notes on 23 species, with an appendix containing a list of the 48 species represented in Mr. Hudson's collection, and observations on the composition of the avifauna of the Rio Negro. *Cnipolegus hudsoni* is described as a new species and figured, and is also illustrated in the text.

585

[Report on the additions to the Society's Menagerie in March, 1872.]

Proc. Zool. Soc. London, 1872, pp. 602-604.

586

[Exhibition of the Skull of a Hairy Tapir (*Tapirus roulini*), and remarks on its differences from that of *T. terrestris*.]

Proc. Zool. Soc. London, 1872, pp. 604, 605.

The nasal bones of *Tapirus terrestris* and *T. roulini* are figured in the text.

587

On the habits of the Swallows of the genus *Progne* met with in the Argentine Republic. By W. H. Hudson, C. M. Z. S. With notes by P. L. Sclater.

Proc. Zool. Soc. London, 1872, pp. 605-609.

Remarks on the habits of *Progne purpurea*, *P. chalybea* and *P. tapera*, with notes by Mr. Sclater on the distribution of the four species of the genus *Progne*.

588

[Report on the additions to the Society's Menagerie in April, 1872.]

Proc. Zool. Soc. London, 1872, pp. 635, 636, pls. l-lii.

Pteromys magnificus, *Tapirus bairdi*, juv., and *T. terrestris*, ♀ adult, are figured.

589

Observations on the Birds of St. Lucia. By the Rev. J. E. Semper, colonial chaplain. With notes by P. L. Sclater.

Proc. Zool. Soc. London, 1872, pp. 647-653.

Notes on the species (31 in number) contained in Mr. Semper's two collections from St. Lucia.

(See also *Proc. Zool. Soc. London*, 1871, p. 263; 1876, p. 13.)

590

On the species of Quadrumana collected by Mr. Buckley in Ecuador.

Proc. Zool. Soc. London, 1872, pp. 663, 664, pl. liv.

Note on the species of monkeys (6 in number) observed by Mr. Buckley in Ecuador, with figure of *Ateles fusciceps*.

591

[Exhibition of a specimen of *Coccyzus erythrophthalmus* killed in Ireland.]

Proc. Zool. Soc. London, 1872, p. 681.

592

Additional notes on rare or little-known Animals now or lately living in the Society's Gardens.

Proc. Zool. Soc. London, 1872, pp. 688-690, pls. lvii-lix.

Notes on *Ateles rufiventris* sp. nov., *Saimaris usta*, *Galago garnetti*, *Capra picta*, *Cervus savannarum*, and *Crax incommoda* sp. nov. The following are figured: *Ateles rufiventris*, *Capra picta* and *Cervus savannarum*. The head of *Saimaris usta* is figured in the text.

(See also *Proc. Zool. Soc. London*, 1871, pp. 221, 489, 743.)

593

Report on additions to the Society's Menagerie in May, 1872.]

Proc. Zool. Soc. London, 1872, pp. 728, 729.

594

[Exhibition, for Mr. Vincent Legge, of a pair of a new Ceylonese Bird, proposed to be called *Prionochilus vincens*.]

Proc. Zool. Soc. London, 1872, pp. 729, 730.

Prionochilus vincens is described.

595

[Report on the additions to the Society's Menagerie during the months of June, July, August, and September, 1872.]

Proc. Zool. Soc. London, 1872, pp. 789-795, pl. lxvii.

Report on the additions to the Zoological Society's Menagerie, of which the most noticeable are remarked upon. The differences between the two rhinoceroses *R. lasiotis* and *R. sumatrensis* are pointed out and the latter figured. The text is illustrated.

596

[Announcement of the birth of a Hippopotamus in the Society's Gardens.]

Proc. Zool. Soc. London, 1872, p. 795.

597

[Remarks on a Mexican Spider Monkey (*Ateles*) in the Berlin Museum.]

Proc. Zool. Soc. London, 1872, p. 798.

Note on *Ateles vellerosus*.

598

[Remarks on the two Livingstone Expeditions into Inner Africa.]

Proc. Zool. Soc. London, 1872, p. 810.

599

[Report on the additions to the Society's Menagerie in October and November, 1872.]

Proc. Zool. Soc. London, 1872, pp. 860-862, pl. lxxii.

Cholopus hoffmanni and *C. didactylus* are figured.

600

[Exhibition of a nest of the Tijereta (*Milvulus tyrannus*) containing eggs of *Molothrus bonariensis*.]

Proc. Zool. Soc. London, 1872, pp. 862, 863.

Exhibition, to a meeting of the Zoological Society of London, of a nest of *Milvulus tyrannus* containing eggs of *Molothrus bonariensis*, with an extract of a letter from Mr. W. H. Hudson concerning it and the parasitic habits of the *Molothri*.

601

A Revision of the species of the Fringilline genus *Sycalis*.

Ibis, 1872, pp. 39–48, pls. ii, iii.

A review of the species (10 in number) of the genus *Sycalis*. *Sycalis pelzelni* is described and the following species are figured: *Sycalis chrysops*, *S. lutea*, and *S. aureiventris* ($\male,\female$).

602

Observations on the systematic position of the genera *Peltops*, *Eurylæmus* and *Todus*.

Ibis, 1872, pp. 177–180.

Each of the genera *Peltops*, *Eurylæmus* and *Todus* is relegated to its proper position in the natural system. *Peltops* is referred to the family *Muscicapidæ*, *Eurylæmus* (the *Eurylæmidæ*) is placed in the order *Passeres*, and *Todus* is made the type of a new family, *Todidæ*, to be placed in the *Coccygomorphæ*, next to the *Momotidæ*. The text is illustrated.

603

On a new Parrakeet of the genus *Loriculus* from the Philippine Islands.

Ibis, 1872, pp. 323–325, pl. xi.

Loriculus chrysonotus is described and figured.

604

Index to the Ornithological Literature of 1871. By Osbert Salvin and P. L. Sclater.

Ibis, 1872, pp. 413–468.

An alphabetical list of the ornithological publications in 1871, with short abstracts of their contents.

605

Notes on *Propithecus bicolor* and *Rhinoceros lasiotis*.

Ann. and Mag. Nat. Hist., ser. 4, X, pp. 298, 299 (1872).

Notes on *Propithecus bicolor*, Gray, which is shown to have been already described by M. A. Grandidier as *P. edwardsi*, and on the distinctness of *Rhinoceros lasiotis*.

*(See also *Nature*, VI, p. 518, 1872; *Rep. Brit. Assoc. Adv. Sci.*, 1872, Pt. II, p. 140.)

606

The new Rhinoceros.

Nature, VI, pp. 518, 519 (1872).

An illustrated account of *Rhinoceros lasiotis*, a new species received by the Zoological Society of London, with notes on the other species of Rhinoceroses living in the Society's Gardens.

(See also *Rep. Brit. Assoc. Adv. Sci.*, 1872, Pt. II, p. 140, *Ann. and Mag. Nat. Hist.*, ser. 4, X, p. 298, 1872.)

607

Proceedings of Zoological Collectors.

Nature, VII, p. 110 (1872).

Note on the whereabouts and doings of zoological collectors in foreign countries.

608

On a new Rhinoceros, with remarks on the recent species of this genus and their distribution.

Rep. Brit. Assoc. Adv. Sci., 1872, Pt. II, p. 140.

Note on *Rhinoceros lasiotis*, n. sp., and a list of the six known species of Rhinoceroses, with remarks.

(See also *Nature*, VI, p. 518, 1872; *Ann. and Mag. Nat. Hist.*, ser. 4, X, p. 298, 1872.)

609

Notice of an apparently new Marine Animal from the Northern Pacific.

Rep. Brit. Assoc. Adv. Sci., 1872, Pt. II, pp. 140, 141.

Note on a remarkable animal from Washington Territory, North America, described by Dr. Gray as *Osteocella septentrionalis*, but supposed by Mr. Sclater to be the ossified notochord of some cartilaginous fish.

(See also *Nature*, VIII, p. 487.)

610

[Report on the additions to the Society's Menagerie in December, 1872.]

Proc. Zool. Soc. London, 1873, pp. 1–3.

The American Darter (*Plotus anhinga*) is illustrated in the text.

611

[Exhibition of some skins of Birds from New Britain and the neighbouring Islands.]

Proc. Zool. Soc. London, 1873, p. 3.

Exhibition to the Zoological Society of London of skins of seven species made up from specimens which had been received in spirit from Dr. Bennett, of Sydney.

612

On Peruvian Birds collected by Mr. Whitely. By P. L. Sclater and Osbert Salvin. Part VI.*

Proc. Zool. Soc. London, 1873, pp. 184–187, pl. xxi.

A list of 78 species, with notes on the more remarkable ones. *Hapalocercus acutipennis* is described as a new species, and *Tanagra olivina* is figured.

* (For Part I see *Proc. Zool. Soc. London*, 1867, p. 982; Pt. II. 1868, p. 173; Pt. III, 1868, p. 568; Pt. IV. 1869, p. 151; Pt. V, 1869, p. 596; Pt. VII. 1873, p. 779; Pt. VIII, 1874, p. 677; Pt. IX, 1876, p. 15.)

613

[Report on the additions to the Society's Menagerie in January, 1873.]

Proc. Zool. Soc. London, 1873, pp. 193, 194, pl. xxii.

Report on the additions to the Zoological Society's Menagerie, with notes on the most noticeable specimens. An apparently new species of fruit bat is named *Pteropus formosus*, and a list of the species of fruit bats (13 in number) living in the Menagerie is given. A figure is given in the text, of a female Tapir from Paraguay.

614

On the Birds of eastern Peru. By P. L. Sclater and Osbert Salvin. With notes on the habits of the Birds, by Edward Bartlett.

Proc. Zool. Soc. London, 1873, pp. 252–311, pls. xxv, xxvi.

An annotated catalogue of 473 species, with remarks on the composition of the east Peruvian avifauna. The new generic name *Cnipodectes* is proposed for the reception of *Cyclorhynchus subbrunneus*, Scl., and the following species are described: *Pithys lunulata*, *Rhynchocyclus viridiceps*, and *Orypturus bartletti*. The first-mentioned is figured. A map showing the localities in which the collections were made is given. The nest of *Furnarius minor* is figured in the text.

615

[Report on the additions to the Society's Menagerie in February, 1873.]

Proc. Zool. Soc. London, 1873, pp. 311, 312, pl. xxvii.

Report on the additions to the Zoological Society's Menagerie, with notes on the more interesting specimens. *Felis aurata* is figured.

616

[Report on the additions to the Society's Menagerie in March and April, 1873.]

Proc. Zool. Soc. London, 1873, pp. 433, 434.

617

[Remarks on the Liberian Hippopotamus.]

Proc. Zool. Soc. London, 1873, p. 434.

Note on and exhibition to the Zoological Society of London of photographs of a young specimen of *Hippopotamus liberiensis.*

618

Notes on the Range of several American *Limicolæ.*

Proc. Zool. Soc. London, 1873, pp. 453–457.

Notes on the range of certain species of the genera *Himantopus, Macrorhamphus, Tringa, Limosa* and *Numenius.* The heads of *Himantopus nigricollis* and *H. brasiliensis* are figured in the text.

619

[Remarks on Animals seen in some of the Continental zoological gardens.]

Proc. Zool. Soc. London, 1873, pp. 473, 474.

Remarks on the most interesting animals observed during visits to the zoological gardens of Antwerp, Rotterdam, Amsterdam, Hamburg and Berlin.

620

On some Venezuelan Birds collected by Mr. James M. Spence. By P. L. Sclater and Osbert Salvin.

Proc. Zool. Soc. London, 1873. pp. 511, 512.

Notes on eight species contained in collections from Venezuela. *Lochmias sororia* and *Crypturus cerviniventris* are described as new.

621

[Report on the additions to the Society's Menagerie in May, 1873.]

Proc. Zool. Soc. London, 1873, pp. 517, 518, pl. xliv.

Clemmys unicolor is figured.

622

[Exhibition of an Egg of the Spotted Bower-bird, a series of photographs, and a specimen of *Casuarius bicarunculatus.*]

Proc. Zool. Soc. London, 1873, pp. 518, 519.

Exhibition to the Zoological Society of London of an egg of *Chlamydodera maculata,* a series of photographs of animals, and a skin of *Casuarius bicarunculatus,* with an extract from a letter from Dr. George Bennett concerning the habitat of *C. bennetti.*

623

[Notice of a new work on American Birds, and remarks on *Turdus subcinereus* and on a supposed species of *Cnipolegus.*]

Proc. Zool. Soc. London, 1873, pp. 554, 555.

Notice of the "Nomenclator Avium Neotropicalium," with a tabular list showing the proposed arrangement. It is pointed out that the introduction into the American avifauna, in the "Catalogue of American Birds," of *Turdus subcinereus,* and *Cnipolegus,* sp. inc., is an error.

624

[Notice of a memoir on the Curassows now or lately living in the Society's Gardens.]

Proc. Zool. Soc. London, 1873, p. 557.

625

[Exhibition of some Birds collected in New Guinea by Signor d'Albertis, and description of a new species of Paradise Bird.]

Proc. Zool. Soc. London, 1873, pp. 557–560, pl. xlvii.

Exhibition to the Zoological Society of London of a series of skins, with notes respecting the more remarkable species. *Paradisea raggiana,* sp. nov., and *Drepanornis* * *albertisi,* gen. et sp. nov., are described. The latter is figured.

* (See also *Nature,* VIII, pp. 192–305.)

626

Note on the genus *Ornithion* of Hartlaub.

Proc. Zool. Soc. London, 1873, pp. 576–578.

A synopsis of the species of the genus *Ornithion.* Four species are enumerated.

627

[Report on the additions to the Society's Menagerie during the months of June, July, August, and September, 1873.]

Proc. Zool. Soc. London, 1873, pp. 682–684.

628

Characters of new species of Birds discovered in New Guinea by Signor d'Albertis.

Proc. Zool. Soc. London, 1873, pp. 690–698, pls. lii–lvii.

The following new species are described: *Eupetes leucostictus, Monarcha frater, Leucophantes* (gen. nov.) *brachyurus, Reetes bennetti, Pachycephala rufinucha, P. soror, Campephaga aurulenta, Climacteris placens, Ptilotis cinerea, P. melanophrys, Melidectes* (gen. nov.) *torquatus, Melipotes* (gen. nov.) *gymnops, Ægotheles albertisi,* and *Ptilonopus bellus. Eupetes leucostictus, Leucophantes brachyurus, Campephaga aurulenta, Melidectes torquatus, Melipotes gymnops* and *Ptilonopus bellus,* are figured. A list of Signor d'Albertis's collection (53 species), with the localities, is given. Each new genus is illustrated in the text.

629

[Exhibition of Birds from Antioquia, Colombia, and descriptions of new species.]

Proc. Zool. Soc. London, 1873, pp. 728, 729.

Exhibition of, to the Zoological Society of London, and descriptions of *Chlorochrysa nitidissima* and *Grallaria rufeceps,* nn. spp.

630

[Exhibition of a pair of horns of *Alcelaphus tora.*]

Proc. Zool. Soc. London, 1873, p. 729.

631

[Report on the additions to the Society's Menagerie during the months of October and November, 1873.]

Proc. Zool. Soc. London, 1873, pp. 701, 702.

632

[Remarks on a fine head of *Alcelaphus tora.*]

Proc. Zool. Soc. London, 1873, p. 762.

The head is figured in the text.

633

On Peruvian Birds collected by Mr. Whitely. Part VII. *

Proc. Zool. Soc. London, 1873, pp. 770–784.

A list of 42 species, with their localities, and notes on the more interesting examples. The following species are described as new: *Thryophilus fulvus, Todirostrum pulchellum, Tyranniscus viridissimus, Myiobius auriventris*, and *Grallaria erythroleuca.*

*(For Part I see *Proc. Zool. Soc. London*, 1867, p. 982; Pt. II, 1868, p. 173; Pt. III, 1868, p. 568; Pt. IV, 1869, p. 151; Pt. V, 1869, p. 596; Pt. VI, 1873, p. 184; Pt. VIII, 1874, p. 677; Pt. IX, 1876, p. 15.)

634

Note on the *Pyranga roseogularis* of Cabot.

Ibis, 1873, pp. 125, 126, pl. iii.

Pyranga roseogularis is remarked upon, characterized and figured.

635

Additions to the List of Birds of Nicaragua.

Ibis, 1873, pp. 372, 373.

A nominal list of 17 species not represented in Mr. Thomas Belt's former collection from Nicaragua.

(See Salvin, *Ibis*, 1872, p. 311.)

636

Notes on Birds observed at Para. By E. L. Layard. With descriptions of two new species by P. L. Sclater.

Ibis, 1873, pp. 374–396, pls. xiv, xv.

Field notes on 120 species by Mr. E. L. Layard, two of which, *Picolaptes layardi* and *Thamnophilus simplex*, are described as new by Mr. Sclater and figured.

637

Index to the Ornithological Literature of 1872. By P. L. Sclater and O. Finsch.

Ibis, 1873, pp. 431–493.

An alphabetical record of the Ornithological publications of 1872, with short abstracts of their contents.

638

Remarks on *Cervus chilensis* and *Cervus antisiensis*.

Ann. and Mag. Nat. Hist., ser. 4, XI, pp. 213, 214 (1873).

Remarks showing that the animals described by Dr. Gray as *Huamela leucotis* and *Xenelaphus anomalocera* are referable to *Cervus chilensis* and *C. antisiensis*, respectively.

(See paper No. 679.)

639

The Zoological Collections in the India House.

Nature, VII, pp. 457, 458 (1873).

Remarks on the inaccessibility of the zoological collections in the India House, and suggestions for properly housing them.

640

[Note on the generic term *Drepanephorus*.]

Nature, VIII, p. 192 (1873).

The generic name *Drepanephorus*, given to a new Bird of Paradise at a meeting of the Zoological Society of London, having been preoccupied, is changed to *Drepanornis*.

(See also *Proc. Zool. Soc. London*, 1873, p. 560; *Nature*, VIII, p. 305.)

641

The Huemul.

Nature, VIII, p. 302 (1873).

Letter on the Huemul (*Cervus chilensis*) of Chili and Patagonia.

642

The new Bird of Paradise.

Nature, VIII, pp. 305, 306 (1873).

A description and figure of *Drepanornis albertisi*, with remarks.

(See also *Proc. Zool. Soc. London*, 1873, p. 560; *Nature*, VIII, p. 192.)

643

The new Marine Animal from Washington Territory.

Nature, VIII, pp. 487, 488 (1873).

Note on *Verrillia blakei*, Stearns, a new Polype from Barraud's Inlet, Washington Territory, the ossified remains of which had been described by Dr. Gray as *Osteocella septentrionalis.*

(See Sel., *Rep. Brit. Assoc. Adv. Sci.*, 1872, Pt. II, p. 140.)

644

[Report on the additions to the Society's Menagerie in December, 1873.]

Proc. Zool. Soc. London, 1874, pp. 1, 2, pl. i.

Ciconia boyciana is figured.

645

On the species of the genus *Synallaxis*, of the family *Dendrocolaptidæ*.

Proc. Zool. Soc. London, 1874, pp. 2–28, pls. ii–iv.

A synopsis of the species of *Synallaxis*, together with a chronological list of the literature on the genus and a table showing the distribution of the species. Fifty-eight valid and four doubtful species are enumerated, of which the following are described as new: *S. hypospodia, S. subpudica, S. mustelina*, Natt. MS., *S. subcristata* and *S. hudsoni*. The following species are figured: *S. stictothorax, S. scutata, S. kollari, S. candæi, S. subcristata* and *S. hyposticta.*

646

[Exhibition of two skulls of Baird's Tapir (*Tapirus bairdi*) from Mexico.]

Proc. Zool. Soc. London, 1874, p. 89.

647

[Exhibition of the horns of a male and female Arkar Sheep (*Ovis arkar*).]

Proc. Zool. Soc. London, 1874, p. 89.

648

[Exhibition of a specimen of the Wild Ibex of Crete.]

Proc. Zool. Soc. London, 1874, pp. 89, 90.

Exhibition to the Zoological Society of London of a stuffed skin of the wild Ibex of Crete, and remarks showing that the species is referable to *Capra ægagrus* (Pallas) and not to *Capra picta*, Erhardt, as had previously been the case.

649

[Report on the additions to the Society's Menagerie in January, 1874.]

Proc. Zool. Soc. London, 1874, p. 110.

650

[Extract from a letter addressed to Mr. Sclater by M. Luigi M. d'Albertis, C. M. Z. S., containing an account of a new species of Kanguroo (*Halmaturus luctuosus*) from New Guinea.]

Proc. Zool. Soc. London, 1874, p. 110.

651

[Report on the additions to the Society's Menagerie in February, 1874.]

Proc. Zool. Soc. London, 1874, pp. 151, 152.

Report on the additions to the Zoological Society's Menagerie, with notes on the more remarkable specimens. *Cervus euopis*, Swinhoe MS., is adopted as the name for a new species of Deer.

652

On a small collection of Birds from Barbados, West Indies.

Proc. Zool. Soc. London, 1874, pp. 174, 175.

Remarks on a small collection, consisting of specimens in spirit of nine species, transmitted from Barbados by Sir Graham Briggs.

653

On *Centropsar*, an apparently new form of the family *Icteridæ*.

Proc. Zool. Soc. London, 1874, pp. 175, 176, pl. xxvi.

Centropsar mirus, gen. et spec. nov., is described and figured. The text is illustrated with the head, wing and foot of the species.

(See paper No. 691.)

654

[Announcement of the arrival in the Society's Menagerie of a Javan Rhinoceros.]

Proc. Zool. Soc. London, 1874, pp. 182, 183, pl. xxviii.

Note on and figure of *Rhinoceros sondaicus*, a specimen of which had been received by the Zoological Society of London.

655

[Report on the additions to the Society's Menagerie in March, 1874.]

Proc. Zool. Soc. London, 1874, p. 206, pl. xxxiv.

Report on the additions to the Zoological Society's Menagerie, of which, among others, *Chrysotis finschi* is remarked upon and figured.

656

[Report on the additions to the Society's Menagerie in April, 1874.]

Proc. Zool. Soc. London, 1874, p. 247, pl. xlii.

Halmaturus luctuosus is figured.

657

[Remarks on a Cassowary in the Society's Gardens, received from the Zoological Society of Amsterdam in 1871.]

Proc. Zool. Soc. London, 1874, pp. 247, 248.

Remarks showing that the Cassowary described and figured (*Proc. Zool. Soc. London*, 1872, p. 147, pl. ix) under the name of *Casuarius kaupi* had been wrongly determined. The new name *Casuarius westermanni* is proposed for it.

(See also *Proc. Zool. Soc. London*, 1872, p. 147; 1875, p. 84.)

658

[Announcement of the appointment of a Naturalist to accompany the Astronomical Expedition to Kerguelen's Land.]

Proc. Zool. Soc. London, 1874, p. 248.

659

[Exhibition of a skin of *Ciconia boyciana*, and remarks upon its distribution.]

Proc. Zool. Soc. London, 1874, pp. 306, 307.

660

[Report on the additions to the Society's Menagerie in May, 1874.]

Proc. Zool. Soc. London, 1874, pp. 323, 324, pl.1. *Nyctereutes procynides* is figured.

661

[Remarks upon two species of Birds from New Guinea, lately described in the Society's "Proceedings."]

Proc. Zool. Soc. London, 1874, p. 419.

Remarks on *Rectes bennetti* and *Campephaga aurulenta*, which had been pointed out by Dr. Meyer, in a communication to Mr. Sclater, to belong to *R. nigrescens* and *O. sloetii*, respectively. Mr. Sclater doubts the identification of the former species.

662

Descriptions of three new species of the genus *Synallaxis*.

Proc. Zool. Soc. London, 1874, pp. 445–447, pl. lviii.

Synallaxis pudibunda, *S. graminicola*, Jelski MS., and *S. virgata*, Jelski MS., are described, of which the first two mentioned are figured. A list of the 10 species of *Synallaxis* inhabiting central Peru is given.

663

[Report on the additions to the Society's Menagerie in June, July, August, and September, 1874.]

Proc. Zool. Soc. London, 1874, pp. 494–496, pl. lxiii.

Felis servalina is figured.

664

[Remarks on some visits recently made to several zoological gardens and museums in France and Italy.]

Proc. Zool. Soc. London, 1874, pp. 496, 497.

Remarks on the more interesting animals observed during visits to the Jardin des Plantes, Paris, and the Museo Civico at Genoa.

665

[Report on the additions to the Society's Menagerie in October, 1874.]

Proc. Zool. Soc. London, 1874, p. 605.

666

[Exhibition of an Egg of *Pareudiastes pacificus*.]

Proc. Zool. Soc. London, 1874, pp. 605, 606.

667

On the Black Wolf of Thibet.

Proc. Zool. Soc. London, 1874, pp. 654, 655, pl. lxxviii.

Remarks on the Black Wolf of Thibet, which had been previously referred to *Lupus laniger* and which is here proposed to be called *Canis niger*. The animal is figured.

668

[Report on the additions to the Society's Menagerie in November, 1874.]

Proc. Zool. Soc. London, 1874, pp. 664–666, pl. lxxxii.

Dasyprocta antillensis is described and figured.

669

Remarks upon a donation to the Society's Library of a MS. work on the Birds of India, by Col. S. R. Tickell.

Proc. Zool. Soc. London, 1874, pp. 667, 668.

This work consists of seven small folio volumes, with 261 plates of birds (illustrating 276 species), descriptions of 448 species, and 5 plates of eggs, containing illustrations of those of 42 species.

670

[List of Humming-Birds obtained by Mr. Whitely in High Peru.]

Proc. Zool. Soc. London, 1874, pp. 676, 677.

A nominal list of the species (30 in number) of Humming-birds collected by Mr. Whitely in Peru, with references to his notes upon them in his former papers in the *Proceedings*.

671

On Peruvian Birds collected by Mr. Whitely. By P. L. Sclater and Osbert Salvin. Part VIII.*

Proc. Zool. Soc. London, 1874, pp. 677–080, pl. lxxxiv.

A list of 32 species and their localities, with notes on the more interesting species. *Nothoprocta taczanowskii* is described as a new species and figured. The six known species of *Nothoprocta* are diagnosed.

*(For Part I see *Proc. Zool. Soc. London*, 1867, p. 982; Pt. II, 1868, p. 173; Pt. III, 1868, p. 568; Pt. IV, 1869, p. 151; Pt. V, 1869, p. 596; Pt. VI, 1873, p. 184; Pt. VII, 1873, p. 779; Pt. IX, 1876, p. 15.)

672

On the *Prionochili* of British India.

Ibis, 1874, pp. 1–3, pl. i.

Notes on *Prionochilus vincens* (which is characterized) and *P. melanoxanthus*. Both species are figured.

673

Notice of Père David's Travels in China.

Ibis, 1874, pp. 167–172.

An abstract of a memoir published by Père Armand David in the "Nouvelles Archives du Muséum d'Histoire Naturelle de Paris," Vol. VII, on his travels in China.

674

On the Neotropical species of the family *Pteroptochidæ*.

Ibis, 1874, pp. 189–206, pl. viii.

A synopsis of the neotropical genera (8 in number) and species (19 in number) of the family *Pteroptochidæ*, with a table of their distribution. *Rhinocrypta fusca* is figured (R. *fulva* on plate). The head of *Liosceles thoracicus* is figured in the text. The genera treated of are: *Scytalopus*, *Merulaxis*, *Rhinocrypta*, *Liosceles*, *Pteroptochus*, *Hylactes*, *Acropternis* and *Triptorhinus*.

675

Dr. A. B. Meyer's Ornithological Discoveries in New Guinea.

Ibis, 1874, pp. 416–420.

A summary of the contents of Dr. Meyer's several papers on the ornithological results of his expedition to New Guinea.

676

The Geographical Distribution of Mammals.

Science Lectures for the People, No. 5, sixth series, Manchester, 1874, pp. 67–84.

A popular lecture on the geographical distribution of mammals delivered in the Hulme town hall, Manchester, on November 25, 1874.

677

[Report on the additions to the Society's Menagerie in December, 1874.]

Proc. Zool. Soc. London, 1875, p. 1.

678

Descriptions of some new species of South American Birds. By P. L. Sclater and Osbert Salvin.

Proc. Zool. Soc. London, 1875, pp. 37–39, pl. vi.

Microcerculus squamulatus, *Automolus striaticeps* and *Tigrisoma salmoni* are described, of which the first named is figured. A synopsis of the four known species of *Tigrisoma* is given. The heads of *Tigrisoma fasciatum* and *T. salmoni* are figured in the text.

679

[Exhibition of a skin and skull of a female Huemul (*Cervus chilensis*) and remarks on the Deer of Chili and western Peru.]

Proc. Zool. Soc. London, 1875, pp. 44–47.

Exhibition, to a meeting of the Zoological Society of London, of a skin and skull of a female, and a pair of horns of a male *Cervus chilensis*, with an extract of a communication from Mr. E. C. Reed containing the synonymy of and remarks upon *Cervus chilensis*. *C. antisiensis*, *C. whitelyi* and *C. peruvianus*. The left horn of *C. chilensis* is figured in the text.

(See paper No. 638.)

680

On some rare Parrots living in the Society's Gardens.

Proc. Zool. Soc. London, 1875, pp. 59–62, pls. x, xi.

The rarer species of parrots living in the Zoological Society's Menagerie are enumerated, and remarks made upon *Chrysotis guatemalæ*, *C. bouqueti*, and the species of the genus *Cacatua*. *Cacatua goffini* and *Chrysotis bouqueti* are figured. The feet of *Cacatua sanguinea* and *C. goffini* are figured in the text.

681

[Report on the additions to the Society's Menagerie in January, 1875, and remarks on *Canis chama*.]

Proc. Zool. Soc. London, 1875, pp. 81, 82, pl. xvii.

Canis chama is remarked upon and figured, and attention directed to the other important additions to the Zoological Society's Menagerie in January, 1875.

682

[Exhibition of a drawing of a supposed new Rhinoceros from the Terai of Bhootan.]

Proc. Zool. Soc. London, 1875, p. 82.

683

[Exhibition of a living specimen of the Pegnan Tree-Shrew (*Tupaia peguana*) and a Squirrel (*Sciurus blanfordi*).]

Proc. Zool. Soc. London, 1875, p. 82.

684

Further remarks on the Cassowaries living in the Society's Gardens and on other species of the genus *Casuarius*.

Proc. Zool. Soc. London, 1875, pp. 84–87, pls. xviii–xx.

Additional notes* on the Cassowaries living in the Gardens of the Zoological Society of London. *Casuarius bennetti*, *C. westermanni*, and *C. picticollis*, sp. n., are diagnosed, *C. beccarii*, sp. n., is described, and an "Index specierum generis Casuarii" appended. *C. picticollis*, *C. westermanni* and *C. unlappendiculatus* are figured. The head and wattles of *C. beccarii* are figured in the text.

*(See also *Proc. Zool. Soc. London*, 1872, p. 147; 1874, p. 247.)

685

[Report on the additions to the Society's Menagerie in February, 1875.]

Proc. Zool. Soc. London, 1875, pp. 156, 157, pl. xxvi.

Chrysotis xanthotora is figured.

686

On Venezuelan Birds collected by Mr. A. Goering. By P. L. Sclater and Osbert Salvin. Part V.*

Proc. Zool. Soc. London, 1875, pp. 234–238, pl. xxxv.

A list of 42 species from Merida, not represented in Mr. Goering's former collection from that locality, and notes on the more interesting species contained in both collections; also a list of 33 species (with notes) collected at San Cristoval. *Chlorospingus chrysophrys*, *Buarremon castaneifrons* and *Chloronerpes xanthochlorus* are described as new species, and the name *Buarremon mystacalis*, Tacz., is changed to *B. taczanowskii*. *B. castaneifrons* and *B. taczanowskii* are figured.

*(For Part I see *Proc. Zool. Soc. London*, 1868, p. 165; Pt. II, 1868, p. 626; Pt. III, 1869, p. 250; Pt. IV, 1870, p. 779.)

687

[Report on the additions to the Society's Menagerie in March, 1875.]

Proc. Zool. Soc. London, 1875, p. 316.

688

[Report on the additions to the Society's Menagerie in April, 1875.]

Proc. Zool. Soc. London, 1875, pp. 348, 349.

689

[Exhibition of and remarks on the skin of a chick of a Cassowary.]

Proc. Zool. Soc. London, 1875, p. 349.

Exhibition to a meeting of the Zoological Society of London, of a skin of a chick of a Cassowary, supposed to be that of *C. picticollis*.

690

[Remarks on animals seen during visits recently made to several zoological gardens in Rotterdam, the Hague, Amsterdam, Antwerp and Ghent.]

Proc. Zool. Soc. London, 1875, pp. 379, 380.

691

[Exhibition of and remarks on the typical specimen of *Centropsar mirus*.]

Proc. Zool. Soc. London, 1875, p. 380.

Note showing that the skin of the typical specimen of *Centropsar mirus* had been "made up," and that the name must therefore be removed from the ornithological category.

(See paper No. 653.)

692

On several rare or little-known Mammals now or lately living in the Society's Collection.

Proc. Zool. Soc. London, 1875, pp. 417–423, pls. xlvii–li.

Remarks on *Macacus speciosus*, *M. rhesosimilis*, *Ateles melanochir*, *Hapale melanura*, *Canis famelicus*, *Procyon cancrivorus*, and *Cervulus micrurus*, sp. n. *Macacus speciosus*, *Ateles melanochir* (2 plates), *Hapale melanura*, *Cervulus micrurus*, and *C. reevesi*, vit., are figured. The species of the genus *Cervulus* are also remarked upon.

693

[Report on the additions to the Society's Menagerie in May, 1875.]

Proc. Zool. Soc. London, 1875, p. 469.

694

[Notice of a Memoir on the Rhinoceroses now or lately living in the Society's Menagerie.]

Proc. Zool. Soc. London, 1875, p. 470.

695

[Report on the additions to the Society's Menagerie in June, July, August, and September, 1875.]

Proc. Zool. Soc. London, 1875, pp. 527–530, pls. lviii, lix.

Casuarius beccarii and *Gazella granti* are figured.

696

Description of two new species of Birds from the State of Antioquia, U. S. C. By P. L. Sclater and Osbert Salvin.

Proc. Zool. Soc. London, 1875, pp. 541, 542.

Catharus phæopleurus and *Automolus holostictus* are described.

697

[Report on the additions to the Society's Menagerie in October, 1875.]

Proc. Zool. Soc. London, 1875, p. 565.

698

[Exhibition of and remarks on the upper horn of a two-horned Rhinoceros from the valley of the Brahmapootra.]

Proc. Zool. Soc. London, 1875, p. 566.

699

[Remarks on the female plumage of *Pauxis galeata*.]

Proc. Zool. Soc. London, 1875, p. 566.

700

[Report on the additions to the Society's Menagerie in November, 1875.]

Proc. Zool. Soc. London, 1875, p. 633.

701

[Exhibition of and remarks on a skin of *Hypocolius ampelinus*, Bp.]

Proc. Zool. Soc. London, 1875, p. 633.

702

Synopsis of the species of the subfamily *Diglossinæ*.

Ibis, 1875, pp. 204–221, pls. iv, v.

A synopsis of the 15 known species of the subfamily *Diglossinæ*, with a table showing their geographical distribution. Bonaparte's name *Agrilorhinus* is emended to *Ancylorhinus*, and *Diglossa pectoralis* and *D. albilateralis* (♂ and ♀) are figured. The genera treated of are *Diglossa* and *Diglossopis*.

703

On *Turdus jaranicus* of Horsfield and its allied form, *Turdus schlegeli*.

Ibis, 1875, pp. 344–347, pl. viii.

Remarks on *Turdus javanicus* and *T. schlegeli*, with their synonyms. The former species is figured.

704

Remarks on the species of the Tanagrine genus *Chlorochrysa*.

Ibis, 1875, pp. 464–467, pl. x.

A review of the three species of the genus *Chlorochrysa*, viz, *C. calliparia*, *C. phœnicotis* and *C. nitidissima*. The last-named species is figured.

705

On the Curassows now or lately living in the Society's Gardens.

Trans. Zool. Soc. London, IX, pp. 273–288 pls. xl–liii (1875).

A synopsis of the species of Curassows, and lists of the specimens now or lately living in the Gardens of the Zoological Society of London. The generic name *Pauxi* is emended to *Pauxis*, and *Crax viridirostris* is described as a new species. The following species are figured: *Crax globicera* (♂, ♀), *C. daubentoni* (♂, ♀), *C. alector* (♂, ♀), *C. sclateri* (♂, ♀), *C. globulosa* (♂, ♀), *C. carunculata* (♂, ♀), *C. alberti* (♂, ♀), *C. incommoda* (♀), *Nothocrax urumutum*, *Mitua tuberosa*, *M. tomentosa*, *Pauxi galeata*, and *P. galeata* var. *rubra*.

(See also *Trans. Zool. Soc. London*, X, p. 543, 1879.)

706

Cassowaries.

Nature, XII, pp. 516, 517 (1875).

A review of the genus *Casuarius*. The nine known species are enumerated and remarked upon.

707

On the Distribution of the Species of Cassowaries.

Rep. Brit. Assoc. Adv. Sci., 1874, pt. 2, p. 138 (1875).

Abstract of a paper read before the Belfast meeting of the British Association for the Advancement of Science, on the systematic position of *Casuarius* and on the characters and distribution of the known species (seven in number) contained in the genus.

708

Fruit-eating Snakes.

Zoologist, 1875, p. 4574.

Note pointing out that the East Indian snake, *Acrochordus javanicus*, is commonly supposed to feed on fruit.

709

Descriptive list of the Cassowaries.

Zoologist, 1875, pp. 4685–4688.

Description of and remarks on the nine known species of the genus *Casuarius*.

710

[Report on the additions to the Society's Menagerie in December, 1875.]

Proc. Zool. Soc. London, 1876, p. 1.

711

On some additional species of Birds from St. Lucia, West India Islands.

Proc. Zool. Soc. London, 1876, pp. 13, 14, pl. ii.

A list of eight species not represented in the two previous collections* from St. Lucia, with their local names. *Thryothorus mesoleucus*, sp. n., and *Leucopeza semperi*, gen. et sp. n., are described. The latter is figured.

* (See also *Proc. Zool. Soc. London*, 1871, p. 263; 1872, p. 647.)

712

On Peruvian Birds collected by Mr. Whitely. By P. L. Sclater and Osbert Salvin. Part IX.*

Proc. Zool. Soc. London, 1876, pp. 15–19, pl. iii.

A list of 65 species, with their localities, and notes on the more interesting species. *Thamnophilus melanochrous* and *Columba albipennis* are described as new. The former is figured.

* (For Part I see *Proc. Zool. Soc. London*, 1867, p. 982; Pt. II, 1868, p. 173; Pt. III, 1868, p. 568; Pt. IV, 1869, p. 151; Pt. V, 1869, p. 596; Pt. VI, 1873, p. 184; Pt. VII, 1873, p. 779; Pt. VIII, 1874, p. 677.)

713

[Extract from a Report of the visit of H. M. S. *Petrel* to the Galapagos Islands.]

Proc. Zool. Soc. London, 1876, pp. 178, 179.

714

[Exhibition of and remarks on an antler of a Rusa Deer.]

Proc. Zool. Soc. London, 1876, pp. 179, 180.

715

Descriptions of new Birds obtained by Mr. C. Buckley in Bolivia. By P. L. Sclater and Osbert Salvin.

Proc. Zool. Soc. London, 1876, pp. 253, 254.

The following four species are described: *Diglossa glauca*, *Buarremon melanops*, *Leptopogon tristis* and *Ilypoxanthus atriceps*.

716

[Report on the additions to the Society's Menagerie in January, 1876.]

Proc. Zool. Soc. London, 1876, pp. 254, 255.

717

[Exhibition of and remarks on a new Parrot (*Conurus illigeri*) belonging to the Museum of Neuchâtel.]

Proc. Zool. Soc. London, 1876, pp. 255, 256.

Ara couloni (*Conurus illigeri*, Tschudi) is described as a new species. The head is figured in the text.

718

Notes on some of the Blue Crows of America. By P. L. Sclater and Osbert Salvin.

Proc. Zool. Soc. London, 1876, pp. 268–272.

Notes on, and the synonymy of, the seven species of the genus *Cyanocitta*, of which *C. germana* is described as new.

719

[Report on the additions to the Society's Menagerie in February, 1876.]

Proc. Zool. Soc. London, 1876, pp. 273, 274.

Lophotragus michianus, ♂, is figured in the text.

720

[Exhibition of and remarks on the skin of a female of Anderson's Pheasant.]

Proc. Zool. Soc. London, 1876, p. 274.

It is here pointed out that *Phasianus crawfurdii*, as described by Dr. Gray, is the female of *Euplocamus andersoni*, Elliot, and that this species should strictly be called *Euplocamus crawfurdi*.

721

[Exhibition of and remarks upon a series of skins of the Parrots of the Fiji Islands, obtained by Mr. E. L. Layard, F. Z. S.]

Proc. Zool. Soc. London, 1876, pp. 307, 308.

Skins of *Pyrrhulopsis atrigularis*, *P. tavinensis*, *P. splendens* and *P. personata* were exhibited to a meeting of the Zoological Society of London, and remarked upon.

722

[Report on the additions to the Society's Menagerie in March, 1876.]

Proc. Zool. Soc. London, 1876, pp. 332, 333, pl. xxv.

Report on the additions to the Zoological Society's Menagerie, with notes on the more interesting species. *Polyborus tharus*, var., is figured.

723

On new species of Bolivian Birds. By P. L. Sclater and Osbert Salvin.

Proc. Zool. Soc. London, 1876, pp. 352–358, pls. xxx–xxxiii.

The genus *Malacothraupis* and the following new species are described: *Catharus mentalis, Basileuterus euophrys, Malacothraupis dentata, Calliste punctulata, C. fulvicervix, C. argyrofenges, Chlorospingus calophrys, Cyanocorax nigriceps, Ochthodiæta fuscorufus, Ochthœca pulchella, Anæretes flavirostris, Lathria uropygialis, Grallaria erythrotis, Thamnophilus subfasciatus* and *Asturina saturata. Chirocylla* is proposed as a new generic name for *Lathria uropygialis*. Figures are given of the following species: *Calliste fulvicervix, C. argyrofenges, Malacothraupis dentata, Lathria uropygialis,* and *Thamnophilus subfasciatus* ($\male, \female$). The head, wing and foot of *Malacothraupis dentata,* and the wing of *Lathria uropygialis,* are figured in the text.

724

A Revision of the Neotropical *Anatidæ*. By P. L. Sclater and Osbert Salvin.

Proc. Zool. Soc. London, 1876, pp. 358–412, pl. xxxiv.

A revision of the neotropical *Anatidæ,* including general remarks on the family, a synopsis of the species (62 in number), and a table of their geographical distribution, with notes thereon. *Querquedula andium* is figured. The male and female of hybrids between *Bernicla dispar* and *B. magellanica* are figured in the text. The following are the genera treated of: *Anser, Bernicla, Chenalopex, Cygnus, Dendrocygna, Sarcidiornis, Cairina, Anas, Heteronetta, Querquedula, Dafila, Mareca, Spatula, Aix, Metopiana, Fuligula, Clangula. Œdemia, Tachyeres, Erismatura, Merganetta* and *Mergus.*

725

[Report on the additions to the Society's Menagerie in April, 1876, and remarks on the Cassowaries in the Society's collection.]

Proc. Zool. Soc. London, 1876, pp. 413, 414, pl. xxxv.

Report on the additions to the Zoological Society's Menagerie, with special reference to a collection from Angola brought home by Lieut. V. R. Cameron. *Colius castanonotus* is figured. A list of the Cassowaries living in the Society's Gardens is given.

726

[Extracts from several letters addressed to Mr. Sclater by Dr. G. Bennett, F. Z. S., referring to the proceedings of Mr. L. M. D'Albertis, C. M. Z. S.]

Proc. Zool. Soc. London, 1876, p. 414.

727

[Exhibition of a rare Pacific Parrot, *Coriphilus kuhli,* and remarks on its habitat.]

Proc. Zool. Soc. London, 1876, pp. 421, 422.

728

On the Birds collected by Dr. Comrie on the southeast coast of New Guinea during the survey of H. M. S. *Basilisk*.

Proc. Zool. Soc. London, 1876, pp. 459–461, pls. xlii, xliii.

A list of 11 species, with remarks upon them. *Manucodia comrii* is described as new and figured. *Megapodius macgillivraii* is also figured.

729

[Report on the additions to the Society's Menagerie in May, 1876, and list of Indian animals deposited by H. R. H. the Prince of Wales.]

Proc. Zool. Soc. London, 1876, pp. 462–464.

730

[Exhibition of Land Crabs from Ascension Island, presented by Dr. S. B. Drew.]

Proc. Zool. Soc. London, 1876, pp. 464, 465.

Exhibition, to a meeting of the Zoological Society of London, of specimens of *Gecarcinus lagostoma,* with an extract from a letter from Dr. Drew containing remarks upon them.

731

[Exhibition of and remarks on the skins of a male and female Pheasant (*Lobiophasis bulweri*).]

Proc. Zool. Soc. London, 1876, p. 465, pl. xliv.

Exhibition, to a meeting of the Zoological Society of London, of the skins of the male and female of *Lobiophasis bulweri,* with the characters of the female. Both male and female are figured.

732

[Exhibition of a drawing of a Fruit-Pigeon, apparently belonging to *Carpophaga paulina,* living in the Society's Gardens.]

Proc. Zool. Soc. London, 1876, p. 519.

733

[Exhibition of a collection of Birds received from Signor L. M. D'Albertis, and descriptions of two new Parrots.]

Proc. Zool. Soc. London, 1876, pp. 519, 520, pl liv.

Trichoglossus subplacens and *Cyclopsitta suavissima* are described. The latter is figured.

734

[Report on the additions to the Society's Menagerie in June, July, August, and September, 1876.]

Proc. Zool. Soc. London, 1876, pp. 693–696, pls. lxvi–lxviii.

Report on the additions to the Zoological Society's Menagerie, with remarks on the most noticeable species. *Corvus capellanus* (described as a new species), *Sarcidiornis melanonota* and *S. carunculata* are figured. *Cervulus micrurus* (described in *Proc. Zool. Soc. London,* 1875, p. 422) is pointed out to be referable to *C. reevesi.*

735

[Report on the additions to the Society's Menagerie in October, 1876.]

Proc. Zool. Soc. London, 1876, p. 751.

736

[Exhibition of and remarks upon a skin of a young Rhinoceros from the Sunderbunds.]

Proc. Zool. Soc. London, 1876, p. 751.

737

[Report on the additions to the Society's Menagerie in November, 1876.]

Proc. Zool. Soc. London, 1876, pp. 775, 776.

738

Ornithological Notes from Constantinople. By P. L. Sclater and E. C. Taylor.

Ibis, 1876, pp. 60–65.

Notes on the birds observed during a short visit
to Constantinople in September and October, 1875.

739

On recent Ornithological Progress in
New Guinea.

Ibis, 1876, pp. 243–259.

A résumé of the contributions to the ornithological literature of New Guinea.

(See also *Ibis*, 1876, p. 357.)

740

Further Ornithological News from New
Guinea.

Ibis, 1876, pp. 357–364.

Additional notes on the contributions to the
literature on the New Guinea avifauna.

(See also *Ibis*, 1876, p. 243.)

741

Description of a new Tanager of the
genus *Calliste*, and remarks on other recently discovered species.

Ibis, 1876, pp. 407–410, pl. xii.

Calliste melanotis is described and figured and
remarks made on some other species of the genus
Calliste. *C. cyanotis* is figured also.

742

On the Rhinoceroses now or lately living in the Society's Menagerie.

Trans. Zool. Soc. London, IX, pp. 645–660,
pls. xcv–xcix (1876).

The following species are remarked upon and
figured: *Rhinoceros unicornis*, *R. sondaicus*, *R.
sumatrensis*, *R. lasiotis* and *R. bicornis*. The examples of Rhinoceroses living in the Zoological
Society's Menagerie from 1834–1875 are enumerated. The text is illustrated.

743

On the present state of our knowledge
of Geographical Zoology. Address delivered to the Biological Section of the British Association, at Bristol, August 25,
1875.

Rep. Brit. Assoc. Adv. Sci., 1875, Pt. II, pp.
85–133. [Also separately printed.]

The presidential address to the Biological
Section of the British Association, at Bristol,
1875, being a review of the distribution of the
terrestrial members of the vertebrate subking-
dom of animals over the earth's surface, which
is divided into seven divisions. Each division is
remarked upon and the works relating thereto
enumerated.

744

[Report on the additions to the Society's Menagerie in December, 1876.]

Proc. Zool. Soc. London, 1877, pp. 1, 2.

745

Descriptions of eight new species of
South American Birds. By P. L. Sclater
and Osbert Salvin.

Proc. Zool. Soc. London, 1877, pp. 18–22, pl. i.

The following species are described: *Euphonia
finschi*, *Pheucticus crissalis*, *Ochthœca leucometopa*,
O. arenacea, *Chloronerpes dignus*, *Oeleus subflavus*,
Chamœpelia buckleyi and *Crax erythrognatha*.
Chloronerpes dignus is figured.

746

[Exhibition of and remarks upon a
collection of Mammals, Birds, and Insects formed by the Rev. George Brown,
C. M. Z. S., in Duke of York Island, New
Britain, and New Ireland.]

Proc. Zool. Soc. London, 1877, p. 28.

(See also *Proc. Zool. Soc. London*, 1877, p. 96;
1878, pp. 289, 670; 1879, p. 446; 1880, p. 65.)

747

[Report on the additions to the Society's Menagerie in January 1877.]

Proc. Zool. Soc. London, 1877, p. 42.

748

[Exhibition of and remarks upon the
original and unique specimen of *Manucodia comrii*.]

Proc. Zool. Soc. London, 1877, p. 43.

749

Notice of an apparently new species of
Spur-winged Goose of the genus *Plectropterus*.

Proc. Zool. Soc. London, 1877, pp. 47, 48, pl.
vii.

Description and figure of *Plectropterus niger*,
with remarks.

750

On the Birds collected by Mr. George
Brown, C. M. Z. S., on Duke of York
Island, and on the adjoining parts of New
Ireland and New Britain.

Proc. Zool. Soc. London, 1877, pp. 96–114, pls.
xiv–xvi.

Remarks on Mr. George Brown's collection of
birds, with an annotated list of the 70 species contained in it. The following 10 species are described as new: *Monarcha verticalis*, *Artamus insignis*, *Dicrurus læmo-stictus*, *Dicæum eximium*,
Philemon cockerelli, *Tanysiptera nigriceps*, *Loriculus tener*, *Ninox odiosa*, *Macropygia browni*, and
Phlogœnas johannæ. *Monarcha melanonotus* is
proposed as a new name for the New Guinea species of *Monarcha*, which is commonly assigned to
M. chrysomelas. *Monarcha verticalis*, *Dicæum eximium*, *Artamus insignis*, and *Phlogœnas johannæ*
are figured. A figure of the head of *Œdirhinus
insolitus*, and an outline map of the Duke of York
Island, New Britain and New Ireland, are given
in the text.

(See also *Proc. Zool. Soc. London*, 1877, p. 28;
1878, pp. 289, 670; 1879, p. 446; 1880, p. 65.)

751

[Report on the additions to the Society's Menagerie in February, 1877.]

Proc. Zool. Soc. London, 1877, pp. 159, 160.

752

[Remarks upon a two-horned Rhinoceros killed in 1876 near Comillah, in Tip-
perah, and on a living specimen of *Rhinoceros sondaicus* from the Sunderbans.]

Proc. Zool. Soc. London, 1877, pp. 269, 270.

753

[Exhibition of a small living Amphisbænian (*Blanus cinereus*).]

Proc. Zool. Soc. London, 1877, p. 270.

754

[Report on the additions to the Society's Menagerie in March, 1877.]

Proc. Zool. Soc. London, 1877, p. 303.

755

[Exhibition of and remarks on young Anacondas, which had been produced dead in the Society's Menagerie.]

Proc. Zool. Soc. London, 1877, p. 303.

756

[Remarks upon two large photographs of the young Gorilla now living in Berlin, and on an example of the Gorilla formerly living in England.]

Proc. Zool. Soc. London, 1877, pp. 303, 304, pl. xxxv.

Troglodytes gorilla is figured.

757

[Report on the additions to the Society's Menagerie in April, 1877.]

Proc. Zool. Soc. London, 1877, pp. 418, 419.

758

[Remarks on the Zoological Gardens of Rotterdam, Amsterdam, Antwerp, Brussels, and Ghent, lately visited by Mr. Sclater.]

Proc. Zool. Soc. London, 1877, p. 419.

759

Descriptions of six new species of South American Birds. By P. L. Sclater and Osbert Salvin.

Proc. Zool. Soc. London, 1877, pp. 521-523, pl. lii.

The following species are described: *Basileuterus castaniceps, Euphonia insignis, Chlorospingus phæocephalus, Todirostrum rufigene, Lathria cryptolopha,* and *Fuligula nationi.* * *Euphonia insignis* and *Chlorospingus phæocephalus* are figured.

*(See also *Proc. Zool. Soc. London*, 1878, p. 477.)

760

[Report on the additions to the Society's Menagerie in May, 1877.]

Proc. Zool. Soc. London, 1877, pp. 530-532, pl. lv.

Report on the additions to the Zoological Society's collection, with remarks on the more noticeable species. An apparently new species of Cheetah, to which the temporary name *Felis lanea* * is applied, is figured. *Manis tricuspis* is figured in the text.

*(See also *Proc. Zool. Soc. London*, 1878, p. 655; 1884, p. 476.)

761

Reports on the collections of Birds made during the voyage of H. M. S. *Challenger.* No. I. General remarks on the collections.

Proc. Zool. Soc. London, 1877, pp. 534, 535.

General remarks on the collections of birds made during the voyage of the *Challenger*.

(See also *Proc. Zool. Soc. London*, 1877, p. 551; 1878, pp. 346, 431, 576, 650.)

762

Reports on the collections of Birds made during the voyage of H. M. S. *Challenger.* No. III. On the Birds of the Admiralty Islands.

Proc. Zool. Soc. London, 1877, pp. 551-557.

An annotated list of 27 species, of which the following are described as new: *Rhipidura semirubra, Monarcha infelix, Philemon albitorques, Myzomela pammelæna, Carpophaga rhodinolæma, Ptilopus johannis* and *Megapodius rubrifrons.*

(See also *Proc. Zool. Soc. London*, 1877, p. 534; 1878, pp. 346, 431, 576, 650.)

763

[Reports on the additions to the Society's Menagerie in June, July, August, and September, 1877.]

Proc. Zool. Soc. London, 1877, pp. 679-683, pls. lxx, lxxi.

Report on the additions to the Zoological Society's collection, with notes on the most interesting species, of which *Hylobates leucogenys* and *Paradoxurus prehensilis* are figured. The head of *Cervus schomburgki* is figured in the text.

764

[Report on the additions to the Society's Menagerie in October, 1877.]

Proc. Zool. Soc. London, 1877, p. 754.

765

[Report on the additions to the Society's Menagerie in November, 1877.]

Proc. Zool. Soc. London, 1877, pp. 805, 806, pl. lxxxi.

Canis jubatus is figured.

766

Note on the South American Song Sparrows.

Ibis, 1877, pp. 46-48, pl. i.

Notes on the species of the genus *Zonotrichia*, with their distribution. *Z. canicapilla* and *Z. strigiceps* are figured.

767

On the Nesting of the Spoonbill in Holland. By P. L. Sclater and W. A. Forbes.

Ibis, 1877. pp. 412-416.

An account of a visit to the nesting place of *Platalea leucorodia* in the Horster Meer, Holland.

768

Description of two new Ant Birds of the genus *Grallaria*, with a list of the known species of the genus.

Ibis, 1877, pp. 437-451, pls. viii, ix.

Grallaria haplonota and *G. flavotincta* are described, and a synopsis of the species (27 in number) of the genus *Grallaria* is given. *G. ruficeps* and *G. flavotincta* are figured.

769

On a recent addition to the species of the genus *Loriculus*.

Rowley's Ornithological Miscellany, II, pp. 375-377, pl. lxxii (1877).

Remarks on the differences between *Loriculus tener* and *L. aurantifrons*. Both species are figured.

770

On the American Parrots of the genus *Pionus.*

Rowley's Ornithological Miscellany, III, pp. 5-9, pls. lxxx, lxxxi (1877).

An arrangement of the nine species of the genus *Pionus*, with remarks and a table showing their geographical distribution. *Pionus corallinus* and *P. tumultuosus* are figured.

771

Remarks on the new Monotreme from New Guinea.

Nature, XV, pp. 257, 258 (1877).

Remarks on the new mammal described by Messrs. W. Peters and G. Doria as *Tachyglossus bruijnii.* The text is illustrated with the skulls of *T. bruijnii* and one of the Australian species of *Tachyglossus.*

772

The Development of Batrachians without Metamorphosis.

Nature, XV, pp. 491, 492 (1877).

Notes on the development of batrachians without metamorphosis, which is shown, in a communication by Dr. Peters to the Royal Academy of Sciences, Berlin, to have taken place in *Hylodes martinicensis.* The egg, young, and adult of *Hylodes martinicensis* are figured in the text.

773

[Report on the additions to the Society's Menagerie in December, 1877.]

Proc. Zool. Soc. London, 1878, p. 1.

774

[Report on the additions to the Society's Menagerie in January, 1878.]

Proc. Zool. Soc. London, 1878, pp. 115, 116.

775

On the collection of Birds made by Professor Steere in South America. By P. L. Sclater and Osbert Salvin.

Proc. Zool. Soc. London, 1878, pp. 135–142, pls. xi–xiii.

Remarks on 22 rare or little-known species contained in a collection of 302 species made by Professor Steere during a journey across South America. The following new species are described: *Oryzoborus atrirostris, Myiarchus semirufus, Furnarius pileatus, Capito steerii,* and *Crypturus transfasciatus. Myiarchus semirufus, Capito steerii* and *Crypturus transfasciatus* are figured.

776

[Exhibition of and remarks upon a skin of a Cassowary in the collection of the British Museum.]

Proc. Zool. Soc. London, 1878, pp. 212–214.

Remarks on *Casuarius salvadorii,* with a figure of its head in the text.

777

[Report on the additions to the Society's Menagerie in February, 1878.]

Proc. Zool. Soc. London, 1878, p. 289.

778

[Exhibition of and remarks on a second collection of Birds from Duke of York Island, New Britain, and New Ireland, received from the Rev. G. Brown, C. M. Z. S.]

Proc. Zool. Soc. London, 1878, pp. 289, 290.

Twenty-three species are enumerated and remarks made upon some of them.

(See also *Proc. Zool. Soc. London,* 1877, pp. 28, 96; 1878, p. 670; 1879, p. 446; 1880, p. 65.)

779

[Exhibition of and remarks upon the typical specimen of *Ninox solomonis,* Sharpe.]

Proc. Zool. Soc. London, 1878, p. 290.

780

[Exhibition of a Coot, probably the typical specimen of *Fulica gallinuloides.*]

Proc. Zool. Soc. London, 1878, p. 291.

781

[Exhibition of and remarks upon the typical specimen of *Dicrurus marginatus* of Blyth.]

Proc. Zool. Soc. London, 1878, p. 339.

782

Reports on the collections of Birds made during the voyage of H. M. S. *Challenger.* No. VIII. On the Birds of the Sandwich Islands.

Proc. Zool. Soc. London, 1878, pp. 346–351.

Thirteen species are enumerated and remarked upon. *Anas wyvilliana* is described as new.

(See also *Proc. Zool. Soc. London,* 1877, pp. 534, 555; 1878, pp. 431, 576, 650.)

783

[Report on the additions to the Society's Menagerie in March, 1878.]

Proc. Zool. Soc. London, 1878, pp. 377–379.

Report on the additions to the Zoological Society's Gardens, with remarks on the more interesting species. A list of the Bears living in the Menagerie is given, and the breeding of the Anaconda (*Eunectes murinus*) in the Society's reptile house is recorded.

784

[Exhibition of and remarks upon a typical specimen of a new Fox (*Vulpes cana,* Blanford).]

Proc. Zool. Soc. London, 1878, p. 392.

The differences between *Vulpes cana* and *Canis famelicus* are pointed out. The dimensions of the former animal are given.

785

Reports on the collections of Birds made during the voyage of H. M. S. *Challenger.* No. IX. On the Birds of Antarctic America. By P. L. Sclater and Osbert Salvin.

Proc. Zool. Soc. London, 1878, pp. 431–438.

A catalogue of 41 species, with notes upon them.

(See also *Proc. Zool. Soc. London,* 1877, pp. 534, 551; 1878, p. 346, 576, 650.)

786

Descriptions of three new species of Birds from Ecuador. By P. L. Sclater and Osbert Salvin.

Proc. Zool. Soc. London, 1878, pp. 438–440, pls. xxvii, xxviii.

Buarremon leucopis, Neomorphus radiolosus and *Aramides calopterus* are described. The last two mentioned are figured.

787

[Report on the additions to the Society's Menagerie in April, 1878.]

Proc. Zool. Soc. London, 1878, p. 441.

788

Further remarks on *Fuligula nationi.*

Proc. Zool. Soc. London, 1878. pp. 477–479, pl. xxxii.

Fuligula nationi is characterized and figured. The trachea of this duck is also figured in the text and remarked upon.

(See also *Proc. Zool. Soc. London,* 1877, p. 522.)

789

Reports on the collections of Birds made during the voyage of H. M. S. Challenger. No. X. On the Birds of the Atlantic Islands and Kerguelen's Land, and on the miscellaneous collections.

Proc. Zool. Soc. London, 1878, pp. 576–579.

A résumé of the contents of several of the collections of the Challenger expedition.

(See also Proc. Zool. Soc. London, 1877, pp. 534, 551; 1878, pp. 346, 431, 650.)

790

[Report on the additions to the Society's Menagerie in May, 1878, and remarks on Tapirus roulini.]

Proc. Zool. Soc. London, 1878, pp. 631, 632, pl. xxxix.

Report on the additions to the Zoological Society's Gardens, with notes on the more remarkable specimens. Tapirus roulini is figured.

791

[Exhibition of and remarks upon a young specimen of Temminck's Manis (Manis temmincki) from Zanzibar.]

Proc. Zool. Soc. London, 1878, pp. 632, 633.

792

[Remarks upon the living examples of Ciconia maguari and Ciconia episcopus now in the Society's Gardens.]

Proc. Zool. Soc. London, 1878, p. 633.

Notes on the mimicry of the rectrices by the elongated upper tail-coverts in Ciconia maguari and C. episcopus. It is also shown that the generic name Euxenura should give place to Dissura.

793

Reports on the collections of Birds made during the voyage of H. M. S. Challenger. No. XI. On the Steganopodes and Impennes. By P. L. Sclater and Osbert Salvin.

Proc. Zool. Soc. London, 1878, pp. 650–655.

Notes on nine species of Steganopodes and six species of Impennes.

(See also Proc. Zool. Soc. London, 1877, pp. 534, 551; 1878, pp. 346, 431, 576.)

794

[Note on a second specimen of Felis lanea.]

Proc. Zool. Soc. London, 1878, pp. 655, 656.

Extract from a letter from Mr. E. L. Layard intimating the existence of an example of Felis lanea in the South African Museum.

(See also Proc. Zool. Soc. London, 1877, p. 530; 1884, p. 476.)

795

[Notice of a supplementary memoir on the Curassows (Cracidae).]

Proc. Zool. Soc. London, 1878, p. 656.

796

On a third collection of Birds made by the Rev. G. Brown, C. M. Z. S., in the Duke of York Group of Islands and its vicinity.

Proc. Zool. Soc. London, 1878, pp. 670–673, pl. xlii.

A tabular list of 30 species, with their localities and remarks upon the more interesting species.

Carpophaga melanochroa is described as new and figured.

(See also Proc. Zool. Soc. London, 1877, pp. 28, 96; 1878, p. 289; 1879, p. 446; 1880, p. 65.)

797

[Report on the additions to the Society's Menagerie in June, July, August, September, and October, 1878.]

Proc. Zool. Soc. London, 1878, pp. 788–791.

798

[Notice of some hybrid Monkeys lately born in the Society's Menagerie.]

Proc. Zool. Soc. London, 1878, p. 791.

Notes on hybrids between Macacus cynomolgus, ♂, and Cercocebus fuliginosus, ♀, and Macacus cynomolgus, ♂, and Cynocephalus mormon. ♀, born in the Menagerie of the Zoological Society of London.

799

[Exhibition of and remarks upon a specimen of Saxicola stapazina killed in Lancashire.]

Proc. Zool. Soc. London, 1878, p. 881.

(See also Proc. Zool. Soc. London, 1878, p. 977.)

800

[Report on the additions to the Society's Menagerie in November, 1878.]

Proc. Zool. Soc. London, 1878, pp. 975, 976, pl. lxi.

Ara spixi is figured.

801

[Further remarks on the occurrence of Saxicola stapazina in Lancashire.]

Proc. Zool. Soc. London, 1878, p. 977.

(See also Proc. Zool. Soc. London, 1878, p. 881.)

802

[Notice of an error in the last part of the Society's Proceedings.]

Proc. Zool. Soc. London, 1878, p. 977.

A correction of an error which had taken place in the "Proceedings" (1878, p. 637) with reference to a collection of butterflies from Billiton.

803

Revision of the species of the Cotingine genus Pipreola.

Ibis, 1878, pp. 164–173, pl. vi.

Swainson's name. Pipreola, for the green Cotingas is adopted, and synonyms of the genus given, together with a synopsis of the species, of which nine are enumerated. Pipreola frontalis is figured.

804

Preliminary remarks on the Neotropical Pipits.

Ibis, 1878, pp. 356–367, pl. x.

A review of the American species of the genus Anthus. Six species are enumerated, of which A. nattereri is described as new and figured. The text is illustrated.

805

Note on the Breeding of the Sacred Ibis in the Zoological Society's Gardens.

Ibis, 1878, pp. 449–451, pl. xii.

Observations on the breeding of Ibis æthiopica in the Gardens of the Zoological Society of London. The young bird and egg are figured.

806

Zoological Distribution and some of its difficulties.

Proc. Roy. Inst. Grt. Brit., VIII, pp. 511–513 (1878).

An abstract of a lecture delivered before the Royal Institution of Great Britain on zoological distribution. The characteristic species of each zoological area are treated of, and some of the species with abnormal distribution enumerated and remarked upon.

807

[Report on the additions to the Society's Menagerie in December, 1878.]

Proc. Zool. Soc. London, 1879, p. 2.

808

[Report on the additions to the Society's Menagerie in January, 1879.]

Proc. Zool. Soc. London, 1879, p. 108.

809

[Remarks upon and diagnosis of *Mitua salvini*, the new Curassow.]

Proc. Zool. Soc. London, 1879, pp. 108, 109.

Extract from a letter from Professor Reinhardt containing remarks on *Mitua salvini*. The species is diagnosed by Mr. Sclater.

810

On the Breeding of the Argus Pheasant and other *Phasianidæ* in the Society's Gardens.

Proc. Zool. Soc. London, 1879, pp. 114–118, pls. vii, viii.

Report on the breeding of several species of *Phasianidæ* in the Zoological Society's Gardens. *Argus giganteus*, ♂ pull., and the eggs of the following species are figured: *Argus giganteus, Polyplectron chinquis, Ceriornis temmincki, C. satyra*, and *Crossoptilon mantchuricum*.

811

[Exhibition and description of a new Humming-Bird, *Thaumasius taczanowskii*, from northern Peru.]

Proc. Zool. Soc. London, 1879, pp. 145, 146.

Thaumasius taczanowskii is described. The generic name *Thaumatius* is emended to *Thaumasius*.

812

[Exhibition of a living Amphisbænian from Monte Video.]

Proc. Zool. Soc. London, 1879, p. 146.

A species apparently referable to *Amphisbæna darwini*.

813

[Report on the additions to the Society's Menagerie in February, 1879.]

Proc. Zool. Soc. London, 1879, p. 218.

814

[Exhibition of and remarks upon two rare Fruit Pigeons.]

Proc. Zool. Soc. London, 1879, p. 218.

Carpophaga van-wicki and *C. rhodinolæma* were exhibited to a meeting of the Zoological Society of London and remarked upon.

815

[Remarks upon the Japanese Deer (*Cervus sika*).]

Proc. Zool. Soc. London, 1879, p. 294.

On the Japanese deer (*Cervus sika*) breeding in captivity, with extracts from a letter from Lord Powerscourt containing remarks upon them.

816

Remarks on some Parrots living in the Society's Gardens.

Proc. Zool. Soc. London, 1879, pp. 299–301, pl. xxviii.

Report on the collection of parrots in the Zoological Society's Menagerie, with remarks on the following species: *Brotogerys tuipara, B. chrysoptera, Palæornis cyanocephalus, P. rosa, P. fasciatus*, and *Caica xanthomera*. The last-mentioned species is figured.

817

[Report on the additions to the Society's Menagerie in March, 1879.]

Proc. Zool. Soc. London, 1879, p. 308.

818

[Exhibition of the Eggs collected by the naturalists of the *Challenger* Expedition.]

Proc. Zool. Soc. London, 1879, pp. 309–311.

Exhibition to a meeting of the Zoological Society of London of a series of 250 eggs referable to about 50 species, which are enumerated, with their localities.

819

[Report on the additions to the Society's Menagerie in April, 1879.]

Proc. Zool. Soc. London, 1879, p. 384.

820

[Report on the dimensions and weights of the Indian Elephants.]

Proc. Zool. Soc. London, 1879, p. 385.

The dimensions and weights of the four Indian elephants living in the Zoological Society's Menagerie are given.

(See also *Proc. Zool. Soc. London*, 1881, p. 450; 1883, p. 465.)

821

[Remarks on the Zoological Gardens of Rotterdam, Amsterdam, Cologne, Frankfurt, and Antwerp.]

Proc. Zool. Soc. London, 1879, p. 438.

Remarks on the interesting animals and other objects observed during a visit to the above-mentioned gardens.

822

On a fourth collection of Birds made by the Rev. G. Brown, C. M. Z. S., on Duke of York Island and its vicinity.

Proc. Zool. Soc. London, 1879, pp. 446–451, pls. xxxvi, xxxvii.

A list of 41 species, with remarks on the more interesting ones. *Graucalus sublineatus, Myzomela cineracea, Donacicola* (emend. ex *Donacola*, Gould) *spectabilis*, and *Munia forbesi* are described as new species and figured.

(See also *Proc. Zool. Soc. London*, 1877, pp. 28, 96; 1878, pp. 289, 670; 1880, p. 65.)

823

[Remarks on two volumes of original drawings of the Birds of India, by Brig. Gen. A. C. M'Master.]

Proc. Zool. Soc. London, 1879, p. 460.

The two volumes contain about 270 figures of the birds of India, and are deposited in the Zoological Society's library.

824

[Exhibition of and remarks upon a collection of Birds from the Argentine Republic.]

Proc. Zool. Soc. London, 1879, pp. 460, 461.

Exhibition to a meeting of the Zoological Society of London of a collection consisting of nine species of birds from Argentina Doring's MS. name. *Phacellodomus sibilatrix*, is adopted as the name of a new species.

825

On the Birds collected by the late Mr. T. K. Salmon in the State of Antioquia, United States of Colombia. By P. L. Sclater and Osbert Salvin.

Proc. Zool. Soc. London. 1879, pp. 486–550, pls. xli–xlii.

An account of Mr Salmon's collections and the localities in which they were made, and a summary of the previous literature on the avifauna of Colombia. The collections (eight in number) consisted of about 3,500 specimens, referable to 468 species, which are enumerated and remarked upon. The following new species are described: *Cyphorhinus dichrous. Buarremon elæoprorus, Automolus ignobilis. Grallaria rufo-cinerea*, and *Brachygalba salmoni. Cyphorhinus dichrous* and the eggs of several species are figured. A map showing Mr. Salmon's collecting stations is also given.

826

[Report on the additions to the Society's Menagerie in May, 1879.]

Proc. Zool. Soc. London, 1879, pp 550 551, pl. xliv.

Nymphicus cornutus is figured.

827

[Exhibition of and remarks upon a skin of *Ara glauca*.]

Proc. Zool. Soc. London, 1879, p. 551.

828

On the Birds collected in Bolivia by Mr. C. Buckley. By P. L. Sclater and Osbert Salvin.

Proc. Zool. Soc. London, 1879, pp. 588–645.

A complete list of Mr. Buckley s two collections, consisting of 700 skins, referable to 501 species, with an account of the previous authorities on the avifauna of Bolivia. *Synallaxis rufipennis* and *Leptoptila megalura* are described as new species.

829

[Report on the additions to the Society's Menagerie in June, July, August, and September, 1879.]

Proc. Zool. Soc. London, 1879, pp. 663, 664.

830

[Report on the additions to the Society's Menagerie in October, 1879.]

Proc. Zool. Soc. London, 1879, p. 713.

831

[Report on the additions to the Society's Menagerie in November, 1879.]

Proc. Zool. Soc. London, 1879, pp. 763, 764.

832

[Exhibition of and remarks upon a small collection of Birds from the island of Montserrat, West Indies.]

Proc. Zool. Soc. London, 1879, pp. 764, 765.

A nominal list of 17 species, with their local names.

833

Note on the American Crows of the subgenus *Xanthura*.

Ibis, 1879, pp 87–89.

Remarks on the synonymy and distribution of the species of *Xanthura*.

834

On recent additions to our knowledge of the Avifauna of the Sandwich Islands.

Ibis, 1879, pp. 89–92, pl. ii.

A summary of the contributions to the ornithological literature of the Sandwich Islands. *Loxioides bailleui* is figured, and a list is given of the 23 known species peculiar to these islands.

835

Note on the name of the Purple Water Hen of southwestern Europe.

Ibis, 1879, pp. 195, 196.

Remarks showing that the specific name "*veterum*," used by authors for the Purple Water Hen, can not stand, and that this species should be called *Porphyrio cœruleus*.

836

Remarks on the Nomenclature of the British Owls, and on the arrangement of the Order *Striges*.

Ibis, 1879, pp. 346–352.

An examination of the nomenclature of the British *Strigidæ*, with remarks on the principal divisions of the order *Striges*.

837

The generic name *Euchætes*.

Ibis, 1879, p. 388.

The name *Euchætes*, Scl., having been previously used in entomology, it is here proposed to change it to *Calochætes*.

838

Descriptions of some new Tanagers of the genus *Buarremon*. By P. L. Sclater and Osbert Salvin.

Ibis, 1879, pp. 425–427.

The following species are described: *Buarremon melanolæmus, B. spodionotus, B. comptus*, and *B. inornatus. B. latinuchus* and *B. melanolæmus* are figured.

839

Supplementary notes on the Curassows now or lately living in the Society's Gardens.

Trans. Zool. Soc. London, X, p. 543–546, pls. lxxxix–xcv (1879).

Supplementary notes to a former communication on the Curassows (cf. *Trans. Zool. Soc. London*, IX, p. 273, 1875). The following species are remarked upon and figured: *Orax globicera, C. erythrognatha, C. globulosa, C. viridirostris, C. incommoda, Nothocrax urumutum* and *Mitua salvini*.

840

The Exploration of Socotra.

Nature, XXI, p. 153 (1879).

An advertisement for a naturalist to visit Socotra.

841

Monkeys in the West Indies.

Nature, XXI, p. 153 (1879).

Letter on the existence of monkeys in the West Indies.

(See also *Proc. Zool. Soc. London*, 1866, p. 79; *Nature*, XLI, p. 368 (1890).)

842

[Report on the additions to the Society's Menagerie in December, 1879, and remarks upon two rare species of *Chrysotis*.]

Proc. Zool. Soc. London, 1880, pp. 22, 23, pl. ii.

Chrysotis bodini and *C. erythrura* are remarked upon. The latter is figured.

843

[Exhibition of an Egg of the Mooruk (*Casuarius bennetti*).]

Proc. Zool. Soc. London, 1880, p. 27.

844

Remarks on some species of the genus *Tyrannus*.

Proc. Zool. Soc. London, 1880, pp 28–30, pl. iii.

A commentary of Mr. Ridgway's paper on the genus *Tyrannus* (*Proc. U. S. Nat. Mus.*, I, p. 166). *Tyrannus niveigularis* is figured. The text is illustrated.

845

On a fifth collection of Birds made by the Rev. G. Brown, C. M. Z. S., on the Duke of York Island and its vicinity.

Proc. Zool. Soc. London, 1880, pp. 65–67, pls. vi–viii.

A list of 13 species, of which the following are described as new: *Megalurus interscapularis*, *Pœcilodryas æthiops*, *Munia melæna*, and *Rallus insignis*. Also notes on a small collection in spirits.

(See also *Proc. Zool. Soc. London*, 1877, pp. 28, 90; 1878, pp. 289, 670; 1879, p. 446.)

846

[Report on the additions to the Society's Menagerie in January, 1880, and exhibition of a drawing of an undescribed Parrot of the genus *Chrysotis* living in the Society's Gardens.]

Proc. Zool. Soc. London, 1880. pp. 67, 68, pl. ix.

*Chrysotis cœligena** is described and figured. *C. dufresniana* is also figured.

**(cf. *Proc. Zool. Soc. London*, 1879, p. 815.)

847

[Remarks upon the probable identity of *Colobus palliatus*, Peters, with *C. angolensis*, Scl.]

Proc. Zool. Soc. London, 1880, p. 68.

848

On new Birds collected by Mr. C. Buckley in eastern Ecuador. By P. L. Sclater and Osbert Salvin.

Proc. Zool. Soc. London, 1880, pp. 155–161, pls. xvi, xvii.

The following species are described: *Hylophilus fuscicapillus*, *Nemosia chrysopis*, *Platyrhynchus senex*, *Serpophaga albogrisea*, *Syristes albocinereus*, *Myiochanes nigrescens*, *Heterocercus aurantiivertex*, *Ptilochloris buckleyi*, *Automolus dorsalis*, *Dysithamnus subplumbeus*, *Herpsilochmus frater*, *Myrmotherula spodionota*, *Terenura humeralis*, *Hypocnemis stellata*, *H. lepidonota*, *Pithys melanosticta*, *Grallaria dignissima*, *Celeus spectabilis*, and *Porzana œnops*. *Ptilochloris buckleyi*, ad. et pull., and *Grallaria dignissima* are figured.

849

[Report on the additions to the Society's Menagerie in February, 1880.]

Proc. Zool. Soc. London, 1880, p. 186.

850

[Report on the additions to the Society's Menagerie in March, 1880.]

Proc. Zool. Soc. London, 1880, p. 288.

851

[Report on the additions to the Society's Menagerie in April, 1880.]

Proc. Zool. Soc. London, 1880, p. 355.

Phascolarctus cinereus is figured in the text.

852

[Exhibition of and remarks upon an Ibis (*Geronticus comatus*).]

Proc. Zool. Soc. London, 1880, p. 356.

Exhibition to a meeting of the Zoological Society of London of a specimen of *Geronticus comatus* obtained by Mr. Danford on the Euphrates, and notes on the distribution of the species.

853

[Remarks on Animals observed in the Zoological Gardens of Berlin, Hamburg, Amsterdam, The Hague, and Antwerp.]

Proc. Zool. Soc. London, 1880, p. 420.

854

[Exhibition of a Spider of the genus *Tegenaria*, forwarded from Cape Town by J. H. Payne.]

Proc. Zool. Soc. London, 1880, p. 421.

855

[Report on the additions to the Society's Menagerie in May, 1880, and description of a new Lemur (*Lemur nigerrimus*).]

Proc. Zool. Soc. London, 1880, pp. 450–452.

Lemur nigerrimus, sp. nov., is described. The head and that of *L. macaco* are figured in the text.

856

[Exhibition of and remarks upon an apparently new species of Antelope.]

Proc. Zool. Soc. London, 1880, p. 452, pl. xliv.

Exhibition to a meeting of the Zoological Society of London of a skin of an antelope, which is described as *Tragelaphus gratus* and figured.

(See also *Proc. Zool. Soc. London*, 1883, p. 34.)

857

List of the certainly known species of *Anatidæ*, with notes on such as have been introduced into the zoological gardens of Europe, and remarks on their distribution.

Proc. Zool. Soc. London, 1888, pp. 496–536.

One hundred and seventy-four species are enumerated and remarked upon. The generic name *Dendrocygna* is emended to *Dendrocycna*.

858

[Report on the additions to the Society's Menagerie in June, July, August, September, and October, 1880.]

Proc. Zool. Soc. London, 1880, pp. 537–539.

859

[Exhibition of and remarks upon a skin of *Numida ellioti*.]

Proc. Zool. Soc. London, 1880, p. 539.

Numida ellioti. Bartlett, is shown to be referable to *N. pucherani*, Hartlaub.

860

[Report on the additions to the Society's Menagerie in November, 1880.]

Proc. Zool. Soc. London, 1880, p. 648.

861

[Exhibition of and remarks upon an example of *Pauxis galcata*.]

Proc. Zool. Soc. London, 1880, p. 648.

862

Notes upon some West-Indian Birds.

Ibis, 1880, pp. 71-74, pl. l.

Notes on seven species, of which *Margarops sanctæ-luciæ* is described as new. A new generic name, *Catharopeza*, is proposed for the reception of *Leucopeza bishopi*, Lawr. *Catharopeza bishopi* is figured. The text is illustrated with the wing, bill and foot of *Catharopeza*.

863

Note on the *Rallus sulcirostris* of Wallace and its allies.

Ibis, 1880, pp. 309-312, pl. vi.

Reichenbach's generic name *Hypotænidia* is adopted for this Rail, and remarks made on the six other species comprising the genus. Salvadori's MS. name *Hypotænidia saturata* is published and the species characterized. *H. sulcirostris* is figured.

864

Remarks on the present state of the Systema Avium.

Ibis, 1880, pp. 340-350, 309-411.

A scheme for the classification of birds.

(See also *Rep. Brit. Assoc. Adv. Sci.*, 1880, p. 606, and *Nature*, XXII, p. 549, 1880.)

865

Waterfowl.

Nature, XXII, pp. 295-298 (1880).

An illustrated abstract of a lecture delivered before the Zoological Society of London on the introduction into, and the acclimatization of waterfowl in, the Society's Gardens.

866

On the classification of Birds.

Rep. Brit. Assoc. Adv. Sci., 1880, pp. 606-609, and *Nature*, XXII, p. 549 (1880) (abstract).

A scheme for the systematic arrangement of the class Aves, with approximate numbers of species belonging to each order.

(See also *Ibis*, 1880, pp. 340, 390.)

867

Illustrations of new or rare Animals in the Zoological Society's Living Collection.

Nature, XXIII, pp. 35-38, 415-417, 487-490 (1880-81); XXIV, pp. 534-536 (1881); XXV, pp. 295-298, 391-393, 608-610 (1882); XXVI, pp. 131-134, 603-606 (1882).

Illustrated chapters on the most noticeable animals living in the Zoological Society's Menagerie.

868

[Exhibition of and remarks upon a skin of a Merganser (*Mergus australis*).]

Proc. Zool. Soc. London, 1881, p. 1.

869

[Report on the additions to the Society's Menagerie in December, 1880.]

Proc. Zool. Soc. London, 1881, p. 165.

870

On the Birds collected in Socotra by Prof. I. Bayley Balfour. By P. L. Sclater and Dr. G. Hartlaub.

Proc. Zool. Soc. London, 1881, pp. 165-175, pls. xv-xvii.

A report on a collection consisting of 126 skins, referable to 36 species, which are enumerated and remarked upon. The genus *Rhynchostruthus* and the following species are described as new: *Cisticola incana. Drymœca hœsitata, Lanius uncinatus, Cinnyris balfouri, Passer insularis, Rhynchostruthus socotranus*, and *Amydrus frater*. *Cisticola incana, Cinnyris balfouri, Passer insularis, and Rhynchostruthus socotranus* are figured. The text is illustrated with the head of *Lanius uncinatus*, and the head, wing and foot of *Rhynchostruthus socotranus*.

871

On some Birds collected by Mr. E. F. im Thurn in British Guiana.

Proc. Zool. Soc. London, 1881, pp. 212-214.

Notes on six species of birds contained in a series of skins collected in British Guiana. *Agelæus inthurni* is described as new, and the head of it is figured in the text.

872

[Report on the additions to the Society's Menagerie in January, 1881.]

Proc. Zool. Soc. London, 1881, pp. 258, 259, pl. xxix.

Pithecia albinasa is figured and its synonyms are given.

873

[Exhibition of and remarks upon the Eggs of *Opisthocomus cristatus* and *Coturnix delegorgii*.]

Proc. Zool. Soc. London, 1881, p. 259.

874

[Exhibition of and remarks upon a large Spider of the genus *Mygale*.]

Proc. Zool. Soc. London, 1881, p. 325.

This species, obtained at Bahia, is referred doubtfully to *Mygale bistriata*, Koch.

875

[Report on the additions to the Society's Menagerie in February, 1881.]

Proc. Zool. Soc. London, 1881, p. 409.

876

[Report on the additions to the Society's Menagerie in March, 1881.]

Proc. Zool. Soc. London, 1881, p. 450.

877

[Note on the weights and measurements of the Indian Elephants in the Society's Menagerie.]

Proc. Zool. Soc. London, 1881, pp. 450, 451.

The dimensions and weights of the four Indian Elephants living in the Society's Gardens, with figures to show the increase in size and weight of the animals since May, 1879.

(See *Proc. Zool. Soc. London*, 1879, p. 385; 1883, p. 465.)

878

[Exhibition of and remarks upon some bird skins brought home by the *Challenger* Expedition.]

Proc. Zool. Soc. London, 1881, p. 451.

Notes on four species of birds from the Island of Rotumeh.

879

[Exhibition and descriptions of two new Birds from New Britain.]

Proc. Zool. Soc. London, 1881, pp. 451-453, pl. xxxix.

Trichoglossus rubrigularis, sp. nov., and *Ortygo cichla rubiginosa*, gen. et. sp. nov., are described. The latter is figured.

880

On the Birds of the vicinity of Lima, Peru. By P. L. Sclater. With notes on their habits by Prof. W. Nation. Part V.*

Proc. Zool. Soc. London, 1881, pp. 484–488, pl. xlvi.

Remarks on a collection consisting of 12 species, two of which—*Buarremon nationi* and *Leptasthenura pileata*—are described as new. The former species is figured.

*(For Part I see *Proc. Zool. Soc. London*, 1866, p. 96; Pt. II, 1867, p. 340; Pt. III, 1869, p. 146; pt. IV, 1871, p. 496.)

881

[Report on the additions to the Society's Menagerie in April, 1881.]

Proc. Zool. Soc. London, 1881, pp. 626, 627, pl. liv.

The adult and young of *Oryx beisa* are figured.

882

[Exhibition of and remarks upon a skin of a *Chrysotis* from St. Lucia, West Indies.]

Proc. Zool. Soc. London, 1881, pp. 627, 628.

Remarks on *Chrysotis versicolor*, with notes on the distribution of the species of *Chrysotis* in the Lesser Antilles.

883

[Remarks upon the Insectarium lately opened in the Society's Gardens.]

Proc. Zool. Soc. London, 1881, pp. 651–656.

Observations on the building and arrangement of the insectarium, together with a report by Mr. W. Watkins on the species exhibited therein during May, 1881.

(See also *Rep. Brit. Assoc. Adv. Sci.*, 1881, p. 668.)

884

[Report on the additions to the Society's Menagerie in May, 1881.]

Proc. Zool. Soc. London, 1881, p. 734.

885

On the generic divisions of the *Bucconidæ*, together with the description of a new species of the genus *Nonnula*.

Proc. Zool. Soc. London, 1881, pp. 775–778.

A summary of the generic divisions of the *Bucconidæ*. Seven genera are enumerated, two of which, *Micromonacha* and *Hapaloptila*, are described as new and illustrated in the text. A new species, *Nonnula cineracea*, is also described. The genera recognized are: *Bucco*, *Malacoptila*, *Micromonacha*, *Nonnula*, *Hapaloptila*, *Monacha* and *Chelidoptera*.

886

[Report on the additions to the Society's Menagerie in June, July, August, September, and October, 1881.]

Proc. Zool. Soc. London, 1881, pp. 818, 819.

887

[Exhibition of a specimen of the Glossy Ibis (*Plegadis falcinellus*) shot at Dogmersfield Park, Hampshire.]

Proc. Zool. Soc. London, 1881, p. 827.

888

[Report on the additions to the Society's Menagerie in November, 1881.]

Proc. Zool. Soc. London, 1881, pp. 967, 968.

889

[Exhibition of two skins of a Rail from Macquarie Island.]

Proc. Zool. Soc. London 1881, p. 908.

These skins apparently belonged to the species described by Captain Hutton as *Rallus macquariensis*.

890

On an apparently new Parrot of the genus *Conurus*.

Ibis, 1881, pp. 130, 131, pl. iv.

Conurus egregius is described and figured.

891

Descriptions of some new species of South American Birds of the families *Tyrannidæ* and *Formicariidæ*. By P. L. Sclater and Osbert Salvin.

Ibis, 1881, pp. 267–271, pl. ix.

The genus *Tyranneutes* and the following species are described as new: *Todirostrum signatum*, *Euscarthmus pelzelni*, *Tyranneutes brachyurus*, *Myiarchus apicalis*, *Myrmotherula gutturalis*, and *Terenura spodioptila*. The last-mentioned species and *Terenura humeralis* (♂, ♀) are figured.

892

On the genus *Hylophilus*.

Ibis, 1881, pp. 293–312, pls. x, xi.

A review of the genus *Hylophilus*, embracing the history of the genus, synopsis of the species (19 in number), list of species unknown to the author, list of species wrongly referred to the genus, and remarks on the geographical distribution. *Hylophilus luteifrons* is described as new, and the following species are figured: *H. muscicapinus*, *H. fuscicapillus*, *H. brunneiceps*, and *H. ferrugineifrons*.

893

Remarks on the recently described Parrots of the genus *Chrysotis*.

Ibis, 1881, pp. 411–414.

Remarks on *Chrysotis lactifrons*, *C. campalliata*, *C. apophœnica*, *C. panamensis*, *C. nichollsi*, and *C. cæligena*.

894

On two apparently new Finches of the genus *Erythrura*, with remarks on other known species of the group.

Ibis, 1881, pp. 543–546, pl. xv.

Erythrura regia and *E. serena** are described and figured, and remarks made on the six other known species of the genus *Erythrura*.

*(These two species are described under the generic name *Erythrospiza*, which, as will be be seen by the context, is a printer's error.)

895

On two new species of Birds discovered by Mr. E. W. White in the Argentine Republic.

Ibis, 1881, pp. 509, 600. pl. xvii.

Poospiza erythrophrys and *Synallaxis whitii* are characterized and figured.

896

Characters of a new Puff-bird of the genus *Nonnula*.

Ibis, 1881, pp. 600, 601.

Nonnula brunnea is described.

897

On the Insect House in the Gardens of the Zoological Society of London.

Rep. Brit. Assoc. Adv. Sci., 1881, pp. 668, 669.

Notice of the addition to the Zoological Society's Gardens of an Insectarium, and report on the Insects exhibited therein during the year 1881.
(See also *Proc. Zool. Soc. London*, 1881, p. 651.)

898

[Report on the additions to the Society's Menagerie in December, 1881.]

Proc. Zool. Soc. London, 1882, p. 97.

899

[Exhibition of (on behalf of Mr. Peter Inchbald, F. Z. S.) and remarks upon two curious Ducks shot near Darlington.]

Proc. Zool. Soc. London, 1882, p. 134.

900

[Report on the additions to the Society's Menagerie in January, 1882.]

Proc. Zool. Soc. London, 1882, pp 233, 234, pl. x.

The female and young of *Bos frontalis* are figured.

901

[Exhibition of living examples of *Helix hæmastoma*.]

Proc. Zool. Soc. London, 1882, p. 286.

These specimens had been sent from Ceylon.

902

[Report on the additions to the Society's Menagerie in February, 1882.]

Proc. Zool. Soc. London, 1882, p. 311.

903

[Remarks on the use of the term "Lipotype."]

Proc. Zool. Soc. London, 1882, pp. 311, 312.

Note on the coining of the word "lipotype" for conveniently designating a type of animal life, the absence of which is characteristic of a particular district or region.

904

[Exhibition of and remarks upon an adult male of *Cyanomyias cœlestis*.]

Proc. Zool. Soc. London, 1882, p. 342.

The head of *Cyanomyias cœlestis*, ♂, is figured in the text.

905

[Exhibition of and remarks upon the skins of two specimens of the Subcylindrical Hornbill (*Buceros subcylindricus*).]

Proc. Zool. Soc. London, 1882, p. 343.

906

[Report on the additions to the Society's Menagerie in March, 1882.]

Proc. Zool. Soc. London, 1882, p. 358.

907

[Exhibition of and remarks upon a drawing of a Tapir living in the Society's Gardens.]

Proc. Zool. Soc. London, 1882, p. 391, pl. xxiii.

Exhibition to a meeting of the Zoological Society of London of a drawing of a Tapir, probably referable to *Tapirus dowii*. *T. dowii* is figured.

908

[Report on the additions to the Society's Menagerie in April, 1882.]

Proc. Zool. Soc. London, 1882, p. 421.

909

Note on an Australian Duck living in the Society's Gardens.

Proc. Zool. Soc. London, 1882, pp. 452–454, pl. xxxiii.

Notes on, and synonyms and figure of, *Anas gibberifrons*.

910

[Remarks upon the mode of feeding of the young Cormorants by the parent birds in the Society's Gardens.]

Proc. Zool. Soc. London, 1882, pp. 458, 459.

An illustration of Cormorants feeding their young is given in the text.

911

[Exhibition of some Lepidoptera bred in the insect house.]

Proc. Zool. Soc. London, 1882, p. 459.

912

[Report on the additions to the Society's Menagerie in May, 1882.]

Proc. Zool. Soc. London, 1882, pp. 546, 547, pl. xxxvii.

Porcula salvanic is figured.

(For figure of young see *Proc. Zool. Soc. London*, 1883, pl. xliii, p. 388.)

913

Exhibition of some Lepidoptera, etc., reared at the insect house in the Society's Gardens.

Proc. Zool. Soc. London, 1882, p. 548.

A list of the insects reared in the Zoological Society's insect house is given.

914

Note on Rüppell's Parrot.

Proc. Zool. Soc. London, 1882, pp. 577, 578, pl. xlii.

The two sexes of *Pæocephalus rüppelli* are figured and remarked upon.

915

On two apparently new species of the genus *Synallaxis*.

Proc. Zool. Soc. London, 1882, pp. 578, 579, pl. xliii.

Synallaxis fusco-rufa and *S. griseo-murina* are described and figured. A list of the species of *Synallaxis* described since 1874 is appended.

916

Notes on Birds collected in the Argentine Republic. By E. W. White. With notes by P. L. Sclater.

Proc. Zool. Soc. London, 1882, pp. 591–629.

Two hundred and one species, accompanied by Mr. White's field notes and remarks by Mr. Sclater, are enumerated.

(See also *Proc. Zool. Soc. London*, 1883, p. 37.)

917

[Report on the additions to the Society's Menagerie in June, July, August, September, and October, 1882.]

Proc. Zool. Soc. London, 1882, pp. 630, 631, pls. xlvi, xlvii.

Report on the additions to the Zoological Society's Menagerie, with notes on the more remarkable species. A provisional name, *Canis microtis*, is given to a supposed new species of Dog, which is figured, as is also *Cyanorhamphus saisseti*.

918

[Report on the insects bred in the insect house in the Society's Gardens.]

Proc. Zool. Soc. London, 1882, pp. 632, 633.

919

[Report on the additions to the Society's Menagerie in November, 1882.]

Proc. Zool. Soc. London, 1882, pp. 719, 720.

920

[Exhibition of and remarks upon some photographs of a new Zebra (*Equus grevyi*).]

Proc. Zool. Soc. London, 1882, p. 721.

Equus grevyi is figured in the text.

921

Second note on the species of the Tyrannine genus *Hirundinea*.

Ibis, 1882, pp. 162-164.

Supplementary remarks to a previous communication (cf. *Ibis*, 1869, p. 195) on the species of the genus *Hirundinea*. Amended diagnoses of the three species are given.

922

[Report on the additions to the Society's Menagerie in December, 1882.]

Proc. Zool. Soc. London, 1883, p. 1.

923

[Report on the additions to the Society's Menagerie in January, 1883.]

Proc. Zool. Soc. London, 1883, p. 32.

924

Further notes on *Tragelaphus gratus*.

Proc. Zool. Soc. London, 1883, pp. 34-37, pl. viii.

Additional remarks on and figures of the male and female of *Tragelaphus gratus*. The head is also figured in the text.

(See also *Proc. Zool. Soc. London*, 1880, p. 452.)

925

Supplementary notes on the Birds of the Argentine Republic. By E. W. White. With remarks by P. L. Sclater.

Proc. Zool. Soc. London, 1883, pp. 37-43, pl. ix.

Field notes by Mr. White and remarks by Mr. Sclater on 34 species not represented in Mr. White's former collection. *Poospiza whitii* is described as new and figured.

(See also *Proc. Zool. Soc. London*, 1882, p. 591.)

926

On Birds collected in the Timor Laut or Tenimber group of islands, by Mr. Henry O. Forbes.

Proc. Zool. Soc. London, 1883, pp. 48-58, pls. xl-xliv.

A list of 54 species and their localities, with descriptions of those that are new and notes on several others imperfectly known. Fifteen new species are described, viz, *Ninox forbesi, Strix sororcula, Tanygnathus subaffinis, Monarcha castus, M. mundus, Rhipidura hamadryas, Myiagra fulviventris, Micræca hemixantha, Graucalus unimodus, Lalage mœsta, Pachycephala arctitorquis, Dicæum fulgidum, Myzomela annabellæ, Calornis crassa,* and *Megapodius tenimberensis*. The following species are figured: *Ninox forbesi, Monarcha castus, M. mundus, Pachycephala arctitorquis (♂, ♀),* and *Calornis crassa (♂, ♀)*. Remarks on the

general character of the avifauna of the Tenimber islands are added. The text is illustrated with the upper surface of the bills of *Monarcha mundus* and *M. castus*.

(See also *Proc. Zool. Soc. London*, 1883, p. 194.)

927

[Report on the additions to the Society's Menagerie in February, 1883.]

Proc. Zool. Soc. London, 1883, pp. 73, 74.

928

[Remarks upon a specimen of *Macropus erubescens* in the Gardens of the Zoological and Acclimatization Society, Melbourne, Australia.]

Proc. Zool. Soc. London, 1883, p. 131.

929

[Remarks on a new list of British Birds.]

Proc. Zool. Soc. London, 1883, pp. 131, 132.

A note on the B. O. U. list of British birds, with a table showing the results of the examination and cataloguing of the British species.

930

[Exhibition of a skin of a Crow sent to Mr. Sclater for examination by Mr. Albert A. C. Le Souëf, C. M. Z. S.]

Proc. Zool. Soc. London, 1883, p. 144.

This skin apparently belonged to a variety of *Corvus australis*.

931

[Report on the additions to the Society's Menagerie in March, 1883.]

Proc. Zool. Soc. London, 1883, p. 178.

932

Additional notes on Birds collected in Timor Laut or Tenimber group of islands by Mr. Henry O. Forbes.

Proc. Zool. Soc. London, 1883, pp. 194-200, pls. xxvi-xxviii.

A list of 40 species and their localities, with descriptions of those that are new and remarks on those of special interest. The following new species are described: *Rhipidura fusco-rufa, R. opistherythra, Pachycephala fusco-flava, Zosterops grisiventris, Gerygone dorsalis,* and *Mimeta decipiens*. Figures are given of *Eclectus riedeli (♂, ♀), Rhipidura fusco-rufa,* and *Pachycephala fusco-flava (♂, ♀)*. A list of the 60 species known to inhabit the Tenimber group is appended.

(See also *Proc. Zool. Soc. London*, 1883, p. 48.)

933

[Exhibition of a skin of a rare Paradise Bird (*Rhipidornis gulielmi-tertii*).]

Proc. Zool. Soc. London, 1883, p. 252.

934

[Remarks on Radde's "Internationale Farbenskala."]

Proc. Zool. Soc. London, 1883, p. 252.

Remarks on and explanation of the use of Radde's work on the nomenclature of colours, a copy of which had been added to the Zoological Society's library.

935

[Report on the additions to the Society's Menagerie in April, 1883.]

Proc. Zool. Soc. London, 1883, p. 346.

936

[List of the species of Lepidopterous Insects bred in the Society's insect house, and exhibition of living specimens of the West Indian Firefly.]

Proc. Zool. Soc. London, 1883, pp. 346, 347.

937

[Exhibition of and remarks upon a selection of Birds from New Britain, New Ireland, and the Solomon Islands sent to Mr. Sclater for examination by the Rev. George Brown, C. M. Z. S.]

Proc. Zool. Soc. London, 1883, pp. 347, 348.

Examples of twelve species of birds were exhibited to a meeting of the Zoological Society of London and remarked upon.

938

[Exhibition of and remarks upon two birds obtained near Lima, Peru, and transmitted by Prof. William Nation, C. M. Z. S.]

Proc. Zool. Soc. London, 1883, pp. 348, 349.

Exhibition of, to a meeting of the Zoological Society of London, and remarks on *Buteo abbreviatus* and *Polyonymus caroli*. *Buarremon nationi*, Scl., is pointed out to be identical with *Pipilo mystacalis*, Tacz., but the specific name *mystacalis* had been previously used. *Nationi* is retained.

939

[Remarks upon a Condor from Peru living in the Society's Gardens.]

Proc. Zool. Soc. London, 1883, p. 349, pl. xxxv.

Remarks on and figure of *Sarcorhamphus æquatorialis*.

940

[Report on the additions to the Society's Menagerie in May, 1883.]

Proc. Zool. Soc. London, 1883, p. 388, pl. xliii.

Porcula salvania, pull., is figured.

(For figure of adult see *Proc. Zool. Soc. London*, 1882, p. 546, pl. xxxvii.)

941

[Report on the additions to the Society's Menagerie during the months of June, July, August, September, and October, 1883.]

Proc. Zool. Soc. London, 1883, pp. 403, 464, pls. xlvi, xlvii.

Report on the additions to the Zoological Society's collection, with notes on those of special interest and figures of *Pelecanus trachyrhynchus* and *Babirussa alfurus*, young.

942

[Remarks upon the opening of the Society's new reptile house.]

Proc. Zool. Soc. London, 1883, p. 464.

The opening of the Zoological Society's new reptile house took place on August 4, 1883. The total number of specimens exhibited therein on October 1 was 211.

943

[Note upon the increase in size and weight of the young male African Elephant purchased July, 1882.]

Proc. Zool. Soc. London, 1883, p. 465.

The weights and dimensions of a young *Elephas africanus*, taken in July, 1882, and again on October 8, 1883, are given.

(See also *Proc. Zool. Soc. London*, 1879, p. 385; 1881, p. 450.)

944

[Exhibition, on behalf of Dr. G. Bennett, F. Z. S., and remarks upon some skins of a species of *Drepanornis* from southern New Guinea.]

Proc. Zool. Soc. London, 1883, p. 578.

Mr. Sclater here refers these skins to a new subspecies of *Drepanornis albertisi*, and calls it *D. albertisi cervinicauda*.

945

[Report on the additions to the Society's Menagerie in November, 1883.]

Proc. Zool. Soc. London, 1883, p. 598.

946

Descriptions of five apparently new species of South American Passeres.

Proc. Zool. Soc. London, 1883, pp. 653, 654, pl. lxi.

The following species are described: *Basileuterus fraseri*, *Calliste cyanopygia*, *Cnipodectes minor*, *Automolus rubidus*, and *Anabazenops oleagineus*. The first-mentioned species is figured.

947

On the genera *Microbates* and *Rhamphocænus* of the family *Formicariidæ*.

Ibis, 1883, pp. 92–96, pl. iii.

A synopsis of the species of the genera *Microbates* and *Rhamphocænus*. *Microbates collaris* is figured and *Rhamphocænus albiventris* described as a new species.

948

Review of the species of the family *Icteridæ*. Part I*, *Cassicinæ*.

Ibis, 1883, pp. 145–163, pls. vi, vii.

Six genera, of which *Eucorystes* is described as new, and 27 species are enumerated. Two of the species, *Ostinops salmoni* and *O. oleagineus*, are described and figured. The text is illustrated. The genera treated in Part I are: *Clypeicterus*, *Ocyalus*, *Eucorystes*, *Ostinops*, *Cassiculus* and *Cassicus*.

*(For Part II. *Icterinæ*, see *Ibis*, 1883, p. 352; Pt. III, *Agelæinæ*, *Ibis*, 1884, p. 1; Pt. IV, *Quiscalinæ*, *Ibis*, 1884, p. 149.)

949

Review of the species of the family *Icteridæ*. Part II*, *Icterinæ*.

Ibis, 1883, pp. 352–374, pl. xi.

Thirty-seven species of the subfamily *Icterinæ* are enumerated, all referred to the single genus *Icterus*. *Icterus grace-annæ* is figured.

*(For Part I, *Cassicinæ*, see *Ibis* 1883, p. 145; Pt. III, *Agelæinæ*, *Ibis*, 1884, p. 1; Pt. IV, *Quiscalinæ*, *Ibis*, 1884, p. 149.)

950

The High Springs of 1883.

Nature, XXVII, p. 529 (1883)

Letter on the extraordinary rising of the springs in 1883, in several localities in North Hampshire, after the excessive rainfall of the winter of 1882.

951

[Report on the additions to the Society's Menagerie in December, 1883.]

Proc. Zool. Soc. London, 1884, p. 1.

952

[Exhibition of a Night Heron (*Nycticorax griseus*) shot in Plumstead Marshes.]

Proc. Zool. Soc. London, 1884, p. 2.

953

On the Lesser Koodoo, *Strepsiceros imberbis*, of Blyth.

Proc. Zool. Soc. London, 1884, pp. 45–48, pl. iv.

Remarks on, synonyms, and figure of *Strepsiceros imberbis*, together with the comparative dimensions of its horns and those of *S. kudu*. The horns of both species are figured in the text.

954

[Report on the additions to the Society's Menagerie in January, 1884.]

Proc. Zool. Soc. London, 1884, p. 55.

955

[Remarks upon a copy of the lately issued "Guide to the Calcutta Zoological Gardens" and on *Rhinoceros lasiotis*.]

Proc. Zool. Soc. London, 1884, pp. 55, 56.

An extract from Dr. John Anderson's "Guide to the Calcutta Zoological Gardens" respecting the capture of an example of *Rhinoceros lasiotis* living in those gardens.

956

[Report on the additions to the Society's Menagerie in February, 1884.]

Proc. Zool. Soc. London, 1884, p. 176, pl. xiv.

Cercopithecus martini is figured.

957

[Exhibition of and remarks upon specimens of the Eggs of two species of Testudinata laid in the Society's Gardens.]

Proc. Zool. Soc. London, 1884, p. 206.

These eggs were laid by the species *Testudo elephantopus* and *Chelys matamata*.

958

[Report on the additions to the Society's Menagerie in April, 1884.]

Proc. Zool. Soc. London, 1884. p. 251.

959

[Report on the additions to the Society's Menagerie in May, 1884.]

Proc. Zool. Soc. London, 1884, p. 389, pl. xxxiii.

Sphingurus spinosus is figured.

960

[Exhibition of and remarks upon the Deciduous Knob of the Culmen of the Beak of the Rough-billed Pelican (*Pelecanus trachyrhynchus*).]

Proc. Zool. Soc. London, 1884, p. 410.

961

[Remarks upon a very singular habit of the Greater Vasa Parrot (*Coracopsis vasa*).]

Proc. Zool. Soc. London, 1884, p. 410.

Remarks on the habit of a specimen of *Coracopsis vasa* producing from its cloaca a mass of dark flesh-coloured substance, and drawing it in again after exposing it for several minutes. This substance was supposed to be the membranous lining of the cloaca blown out during the period of sexual excitement.

(See also *Proc. Zool. Soc. London*, 1884, p. 562; 1893, p. 435.)

962

[Report on the additions to the Society's Menagerie in June, July, August, and September, 1884.]

Proc. Zool. Soc. London, 1884, pp. 475, 476, pl. xlv, figs. 2, 3.

Colius erythromelon is figured.

963

[Exhibition of and remarks upon a skin of a Woolly Cheetah (*Felis lanea*) from South Africa.]

Proc. Zool. Soc. London, 1884, p. 476.

(See also *Proc. Zool. Soc. London*, 1877, p. 530, pl. lv; 1878, p. 655.)

964

[Report on the additions to the Society's Menagerie in October, 1884.]

Proc. Zool. Soc. London, 1884, p. 530, pl. xlv, fig. 1.

Colius nigricollis is figured.

965

On some Mammals from Somaliland.

Proc. Zool. Soc. London, 1884, pp. 538–542, pls. xlix, l.

Notes on five species of mammals. *Equus asinus somalicus* [*] is described as a new subspecies and figured. *Gazella walleri* and *Equus asinus africanus* are also figured.

[*] (See also *Proc. Zool. Soc. London*, 1892, p. 195.)

966

[Report on the additions to the Society's Menagerie in November, 1884.]

Proc. Zool. Soc. London, 1884, pp. 561, 562.

967

[Remarks upon the death of a Greater Vasa Parrot (*Coracopsis vasa*) which had passed fifty-four years in the Society's Menagerie.]

Proc. Zool. Soc. London, 1884, p. 562.

(See also *Proc. Zool. Soc. London*, 1884, p. 410; 1893, p. 435.)

968

A review of the species of the family *Icteridæ*. Part III[*], *Agelæinæ*.

Ibis, 1884, pp. 1–27, pl. i.

Of the subfamily *Agelæinæ* 38 species are enumerated and referred to 13 genera. Subspecific names are applied to 4 local varieties of *Sturnella ludoviciana*, viz. *Sturnella ludoviciana neglecta*, *S. ludov. hippocrepis*, *S. ludov. mexicana*, and *S. ludov. meridionalis*. *Agelæus cyanopus* is figured. The genera included in Part II are *Dolichonyx*, *Molothrus*, *Oyrtotes*, *Agelæus*, *Xanthocephalus*, *Xanthosomus*, *Amblyrhamphus*, *Gymnomystax*, *Pseudoleistes*, *Curæus*, *Leistes*, *Trupialis* and *Sturnella*.

[*] (For Part I, *Cassicinæ*, see *Ibis*, 1883, p. 145; Pt. II, *Icterinæ*, *Ibis*, 1883, p. 352; Pt. IV, *Quiscalinæ*, *Ibis*, 1884, p. 149.)

969

A review of the species of the family *Icteridæ*. Part IV[*], *Quiscalinæ*.

Ibis, 1884, pp. 149–167, pl. v.

Eight genera, embracing 25 species, are referred to the subfamily *Quiscalinæ*. *Quiscalus graysoni* is described as new, and *Q. tenuirostris* figured.

The genera treated of are: *Lamproxar, Scolecophagus, Dives, Quiscalus, Macragelœus, Hypopyrrhus, Aphobus* and *Cassidix.*

*(For Part I, *Cassicinœ* see *Ibis*, 1883, p. 145; Pt. II, *Icterinœ, Ibis,* 1883, p. 352; Pt. III, *Agelœinœ, Ibis,* 1884, p. 1.)

970

Remarks on two rare American Oscines.

Ibis, 1884, pp. 240, 241, pl. vii.

Remarks on *Idiopsar brachyurus* and *Acanthidops bairdi.* The former species is figured.

971

[Report on the additions to the Society's Menagerie in December, 1884, and description of a new species of *Cervulus.*]

Proc. Zool. Soc. London, 1885, pp. 1 2, pl. i.

Cervulus crinifrons is described and figured. The head is also figured in the text.

972

[Remarks on the breeding of the Chinese Blue Magpie (*Cyanopolius cyanus*) in the Society's Gardens in 1884.]

Proc. Zool. Soc. London, 1885, pp. 2, 3.

973

[Exhibition of a rare South American Lizard (*Heterodactylus imbricatus*) presented to the Society by Mr. G. Lennon Hunt.]

Proc. Zool. Soc. London, 1885, p. 63.

974

[Exhibition of a Beetle of the family *Buprestidœ*, transmitted to the Society by Mr. B. F. Ffinch.]

Proc. Zool. Soc. London, 1885, pp. 63, 64.

Julodis finchi is remarked upon and figured in the text.

975

[Exhibition of Lepidopterous Insects bred in the Insect house during the past season, and report on the insect house.]

Proc. Zool. Soc. London, 1885, pp. 65, 66.

A list of the insects exhibited in the Zoological Society's Insectarium, and remarks upon some of them.

976

[Report on the additions to the Society's Menagerie in January, 1885.]

Proc. Zool. Soc. London, 1885, p. 168.

977

[Report on the additions to the Society's Menagerie in February, 1885.]

Proc. Zool. Soc. London, 1885, pp. 245, 246.

A list of the species of Pelicans living in the Zoological Society's Gardens is given.

978

[Exhibition of and remarks upon a curious Duck shot in Yorkshire.]

Proc. Zool. Soc. London, 1885, p. 246.

This bird was apparently a variety of *Fuligula marila.*

979

[Report on the additions to the Society's Menagerie in March, 1885.]

Proc. Zool. Soc. London, 1885, p. 322.

980

[Exhibition of and remarks upon a pair of Pheasants from northern Afghanistan, belonging to H. R. H. the Prince of Wales.]

Proc. Zool. Soc. London, 1885, pp. 322–324, pl. xxii.

Phasianus principalis is characterized, figured, and remarked upon.

981

[Exhibition of and remarks upon some Eggs of Darwin's Rhea.]

Proc. Zool. Soc London, 1885, pp. 324–327.

Exhibition to a meeting of the Zoological Society of London of some eggs of *Rhea darwinii*, and an extract of a letter from M G. Claraz concerning them.

982

[Report on the additions to the Society's Menagerie in April, 1885.]

Proc. Zool. Soc. London, 1885, p. 421.

983

[Remarks upon the Colies now or lately living in the Society's Gardens.]

Proc. Zool. Soc. London, 1885, p. 542.

A list of the species of *Colius* represented in the Zoological Society's collection is given.

984

[Report on the additions to the Society's Menagerie in May, 1885.]

Proc. Zool. Soc. London, 1885, p. 609.

985

Description of a new species of *Icterus.*

Proc. Zool. Soc. London, 1885, p. 671.

Icterus hauxwelli is described.

986

Note on *Lemur macaco* and the way in which it carries its young.

Proc. Zool. Soc. London, 1885, pp. 672, 673.

An illustration of the female of *Lemur macaco* carrying its young, with remarks.

987

[Report on the additions to the Society's Menagerie in June, July, August, and September, 1885.]

Proc. Zool. Soc. London, 1885, pp. 717, 718.

988

[Exhibition of and remarks upon a Skull of an American Tapir.]

Proc. Zool. Soc. London, 1885, p. 718.

Exhibition to a meeting of the Zoological Society of London of a skull of a Tapir, which had been described as *Tapirus roulini*, but which, as evidenced by an examination of the skull, was only a dark variety of *T. americanus.*

989

[Report on the additions to the Society's Menagerie in October, 1885.]

Proc. Zool. Soc. London, 1885, p. 833.

990

[Remarks upon a Newt (*Molge vittata*) and its distribution.]

Proc. Zool. Soc. London, 1885, pp. 834, 835.

991

Characters of an apparently new species of Tanager of the genus *Calliste*.

Proc. Zool. Soc. London, 1885, pp. 849, 850.

Calliste gouldi is characterized.

992

[Report on the additions to the Society's Menagerie in November, 1885.]

Proc. Zool. Soc. London, 1885, p. 851.

993

[Exhibition of and remarks upon an African Hornbill and other birds belonging to Mr. H. Whitely.

Proc. Zool. Soc. London, 1885, p. 851.

Exhibition to the Zoological Society of London of several bird skins belonging to Mr. H. Whitely, and remarks on the species *Buceros casuarinus*, which is supposed to have been founded on a young specimen of *B. cylindricus*.

994

On the Muscicapine genus *Chasiempis*.

Ibis, 1885, pp. 17–19, pl. i.

Remarks on, and figures of, the male and female of *Chasiempis sandwichensis*.

995

On some little-known species of Tanagers.

Ibis, 1885, pp. 271–275, pl. vi.

Notes on nine species of Tanagers. *Nesospingus* is proposed as a new generic name for the reception of *Chlorospingus speculiferus*, Lawr., and *Lanio lawrencii* is described as a new species and figured. *Tachyphonus nattereri* is also figured. *Nesospingus speculiferus* is illustrated in the text.

996

" Furculum " or " Furcula."

Nature, XXXII, p. 466 (1885).

Letter on the correct term to be employed as an equivalent of the *os furculatorium* of birds.

997

[Report on the additions to the Society's Menagerie in December, 1885.]

Proc. Zool. Soc. London, 1886, pp. 1, 2.

998

[Exhibition of Lepidopterous Insects bred in the insect house during the past season.]

Proc. Zool. Soc. London, 1886, pp. 2–4.

Exhibition to a meeting of the Zoological Society of London, of a series of specimens of Lepidoptera bred in the Society's insect house, together with a list of the species exhibited therein, with remarks.

999

[Report on the additions to the Society's Menagerie in January, 1886.]

Proc. Zool. Soc. London, 1886, pp. 124, 125.

1000

[Exhibition of and remarks upon a specimen of a newly described Paradise Bird (*Paradisornis rudolphi*).]

Proc. Zool. Soc. London, 1886, p. 125.

1001

[Report on the additions to the Society's Menagerie in February, 1886.]

Proc. Zool. Soc. London, 1886, p. 137.

1002

Note on the external characters of *Rhinoceros simus*.

Proc. Zool. Soc. London, 1886, pp. 143, 144, pl. xvi.

The distinctive features of *Rhinoceros simus* and *R. bicornis* are pointed out. The heads of the two species are figured.

1003

[Report on the additions to the Society's Menagerie in March, 1886.]

Proc. Zool. Soc. London, 1886, p. 176.

1004

[Exhibition of and remarks upon the heads and horns of two species of Antelopes from Lamoo, East Africa (*Strepsiceros imberbis* and *Damalis senegalensis*).]

Proc. Zool. Soc. London, 1886, p. 176.

1005

[Report on the additions to the Society's Menagerie in April, 1886.]

Proc. Zool. Soc. London, 1886, p. 266.

1006

Remarks on the various species of Wild Goats.

Proc. Zool. Soc. London, 1886, pp. 314–318, pls. xxxi, xxxii.

Remarks on 10 species of the genus *Capra*. *C. ægagrus* and *C. sinaitica* are figured.

(See also *Proc. Zool. Soc. London*, 1887, p. 552.)

1007

[Report on the additions to the Society's Menagerie in May, 1886.]

Proc. Zool. Soc. London, 1886, p. 318.

1008

[Remarks on interesting animals observed during a visit to the Zoological Gardens of Rotterdam, Amsterdam, Cologne, Antwerp, and Ghent.]

Proc. Zool. Soc. London, 1886, p. 320.

1009

[Exhibition, on behalf of Mr. J. Brazier, C. M. Z. S., of a series of 55 eggs laid by a Pacific Porphyrio.]

Proc. Zool. Soc. London, 1886, p. 330.

A specimen of this bird—*Porphyrio vitiensis*—was captured at Maré, Loyalty Islands, in 1873, and was kept in captivity till 1882, during which period she laid 491 eggs.

1010

List of a collection of Birds from the Province of Tarapacá, northern Chili.

Proc. Zool. Soc. London, 1886, pp. 395–404, pl. xxxvi.

Fifty-three species are enumerated and remarked upon. *Phœnicopterus jamesi* is described as a new species and figured. A map, showing the localities where the collection was made, is given. The bills of *P. jamesi* and *P. andinus* are figured in the text.

(See also *Proc. Zool. Soc. London*, 1891, p. 131.)

1011

[Report on the additions to the Society's Menagerie in June, July, August, September, and October, 1886.]

Proc. Zool. Soc. London, 1886, pp. 417, 418.

1012

On two species of Antelopes from Somaliland.

Proc. Zool. Soc. London, 1886 pp. 504, 505. pl. li.

Remarks on *Gazella naso*, n. sp., and *Neotragus kirki*. The head of the former species is figured.

1013

On an apparently new Parrot of the genus *Conurus* living in the Society's Gardens.

Proc. Zool. Soc. London, 1886, pp. 538, 539, pl. lvi.

Conurus rubritorquis is described and figured

1014

[Report on the additions to the Society's Menagerie in November, 1886.]

Proc. Zool. Soc. London, 1886, p. 549.

1015

On the Claws and Spurs of Birds' Wings.

Ibis, 1886, pp. 147–151, 300–301.

Remarks on and illustrations of the spurs and claws on the wings of *Gypagus papa*, *Chauna derbiana*, *Plectropterus gambensis*, and *Parra jacana*.

1016

Description of a new Ground Finch from western Peru.

Ibis, 1886, pp. 258, 259, pl. viii.

Hæmophila pulchra is described and figured.

1017

[Report on the addition to the Society's Menagerie in December, 1886.]

Proc. Zool. Soc. London, 1887, pp. 1, 2.

1018

[Exhibition of and remarks upon a specimen of a rare Parrot. (*Chrysotis bodini*).]

Proc. Zool. Soc. London, 1887, p. 2.

1019

Characters of new species of Birds of the family *Tyrannidæ*.

Proc. Zool. Soc. London, 1887, pp. 47–50, pl. ix.

The following species are characterized and remarked upon : *Tænioptera holospodia*, *Euscarthmus apicalis*, *Pogonotriccus gualaquizæ*, *Leptopogon godmani*, *L. oustaleti*, *Phyllomyias berlepschi*, *Elainea hypospodia*, *E. flavivertex*, *Myiobius subochraceus*, and *Empidonax ridgwayi*. *Euscarthmus apicalis* and *Leptopogon oustaleti* are figured.

1020

[Report on the additions to the Society's Menagerie in January, 1887.]

Proc. Zool. Soc. London, 1887, pp. 138, 139.

1021

[Report on the additions to the Society's Menagerie in February, 1887.]

Proc. Zool. Soc. London, 1887, p. 319.

1022

[Report on the additions to the Society's Menagerie in March, 1887.]

Proc. Zool. Soc. London, 1887, p. 340.

1023

[Extracts from a letter addressed to Mr. Sclater by Rev. G. H. R. Fisk, C. M. Z. S., respecting the killing and eating, by a Mouse, of a young venomous Snake.]

Proc. Zool. Soc. London, 1887, pp. 340–342.

The Mouse was a specimen of *Dendromys melanotis*, and the snake *Sepedon hæmachates*.

1024

[Exhibition of and remarks upon a set of eleven photographs, representing objects of Natural History, collected by General Prejevalski in Central Asia.]

Proc. Zool. Soc. London, 1887, p. 302.

These photographs represented objects of General Prejevalski's collection, as arranged for exhibition in the Museum of the Imperial Academy of St. Petersburg. They had been presented to the Library of the Zoological Society of London, where they are now located.

1025

[Extract from a letter addressed to Mr. Sclater by Mr. Albert A. C. Le Souef, C. M. Z. S., containing remarks upon some living Duckbills (*Ornithorhynchus paradoxus*) in confinement at Melbourne.]

Proc. Zool. Soc. London, 1887, p. 363.

1026

[Report on the additions to the Society's Menagerie in April, 1887.]

Proc. Zool. Soc. London, 1887, p. 396.

1027

[Extracts from a letter addressed to Mr. Sclater by Mr. Roland Trimen, F. Z. S., respecting the obtaining of a second example of *Laniarius atrococceus*.]

Proc. Zool. Soc. London, 1887, pp. 396, 397.

1028

[Report on the additions to the Society's Menagerie in May, 1887.]

Proc. Zool. Soc. London, 1887, p. 482.

1029

[Remarks upon specimens of two species of North American Foxes living in the Society's Gardens.]

Proc. Zool. Soc. London, 1887, p. 482.

Remarks on specimens of *Canis velox* and *C. virginianus*.

1030

[Exhibition of and remarks upon the Skin of a White-nosed Monkey (*Cercopithecus ascanias ?*).]

Proc. Zool. Soc. London, 1887, p. 502.

This monkey was obtained in eastern Equatorial Africa and is here doubtfully referred to *C. ascanias*.

1031

[Exhibition of and remarks upon a specimen of a Pheasant from northern Afghanistan (*Phasianus principalis*).]

Proc. Zool. Soc. London, 1887, p. 502.

1032

Note on the Wild Goats of the Caucasus.

Proc. Zool. Soc. London, 1887, pp. 552, 553.

Remarks on *Capra caucasica* and *C. pallasi*, and an extract from a communication from Dr. G. Radde concerning them The two species are shown to be distinct, and the author points out that he was in error in uniting them in a former paper. (cf. *Proc. Zool Soc. London*, 1886, p. 314).

1033

[Report on the additions to the Society's Menagerie in June, July, August, September, and October, 1887.]

Proc. Zool. Soc. London. 1887, pp. 558, 559.

1034

[Report on the additions to the Society's Menagerie in November, 1887.]

Proc. Zool. Soc. London, 1887, p. 638.

1035

[Extract of a letter from Dr. Burmeister, F. M. Z. S., and remarks on a supposed new Humming Bird (*Chætocercus burmeisteri*).]

Proc. Zool. Soc. London, 1887, pp. 638, 639.

Mr. Sclater proposes the name *Chætocercus burmeisteri* for the species characterized in Dr. Burmeister's letter.

1036

On *Empidonax brunneus* and its allied species.

Ibis, 1887, pp. 64–66.

Observations on *Empidonax brunneus* (which is referred to *E. bimaculatus*, d'Orb. et Lafr.), *E. oliva*, *Empidochanes fringillaris*, *E. fuscatus*, and *E. oliva aut vireoninus* (referred to *E. arenaceus*).

1037

Remarks on the species of the genus *Cyclorhis*.

Ibis, 1887, pp. 320–324, pl. x.

An arrangement of the species (10 in number) of the genus *Cyclorhis*, with remarks upon them. *Cyclorhis atrirostris* is described as new and figured.

1038

[Report on the additions to the Society's Menagerie in December, 1887, and list of specimens of the genus *Canis*.]

Proc. Zool. Soc. London, 1888, pp. 1, 2.

A list of the specimens (36 in number) of the genus *Canis* living in the Zoological Society's Gardens is given.

1039

[Report on the additions to the Society's Menagerie in January, 1888.]

Proc. Zool. Soc. London, 1888, p. 87.

1040

[Report on the additions to the Society's Menagerie in February, 1888.]

Proc. Zool. Soc. London, 1888, p. 140.

1041

[Exhibition on behalf of Lieut. Col. H. M. Drummond-Hay, C. M. Z. S., of a specimen of the Desert Wheatear (*Saxicola deserti*) killed in Scotland.]

Proc. Zool. Soc. London, 1888, p. 140.

1042

[Report on the additions to the Society's Menagerie in March, 1888.]

Proc. Zool. Soc. London, 1888, p. 219.

1043

[Report on the additions to the Society's Menagerie in April, 1888.]

Proc. Zool. Soc. London, 1888, p. 265.

1044

[Report on the additions to the Society's Menagerie in May, 1888]

Proc. Zool. Soc. London, 1888, p. 291.

1045

[Exhibition on the part of Mr. F. M. Campbell, F. Z. S., of a pair of Pallas's Sand Grouse, and remarks on the numerous recent occurrences of this bird in western Europe.]

Proc. Zool. Soc. London, 1888, p. 291.

1046

[Exhibition, on behalf of Prof. R. Collett, C. M. Z. S., of a nest, eggs, and two young ones in down of the Ivory Gull (*Larus eburneus*).]

Proc. Zool. Soc. London, 1888, pp. 291, 292.

1047

[Report on the additions to the Society's Menagerie in June, July, August, September, and October, 1888.]

Proc. Zool. Soc. London, 1888, p. 413.

1048

[Report on the additions to the Society's Menagerie in November, 1888.]

Proc. Zool. Soc. London, 1888, p. 564.

1049

Notes on the Emperor Penguin (*Aptenodytes forsteri*).

Ibis, 1888, pp. 325–334.

The history and synonymy of *Aptenodytes forsteri*. The differences in coloration and structure between this species and *A. pennanti* are pointed out. The upper surface of the skull and the sterna of both species are figured in the text.

1050

Electric Fishes in the River Uruguay.

Nature, XXXVIII, p. 148 (1888).

Letter on the occurrence of an electric eel (*Gymnotus*) in the Rio Uruguay.

1051

The "Tamaron" of the Philippine Islands.

Nature, XXXVIII, pp. 363, 364 (1888).

Letter on the discovery in the Philippine Islands, by Prof. J. B. Steere, of a new species of *Anoa—Anoa mindorensis*.

1052

The Barbary Ape in Algeria.

Nature, XXXIX, p. 30 (1888).

Letter on his having seen wild specimens of the Barbary ape in Algeria.

1053

[Report on the additions to the Society's Menagerie in December, 1888.]

Proc. Zool. Soc. London, 1889, p. 1.

1054

[Report on the additions to the Society's Menagerie in January, 1889.]

Proc. Zool. Soc. London, 1889, p. 26.

1055

[Exhibition of and remarks upon a living specimen of the Thick-billed Lark (*Rhamphocorys clot-beyi*).]

Proc. Zool. Soc. London, 1889, pp. 26, 27.

1056

On some new species and genera of Birds of the family *Dendrocolaptidæ*.

Proc. Zool. Soc. London, 1889, pp. 32-34.

Two new generic terms, *Limnophyes* and *Hylexetastes*, are proposed for the reception of *Limnornis curvirostris* and *Dendrocolaptes perroti*, respectively, and the following new species are described: *Upucerthia bridgesi*, *Phacellodomus ruppennis*, *Thripophaga fusciceps*, *Philydor cervicalis*, and *Picolaptes parvirostris*.

1057

[Exhibition of and remarks upon a series of specimens of the eggs and chicks of the Hoatzin (*Opisthocomus cristatus*).]

Proc. Zool. Soc. London, 1889, p. 57.

1058

[Exhibition of and remarks upon some heads and skins of a new Antelope obtained by Mr. H. C. V. Hunter, F. Z. S., in northeastern Africa.]

Proc. Zool. Soc. London, 1889, pp. 58, 59.

The heads and skins of a new species of antelope, proposed to be called *Damalis hunteri*, were exhibited to a meeting of the Zoological Society of London, and remarked upon. The head is figured in the text.

1059

[Report on the additions to the Society's Menagerie in February, 1889.]

Proc. Zool. Soc. London, 1889, p. 85.

1060

[Remarks upon the collections of Fishes made at Constantinople by Dr. E. D. Dickson, C. M. Z. S.]

Proc. Zool. Soc. London, 1889, p. 135.

1061

[Report on the additions to the Society's Menagerie in March, 1889.]

Proc. Zool. Soc. London, 1889, pp. 160, 161.

1062

[Exhibition of and remarks upon a pair of Buprestine Beetles (*Julodis finchi*) obtained by Mr. B. T. Ffinch, near Karachi.]

Proc. Zool. Soc. London, 1889, p. 219.

1063

[Exhibition of and remarks upon a specimen of the Mole Cricket (*Gryllotalpa vulgaris*) found at Bagdad and transmitted by Mrs. Talbot.]

Proc. Zool. Soc. London, 1889, p. 219.

1064

[Remarks on interesting animals observed during a visit to the Zoological Gardens of Rotterdam, Amsterdam, and Antwerp.]

Proc. Zool. Soc. London, 1889, pp. 219, 220.

1065

[Report on the additions to the Society's Menagerie in April, 1889.]

Proc. Zool. Soc. London, 1889, p. 246.

1066

[Exhibition of and remarks upon a living specimen of an albino variety of the Cape Mole Rat.]

Proc. Zool. Soc. London, 1889, pp. 246, 247.

1067

[Exhibition of and remarks upon a mummy of a Falcon obtained at Thebes, in Egypt.]

Proc. Zool. Soc. London, 1889, p. 262.

Apparently a mummified specimen of *Tinnunculus alaudarius*.

1068

[Exhibition of and remarks upon a series of Photographs taken at Antipodes Island.]

Proc. Zool. Soc. London, 1889, p. 262.

These photographs represented groups of marine birds and sea lions which frequent Antipodes Island for breeding purposes.

1069

[Exhibition of and remarks upon a Leaf Insect (*Phyllium gelonus*) living in the Society's insect house.]

Proc. Zool. Soc. London, 1889, p. 262.

An illustration of *Phyllium gelonus* (immature) is given.

1070

[Report on the additions to the Society's Menagerie in May, 1889.]

Proc. Zool. Soc. London, 1889, p. 316.

1071

List of Birds collected by Mr. Ramage in Dominica, West Indies.

Proc. Zool. Soc. London, 1889, pp. 326, 327.

A list of 30 species, with general remarks on the avifauna of Dominica.

1072

Description of Hunter's Antelope.

Proc. Zool. Soc. London, 1889, pp. 372-377, pl. xlii.

Damalis hunteri is characterized and figured, and remarks made on a series of horns and skins of this animal. The text is illustrated with figures of the head, skull and horns, of the male and female.

1073

[Report on the additions to the Society's Menagerie in June, July, August, and September, 1889.]

Proc. Zool. Soc. London, 1889, pp. 393, 394.

1074

List of Birds collected by Mr. Ramage in St. Lucia, West Indies.

Proc. Zool. Soc. London, 1889, pp. 394, 395.

A list of 30 species, with general notes on the ornithology of St. Lucia.

1075

[Report on the additions to the Society's Menagerie in October, 1889.]

Proc. Zool. Soc. London, 1889, pp. 447, 448.

1076

[Exhibition of a Skin of an albino variety of the Cape Mole Rat (*Georychus capensis*).]

Proc. Zool. Soc. London, 1889, p. 449.

1077

[Report on the additions to the Socie-ty's Menagerie in November, 1889.]

Proc. Zool. Soc. London, 1889, p. 586.

1078

[Exhibition of and remarks upon an Egg of the Crested Screamer (*Chauna chararia*).]

Proc. Zool. Soc. London, 1889, pp. 586, 587.

1079

Notes on some recently described spe-cies of *Dendrocolaptidæ*.

Ibis, 1889, pp. 350-354, pl. xi.

Notes on *Berlepschia rikeri*, *Phacellodomus inornatus*, *Dendrornis punctigula*, Ridgw. MS., *D lawrencii*, *D. lawr. costaricensis*, *Picolaptes gracilis*, *Dendrocincla rufo-olivacea*, *D. castanop-tera*, *Dendrocolaptes obsoletus*, and *Sclerurus cani-gularis*. *Berlepschia rikeri* is figured.

1080

The Rabbit Post.

Nature, XXXIX, pp. 493, 494 (1889).

Note on the plan advocated by Mr. W. Rodier, of New South Wales, for the extermination of rabbits in Australia.

1081

"La Pietra Papale."

Nature, XLI, pp. 30, 31 (1889).

A description of an enormous granite boulder, near Stresa, in Italy.

1082

[Report on the additions to the Socie-ty's Menagerie in December, 1889.]

Proc. Zool. Soc. London, 1890, p. 1.

1083

[Exhibition of and remarks upon a hybrid Duck.]

Proc. Zool. Soc. London, 1890, pp. 1, 2, pl. i.

Exhibition to a meeting of the Zoological So-ciety of London of a hybrid between *Tadorna casarca* and *Querquedula falcata*. The bird is figured.

1084

[Report on the additions to the Socie-ty's Menagerie in January, 1890.]

Proc. Zool. Soc. London, 1890, p. 44.

1085

On a Guinea Fowl from the Zambesi, allied to *Numida cristata*.

Proc. Zool. Soc. London, 1890, pp. 86, 87, pl. xii.

Remarks on and figure of an undetermined species of *Numida* from the Zambesi.

1086

[Report on the additions to the Socie-ty's Menagerie in February, 1890.]

Proc. Zool. Soc. London, 1890, p. 94.

1087

[Exhibition of and remarks upon some Mammals obtained in the Upper Magda-lena Valley of Colombia by Mr. R. B. White, C. M. Z. S.]

Proc. Zool. Soc. London, 1890, p. 98.

Examples of four species of mammals, determ-ined by Mr. Oldfield Thomas, were exhibited to a meeting of the Zoological Society of London and remarked upon.

1088

[Report on the additions to the Socie-ty's Menagerie in March, 1890.]

Proc. Zool. Soc. London, 1890, p. 147, pl. xv.

Hypocolius ampelinus is figured.

1089

[Report on the additions to the Socie-ty's Menagerie in April, 1890.]

Proc. Zool. Soc. London, 1890, p. 354.

1090

[Exhibition of and remarks upon the Head of an Antelope (*Damalis senegalensis*) from East Africa.]

Proc. Zool. Soc. London, 1890, pp. 354-357.

The head and skull of *Damalis senegalensis* are figured in the text, and remarks made upon the animal. A list of its synonyms is given.

1091

On a new Toucan of the genus *Ptero-glossus*.

Proc. Zool. Soc. London, 1890, p. 403.

Pteroglossus didymus is characterized.

1092

[Report on the additions to the Socie-ty's Menagerie in May, 1890.]

Proc. Zool. Soc. London, 1890, pp. 411, 412.

1093

[Exhibition of and remarks upon two young specimens of Darwin's Rhea (*Rhea darwini*) from the Province of Tarapacá.]

Proc. Zool. Soc. London, 1890, p. 412.

1094

[Exhibition of and remarks upon the Flat Skin of a Zebra received from Ber-bera, northern Somaliland.]

Proc. Zool. Soc. London, 1890, pp. 412-414.

The skins of *Equus grevyi* and *E. burchelli* are figured in the text.

1095

[Exhibition of and remarks upon a Mounted Head of a rare Antelope (*Æpy-ceros petersi*).]

Proc. Zool. Soc. London, 1890, pp. 460, 461.

A figure of the head is given in the text.

1096

[Exhibition of a photograph of Gré-vy's Zebra.]

Proc. Zool. Soc. London, 1890, p. 461.

This photograph of *Equus grevyi* was taken by Mr. Gambier Bolton from the type specimen in the Paris Museum.

1097

[Remarks upon a map transmitted by M. P. A. Pichot, C. M. Z. S., showing the exact locality in which the Beaver is now found in the Delta of the Rhone.]

Proc. Zool. Soc. London, 1890, p. 463.

1098

[Report on the additions to the Socie-ty's Menagerie in June, July, August, September, and October, 1890.]

Proc. Zool. Soc. London, 1890, pp. 589, 590, pls. xlvii, xlviii.

Tragelaphus spekii and *Colobus ferrugineus* are figured.

1099

[Report on the additions to the Society's Menagerie in November, 1890.]

Proc Zool. Soc. London, 1890, pp. 646, 647.

1100

Remarks on the fifth cubital remex of the wing in the Carinatæ.

Ibis, 1890, pp. 77-83

Observations on the presence or absence of the fifth cubital remex in the wing of the various orders of the Carinate birds. The distal cubital remiges, with their attached tectrices majores, of *Phasianus colchicus* and *Aquila chrysaetus* are figured in the text.

1101

On the Range of the Guácharo (*Steatornis caripensis*) in South America.

Ibis, 1890, pp. 335-339.

A history of the occurrences of *Steatornis caripensis* in various localities in South America, with a list of the principal references to this species

1102

On some Birds of the Argentine Republic. By A. H. Holland. With notes by P. L. Sclater.

Ibis, 1890, pp. 424-428.

A nominal list of 65 species, accompanied by Mr. Holland's field notes and remarks by Mr. Sclater on some of the more interesting species.

(See also *Ibis*, 1891, p. 16.)

1103

African Monkeys in the West Indies.

Nature XLI, pp. 368, 369 (1890).

Letter on the occurrence of *Cercopithecus callitrichus* in the West Indies.

(See also *Proc. Zool. Soc. London*, 1866, p. 79; *Nature*, XXI, p. 153, 1879.)

1104

The White Rhinoceros.

Nature, XLII, pp. 520, 521 (1890).

Remarks on *Rhinoceros simus*, which is shown to differ in many respects from *R. bicornis*. The heads of the two species are figured.

1105

The New Australian Mammal.

Nature, XLII, p 645 (1890).

Notes on the curious new mammal discovered in Central Australia by Dr. E. C. Stirling.

(See also *Nature*, XLIV, p. 440, 1891.)

1106

[Report on the additions to the Society's Menagerie in December, 1890.]

Proc. Zool. Soc. London, 1891, p. 1.

1107

[Exhibition of and remarks upon some sketches made by Lieut. W. E. Stairs, R. E., of the horns of a large Antelope apparently unknown to science.]

Proc. Zool. Soc. London, 1891, pp. 1-3.

The horn is figured in the text.

1108

[Exhibition of and remarks upon specimens of three species of Purple Water Hens (*Porphyrio poliocephalus*, *P. caruleus*, and *P. smaragdonotus*).]

Proc. Zool. Soc. London, 1891, pp. 47, 48.

1109

[Report on the additions to the Society's Menagerie in January, 1891.]

Proc. Zool. Soc. London, 1891, p. 121.

1110

On a second collection of Birds from the Province of Tarapacá, northern Chili.

Proc. Zool. Soc. London, 1891, pp. 131-137, pl. xiii.

An annotated list of 53 species, of which *Phrygilus coracinus* is described as new and figured. A map of the vicinity of Tarapacá is given.

(See also *Proc. Zool. Soc. London*, 1886, p. 395).

1111

[Report on the additions to the Society's Menagerie in February, 1891.]

Proc. Zool. Soc. London, 1891, p. 179.

1112

[Exhibition of and remarks upon a specimen of Macgregor's Paradise Bird (*Cnemophilus macgregori*).]

Proc. Zool. Soc. London, 1891, p. 179.

1113

[Exhibition of and remarks upon two specimens of the Horns of an Antelope from Somaliland.]

Proc. Zool. Soc. London, 1891, p. 197.

These horns undoubtedly belonged to the species of antelope which had been recently described by Mr. Thomas as *Cervicapra clarkei*.

1114

[Exhibition of skins of the Ounce (*Felis uncia*) and remarks upon its geographical distribution.]

Proc Zool. Soc. London, 1891, p. 197.

1115

[Report on the additions to the Society's Menagerie in March, 1891.]

Proc. Zool. Soc. London, 1891, p. 212.

1116

[Remarks upon the breeding of *Tragelaphus gratus* in the Gardens of the Zoological Society of Amsterdam.]

Proc. Zool. Soc. London, 1891, p. 213.

1117

[Report on the additions to the Society's Menagerie in April, 1891.]

Proc. Zool. Soc. London, 1891, p. 301.

1118

[General remarks upon the Fauna of British Central Africa.]

Proc. Zool. Soc. London, 1891, pp. 301-305.

A summary of the state of knowledge of the fauna of British Central Africa, and a list of the literature relating thereto.

1119

[Report on the additions to the Society's Menagerie in May, 1891.]

Proc. Zool. Soc. London, 1891, p. 326.

1120

[Remarks on interesting animals observed during a visit to the Zoological

Gardens of Paris, Ghent, Antwerp, Rotterdam, Amsterdam, and The Hague.]

Proc Zool. Soc. London, 1891, pp. 326, 327.

1121

[Remarks on the Sea Eagles, referred to *Haliaëtus pelagicus*, living in the Hamburg Zoological Gardens.]

Proc. Zool. Soc. London, 1891, p. 374.

One of these specimens having been incorrectly determined, as pointed out in a communication from Dr. Bolau, Mr. Sclater refers it to *Haliaëtus branickii.* Tacz.

1122

[Report on the additions to the Society's Menagerie in June, July, August, and September, 1891.]

Proc. Zool. Soc. London, 1891, pp. 464, 465.

1123

[Report on the additions to the Society's Menagerie in October, 1891.]

Proc. Zool. Soc. London, 1891, p. 486.

1124

[Exhibition of and remarks upon a specimen of a Shearwater (*Puffinus gavia*) from Australia.]

Proc. Zool. Soc. London, 1891, p. 627.

1125

Further notes on the Birds of the Argentine Republic. By A. H. Holland. With remarks by P. L. Sclater.

Ibis, 1891, pp. 16-20.

A list of 46 species, accompanied by Mr. Holland's field notes and remarks by Mr. Sclater.

(See also *Ibis*, 1890, p. 424.)

1126

The Spotted-billed Pelican (*Pelecanus manillensis*).

Ibis, 1891, pp. 151, 152.

Note on the most likely locality in India to procure specimens of *Pelecanus manillensis.*

1127

Remarks on Macgregor's Paradise Bird (*Cnemophilus macgregori*).

Ibis, 1891, pp. 414, 415, pl. x.

Cnemophilus macgregori is figured and remarked upon.

1128

On recent advances in our knowledge of the Geographical Distribution of Birds.

Ibis, 1891, pp. 514-557.

A reprint, with slight modifications, of an address delivered to the Second International Ornithological Congress, at Budapest, in May, 1891, being a review of the principal additions to the literature of geographical ornithology since 1875.

1129

Porpoises in the Victoria Nyanza.

Nature, XLIV, p. 124 (1891).

Letter on the improbability of Porpoises occurring in Lake Victoria Nyanza, as had been asserted by Dr. Carl Peters.

1130

The new Australian Marsupial Mole, *Notoryctes typhlops*.

Nature, XLIV, p. 449 (1891).

Remarks on *Notoryctes typhlops*, with an extract of a letter from Dr. E. C. Stirling, containing notes on its habits and habitat.

(See also *Nature*, XLII, p. 645, 1890.)

1131

The Bird collections in the Oxford University Museum.

Nature, XLIV, p. 518 (1891).

Letter on the condition of the collections of birds in the Oxford University Museum, and suggestions for their arrangement.

(See also *Ibis*, 1892, p. 186; 1893, p. 156.)

1132

Opportunity for a Naturalist.

Nature, XLV, pp. 174, 269 (1891-92).

Letters on an opportunity for a naturalist to visit Argentina for the purpose of collecting bird skins.

1133

[Report on the additions to the Society's Menagerie in November and December, 1891.]

Proc. Zool. Soc. London, 1892, pp. 1, 2.

1134

[Report on the additions to the Society's Menagerie in January, 1892.]

Proc. Zool. Soc. London, 1892, p. 76.

1135

[Exhibition of and remarks upon the Egg and Young of the Partridge Bronzewing Pigeon (*Geophaps scripta*).]

Proc. Zool. Soc. London, 1892, pp. 76, 77.

Critical remarks on Dr. Sharpe's proposal to alter the systematic position of the *Geophaps.*

1136

On a small collection of Mammals brought by Mr. A. Sharpe from Nyassaland.

Proc. Zool. Soc. London, 1892, pp. 97, 98.

Notes on eight species of mammals.

1137

On a new Antelope from Somaliland and on some other specimens of Antelopes from the same country.

Proc. Zool. Soc. London, 1892, pp. 98-102, pl. v.

Bubalis swaynei is described and its head figured. Ten other species of antelopes from Somaliland are enumerated and remarked upon. The head and neck of *Lithocranius walleri*, and the skull and horns of *Bubalis swaynei*, are figured in the text.

(See also *Proc. Zool. Soc. London*, 1892, pp. 117, 257.)

1138

[Exhibition of, and remarks upon, some "Spinning" or "Japanese" Mice.]

Proc. Zool. Soc. London, 1892, p. 117.

1139

[Exhibition of and remarks upon a series of Mounted Heads of Antelopes belonging to Captain Swayne, including one of *Bubalis swaynei*.]

Proc. Zool. Soc. London, 1892, pp. 117, 118.

These heads belonged to eight different species. A list of the species of Somaliland antelopes (12 in number), with their native names, is given.

(See also *Proc. Zool. Soc. London*, 1892, pp. 98, 257.)

1140

[Report on the additions to the Society's Menagerie in February, 1892.]

Proc. Zool. Soc. London, 1892, p. 174.

1141

[Exhibition of and remarks upon a Skin of the Wild Ass of Somaliland (*Equus asinus somalicus*).]

Proc. Zool. Soc. London, 1892, p. 195.

(See also *Proc. Zool. Soc. London*, 1884, p.538.)

1142

[Report on the additions to the Society's Menagerie in March, 1892, and list of Giraffes that have lived in the Society's Gardens.]

Proc. Zool. Soc. London, 1892, pp. 256, 257.

1143

[Exhibition of and remarks upon two mounted heads of Swayne's Antelope (*Bubalis swaynei*).]

Proc. Zool. Soc. London, 1892, pp. 257, 258.

(See also *Proc. Zool. Soc. London*, 1892, pp. 98, 117.)

1144

[Report on the additions to the Society's Menagerie in April, 1892.]

Proc. Zool. Soc. London, 1892, p. 299.

1145

[Exhibition of and remarks upon a nearly perfect Egg of *Æpyornis medius*.]

Proc. Zool. Soc. London, 1892, p. 299.

1146

[Report on the additions to the Society's Menagerie in May, 1892.]

Proc. Zool. Soc. London, 1892, pp. 470, 471.

The male and female of *Hypocolius ampelinus* are figured in the text.

1147

[Remarks on interesting animals observed during a visit to the Zoological Gardens of Rotterdam, The Hague, Amsterdam, and Antwerp.]

Proc. Zool. Soc. London, 1892, pp. 471, 472.

1148

[Remarks upon the habits of a South African Snake (*Dasypeltis scabra*).]

Proc. Zool. Soc. London, 1892, p. 476.

1149

[Extracts from a letter from Mr. H. H. Johnston, announcing the dispatch of specimens from the Shiré Highlands.]

Proc. Zool. Soc. London, 1892, p. 477.

1150

On a collection of Birds from the Island of Anguilla, West Indies.

Proc. Zool. Soc. London, 1892, pp. 498–500.

A list of 16 species, with remarks upon them.

1151

[Report on the additions to the Society's Menagerie in June, July, August, and September, 1892.]

Proc. Zool. Soc. London, 1892, p. 541.

1152

[Report on the additions to the Society's Menagerie in October, 1892, and description of a new Monkey of the genus *Cercopithecus*.]

Proc. Zool. Soc. London, 1892, pp. 579–581, pl. xl.

Cercopithecus stairsi is described and figured.

1153

[Exhibition of, on behalf of Thomas Ground, and remarks upon a specimen of the Siberian Pectoral Sandpiper, shot on Breydon mudflats, Norfolk.]

Proc. Zool. Soc. London, 1892, p. 581.

1154

[Report on the additions to the Society's Menagerie in November, 1892.]

Proc. Zool. Soc. London, 1892, p. 594.

1155

The Bird Collections in the Oxford University Museum.]

Ibis, 1892, pp. 186, 187.

Remarks on the condition of the bird collections in the Oxford University Museum, and suggestions for properly arranging them.

(See also *Nature*, XLIV, p. 518 (1891); *Ibis*, 1893, p. 156.)

1156

On the Avifauna of the Lower Pilcomayo. By J. Graham Kerr. With notes by the editor [P. L. Sclater].

Ibis, 1892, pp. 120–152, pl. iii.

A list of 174 species, accompanied by Mr. Graham Kerr's field notes and remarks by Mr. Sclater.

1157

Note on *Calliste margarethæ*.

Ibis, 1892, p. 351.

Note on the probable identity of Mr. Allen's newly described *Calliste margarethæ* and Vieillot's *Tanagra formosa*.

1158

Remarks on the correct generic name of the Linnets.

Ibis, 1892, pp. 555–557.

Remarks showing that *Cannabina* should be adopted as the generic name for the Linnets. The synonyms of the genus are given.

1159

[Exhibition of, to a meeting of the British Ornithologists' Club, and remarks upon a specimen of *Paramythia montium*.]

Bull. British Orn. Club, I, pp. xvi, xvii (1892).

1160

The Antelopes of Somaliland.

Natural Science, I, pp. 255–265 (1892).

An illustrated résumé of the antelopes of Somaliland. Twelve species known to inhabit that country are enumerated.

1161

[Report on the additions to the Society's Menagerie in December, 1892.]

Proc. Zool. Soc. London, 1893, p. 1.

1162

Remarks on a rare Argentine Bird, *Xenopsaris albinucha.*

Proc. Zool. Soc. London, 1893, pp. 166–168, pl. vii.

Xenopsaris albinucha (Burm.) is characterized, figured, and remarked upon.

1163

[Report on the additions to the Society's Menagerie in January, 1893.]

Proc. Zool. Soc. London, 1893, p. 168.

1164

[Exhibition of and remarks on behalf of Mr. R. M. Barrington upon an example of the Antarctic Sheathbill (*Chionis alba*) killed on the coast of Ireland.]

Proc. Zool. Soc. London, 1893, p. 178.

1165

[Report on the additions to the Society's Menagerie in February, 1893.]

Proc. Zool. Soc. London, 1893, p. 237.

1166

On a new African Monkey of the genus *Cercopithecus,* with a list of the known species.

Proc. Zool. Soc. London, 1893, pp. 243–258, pls. xvi, xvii.

A review of the species of the genus *Cercopithecus.* Thirty-three species known and 15 not known to the author are enumerated. *Cercopithecus schmidti* and *C. moloneyi* are figured. the latter of which is described as a new species. The head of *C. brazzæ* is figured in the text.

(See also *Proc. Zool. Soc. London,* 1893, p. 441).

1167

[Report on the additions to the Society's Menagerie in March, 1893.]

Proc. Zool. Soc. London, 1893, p. 325.

1168

[Exhibition of and remarks upon a Skin of a variety of the Pig-tailed Monkey (*Macacus nemestrinus.*)]

Proc. Zool. Soc. London, 1893, p. 325.

1169

[Report on the additions to the Society's Menagerie in April, 1893.]

Proc. Zool. Soc. London, 1893, p. 435

1170

[Remarks on the protrusion of a fleshy mass from the cloaca occasionally exhibited by the Greater Vasa Parrot.]

Proc. Zool. Soc. London, 1893, p. 435.

This habit of the female *Coracopsis vasa,* presumably due to sexual excitement, had been previously noticed on two occasions (cf. *Proc. Zool. Soc. London,* 1884, pp. 410, 502).

1171

[List of the dates of receipt from the printers of the sheets of the Society's "Proceedings" from 1831 to 1859, inclusive.]

Proc. Zool. Soc. London, 1893, pp. 435–440.

1172

Additional notes on the Monkeys of the genus *Cercopithecus.*

Proc. Zool. Soc. London, 1893, pp. 441–444, pl. xxxiii.

Supplementary notes to a former communication (cf. *Proc. Zool. Soc. London,* 1893, p. 243), containing remarks on *Cercopithecus bourtourlinii* and *C. brazzæ.* The former species is figured in the text, the latter on a plate.

1173

[Report on the additions to the Society's Menagerie in May, 1893.]

Proc. Zool. Soc. London, 1893, p. 505, pl. xxxix.

The female and young of *Cobus ellipsiprymnus* are figured.

1174

[Exhibition of and remarks upon some Skins of Mammals obtained in the Shiré Highlands, British Central African Protectorate.]

Proc. Zool. Soc. London, 1893, pp. 506, 507.

Remarks on the skins of eight species of mammals from the Shiré Highlands, which were exhibited to a meeting of the Zoological Society of London.

1175

On some Horns belonging, apparently, to a new form of African Rhinoceros.

Proc. Zool. Soc. London, 1893, pp. 514–517.

The dimensions and wood-cut illustrations are given of two remarkable horns of a species of Rhinoceros from Udulia, near Speke Gulf, East Africa. to which the provisional name *Rhinoceros bicornis holmwoodi* is applied.

1176

[Exhibition of and remarks upon two Eggs of the Cape Coly (*Colius capensis*) laid in the Society's Gardens.]

Proc. Zool. Soc. London, 1893, pp. 528, 529.

1177

[Report on the additions to the Society's Menagerie in June, July, August, and September, 1893.]

Proc. Zool. Soc. London, 1893, pp. 612, 613.

1178

[Remarks on the Zoological Gardens of Stuttgart, Frankfort, and Cologne.]

Proc. Zool. Soc. London, 1893, p. 613.

1179

[Remarks upon the breeding of Monkeys during the last ten years in the Society's Gardens.]

Proc. Zool. Soc. London, 1893, pp. 615, 616.

A list of the species of the genera *Macacus* and *Cercopithecus* that have bred during the last ten years in the Zoological Society's Menagerie, with an illustration of a female *Cercopithecus lalandii,* and its young in the act of sucking its two teats at once.

1180

[Report on the additions to the Society's Menagerie in October, 1893.]

Proc. Zool. Soc. London, 1893, p. 691.

1181

[Exhibition of and remarks upon a mounted specimen of *Cercopithecus albigularis* from the Leyden Museum.]

Proc. Zool. Soc. London, 1893, p. 691.

Note on the strange fact that *Cercopithecus albigularis* should inhabit both East and West Africa.

1182

On some specimens of Mammals from Lake Mweru, British Central Africa, transmitted by Vice-Consul Alfred Sharpe.

Proc. Zool. Soc. London, 1893, pp. 723–729.

An extract from Mr. Sharpe's letter containing an account of the animals met with by him during his journey from the north end of Lake Nyassa to Lake Mweru and the Luapula, with a list of and remarks upon 17 species of mammals, of which *Cercopithecus opisthostictus* and *Cobus crawshayi* are described as new. The skull and horns of *Cobus crawshayi* are figured in the text.

1183

[Report on the additions to the Society's Menagerie in November, 1893.]

Proc. Zool. Soc. London, 1893, pp. 729, 730.

Capra caucasica, ♀, is figured in the text.

1184

List of Birds collected by Mr. Alexander Whyte, F. Z. S., in Nyassaland. By Capt. G. E. Shelley, F. Z. S. With a preface by the editor.

Ibis, 1893, pp. 1–6, pls. i–iii.

Prefatory notes to Captain Shelley's paper on Mr. Whyte's collection of birds from Nyassaland.

1185

[The Bird Collections in the Oxford University Museum.]

Ibis, 1893, pp. 156, 157.

Note on the progress made in the arrangement of the bird collections in the the Oxford University Museum.

(See also *Nature*, XLIV, p. 518 (1891); *Ibis*, 1892, p. 186.)

1186

Birds of Antigua, West Indies.

Ibis, 1893, p. 158.

A correction with regard to a statement made by the author that the ornis of Anguilla was entirely unknown.

(See *Proc. Zool. Soc. London*, 1892, p. 498.)

1187

On the occurrence of the Sharp-tailed Sandpiper (*Tringa acuminata*) in Norfolk. By Henry Seebohm. With an appendix by the editor.

Ibis, 1893, pp. 181–185, pl. v.

The synonymy of *Tringa acuminata* is appended to Mr. Seebohm's remarks on this bird. A figure of the bird, and an illustration, in the text, of its tail, are also given.

1188

Notes on *Paramythia montium* and *Amalocichla sclateriana*.

Ibis, 1893, pp. 243–246, pl. vii.

Notes on the systematic positions of *Paramythia montium* and *Amalocichla sclateriana*, and reprints of Mr. De Vis's original descriptions of them. The former species is figured, and its bill, head and foot are illustrated in the text.

1189

Note on the proper use of the generic terms *Certhiola* and *Cœreba*.

Ibis, 1893, pp. 246, 247.

Notes pointing out that the terms *Certhiola* and *Cœreba* should be employed, respectively, for the Sugar Birds of the West Indies and the Blue Creepers of South America.

1190

[Note on the "Crocodile Bird" of the Nile.]

Ibis, 1893, p. 277.

A postscript to Mr. Cook's letter on the "Crocodile Bird" (*Hoplopterus spinosus*) of the Nile.

1191

Great Bustards in the Zoological Society's Gardens.

Ibis, 1893, pp. 476, 477.

Note on the Great Bustard (*Otis tarda*) breeding in the Gardens of the Zoological Society of London.

1192

Field notes on the Birds of Estancia Sta. Elena, Argentine Republic. By A. H. Holland. With remarks by P. L. Sclater.

Ibis, 1893, pp. 483–488.

Fifteen species are enumerated, accompanied by Mr. Holland's field notes and remarks by Mr. Sclater.

1193

The Jellyfish of Lake Urumiah.

Nature, XLVIII, p. 294 (1893).

Letter on the occurrence of a "Jellyfish" or Medusa in Lake Urumiah, Persia.

1194

The "Zoological Record."

Nature, XLIX, pp. 123, 124 (1893).

A reply to Messrs. Pocock and Bather's letter (cf. *Nature*, XLIX, p. 53) on the desirability of including Palæozoology in the "Zoological Record," and a copy of the correspondence with the Geological Society on this subject.

1195

[Exhibition to a meeting of the British Ornithologists' Club of a prepared wing and tail of the Martineta Tinamou.]

Bull. British Orn. Club, I, p. xxiv (1893).

1196

[Extract from a letter from Dr. Hartlaub on the distinctness of *Pennula ecaudata* (King) and *P. sandwichensis* (Gm.).]

Bull. British Orn. Club, I, p. xxiv (1893).

1197

[Aden suggested as a convenient place for an Ornithological Excursion.]

Bull. British Orn. Club, I, pp. xxxiii, xxxiv (1893).

1198

[Remarks on the series of mounted specimens of Italian Birds in the Florence Museum, and on the migratory birds which had visited the S. S. *Oruba* between Gibraltar and Malta from March 29 to April 1, 1893.]

Bull. British Orn. Club, I, p. xliii (1893).

1199

[Exhibition of, to a meeting of the British Ornithologists' Club, and remarks upon a specimen of *Phalaropus fulicarius* from Chili.]

Bull. British Orn. Club, I, p. lv (1893)

1200

[Exhibition of, to a meeting of the British Ornithologists' Club, and remarks on a specimen of *Geophaps plumifera*.]

Bull. British Orn. Club, I, pp. lv, lvi (1893).

1201

Chairman's address on opening the second session of the British Ornithologists' Club (October 18, 1893).

Bull. British Orn. Club, III, pp. 1–4 (1893).

A sketch of the recent events in the ornithological world.

1202

[Exhibition of, to a meeting of the British Ornithologists' Club, and remarks upon a variety of *Psittacus erithacus*.]

Bull. British Orn. Club, III, p. vii (1893).

1203

[Exhibition to a meeting of the British Ornithologists' Club of specimens of the eggs of *Podager nacunda* and *Hydropsalis furcifera*.]

Bull. British Orn. Club, III, p. vii (1893).

1204

The Mammals of Kilima-Njaro.

Natural Science, II, p. 257 (1893).

An illustrated account of the mammal fauna of Kilima-Njaro, with a list of literature on this subject.

1205

The Nearctic Region and its Mammals.

Natural Science, III, pp. 288–292 (1893).

Critical remarks on Messrs. J. A. Allen's and C. Hart Merriam's papers on the geographical distribution of mammals in North America.

1206

On the typical forms of Vertebrated Life suitable for Exhibition in Local Museums.

Rep. of Proc. of the Museums Assoc., pp. 95–99, July, 1893.

An abstract of a paper, read before the Museums Association at their London meeting in July, 1893, on the most desirable objects to be exhibited in a local museum. A list of the existing orders of vertebrates, with the type of each order suitable for exhibition, is given.

1207

[Report on the additions to the Society's Menagerie in December, 1893.]

Proc. Zool. Soc. London, 1894, p. 1.

1208

[Exhibition of and remarks upon a coloured drawing of the head of *Cercopithecus erythrogaster*.]

Proc. Zool. Soc. London, 1894, p. 1.

1209

[Report on the additions to the Society's Menagerie in January, 1894.]

Proc. Zool. Soc. London, 1894, p. 92.

1210

[Exhibition of and remarks upon a mounted specimen of the River Hog of Madagascar (*Potamochœrus edwardsi*), with notes on its habits by Mr. J. T. Last.]

Proc. Zool. Soc. London, 1894, pp. 92–94.

1211

[Exhibition of and remarks upon a stuffed specimen of the White-billed Great Northern Diver (*Colymbus adamsi*) from Norway.]

Proc. Zool. Soc. London, 1894, p. 94.

1212

[Report on the additions to the Society's Menagerie in February, 1894.]

Proc. Zool. Soc. London, 1894, pp. 162–164.

A figure of the young King Vulture in down plumage is figured in the text.

1213

[Exhibition of and remarks upon a photograph of a young male Gaur or Indian Bison (*Bos gaurus*).]

Proc. Zool. Soc. London, 1894, pp. 249, 250

1214

[Report on the additions to the Society's Menagerie in March, 1894.]

Proc. Zool. Soc. London, 1894, p. 316.

1215

Remarks on the specimens of *Protopterus annectens* living in the Society's reptile house.

Proc. Zool. Soc. London, 1894, pp. 353, 354.

1216

[Report on the additions to the Society's Menagerie in April, 1894.]

Proc. Zool. Soc. London, 1894, pp. 390, 391.

1217

[Report on the additions to the Society's Menagerie in May, 1894.]

Proc. Zool. Soc. London, 1894, p. 450.

1218

[Remarks upon animals observed in the Zoological Gardens of Rotterdam, Amsterdam, Hanover, Berlin, and Hamburg.]

Proc. Zool. Soc. London, 1894, pp. 456, 457.

1219

[Exhibition of and remarks upon a Skin of an African Monkey (*Cercopithecus diana ignitus*).]

Proc. Zool. Soc. London, 1894, p. 484.

1220

[Exhibition of and remarks upon the typical specimen of *Cercopithecus grayi*, Fraser.]

Proc. Zool. Soc. London, 1894, pp. 484, 485.

1221

[Report on the additions to the Society's Menagerie in June, July, August, and September, 1894.]

Proc. Zool. Soc. London, 1894, pp. 594–596.

1222

[Report on the additions to the Society's Menagerie in October, 1894.]

Proc. Zool. Soc. London, 1894, p. 654.

1223

[Report on the additions to the Socie-ty's Menagerie in November, 1894.]

Proc. Zool. Soc. London, 1894, pp. 693, 694, pl. xlvi.

Dendrolagus bennettianus is figured and char-acterized.

1224

Ornithology at Munich, Stuttgart, Darmstadt, Frankfort, and Cassel.

Ibis, 1894, pp. 100–108.

Remarks upon the collections of birds in the museums of the above-mentioned cities.

1225

On the Birds of Uruguay. By O. V. Aplin. With an introduction and notes by P. L. Sclater.

Ibis, 1894, pp. 149–215, pl. v.

Observations on 139 species, with figures of the eggs of 7 species.

1226

Remarks on the Birds of Antarctica.

Ibis, 1894, pp. 494–501.

Remarks on the present state of knowledge of the avifauna of the Antarctic Continent.

1227

[Exhibition to a meeting of the British Ornithologists' Club of a needle used by the natives of North Queensland made from the stem of a feather.]

Bull. British Orn. Club, III, pp. xxii, xxiii (1894).

1228

[Exhibition to a meeting of the British Ornithologists' Club of a skin of a Rail (*Amaurolimnas concolor*) from Lima, Peru.]

Bull. British Orn. Club, III, p. xxiii (1894).

1229

[Exhibition to a meeting of the British Ornithologists' Club of a skin of a Hemi-pode from Nyassaland.]

Bull. British Orn. Club, III, p. xxx (1894).

1230

[Remarks on the great inconvenience that would arise if the "*Scomber scom-ber*" principle was adopted in ornitho-logical nomenclature.]

Bull. British Orn. Club, III, p. xxxiii (1894).

1231

[Exhibition to a meeting of the Brit-ish Ornithologists' Club of Skins of *Ara auricollis*, *Pionus laccrus*, and *Chrysotis tucumana* from Argentina.]

Bull. British Orn. Club, III p. xlv (1894).

1232

[Exhibition to a meeting of the Brit-ish Ornithologists' Club of two Eggs of *Phibalura flavirostris*.]

Bull. British Orn. Club, III, p. xlvi (1894)

1233

Chairman's address on opening the third session of the British Ornitholo-gists' Club, 1894.

Bull. British Orn. Club, IV, pp. 1–6 (1894).

1234

[Exhibition to a meeting of the Brit-ish Ornithologists' Club of the Eggs of two species of Macaw, *Ara militaris* and *A. ararauna*, which had been laid in cap-tivity.]

Bull. British Orn. Club, IV, p. vi (1894).

1235

[Exhibition to a meeting of the British Ornithologists' Club of a Skin of *Phalaro-pus wilsoni* from the Falkland Islands.]

Bull. British Orn. Club, IV, p. vi (1894).

1236

[Exhibition to a meeting of the British Ornithologists' Club of a skin of *Falco punicus* which had been captured in the Mediterranean.]

Bull. British Orn. Club, IV, p. xv (1894).

1237

[Remarks on Reiser's work "Materia-len zu einer Ornis Balkanica."]

Bull. British Orn. Club, IV, p. xv (1894).

1238

The new Cypress of Nyassaland.

Nature, LI, pp. 85–87 (1894).

Remarks upon and figure of the cypress (*Wid-dringtonia whytei*) discovered on the plateau of Milanji in Nyassaland by Mr. Alexander Whyte.

1239

Animals not yet in the Zoo.

Science Gossip, N. S., I, pp. 25–28 (1894).

An illustrated account of certain animals that have never been exhibited in the Gardens of the Zoological Society of London, with suggestions for the best means of capturing them and send-ing them home.

(For list of publications subsequent to December, 1894, see APPENDIX.)

Name.	Type species.	Place of description.	No. of paper.
Agathopus	Agathopus micropterus, Scl..	Proc. Zool. Soc. London, 1858, p. 69....	116
Ancistrops, Scl. MS....	Anabates lineaticeps, Scl....	Cat. American Birds, p. 157 (1862).....	8
Aucylorhinus, nom. emend. pro Agrilorhinus, Bp.	....	Ibis, 1875, p. 204....................	702
Antilocapridæ........	Antilocapra americana, Gray.	Rep. Brit. Assoc. Adv. Sci., 1866, pt. 2, p. 78.	397
Cænotriccus	Muscicapa (Todirostrum) ruficeps, Lafr.	Cat. B. Brit. Mus., XIV, pp. 64, 80, (1888).	20
Calochætes	Euchætes coccineus, Scl....	Ibis, 1879, p. 388...................	837
Calodromas.............	Eudromia elegans, d'Orb. et Geoffr.	Nomencl. Av. Neotrop., pp. 153, 156 (1873).	13
Calopitta (sect.).......	Pitta maxima, Müll. et Schleg.	Cat. B. Brit. Mus., XIV, pp. 414, 419 (1888).	20
Camptostoma..........	Camptostoma imberbe, Scl...	Proc. Zool. Soc. London, 1857, p. 203....	108
Carenochrous (n. sect.).	Arremon rufinucha, Tschudi.	Proc. Zool. Soc. London, 1856, p. 87.....	86
Catharopeza...........	Leucopeza bishopi, Lawr.....	Ibis, 1880, p. 74, pl. 1..............	862
Centropelma...........	Podiceps micropterus, Gould.	Exotic Ornith., p. 189, pl. xcv (1860)....	12
Centropsar	Centropsar mirus, Scl.......	Proc. Zool. Soc. London, 1874, p. 176, pl. xxvi.	653
Cercomacra...........	Myrmothera cœrulescens, Vieill.	Proc. Zool. Soc. London, 1858, p. 244....	122
Chætoptila	Entomyza angustipluma, Cass.	Ibis, 1871, p. 358...................	567
Chamæospiza	Pipilo torquatus, Du Bus...	Proc. Zool. Soc. London, 1858, p. 304....	126
Chirocylla	Lathria uropygialis, Scl. et Salv.	Proc. Zool. Soc. London, 1876, p. 357, pl. xxxii.	723
Chloreuphonia, nom. emend. pro Chlorophonia, Bp.	....	Contr. to Ornithology, 1851, p. 94.....	37
Chlorura...............	Fringilla chlorura, Aud......	Cat. American Birds, p. 117 (1862).....	8
Chroocephalus, nom. emend. pro Chroicocephalus, Eyton.	....	Proc. Zool. Soc. London, 1871, p. 576....	554
Clibanornis............	Anabates dendrocolaptoides, Temm. MS. et Pelz.	Nomencl. Av. Neotrop., pp. 61, 155 (1873).	13
Cnipodectes	Cyclorhynchus subbrunneus, Scl.	Proc. Zool. Soc. London, 1873, p. 281....	614
Coracopitta...........	Melampitta lugubris, Schleg.	Cat. B. Brit. Mus., XIV, pp. 412, 449 (1888).	20
Creurgops, Verr. MS..	Creurgops verticalis, Verr. MS.	Proc. Zool. Soc. London, 1858, p. 73, pl. cxxxii, fig. 2.	116
Curæus................	Turdus curæus, Molina......	Cat. American Birds, p. 139 (1862).....	8
Delothraupis..........	Calliste castaneoventris, Scl..	Cat. B. Brit. Mus., XI, pp. 139, 142 (1886).	19
Dendrocycna, nom. emend. pro Dendrocygna.	....	Proc. Zool. Soc. London, 1880, p. 508....	857
Dendromanes..........	Dendrocincla anabatina, Scl..	Proc. Zool. Soc. London, 1859, p. 382....	153
Diglossopis............	Diglossopis cærulescens, Scl..	Ann. and Mag. Nat. Hist., ser. 2, XVII, p. 467 (1856).	94
Diplopsalis	Hydropsalis climacocercus, Tsch.	Proc. Zool. Soc. London, 1866, p. 141....	378
Dissodectes...........	Falco ardesiacus, Vieill.....	Proc. Zool. Soc. London, 1864, p. 248....	317
Diva..................	Tanagra (Euphone?) vassorii, Lafr. et Bolss.	Tanagrarum Catalogue Specificus, pp. 13, 16 (1854).	2
Donacicola, nom. emend. pro Donacola, Gould.	....	Proc. Zool. Soc. London, 1879, p. 449....	822
Drepanornis...........	Drepanornis albertisi, Scl...	Proc. Zool. Soc. London, 1873, p. 560, pl. xlvii.	625
Empidochanes..........	Muscicapa oliva, Bodd.......	Proc. Zool. Soc. London, 1862, p. 112....	255
Euchætes, Verr. MS...	Euchætes coccineus, Verr. MS.	Proc. Zool. Soc. London, 1858, p. 73, pl. cxxxii, fig. 1.	116
Eucometis	Tanagra penicillata, Spix....	Proc. Zool. Soc. London, 1856, p. 117....	86a

List of new families and genera described—Continued.

Name.	Type species.	Place of description.	No. of paper.
Eucorystes	Cassicus wagleri, Gray and Mitch.	Ibis, 1883, p. 147......................	948
Eumomota............	Prionites (Crypticus) superciliaris, Jard. and Selb.	Proc. Zool. Soc. London, 1857, p. 257....	112
Euprepiste	Tanagra brasiliensis, Linn...	Contr. to Ornithology, 1851, p. 95	37
Eupsilostoma.........	Muscicapa eximia, Temm....	Proc. Zool. Soc. London, 1860, p. 69	163
Euschemon	Tanagra flava, Gm	Contr. to Ornithology, 1851, p. 94.......	37
Eutrygon, nom.emend. pro. Trugon, Puch.	....	Journ. of Proc. of Linn. Soc. London (Zool.), II, p. 168 (1858).	138
Glossiptila	Motacilla campestris, Linn...	Proc. Zool. Soc. London, 1856, p. 269....	86b
Grallaricula	Grallaria flavirostris, Scl.....	Proc. Zool. Soc. London, 1858. p. 283...	123
Gymnocichla	Mylothera nudiceps, Cass....	Proc. Zool. Soc. London, 1858, p. 274....	123
Gymnopelia	Columba erythrothorax, Moyen.	Nomencl. Av. Neotrop., pp. 133, 156 (1873).	13
Gymnostinops........	Cacicus montezuma, Less....	Cat. B. Brit. Mus., XI, pp 309, 312 (1886).	19
Hapaloptila..........	Malacoptila castanea, Verr...	Proc. Zool. Soc. London, 1881, p 777....	885
Heleothreptus, nom. emend. pro Eleothreptus. Gray.	....	Proc. Zool. Soc. London, 1866, p. 143....	378
Helicura, nom. emend. pro. Ilicura, Reichenb., et Hoilicura, Salv.	....	Cat. B. Brit. Mus., XIV, p. 311 (1888)...	20
Hemidacnis............	Pipræidea albiventris, Scl....	Cat. American Birds, p. 50 (1862).......	8
Henicorhina, nom. emend. pro Heterorhina, Baird.	....	Proc. Zool. Soc. London, 1868, p. 170....	435
Heterocercus, Hartl. MS.	Elænia linteata, Strickl......	Cat. American Birds, p. 245 (1862)	8
Heterocnemis..........	Sitta nævia, Gmel............	Proc. Zool. Soc. London, 1855, p. 146....	77
Hirundinapus (n. sect.)	Hirundo caudacuta, Lath.....	Proc. Zool. Soc. London, 1865, p. 607....	354
Hyetornis	Cuculus pluvialis, Gm.......	Cat. American Birds. p. 321 (1862)	8
Hylexetastes........,....	Dendrocolaptes perroti, Lafr.	Proc. Zool. Soc. London, 1889, p. 34.....	1056
Hylophorba	Hylophorba ruticilla, Scl.....	Proc. Zool. Soc. London, 1865, p. 326, pl. xiii.	343
Indicatoridæ	....	Ibis, 1870, p. 180	525
Iridornis, nom. emend. pro Iridosornis, Less.	....	Proc. Zool. Soc. London, 1855, p. 227....	81
Laletes ....:.......	Laletes osburni, Scl..........	Proc. Zool. Soc. London, 1861, p. 72, pl. xiv, fig. 2.	212
Lathriosoma, Bp. MS..	Lipaugus rufescens, Scl......	Cat. B. Brit. Mus., XIV, p. 354 (1888)...	20
Legatus	Tyrannus albicollis, Vieill ..	Proc. Zool. Soc. London, 1859, p. 46.....	139
Leucopeza.............	Leucopeza semperi, Scl.......	Proc. Zool. Soc. London, 1876, p. 14, pl. ii.	711
Leucophantes	Leucophantes brachyurus, Scl.	Proc. Zool. Soc. London, 1873, p. 691, pl. liii.	628
Limnophyes	Limnornis curvirostris, Gould.	Proc. Zool. Soc. London, 1889, p. 34.....	1056
Liosceles	Pteroptochus thoracicus, Scl.	Proc. Zool. Soc. London, 1864, p. 600, pl. xxxviii.	328
Macropsalis	Caprimulgus forcipatus, Nitzsch.	Proc. Zool. Soc. London, 1866, p. 143....	378
Malacothraupis........	Malacothraupis dentata, Scl. et Salv.	Proc. Zool. Soc. London, 1876, p. 353, pl. xxxi.	723
Margarops	Turdus fuscatus, Vieill.......	Proc. Zool. Soc. London, 1859, p. 335....	149
Mecocerculus..........	Fluvicola leucophrys, Lafr. et D'Orb.	Proc. Zool. Soc. London, 1862, p. 113....	256
Melanocharis	Dicæum nigrum, Less........	Journ. of Proc. of Linn. Soc. London (Zool.), II, p. 157 (1858).	138
Melanoptila	Melanoptila glabrirostris, Scl.	Proc. Zool. Soc. London, 1857, p. 275....	114
Melidectes............	Melidectes torquatus, Scl....	Proc. Zool. Soc. London, 1873, p. 694, pl. lv.	628
Melipotes	Melipotes gymnops, Scl......	Proc. Zool. Soc. London, 1873, p. 695, pl. lvi.	628
Metopothrix..........	Metopothrix aurantiacus, Scl. et Salv.	Proc. Zool. Soc. London, 1866, p 190, pl. xviii.	390
Microbates	Microbates torquatus, Scl. et Salv.	Nomencl. Av. Neotrop., pp. 72, 155 (1873).	13
Microcerculus	Turdus bambla, Bodd........	Cat. American Birds, p. 19 (1862)......	8
Microchelidon (changed to Neochelidon).	Petrochelidon tibialis, Cass..	Cat. American Birds, p. 39 (1862)......	8
Micromonacha..........	Bucco lanceolatus, Deville...	Proc. Zool. Soc. London, 1881, p. 777....	885
Microrhopias..........	Thamnophilus quixensis, Corn.	Cat. American Birds, p. 182 (1862)......	8
Mimocichla (n. sect.)..	Turdus rubripes, Temm......	Proc. Zool. Soc. London, 1859, p. 336....	149
Mitrephorus...........	Tyrannula, ? Sclater, P. Z. S., 1856, p. 296.	Proc. Zool. Soc. London, 1859, p. 44.....	139
Momotidæ, new family name instead of Prionitidæ.	....	Proc. Zool. Soc. London, 1857, p. 248....	112

List of new families and genera described—Continued.

Name.	Type species.	Place of description.	No. of paper.
Morococcyx	Piaya erythropygia, Less....	Cat. American Birds, p. 322 (1862).....	8
Myiozetetes, nom. emend. pro Myiozeta, Bp.	....	Proc. Zool. Soc. London, 1859, p. 46.....	139
Myrmelastes	Myrmelastes plumbeus, Scl..	Proc. Zool. Soc. London, 1858, p. 274, pl. cxliii.	123
Myrmotherula.........	Muscicapa pygmæa, Gmel...	Proc. Zool. Soc. London, 1858, p. 234....	122
Neochelidon	Petrochelidon tibialis, Cass..	Cat. American Birds, p. xvi (1862)....	8
Neochloe	Neochloe brevipennis, Scl....	Proc. Zool. Soc. London, 1857, p. 213....	109
Neocorys	Alauda spraguii, Aud.......	Proc. Zool. Soc. London, 1857, p. 4.....	98
Neocrex	Porzana erythrops, Scl	Proc. Zool. Soc. London, 1866, p. 457....	448
Neoctantes	Xenops niger, Natt. MS. Pelz.	Proc. Zool. Soc. London, 1868, p. 572....	454
Neopelma (n. sect.)....	Muscicapa aurifrons, Max...	Proc. Zool. Soc. London, 1860, p. 467....	197
Neopipo	Neopipo rubicunda, Scl. et Salv.	Proc. Zool. Soc. London, 1869, p. 438, pl. xxx. fig. 3.	483
Neorhynchus (to replace Callirhynchus, preoccupied).	Callirhynchus mascsus, Bp..	Proc. Zool. Soc. London, 1869, p. 147, pl. xii.	467
Nephœcetes (n. sect.)..	Hirundo nigra, Gm..........	Proc. Zool. Soc. London, 1865, p. 615....	354
Nesocelous	Colaptes fernandinæ, Vig....	Nomencl. Av. Neotrop., pp. 101, 155 (1873).	13
Nesopsar	Icterus nigerrimus, Osburn..	Ibis, 1859, p. 457......................	160
Nesospingus...........	Chlorospingus speculiferus, Lawr.	Ibis, 1885, p. 273......................	995
Nonnula..............	Bucco rubecula, Spix.......	Proc. Zool. Soc. London, 1853, p. 124....	55
Nothoprocta...........	Crypturus perdicarius, Kittl.	Nomencl. Av. Neotrop., pp. 153, 156 (1873).	13
Ochthornis	Elainea littoralis, Pelz.......	Cat. B. Brit. Mus., XIV, pp. 3, 31 (1888)..	20
Onmatornis, Scl. MS...	Merulaxis orthonyx, Lafr....	Cat. American Birds, p. 169 (1862)....	8
Oncostoma............	Todirostrum cinereigulare, Scl.	Cat. American Birds, p. 208, pl. xviii, fig. 1 (1862).	8
Opopsitta.............	Psittacula diophthalma, Hombr. et Jacq.	Proc. Zool. Soc. London, 1860, p. 227....	174
Oreomanes............	Oreomanes fraseri, Scl........	Proc. Zool. Soc. London, 1860, p. 75, pl. clix.	164
Oreothraupis	Saltator arremonops, Jardine.	Proc. Zool. Soc. London, 1856, p. 80.....	86
Ortygocichla..........	Ortygocichla rubiginosa, Scl..	Proc. Zool. Soc. London, 1881, p. 452, pl. xxxix.	879
Pauxis, nom. emend. pro. Pauxi, Temm.	....	Trans. Zool. Soc. London, IX, p. 285 (1875).	705
Phæornis.............	Tænioptera obscura, Cass....	Ibis, 1859, p. 327.....................	158
Phainopepla	Ptilogonys nitens, Swains....	Proc. Zool. Soc. London, 1858, p. 543....	133
Phlegopsis, nom. emend. pro Phlegopsis, Reich.	....	Proc. Zool. Soc. London, 1858, p. 276....	123
Phlogothraupis.......	Tanagra (Tachyphonus) sanguinolentus, Less.	Nomencl. Av. Neotrop., pp. 21, 155 (1873).	13
Pipridea, nom. emend. pro Pipræidea, Swains.	....	Proc. Zool. Soc. London, 1856, p. 265....	86b
Phacellodomus, err. pro Phacellodomus, Reichenb.	....	Proc. Zool. Soc. London, 1868, p. 141....	434
Podochætes...........	Caprimulgus leucopygius, Spix.	Proc. Zool. Soc. London, 1866, p. 135....	378
Polioptila.............	Motacilla cærulea, Linn......	Proc. Zool. Soc. London, 1855, p. 11.....	68
Polychlorus	Psittacus polychlorus, Scopoli, and Psittacodes westermanni, Bp.	Proc. Zool. Soc. London, 1857, p. 226....	110
Porphyrospiza.........	Cyanospiza cyanella, Pelz....	Nomencl. Av. Neotrop., pp. 30, 155 (1873).	13
Potamopsar...........	Icterus minor, Spix.........	Cat. American Birds, p. 141 (1862)....	8
Priotrhynchus	Momotus platyrhynchus, Leadb.	Proc. Zool. Soc. London, 1857, p. 256....	112
Pseudodacnis.........	Dacnis hartlaubi, Scl........	Cat. B. Brit. Mus., XI, pp. 80, 138 (1886).	19
Pseudoloistos.........	Oriolus viridis, Gm..........	Cat. American Birds, p. 137 (1862)....	8
Psilorhamphus	Leptorhynchus guttatus, Ménét.	Proc. Zool. Soc. London, 1855, p. 90....	75
Pygiptila	Thamnophilus stellaris, Scl...	Proc. Zool. Soc. London, 1858, p. 220....	121
Rhynchostruthus......	Rhynchostruthus socotranus, Scl. et Hartl.	Proc. Zool. Soc. London, 1881, p. 170, pl. xvii.	870
Somimerula (n. sect.)...	Turdus gigas, Fraser........	Proc. Zool. Soc. London, 1859, p. 332....	149
Siphonorhis	Caprimulgus americanus, Linn.	Proc. Zool. Soc. London, 1861, p. 77....	212
Sphenopsis............	Sphenopsis ignobilis, Scl.....	Proc. Zool. Soc. London, 1861, p. 379....	229
Spodiornis............	Spodiornis jardinii, Scl......	Proc. Zool. Soc. London, 1856, p. 323....	387
Stegnolæma	Ortalida montagnii, Bp......	Proc. Zool. Soc. London, 1870, p. 521....	516
Stigmatura...........	Culicivora budytoides, Lafr. et D'Orb.	Proc. Zool. Soc. London, 1866, p. 188....	380
Sublegatus	Sublegatus glaber, Scl. et Salv.	Proc. Zool. Soc. London, 1868, p. 172, pl. xiii. fig. 2.	435
Tabara, err. pro Taraba, Less.	Thamnophilus major, Vieill..	Cat. American Birds, p. 172 (1862).....	8

List of new families and genera described—Continued.

Name.	Type species.	Place of description.	No. of paper.
Thamnistes............	Thamnistes anabatinus, Scl. et Salv.	Proc. Zool. Soc. London, 1860, p. 209....	182
Thamnocharis........	Grallaria dignissima, Scl. and Salv.	Cat. B. Brit. Mus., XV, pp. 306, 310 (1890).	22
Thaumasius, n o m . emend. pro Thaumatias, Gould.	....	Proc. Zool. Soc. London, 1870, p. 146....	811
Thripadectes, Scl. MS..	Anabates flammulatus, Eyton	Cat. American Birds, p. 157 (1862).....	8
Thryomanes...........	Troglodytes bewickii, Aud...	Cat. American Birds, p. 22 (1862)......	8
Thyrorhina............	Crex schomburgki, Cab......	Proc. Zool. Soc. London, 1868, p. 458....	448
Todidæ................	....	Ibis, 1872, p. 160......................	602
Tyranneutes	Tyranneutes brachyurus, Scl. et Salv.	Ibis, 1881, p. 268.....................	891
Uropsila...............	Troglodytes leucogastra, Gould.	Nomencl. Av. Neotrop., pp. 7, 155 (1873).	13

PART IV

LIST OF NEW SPECIES DESCRIBED.

Name.	Locality.	Location of type.	Place of description.	No. of paper.
Accipiter collaris (Kaup MS.).	Colombia	Brit. Mus.	Ibis, 1860, p. 148, pl. vi	201
—— haplochrous	New Caledonia	Gurney Coll	Ibis, 1859, p. 275, pl. viii	157
—— ventralis	Colombia	……do	Proc. Zool. Soc. London, 1866, p. 303.	385
Ægotheles albertisi	Atam, Arfak Mountains, New Guinea.	D'Albertis Coll	Proc. Zool. Soc. London, 1873, p. 696.	628
Agathopus micropterus.	Rio Napo	Sclater Coll. in Brit. Mus.	Proc. Zool. Soc. London, 1858, p. 69.	116
Agelæus forbesi	Pernambuco	……do	Cat. B. Brit. Mus., XI, p. 345 (1886).	19
—— inuthurni	British Guiana	……do	Proc. Zool. Soc. London, 1881, p. 213.	871
Agriornis andicola	Panza, Ecuador	……do	Proc. Zool. Soc. London, 1860, p. 78.	164
—— insolens	Tinta, Peru	……do	Proc. Zool. Soc. London, 1869, p. 153.	471
—— pollens, new name for A. andicola, preoccupied.	Panza, Ecuador	……do	……do	471
—— solitaria	Titiacun, Ecuador.	……do	Proc. Zool. Soc. London, 1858, p. 553.	134
Amydrus frater	Socotra	Brit. Mus.	Proc. Zool. Soc. London, 1881, p. 171.	870
—— tristramii	Palestine	Tristram Coll	Ann. and Mag. Nat. Hist., ser. 3, II, p. 465 (1858).	136
Anabates cervinigularis.	Cordova, S. Mexico.	Salló Coll	Proc. Zool. Soc. London, 1856, p. 288.	92
—— erythropterus	Bogota	Sclater Coll. in Brit. Mus.	Proc. Zool. Soc. London, 1856, p. 27.	84
—— infuscatus	E. Peru	……do	Ann. and Mag. Nat. Hist., ser. 2, XVII, p. 468 (1856).	94
—— lineaticeps	……do	……do	……do	94
—— melanopezus	Rio Napo	……do	Proc. Zool. Soc. London, 1858, p. 61.	116
—— pulvericolor (Lafr. MS.).	……do	Lafresnaye Coll	Proc. Zool. Soc. London, 1858, p. 62.	116
—— rubiginosus	Cordova, S. Mexico.	Salló Coll.	Proc. Zool. Soc. London, 1856, p. 288.	92
—— striaticollis (Lafr. MS.).	Bogota	Sclater Coll. in Brit. Mus.	Proc. Zool. Soc. London, 1857, p. 17.	99
—— subataris	Pallatanga, Ecuador.	……do	Proc. Zool. Soc. London, 1859, p. 141.	143
—— temporalis	……do	……do	……do	143
Anabazenops guttulatus.	Caracas, Venezuela.	Paris Mus	Proc. Zool. Soc. London, 1857, p. 272, pl. cxxx.	114
—— oleagineus	Catamarca, Argentine Republic.	Sclater Coll. in Brit. Mus.	Proc. Zool. Soc. London, 1883, p. 654.	946
—— variegaticeps	Cordova, S. Mexico.	Salló Coll	Proc. Zool. Soc. London, 1856, p. 289.	92
Anæretes flavirostris.	Tilotilo, Yungas, Bolivia.	Salvin-Godman Coll. in Brit. Mus.	Proc. Zool. Soc. London, 1876, p. 355.	723
Anas melleri	Madagascar	Royal Inst., Woolwich.	Proc. Zool. Soc. London, 1864, p. 487, pl. xxxiv.	326
—— wyvilliana	Sandwich Islands.	Challenger Coll. in Brit. Mus.	Proc. Zool. Soc. London, 1878, p. 350.	782
Anthus bogotensis	Santa Fé di Bogota.	Sclater Coll. in Brit. Mus.	Proc. Zool. Soc. London, 1855, p. 109, pl. cf.	76
—— nattereri	Sao Paulo, Brazil.	……do	Ibis, 1878, p. 366, pl. x	804
Antrostomus ornatus.	Brazil	Brit. Mus.	Proc. Zool. Soc. London, 1866, p. 586, pl. xlv.	392
Ara couloni	Peru	Neuchâtel Mus	Proc. Zool. Soc. London, 1876, p. 255.	717
Aramides calopterus	Sarayacu, Ecuador	Salvin-Godman Coll. in Brit. Mus.	Proc. Zool. Soc. London, 1878, p. 439, pl. xxviii.	786

List of New Species Described—Continued.

Name.	Locality.	Location of type.	Place of description.	No. of paper.
Arremon axillaris.....	Colombia	Sclater Coll. in Brit. Mus.	Tanagrarum Catalogus Specificus,pp.3,15(1854); Proc. Zool. Soc. London, 1854, p. 97.	2,58
—— dovillii,Bp. MS...	Goyaz, Brazil.....	Paris Mus.............	Proc. Zool. Soc. London, 1856, p. 81.	86
—— d'orbignii.........	Yungas, Bolivia .	.....do	.....do	86
—— erythrorhynchus.	Bogota............	Gould Coll.............	Proc. Zool. Soc. London, 1855, p. 83, pl. lxxxix.	74
—— mysticalis........	Colombia	Mus. d'Hist.Nat. Paris	Rev.et Mag. de Zool.,1852, p. 8.	49
—— nigrirostris	Cosnipata, S. Peru	Sclater Coll. in Brit. Mus.	Cat. B. Brit. Mus., XI, p. 276 (1886).	19
—— spectabilis	Quijos, Ecuador...	Gould Coll.............	Proc. Zool. Soc. London, 1854, p. 114, pl. lxvii.	59
—— wuchereri........	Bahia, Brazil......	Salvin-Godman Coll. in Brit. Mus.	Nomencl.Av.Neotrop.,pp. 25, 157 (1873).	13
Artamus insignis.....	New Ireland......	Tweeddale Coll. in Brit. Mus.	Proc. Zool. Soc. London, 1877, p. 101, pl. xv.	750
Asturina ruficauda...	(?)	(?)	Proc. Zool. Soc. London, 1869, p. 133.	465
—— saturata..........	Tilotilo and Apollo, Yungas, Bolivia.	Salvin-Godman Coll. in Brit. Mus.	Proc. Zool. Soc. London, 1876, p. 357.	723
Ateles rufiventris....	R. Atrato, Columbia.	Zool. Soc. Menagerie..	Proc. Zool. Soc. London, 1872, p. 688, pl. lvii.	592
Attagis chimborazensis.	Chimborazo, Ecuador.	Sclater Coll. in Brit. Mus.	Proc. Zool. Soc. London, 1860, p. 82.	164
Attila citriniventris..	R. Ucayali	.....do	Proc. Zool. Soc. London, 1859, p. 40.	139
—— torridus..........	Babahoyo, Ecuador.	.....do	Proc. Zool. Soc. London, 1860, p. 280.	180
Automolus dorsalis...	Sarayacu,Ecuador	Salvin-Godman Coll. in Brit. Mus.	Proc. Zool. Soc. London, 1880, p. 158.	848
—— holostictus.......	Antioquia,Colombia.	Sclater Coll. in Brit. Mus.	Proc. Zool. Soc. London, 1875, p. 542.	696
—— ignobilis	.....do	.....do	Proc. Zool. Soc. London, 1879, p. 522.	825
—— rubidus	Brazil (?)	.....do	Proc. Zool. Soc. London, 1883, p. 654.	946
—— striaticeps	Bogota,Colombia..	.....do	Proc. Zool. Soc. London, 1875, p. 37.	678
Basileuterus castaneiceps.	Jima, Ecuador	Salvin-Godman Coll. in Brit. Mus.	Proc. Zool. Soc. London, 1877, p. 521.	759
—— cinereicollis	Colombia	Sclater Coll. in Brit. Mus.	Proc. Zool. Soc. London, 1864, p. 166.	311
—— euophrys.........	Tilotilo, Yungas, Bolivia.	Salvin-Godman Coll. in Brit. Mus.	Proc. Zool. Soc. London, 1876, p. 352.	723
—— fraseri...........	Pallatanga, Ecuador.	Sclater Coll. in Brit. Mus.	Proc. Zool. Soc. London, 1883, p. 653, pl. lxi.	946
—— griseiceps	Caripé, Venezuela	.....do	Proc. Zool. Soc. London, 1868, p. 170.	435
—— leucopygius	Costa Rica........	Sclater and Salvin-Godman Coll. in Brit. Mus.	Nomencl.Av.Neotrop.,pp. 10, 156 (1873).	13
—— mesochrysus	Bogota............	Sclater Coll. in Brit. Mus.	Proc. Zool. Soc. London, 1860, p. 251.	178
—— mesoleucus.......	Demerara.........	Hartlaub Coll........	Proc. Zool. Soc. London, 1865, p. 286, pl. ix, fig. 1.	341
—— semicervinus.....	Nanegal, Ecuador.	Sclater Coll. in Brit. Mus.	Proc. Zool. Soc. London, 1860, p. 84.	165
—— uropygialis......	Brazil	.....do	Proc. Zool. Soc. London, 1861, p. 128.	215
Brachygalba fulviventris.	Bogota............	.....do	Cat. B. Brit. Mus., XIX, p. 172 (1891).	24
—— goeringi..........	Lake of Valentia, Venezuela.	.....do	Proc. Zool. Soc. London, 1860, p. 253, pl. xviii.	473
—— melanosterna	Goyaz, Brazil; Guarayos Bolivia.	Professor Bohn Coll., Kiel.	Proc. Zool. Soc. London, 1855, p. 15.	69
—— salmoni	Neche, Antioquia.	Sclater Coll. and Salvin-Godman Coll. in Brit. Mus.	Proc. Zool. Soc. London, 1879, p. 535.	825
Brotogerys chrysosema, Natt. MS.	Brazil	Bremen Mus........	Proc. Zool. Soc. London, 1864, p. 208.	320
Buarremon castaneiceps.	Rio Napo, Ecuador.	Sclater Coll. in Brit. Mus.	Proc. Zool. Soc. London, 1859, p. 441.	154
—— castaneifrons	Paramo de la Culata, Merida, Venezuela.	.....do	Proc. Zool. Soc. London, 1875, p. 235, pl. xxxv, fig. 1.	686
—— comptus	Maraviña, Ecuador.	Salvin-Godman Coll. in Brit. Mus.	Ibis, 1879, p. 427...........	838

List of new species described—Continued.

Name.	Locality.	Location of type.	Place of description.	No. of paper.
Buarremon elæoprorus	Santa Elena, Antioquia.	Salvin-Godman Coll. in Brit. Mus.	Proc. Zool. Soc. London, 1879, p. 504.	825
—— inornatus	Pallatauga, Ecuador.	Sclater Coll. in Brit. Mus.	Ibis, 1879, p. 427	838
—— leucopis	Yauayaca, Ecuador.	Salvin-Godman Coll. in Brit. Mus.	Proc. Zool. Soc. London, 1878 p. 439.	786
—— melanolæmus	Khachupata, Peru.	..... do	Ibis, 1879, p. 425, pl. x, fig 2.	838
—— melanops	Simacu, Bolivia	..... do	Proc. Zool. Soc. London, 1876, p. 253.	715
—— meridæ	Merida, Venezuela.	Sclater Coll. in Brit. Mus.	Proc. Zool. Soc. London, 1870, p. 785.	520
—— nationi	Lima, Peru	..... do	Proc. Zool. Soc. London, 1881, p. 485, pl. xlvi.	680
—— phæopleurus	Caracas, Venezuela.	Paris Mus	Proc. Zool. Soc. London, 1856, p. 85.	86
—— spodionotus	Guapulo, Ecuador.	Sclater Coll. in Brit. Mus.	Ibis, 1879, p. 425	838
—— taczanowskii	Higos, Peru	..... do	Proc. Zool. Soc. London, 1875, p. 236, pl. xxxv, fig. 2.	686
Bubalis swaynei	Somaliland	Brit. Mus	Proc. Zool. Soc. London, 1892, p. 100, pl. v.	1137
Bucco dysoni, Gray MS.	Honduras	..... do	Proc. Zool. Soc. London, 1855, p. 193.	78
—— leucocrissus	Babahoyo, Ecuador.	Sclater Coll. in Brit. Mus.	Proc. Zool. Soc. London, 1860, p. 284.	180
—— napensis, Scl. MS.	Rio Napo	..... do	Cat. American Birds, p. 260 (1862).	8
—— picatus	Chamicuros	Gould Coll	Proc. Zool. Soc. London, 1855, p. 194.	78
—— pulmentum (Bp. et Verr. MS.)	Upper Amazon	Sclater Coll. in Brit. Mus.	Proc. Zool. Soc. London, 1855, p. 194, pl. cvi.	78
—— radiatus	Colombia	Brit. Mus	Proc. Zool. Soc. London, 1853, p. 122, pl. l.	55
—— striatipectus	Bolivia	Derby Mus	Proc. Zool. Soc. London, 1853, p. 123.	55
—— subtectus	Esmeraldas, Ecuador.	Sclater Coll. in Brit. Mus.	Proc. Zool. Soc. London, 1860, p. 296.	181
Buceros subcylindricus.	West Africa	Brit. Mus	Proc. Zool. Soc. London, 1870, p. 668, pl. xxxix.	518
Buteo fuliginosus	North Mexico	Norwich Mus	Proc. Zool. Soc. London, 1858, p. 356.	127
—— zonocercus	Guatemala	..... do	Proc. Zool. Soc. London, 1858, p. 130.	118
Buthraupis aroæi	Cordillera de Chucu, Veragua.	Salvin-Godman Coll. in Brit. Mus.	Proc. Zool. Soc. London, 1869, p. 439, pl. xxxi.	484
—— chloronota	Ecuador	Sclater Coll. in Brit. Mus.	Tanagrarum Catalogue Speciticus, pp. 10, 15 (1854); Proc. Zool. Soc. London, 1854, p. 97, pl. lxiv.	2, 58
Cacatua gymnopis	South Australia.	Zool. Soc. Menagerie.	Proc. Zool. Soc. London, 1871, p. 493.	550
—— ophthalmica	Solomon Islands.	Brit. Mus	Proc. Zool. Soc. London, 1864, p. 188.	315
Cactornis abingdoni	Abingdon Island, Galapagos.	Salvin-Godman Coll. in Brit. Mus.	Proc. Zool. Soc. London, 1870, p. 326.	513
—— pallida	Indefatigable Island.	..... do	Proc. Zool. Soc. London, 1870, p. 327.	513
Callisto argyrofenges.	Tilotilo, Yungas, Bolivia.	..... do	Proc. Zool. Soc. London, 1876, p. 354, pl. xxx fig. 2.	723
—— cabanisi (C. sclateri, Cab.).	Guatemala	Berlin Mus	Ibis, 1868, p. 71, pl. iii	460
—— castaneoventris.	Bolivia	Earl of Derby	Contr. to Ornith., 1851, p. 61.	35
—— castanonota	South Brazil	Strickland Coll	Contr. to Ornith., 1851, p. 63.	35
—— chrysonota	Cayenne	Sclater Coll. in Brit. Mus.	Contr. to Ornith., 1850, p. 50.	33
—— chrysophrys	Colombia, Venezuela, Trinidad.	..... do	Contr. to Ornith., 1851, p. 24, pl. lxix, fig. 2.	34
—— cœlicolor	Colombia	..... do	Contr. to Ornith., 1851, p. 51.	35
—— cyanescens	Caracas, Venezuela.	Brit. Mus	Proc. Zool. Soc. London, 1850, p. 260.	86b
—— cyanopygia	Esmeraldas, Ecuador.	Sclater Coll. in Brit. Mus.	Proc. Zool. Soc London, 1883, p. 653.	946
—— cyanotis	Peru	..... do	Proc. Zool. Soc. London, 1858, p. 294.	125

List of new species described—Continued.

Name.	Locality.	Location of type.	Place of description.	No. of paper.
Calliste florida	Costa Rica........	Salvin-Godman Coll. in Brit. Mus.	Proc. Zool. Soc. London, 1869, p. 416, pl. xxviii.	479
—— franciscæ, nom. emend. pro C. fauny.	....	....	Proc. Zool. Soc. London, 1856, p. 142.	89
—— fulvicervix......	Tilotilo, Yungas, Bolivia.	Salvin-Godman Coll. in Brit. Mus.	Proc. Zool. Soc. London, 1876, p. 354, pl. xxx, fig. 1.	723
—— gouldi...........	S. Brazil........	Brit. Mus.............	Proc. Zool. Soc. London, 1885, p. 849.	991
— - lamprotis	Bolivia	...do	Contr. to Ornith., 1851, p. 65.	35
—— leucotis	Ecuador	Sclater Coll. in Brit. Mus.	Contr. to Ornith., 1851, p. 58.	35
—— lunigera..........	Rio Negro	Edward Wilson.......	Contr. to Ornith., 1851, p. 65, pl. lxx, fig. 2.	35
—— melanotis	Rio Napo, Ecuador.	Sclater Coll. in Brit. Mus.	Ibis, 1876, p. 408, pl. xii, fig. 1.	741
—— punctulata	Tilotilo, Yungas, Bolivia.	Salvin-Godman Coll. in Brit. Mus.	Proc. Zool. Soc. London, 1876, p. 353.	723
—— ruficapilla.......	Bogota............	Sclater Coll. in Brit. Mus.	Contr. to Ornith., 1851, p. 61.	35
—— rufigenis	Venezuela.........	...do	Proc. Zool. Soc. London, 1856, p. 311.	98
—— venusta	Colombia and Quijos, Ecuador.	...do	Proc. Zool. Soc. London, 1854, p. 248.	61
—— vieilloti	Trinidad..........	...do	Proc. Zool. Soc. London, 1856, p. 257.	86b
—— virescens.........	Cayenne	...do	Contr. to Ornith., 1851, p. 22, pl. lxix, fig. 1.	34
—— xanthogastra.....	Rio Negro	Edward Wilson.......	Contr. to Ornith., 1851, p. 23.	34
Calornis crassa.......	Larat, Tenimber Islands.	Brit. Mus.............	Proc. Zool. Soc. London, 1883, p. 56, pl. xiv.	926
Camarhynchus habeli.	Abingdon and Bindloes islands, Galapagos.	Salvin-Godman Coll. in Brit. Mus.	Proc. Zool. Soc. London, 1870, p. 325.	513
—— prosthemelas.....	Indefatigable Island.	...do	Proc. Zool. Soc. London, 1870, p. 325.	513
—— variogatus	Abingdon and Bindloes islands, Galapagos.	...do	Proc. Zool. Soc. London, 1870, p. 324.	513
Campephaga aurulenta.	Sorong, New Guinea.	D'Albertis Coll	Proc. Zool. Soc. London, 1873, p. 692, pl. liv.	628
Camptostoma flaviventre.	Isthmus of Panama.	Salvin-Godman Coll. in Brit. Mus.	Proc. Zool. Soc. London, 1864, p. 358.	322
—— imberbe..........	S. Andres Tuxtla, Mexico.	Sallé Coll	Proc. Zool. Soc. London, 1857, p. 203.	108
Campylorhynchus gularis.	Mexico	Sclater Coll. in Brit. Mus.	Proc. Zool. Soc. London, 1860, p. 462.	197
—— humilis	Mazatlan, Mexico.	Acad. of Nat. Sci. Philadelphia.	Proc. Acad. Nat. Sci. Philadelphia, 1856, p. 263.	96
—— jocosus...........	Oaxaca, Mexico...	Sclater Coll. in Brit. Mus.	Proc. Zool. Soc. London, 1859, p. 371.	153
—— nigriceps.........	Vera Cruz, Mexico.	...do	Proc. Zool. Soc. London, 1860, p. 461.	197
—— pardus	Santa Marta, Colombia.	G. N. Lawrence Coll ..	Proc. Zool. Soc. London, 1857, p. 271.	114
—— striaticollis	Colombia..........	Sclater Coll. in Brit. Mus.	Proc. Zool. Soc. London, 1857, p. 272.	114
Canis lateralis........	Gaboon, W. Africa.	Zool. Soc. Menagerie...	Proc. Zool. Soc. London, 1870, p. 279, pl. xxiii.	512
—— microtis..........	Amazons	Zool. Soc. Menagerie (Now in Brit. Mus.)	Proc. Zool. Soc. London, 1882, p. 631, p. xlvii.	917
—— niger	Lanak Pass, Thibet.	Zool. Soc. Menagerie (Now in Paris Mus.)	Proc. Zool. Soc. London, 1874, p. 655, pl. lxxviii.	667
Capito melanotis, Hartl. MS.	Rio Javari........	Sclater Coll. in Brit. Mus.	Ibis, 1861, p. 190	230
—— steerii...........	Moyobamba, Peru.	Steere Coll	Proc. Zool. Soc. London, 1878, p. 140, pl. xii.	775
—— tschudii.........	E. Peru	Bremen Mus..........	Ibis, 1861, p. 188	236
Carpophaga melanochroa.	Duke of York Island.	Salvin-Godman Coll. in Brit. Mus.	Proc. Zool. Soc. London, 1878, p. 672, pl. xlii.	796
—— rhodinolæma.....	Admiralty Islands.	Challenger Coll.......	Proc. Zool. Soc. London, 1877, p. 555.	762
Casiornis fusca.......	Bahia, Brazil	Sclater Coll. in Brit. Mus.	Nomencl. Av. Neotrop., pp. 57, 159 (1873).	13
Cassiculus flavicrissus.	Babahoyo, Ecuador.	...do	Proc. Zool. Soc. London, 1860, p. 276.	180
—— microrhynchus...	Isthmus of Panama.	...do	Proc. Zool. Soc. London, 1864, p. 353.	322

List of new species described—Continued.

Name.	Locality.	Location of type.	Place of description.	No. of paper.
Casuarius beccarii....	Wokan, Aroo Islands.	Genoa Mus. (Museo Civico).	Proc. Zool. Soc. London, 1875, p. 87.	684
—— bicarunculatus...	Moluccas (?)......	Zool. Soc. Menagerie...	Proc. Zool. Soc. London, 1860, p. 248.	177
—— picticollis........	New Guinea......	.....do	Proc. Zool. Soc. London, 1875, p. 85, pl. xviii.	684
—— westermanni.....	Munsinam, New Guinea.	.....do	Proc. Zool. Soc. London, 1874, p. 248.	657
Catamenia homochroa.	Matos, Ecuador ..	Sclater Coll. in Brit. Mus.	Proc. Zool. Soc. London, 1858. p. 552.	134
Catharus montalis....	Tilotilo, Yungas, Bolivia.	Salvin-Godman Coll. in Brit. Mus.	Proc. Zool. Soc. London, 1870, p. 352.	723
—— occidentalis	Oaxaca, W. Mexico.	Sclater Coll. in Brit. Mus.	Proc. Zool. Soc. London, 1859, p. 323.	149
—— phæopleurus.....	Antioquia, Colombia.	.....do	Proc. Zool. Soc. London, 1875, p. 541.	696
Celeus citreopygius, Bp. MS.	Yurimaguas, Peru.	..... do	Proc. Zool. Soc. London, 1867, p. 758.	417
—— spectabilis	Sarayacu, Ecuador.	Salvin-Godman Coll. in Brit. Mus.	Proc. Zool. Soc. London, 1880, p. 161.	848
—— subflavus	Bahia, Brazil	Sclater Coll. in Brit. Mus.	Proc. Zool. Soc. London, 1877, p. 21.	745
Centrites oreas	Tinta, Peru......	.....do	Proc. Zool. Soc. London, 1869, p. 154.	471
Centropsar mirus.....	Western Mexico...	.....do	Proc. Zool. Soc. London, 1871, p. 176, pl. xxvi.	653
Cephalopterus penduliger.	Pallatanga, Ecuador.	.....do	Ibis, 1859, p. 114, pl. iii; Proc. Zool. Soc. London, 1859, p. 142.	143
Cercomacra carbonaria, Natt. MS.	Rio Brancho, Guiana.	.....do	Nomencl. Av. Neotrop., pp. 73, 161 (1873).	13
—— hypomelæna	Cosnipata, S. W. Peru.	Salvin-Godman Coll. in Brit. Mus.	Cat. B. Brit. Mus. XV, p. 268 (1890).	22
—— maculosa	Babahoyo, Ecuador.	Sclater Coll. in Brit. Mus.	Proc. Zool. Soc. London, 1860, p. 279.	180
—— naponsis, Scl. MS.	Rio Napo, Ecuador.	.....do	Proc. Zool. Soc. London, 1868, p. 572.	454
—— nigricans	Santa Marta, Colombia.	.....do	Proc. Zool. Soc. London, 1858, p. 245.	122
Cercopithecus moloneyi.	Lake Nyassa.....	Mus. P. L. S	Proc. Zool. Soc. London, 1893, p. 252, pl. xvii.	1166
—— opisthostictus ...	Lake Mweru, British Central Africa.	.....do	Proc. Zool. Soc. London, 1893, p. 725.	1182
—— stairsi	Zambezi River....	Zool. Soc. Menagerie (Now in Brit. Mus.).	Proc. Zool. Soc. London, 1892, p. 580, pl. xl.	1152
Certhidea fusca.......	Abingdon and Bindloes islands, Galapagos.	Salvin-Godman Coll. in Brit. Mus.	Proc. Zool. Soc. London, 1870, p. 324.	513
Certhiola mexicana...	South Mexico.....	Sallé Coll	Proc. Zool. Soc. London, 1856, p. 286.	92
Cervulus crinifrons...	Ningpo, China	Zool. Soc. Menagerie (?)	Proc. Zool. Soc. London, 1885, p. 1, pl. i.	971
—— micrurus.........	China............	.....do	Proc. Zool. Soc. London, 1875, p. 421, pl. li, fig. 1.	692
Cervus alfredi	Malayan Peninsula.	.....do	Proc. Zool. Soc. London, 1870, p. 381, pl. xxviii.	515
—— cuopis, Swinhoe MS.	Northern China ..	.....do	Proc. Zool. Soc. London, 1874, p. 151.	651
—— swinhoei	Formosa.........	.....do	Proc. Zool. Soc. London, 1862, p. 152, pl. xvii.	260
Chætoceras burmeisteri.	Tucuman	Nat. Mus. Buenos Aires.	Proc. Zool. Soc. London, 1887, p. 639.	1035
Chætura biscutata....	Ypanema, Brazil..	Sclater Coll. in Brit. Mus.	Proc. Zool. Soc. London, 1865, p. 609, pl. xxxiv.	354
—— brachycerca......	Xeberos, E. Peru..	.....do	Proc. Zool. Soc. London, 1867, p. 758, pl. xxxiv.	417
—— cassini	Gaboon..........	Brit. Mus	Proc. Zool. Soc. London, 1863, p. 205, pl. xiv, fig. 2.	287
—— cinereiventris, Scl. MS.	Brazil	Sclater Coll. in Brit. Mus.	Cat. American Birds, p. 283 (1862).	8
Chamæpelia buckleyi.	Santa Rita, Ecuador.	Salvin-Godman Coll. in Brit. Mus.	Proc. Zool. Soc. London, 1877, p. 21.	745
Chamæza mollissima .	Santa Fé di Bogota.	Brit. Mus	Proc. Zool. Soc. London, 1855, p. 89. pl. xcv.	75
Chauna nigricollis...	Rio Dekke, Colombia.	Zool. Soc. Menagerie..	Proc. Zool. Soc. London, 1864. p. 75, pl. xi.	305
Chelidoptera brasiliensis.	S. E. Brazil.......	Sclater Coll. in Brit. Mus.	Cat. American Birds, p. 275 (1862).	8
Chiroxiphia regina (Natt. MS.).	Borba, Brazil	Vienna Mus	Ann. and Mag. Nat. Hist., ser. 2, XVII, p. 469 (1856).	94

List of new species described—Continued.

Name.	Locality.	Location of type.	Place of description.	No. of paper.
Chloëphaga rubidi-ceps.	Falkland Islands.	Brit. Mus..............	Proc. Zool. Soc. London, 1860, p. 387, pl. clxxiii.	189
Chlorochrysa nitidis-sima.	Antioquia........	Sclater Coll. in Brit. Mus.	Proc. Zool. Soc. London, 1873, p. 728.	029
Chloronerpes dignus..	.....do	.....do	Proc. Zool. Soc. London, 1877, p. 20, pl. i.	745
—— malherbii	Ecuador	.....do	Cat. American Birds, p. 338 (1862).	8
—— xanthochlorus ...	San Cristoval, Venezuela.	.....do	Proc. Zool. Soc. London, 1875, p. 238.	686
Chlorophanes guate-malensis.	Guatemala	.....do	Proc. Zool. Soc. London, 1861, p. 129.	215
—— purpurascens	Caracas, Venezu-ela.	.....do .	Nomencl. Av. Neotrop., pp. 16, 157 (1873).	13
Chlorophoniaflaviros-tris.	Ecuador	.....do	Proc. Zool. Soc. London, 1861, p. 129.	215
Chloropipo holo-chlora.	Bogota.............	.....do	Cat. B. Brit. Mus., XIV, p. 287 (1888).	20
Chlorospingus calo-phrys.	Tilotilo, Yungas, Bolivia.	Salvin-Godman Coll. in Brit. Mus.	Proc. Zool. Soc. London, 1876. p. 354.	723
—— castaneicollis	Peru............	Sclater Coll. in Brit. Mus.	Proc. Zool. Soc. London, 1858, p. 293.	125
—— chrysophrys	Merida, Venezu-ela.	.....do	Proc. Zool. Soc. London, 1875, p. 235.	686
—— flaviventris	Trinidad..........	Jardine Coll	Proc. Zool. Soc. London, 1856, p. 91.	86
—— goeringi	Paramos of Meri-da, Venezuela.	Sclater Coll. in Brit. Mus.	Proc. Zool. Soc. London, 1870, p. 784, pl. xlvi, fig. 1.	520
—— hypophæus	Calovevora, Ver-agua.	Salvin-Godman Coll. in Brit. Mus.	Proc. Zool. Soc. London, 1868, p. 389.	445
—— lichtensteini.....	Bogota............	Berlin Mus	Proc. Zool. Soc. London, 1856, p. 30.	84
—— melanotis	Colombia	Brit. Mus.............	Proc. Zool. Soc. London, 1854, p. 157, pl. lxviii.	60
—— oleagineus	.....do	Sclater Coll. in Brit. Mus.	Proc. Zool. Soc. London, 1862, p. 110.	255
—— phæocephalus....	Jina, Ecuador....	Salvin-Godman Coll. in Brit. Mus.	Proc. Zool. Soc. London, 1877, p. 521, pl. lii. fig. 2.	759
—— punctulatus......	Cordillera de Chucu, Veragua.	.....do	Proc. Zool. Soc. London, 1869, p. 440.	484
—— semifuscus......	Quito, Ecuador...	.....do	Nomencl. Av. Neotrop., pp. 24, 157 (1873).	13
—— xanthophrys....	Bogota	Sclater Coll. in Brit. Mus.	Proc. Zool. Soc. London, 1856, p. 30.	84
Chrysomitris uropy-gialis, Scl. MS.	Chili	.....do	Cat. American Birds, p. 125 (1862).	8
Chrysotis cœligena, Lawr. MS.	(?)	Zool. Soc. Menagerie ..	Proc. Zool. Soc. London, 1879, p. 815; 1880, p. 68, pl. ix, fig. 1.	846
—— finschi	Mexico	Brit. Mus...........	Proc. Zool. Soc. London, 1864, p. 298.	320
—— guatemalæ, Hartl. MS.	Honduras	Sclater Coll. in Brit. Mus.	Ibis, 1860, p. 44............	200
—— sallæi	San Domingo.....	Paris Mus...........	Proc. Zool. Soc. London, 1857, p. 224.	110
Ciccaba nigrolineata..	Southern Mexico.	Norwich Mus........	Proc. Zool. Soc. London, 1859, p. 131.	140
Cinclocerthia macro-rhyncha.	St. Lucia, West Indies.	Paris Mus...........	Proc. Zool. Soc. London, 1866, p. 320.	387
Cinclodes albidiven-tris.	Chimborazo, Ec-uador.	Sclater Coll. in Brit. Mus.	Proc. Zool. Soc. London, 1860, p. 77.	164
—— bifasciatus.......	Bolivia	Derby Mus..........	Proc. Zool. Soc. London, 1858, p. 448.	130
—— excelsior.........	Chimborazo, Ec-uador.	Sclater Coll. in Brit. Mus.	Proc. Zool. Soc. London, 1860, p. 77.	164
Cinclus leuconotus...	Bogota	.....do	Proc. Zool. Soc. London, 1857, p. 274.	114
Cinnyris balfouri.....	Socotra	Brit. Mus............	Proc. Zool. Soc. London, 1881, p. 169, pl. xv, fig. 2.	870
Cisticola incana......	.....do	.....do	Proc. Zool. Soc. London, 1881, p. 166, pl. xv, fig. 1.	870
Clatothcrus elegans...	Dueñas, Guate-mala.	Salvin-Godman Coll. in Brit. Mus.	Ibis, 1859, p. 8............	156
Climacteris placens...	Atam, Arfak Mountains, New Guinea.	D'Albertis Coll.......	Proc. Zool. Soc. London, 1873, p. 693.	628
Cnipodectes minor....	Chamicuros, Peru.	Sclater Coll. in Brit. Mus.	Proc. Zool. Soc. London, 1883, p. 654.	946
Cnipolegus cinereus..	Corumba, Para-guay.	Smithsonian Institu-tion.	Proc. Zool. Soc. London, 1870, p. 58.	501
—— hudsoni.........	Rio Negro, Pata-gonia.	Sclater Coll. in Brit. Mus.	Proc. Zool. Soc. London, 1872, p. 541, pl. xxxi.	584

List of new species described—Continued.

Name.	Locality.	Location of type.	Place of description.	No. of paper.
Cnipolegus pusillus...	Lower Amazons..	Sclater Coll. in Brit. Mus.	Nomencl. Av. Neotrop., pp. 43, 158 (1873).	13
Cobus crawshayi.....	Lake Mweru, British Central Africa.	Brit. Mus. (?).........	Proc. Zool. Soc. London, 1893, p. 726.	1182
Coccothraustes maculipennis.	Mexico......	Sclater Coll. in Brit. Mus.	Proc. Zool. Soc. London, 1860, p. 251, pl. clxiii.	178
Coccyzus bairdi......	Jamaica	....do	Proc. Zool. Soc. London, 1864, p. 120.	308
Cœreba carneipes (?).	Playa Viconto, Mexico.	....do	Proc. Zool. Soc. London, 1859, p. 376.	153
—— lucida............	Guatemala.......	....do	Ibis, 1859, p. 14............	156
Colobus angolensis..	Angola	Brit. Mus............	Proc. Zool. Soc. London, 1860, p. 245.	176
Columba albipennis...	Pitumarca, Peru..	Salvin-Godman Coll. in Brit. Mus.	Proc. Zool. Soc. London, 1870, p. 18.	712
—— nigrirostris	Oaxaca, Mexico...	Sclater Coll. in Brit. Mus.	Proc. Zool. Soc. London, 1859, p. 390.	153
Conirostrum ferrugineiventre.	Bolivia	Derby Mus.........	Proc. Zool. Soc. London, 1855, p. 74, pl. lxxxv.	73
—— fraseri	Cuenca, Ecuador..	Sclater Coll. in Brit. Mus.	Proc. Zool. Soc. London, 1858, p. 452.	131
Conopophaga castaneiceps.	Bogota...........	....do	Proc. Zool. Soc. London, 1857, p. 47.	100
—— cucullata........	....do	....do	Proc. Zool. Soc. London, 1856, p. 29, pl. cxix.	84
—— gutturalis........	Colombia	....do	Proc. Zool. Soc. London, 1868, p. 574.	454
—— torrida..........	Rio Napo.........	....do	Proc. Zool. Soc. London, 1858, p. 68.	116
Contopus mesoleucus.	Orizaba...........	....do	Proc. Zool. Soc. London, 1859, p. 43.	139
—— ochraceus........	Costa Rica........	Salvin-Godman Coll. in Brit. Mus.	Proc. Zool. Soc. London, 1869, p. 419.	479
—— sordidulus	Mexico	Sclater Coll. in Brit. Mus.	Proc. Zool. Soc. London, 1859, p. 44.	139
Conurus egregius.....	Demerara........	Salvin-Godman Coll. in Brit. Mus.	Ibis, 1881, p. 130, pl. iv.....	890
—— holochlorus	Jalapa, Mexico....	Sclater Coll. in Brit. Mus.	Ann. and Mag. Nat. Hist., ser. 3, IV, p. 224 (1859).	161
—— ocularis..........	Isthmus of Panama.	Salvin-Godman Coll. in Brit. Mus.	Proc. Zool. Soc. London, 1864, p. 367.	322
—— propinquus, Scl. MS.	S. E. Brazil.......	Sclater Coll. in Brit. Mus.	Cat. American Birds, p. 340 (1862).	8
—— rhodocephalus ...	Merida, Venezuela	....do	Proc. Zool. Soc. London, 1870, p. 787.	520
—— rhodogaster, Natt. MS.	Borba, Brazil	Bremen Mus..........	Proc. Zool. Soc. London, 1864, p. 298. pl. xxiv.	320
—— rubritorquis	South America (?).	Sclater Coll. in Brit. Mus.	Proc. Zool. Soc. London, 1886, p. 539, pl. lvi.	1013
—— xantholæmus ...	St. Thomas, West Indies.	Newton Coll..........	Ann. and Mag. Nat. Hist., ser. 3. IV, p. 225 (1859).	161
Copsychus suavis.....	S. Borneo.........	Sclater Coll. in Brit. Mus.	Proc. Zool. Soc. London, 1861, p. 185.	216
Copurus fuscicapillus.	Colombia	....do	Proc. Zool. Soc. London, 1861, p. 381.	229
Corethrura rubra.....	Vera Paz, Guatemala.	Salvin-Godman Coll. in Brit. Mus.	Proc. Zool. Soc. London, 1860, p. 300.	182
Corvus capellanus....	Fao, Persian Gulf.	Zool.Soc.Menagerie ..	Proc. Zool. Soc. London, 1876, p. 694. pl. lxvi.	734
Cotinga porphyrolæma.	Sarayacu,Ucayali.	Mus.d'Hist.Nat.Paris	Rev. et Mag. de Zool., 1852, p. 226.	50
Cotyle fulvipennis....	Jalapa, S. Mexico.	Sclater Coll. in Brit. Mus.	Proc. Zool. Soc. London, 1859, p. 364.	152
Cracticus personatus, Temm. MS.	Lobo.............	Leyden Mus..........	Journ. of Proc. of Linn. Soc. London (Zool.), ser. 3, II, p. 162 (1858).	138
Crax erythrognatha..	Bogota, Colombia.	Salvin-Godman Coll. in Brit. Mus.	Proc. Zool. Soc. London, 1877, p. 22.	745
—— incommoda.......	(?).................	....do	Proc. Zool. Soc. London, 1872, p. 690.	592
—— viridirostris.....	(?).................	....do	Trans. Zool. Soc. London, IX, p. 282 (1875).	705
Creurgops verticalis, Verr. MS.	Rio Napo.........	Sclater Coll. in Brit. Mus.	Proc. Zool. Soc. London, 1858, p. 72, pl. cxxxii, fig. 2.	116
Crypturus bartletti...	E. Peru..........	Salvin-Godman Coll. in Brit. Mus.	Proc. Zool. Soc. London, 1873, p. 311.	614
—— corviniventris....	Venezuela	Sclater Coll. in Brit. Mus.	Proc. Zool. Soc. London, 1873, p. 512.	620
—— transfasciatus....	Santa Rosa, Ecuador.	Steere Coll..........	Proc. Zool. Soc. London, 1878, p. 141, pl. xiii.	775

List of new species described—Continued.

Name.	Locality.	Location of type.	Place of description.	No. of paper.
Culicivora boliviana..	Bolivia	Sclater Coll. in Brit. Mus.	Proc. Zool. Soc. London, 1852. p. 34, pl. xlvii.	53
Cyanocitta germana..	Belize.............	Salvin-Godman Coll. in Brit. Mus.	Proc. Zool. Soc. London, 1876, p. 270.	718
Cyanocorax nigriceps.	Tilotilo, Yungas, Bolivia.	Salvin-Godman Coll. in Brit. Mus.	Proc. Zool. Soc. London, 1876, p. 354.	723
Cyclopsitta suavissi- ma.	N a i a b u i, New Guinea.	D'Albertis Coll.......	Proc. Zool. Soc. London, 1876, p. 520, pl. liv.	733
Cyclorhis albiventris.	Bahia, Brazil......	Sclater Coll. and Salvin-Godman Coll. in Brit. Mus.	Nomencl. Av. Neotrop., pp. 13, 156 (1873).	13
—— atrirostris........	Ecuador	Salvin-Godman Coll. in Brit. Mus.	Ibis, 1887, p. 324, pl. x......	1037
—— flavipectus	Trinidad. Venezuela, Colombia.	Sclater Coll. in Brit. Mus.	Proc. Zool. Soc. London, 1858, p. 448.	130
—— virenticeps.......	Babahoyo, Ecuador.	.....do	Proc. Zool. Soc. London, 1860, p. 274, pl. clxiv.	180
Cyclorhynchus æqui- noctialis.	Rio Napo..........	.....do	Proc. Zool. Soc. London, 1858. p. 70.	116
—— cinereiceps.......	Oaxaca, Mexico...	.....do	Ibis, 1859, p. 443	159
—— fulvipectus	Nanegal, Ecuador.	.....do	Proc. Zool. Soc. London, 1860, p. 92.	165
—— subbrunneus......	Babahoyo, Ecuador.	.....do	Proc. Zool. Soc. London, 1860, p. 282.	180
Cyphorinus albigularis.	Isthmus of Panama.	Derby Mus..........	Proc. Zool. Soc. London, 1855, p. 76, pl. lxxxviii.	73
—— dichrous	Remedios, Antioquia.	Sclater Coll. in Brit. Mus.	Proc. Zool. Soc. London, 1879, p. 492, pl. xli.	825
—— phæocephalus....	Esmeraldas, Ecuador.	.....do	Proc. Zool. Soc. London, 1860, p. 291.	181
—— pusillus..........	Oaxaca, Mexico...	.....do	Proc. Zool. Soc. London, 1859, p. 372.	153
Cypselus infumatus..	Banjermassing, Borneo.	Wallace Coll..........	Proc. Zool. Soc. London, 1865, p. 602.	354
Dacnis cærebicolor....	Colombia (?)	Sclater Coll. in Brit. Mus.	Contr. to Ornith., 1851. p. 106.	40
—— egregia...........	Colombia	Brit. Mus..........	Proc. Zool. Soc. London, 1854, p. 251.	63
—— hartlaubi........	..do	.. do	Proc. Zool. Soc. London. 1854, p. 251.	63
—— pulcherrima......	..do	Sclater Coll. in Brit. Mus.	Rev. et Mag. de Zool., 1853. p. 480.	56
—— salmoni	Remedios, Antioquia.	....do	Cat. B. Brit. Mus., XI, p. 27, pl. ii, fig. 2 (1886).	19
Damalis hunteri	Tana River, N. E. Africa.	H. C. V. Hunter Coll ..	Proc. Zool. Soc. London, 1889, pp. 58. 372, pl. xlii.	1058 1072
Dasyprocta antillensis.	St. Lucia, West Indies.	Zool. Soc. Menagerie..	Proc. Zool. Soc. London, 1874, p. 666, pl. lxxxii.	668
Dendrocincla ruficeps	Isthmus of Panama.	Sclater Coll. in Brit. Mus.	Proc. Zool. Soc. London, 1868, p. 54.	431
Dendrocolaptes cytoni.	Capim River, Para, Brazil.	.....do	Proc. Zool. Soc. London, 1853, p. 69, pl. lii.	54
—— puncticollis	Vera Paz, Guatemala.	Sclater Coll. and Salvin-Godman Coll. in Brit. Mus.	Proc. Zool. Soc. London, 1868, p. 54, pl. v.	431
—— radiolatus, Scl. MS.	Yurimaguas, Peru	Sclater Coll. in Brit. Mus.	Proc. Zool. Soc. London, 1867, p. 755.	417
Dendrocygna discolor.	Venezuela, Guiana, and Brazil.	Salvin-Godman Coll. in Brit. Mus.	Nomencl. Av. Neotrop., pp. 129, 161 (1873).	13
Dendrœca chrysoparia.	Vera Paz, Guatemala.	.....do	Proc. Zool. Soc. London, 1860, p. 298.	182
Dendromanes homochrous.	Oaxaca, Mexico...	Sclater Coll. in Brit. Mus.	Proc. Zool. Soc. London, 1859, p. 382.	153
Dendrornis erythropygia.	Vera Cruz, S. Mexico.	..... do	Proc. Zool. Soc. London, 1859, p. 366.	152
Dicæum eximium.....	New Ireland......	Wardlaw Ramsay Coll.	Proc. Zool. Soc. London, 1877, p. 102, pl. xlv, fig. 2.	750
—— fulgidum.........	Larat and Loetoe, Tenimber Islands.	Brit. Mus.............	Proc. Zool. Soc. London, 1883, p. 56.	926
Dicrurus læmostictus.	New Britain......	.....do	Proc. Zool. Soc. London, 1877, p. 101.	750
Diglossa glauca.......	Nairapi, Bolivia..	Salvin-Godman Coll. in Brit. Mus.	Proc. Zool. Soc. London, 1876. p. 253.	715
—— gloriosa..........	Paramo de la Culata, Venezuela.	Sclater Coll. in Brit. Mus.	Proc. Zool. Soc. London, 1870, p. 784, pl. xlvi, fig. 2.	520
—— indigotica, Verr. MS.	Ecuador	.....do	Ann. and Mag. Nat. Hist., ser.2, XVII, p. 467 (1856).	94
Diglossopis cærulescens.	C a r a c a s, Venezuela.	Paris Mus.............	....do	94

List of new species described—Continued.

Name.	Locality.	Location of type.	Place of description.	No of paper.
Diplopterus excellens.	S. Mexico.........	Sallé Coll.............	Proc. Zool. Soc. London, 1857, p. 229.	111
Donacicola spectabilis.	New Britain	Brit. Mus.............	Proc. Zool. Soc. London, 1879, p. 449, pl. xxxvii, fig. 2.	822
Drepanornis albertisi.	Mount Arfak, New Guinea.	D'Albertis Coll......	Proc. Zool Soc. London, 1873, p. 558, pl. xlvii.	625
—— cervinicauda.	Port Moresby, New Guinea.	Dr. G. Bennett Coll.(?)	Proc. Zool. Soc. London, 1883. p. 578.	944
Drymœca hœsitata...	Socotra...........	Brit. Mus.............	Proc. Zool. Soc. London, 1881. p. 166.	870'
Dryocopus fuscipennis.	Babahoyo, Ecuador.	Sclater Coll. in Brit. Mus.	Proc. Zool. Soc. London, 1860, p. 286.	180
Dubuaia aurierissa....	Bogota	....do	Proc. Zool. Soc. London, 1855, p. 227.	81
Dysithamnus ardesiacus.	Rio Napo, Ecuador.	....do	Proc. Zool. Soc. London, 1867, p. 756.	417
—— leucostictus	Rio Napo	....do	Proc. Zool. Soc. London, 1858, p. 60.	116
—— semicinerous	Santa Fé di Bogota.	Brit. Mus.............	Proc. Zool. Soc. London, 1855, p. 90, pl. xcvii.	75
—— subplumbeus ...	Sarayacu, Ecuador.	Salvin-Godman Coll. in Brit. Mus.	Proc. Zool. Soc. London, 1880, p. 158.	848
—— unicolor.........	Pallatanga, Ecuador.	Sclater Coll. in Brit. Mus.	Proc. Zool. Soc. London, 1859, p. 141.	143
Elainea fallax........	Jamaica	....do ....,..	Proc. Zool. Soc. London, 1861, p. 76; 1870, p. 832.	212, 522
—— flavivertex	Upper Amazon...	....do	Proc. Zool. Soc. London, 1887. p. 49.	1019
—— gigas.............	Rio Napo, Ecuador.	....do	Proc. Zool. Soc. London. 1870, p. 831.	522
—— griseigularis....	Riobamba, Ecuador.	....do	Proc. Zool. Soc. London, 1858, p. 554, pl. cxlvi, fig. 1.	134
—— hypospodia	Venezuela........	....do	Proc. Zool. Soc. London. 1887, p. 49.	1019
—— implacens........	Esmeraldas, Ecuador.	....do	Proc. Zool. Soc. London, 1861, p. 408.	233
—— luteiventris	Rio Napo	....do	Proc. Zool. Soc. London, 1858, p. 71.	116
—— pallatangœ.......	Pallatanga, Ecuador.	....do	Proc. Zool. Soc. London, 1861, p. 407, pl. xli.	233
—— placens...........	Cordova, Mexico..	Sallé Coll.............	Proc. Zool. Soc. London, 1859, p. 46.	139
—— pudica	Bogota, Colombia.	Sclater Coll. in Brit. Mus.	Proc. Zool. Soc. London, 1870, p. 833.	522
—— riisii	St. Thomas, West Indies.	....do	Proc. Zool. Soc. London, 1860, p. 314.	185
—— semipagana	Ecuador	....do	Proc. Zool. Soc. London, 1861, p. 406.	233
—— stictoptera	Matos, Ecuador...	....do	Proc. Zool. Soc. London, 1858, p. 554, pl. cxlvi, fig. 2.	134
—— subpagana	Dueñas, Guatemala.	Salvin-Godman Coll. in Brit. Mus.	Ibis, 1860, p. 36.............	200
—— subplacens......	Pallatanga, Ecuador.	Sclater Coll. in Brit. Mus.	Proc. Zool. Soc. London, 1861, p. 407.	233
—— variegata.........	Cordova, S. Mexico.	Sallé Coll.............	Proc. Zool. Soc. London, 1856, p. 297.	92
—— vilissima.........	Central America..	Sclater Coll. in Brit. Mus.	Ibis, 1859, p. 122, pl. iv, fig. 1.	156a
Equus asinus somalicus.	Somaliland	(?)..................	Proc. Zool. Soc. London, 1884, p. 542, pl. l, fig. 1.	965
Erythrura regia (Erythrospiza in text).	Api, New Hebrides.	J. K. Howard Coll. (Now in Brit. Mus.).	Ibis, 1881, p. 544, pl. xv, fig. 2.	894
—— serona (Erythrospiza in text).	Aneitenm, New Hebrides.	Brit. Mus	Ibis, 1881, p. 544, pl. xv fig. 1.	894
Euburnagra chrysoma.	Babahoyo, Ecuador.	Sclater Coll. in Brit. Mus.	Proc. Zool. Soc. London, 1860, p. 275.	180
Empidochanes pœcilurus.	Colombia	....do	Proc. Zool. Soc. London, 1862, p. 112.	255
—— salvini	Roraima, British Guiana.	Salvin-Godman Coll. in Brit. Mus.	Cat. B. Brit. Mus., XIV, p. 218 (1888).	20
Empidonax albigularis.	Dueñas, Guatemala.	....do	Ibis, 1859, p. 122............	156a
—— bairdi............	Oaxaca, S. Mexico.	Sclater Coll. in Brit. Mus.	Proc. Zool. Soc. London, 1858, p. 301.	126
—— brachytarsus.....	Cordova, Mexico..	....do	Ibis, 1859, p. 441............	159
—— ridgwayi..........	Bogota, Colombia.	....do	Proc. Zool. Soc. London, 1887, p. 50.	1019

List of new species described—Continued.

Name.	Locality.	Location of type.	Place of description.	No. of paper.
Eubucco aurantiicollis.	Upper Amazon ...	Brit. Mus.............	Proc. Zool. Soc. London, 1857, p. 267.	131
Euchœtes coccineus, Verr. MS.	Rio Napo.........	Sclater Coll. in Brit. Mus.	Proc. Zool. Soc. London, 1858, p. 73, pl. cxxxii, fig 1.	116
Euchlornis frontalis..	Bolivia	Derby Mus...........	Proc. Zool. Soc. London, 1858, p. 446.	130
Eupetes leucostictus..	A t a m , A r f a k Mountains, New Guinea.	D'Albertis Coll	Proc. Zool. Soc. London, 1873, p. 690, pl. lii	628
Eupherusa egregia....	Castello and Calovevora, V e r a gua.	Salvin Godman Coll. in Brit. Mus.	Proc. Zool. Soc. London, 1868, p. 389.	445
Euphonia chalcopasta..	Colombia	Sclater Coll. in Brit. Mus.	Nomencl. Av. Neotrop., pp. 19. 157 (1873).	13
—— chrysopasta......	River U c a y a l i , Peru.	.....do	Proc. Zool. Soc. London, 1869, p. 438, pl. xxx, figs. 1, 2.	483
—— concinna.........	Colombia	.....do	Tanagrarum Catalogus Specificus, pp. 14, 16 (1854) ; Proc. Zool. Soc. London 1854, p. 98, pl. lxv, fig. 2.	2, 58
—— crassirostris	Bogota.............	.....do	Proc. Zool. Soc. London, 1856, p. 277.	86b
—— finschi	Demerara..........	.....do	Proc. Zool. Soc. London, 1877, p. 19.	745
—— frontalis (B p . MS.).	Ecuador	Edward Wilson Coll..	Contr. to Ornith., 1851, p. 89.	36
—— fulvicrissa	Santa Marta, Colombia.	Sclater Coll. in Brit. Mus.	Proc. Zool. Soc. London, 1856, p. 276.	86b
—— gouldi............	Guatemala.......	Gould Coll...........	Proc. Zool. Soc. London, 1857, p. 66, pl. cxxiv.	101
—— h i r u n d i n a c e a, Bp. MS.	Central America..	Sclater Coll. in Brit. Mus.	Tanagrarum C a t a l o g u s Specificus, pp. 14, 16 (1854).	2
—— insignis..........	Jina, Ecuador.....	Salvin-Godman Coll. in Brit. Mus.	Proc. Zool. Soc. London, 1877, p. 521, pl. lii, fig. 1.	759
—— melanura	Barra do Rio Negro.	Sclater Coll. in Brit. Mus.	Contr. to Ornith., 1851, p. 86.	36
—— pyrrhophrys	Colombia (?)........	.....do	Contr. to Ornith., 1851, p. 89, pl. lxxv, fig. 2.	36
—— vittata	Brazil	.....do	Proc. Zool. Soc. London, 1861, p. 129.	215
Euplocamus nobilis...	Borneo............	Brit. Mus...........	Proc. Zool. Soc. London, 1863, p. 119, pl. xvi.	285
Eupsilostoma pusillum.	Pallatanga, Ecuador.	Sclater Coll. in Brit. Mus.	Proc. Zool. Soc. London, 1860, p. 68.	163
Eurystomus crassirostris.	Solomon Islands..	Brit. Mus. (?)........	Proc. Zool. Soc. London, 1869, p. 121.	464
Euscarthmus agilis...	Bogota............	Sclater Coll. in Brit. Mus.	Proc. Zool. Soc. London, 1856, p. 29, pl. cxviii.	84
—— apicalis	Brazil	Paris Mus...........	Proc. Zool. Soc. London, 1887, p. 47, pl. ix, fig. 1.	1019
—— fulviceps.........	Lima, Peru	Sclater Coll. in Brit. Mus.	Proc. Zool. Soc. London, 1871, p. 497.	551
—— impiger	Venezuela	.....do	Proc. Zool. Soc. London, 1868, p. 171, pl. xiii, fig. 1.	435
—— pelzelni	Cuyaba, Brazil....	.....do	Ibis, 1881, p. 268.	891
—— wuchereri........	Bahia, Brazil.....	.....do	Nomencl. Av. Neotrop., pp. 45. 158 (1873).	13
Falco dickinsoni......	River Shiró, E. Africa.	Dickinson Coll.......	Proc. Zool. Soc. London, 1864, p. 248.	317
Felis lanea...........	Cape Colony (?)...	Zool. Soc. Menagerie..	Proc. Zool. Soc. London, 1877. p. 532, pl. lv.	760
—— passerum, n e w name for F. pajeros, Desm.	....	....	Proc. Zool. Soc. London, 1871, p. 700.	560
Fluvicola atripennis.	Babahoyo, Ecuador.	Sclater Coll. in Brit. Mus.	Proc. Zool. Soc. London, 1860, p. 280.	180
Formicarius moniliger.	Cordova, S. Mexico.	Salló Coll...........	Proc. Zool. Soc. London, 1856, p. 294.	92
—— trivittatus	River Amazon....	Brit. Mus...........	Proc. Zool. Soc. London, 1857, p. 46.	100
Formicivora boucardi.	Acatepec, S. Mexico.	Sclater Coll. in Brit. Mus.	Proc. Zool. Soc. London, 1858, p. 300.	126
—— callinota	Santa Fé di Bogota.	Brit. Mus...........	Proc. Zool. Soc. London, 1855, p. 89, pl. xcvi.	75
—— caloptera.........	Pallatanga, Ecuador.	Sclater Coll. in Brit. Mus.	Proc. Zool. Soc. London, 1859, p. 142.	143

List of new species described—Continued.

Name.	Locality.	Location of type.	Place of description.	No. of paper.
Formicivora caudata .	Colombia	Sclater Coll. in Brit. Mus.	Proc. Zool. Soc. London, 1854, p. 254, pl. lxxiv.	64
—— cinerascens	Chamicuros, E. Peru.	Brit. Mus.............	Proc. Zool. Soc. London, 1857, p. 131.	107
—— consobrina	Babahoyo Ecuador.	Sclater Coll. in Brit. Mus.	Proc. Zool. Soc. London, 1860, p. 279.	180
—— erythrocerca	Brazil (?).........	Eyton Coll.............	Proc. Zool. Soc. London, 1858, p. 240, pl. cxlii.	122
—— hæmatonota......	Chamicuros, E. Peru.	Brit. Mus.............	Proc. Zool. Soc. London, 1857, p. 48.	100
—— hauxwelli........	E. Peru.............	.....do	Proc. Zool. Soc. London, 1857,p.131,pl.cxxvi,fig.2.	107
—— melœna	Bogota.............	Sclater Coll. in Brit. Mus.	Proc. Zool. Soc. London, 1857, p. 130.	107
—— ornata............	Colombia	Eyton Coll.............	Rev. et Mag. de Zool.,1853, p. 480.	56
—— urosticta.........	E. Brazil...........	Sclater Coll. in Brit. Mus.	Proc. Zool. Soc. London, 1857,p.130,pl.cxxvi,fig.1.	107
Fuligula nationi......	Lima,Peru........	Salvin-Godman Coll. in Brit.Mus.	Proc. Zool. Soc. London, 1877, p. 522; 1878, p. 477, pl. xxxii.	750, 788
Furnarius agnatus....	Santa Marta, Colombia.	Sclater Coll. in Brit. Mus.	Nomencl. Av. Neotrop., pp. 61, 159 (1873).	13
—— pileatus...........	Santarem. Amazons.	Steere Coll.............	Proc. Zool. Soc. London, 1878, p 139.	775
—— torridus..........	Ucayali.............	Sclater Coll. in Brit. Mus.	Proc. Zool. Soc. London, 1860, p. 183.	380
Galbula chalcothorax.	Quijos, Ecuador...	Gould Coll.............	Proc. Zool. Soc. London, 1854, p. 110.	59
—— fuscicapilla	Bogota.............	Sclater Coll. in Brit. Mus.	Proc. Zool. Soc. London, 1855, p. 13.	69
—— inornata	Brazil	.....do	Contr. to Ornith., 1852, p. 32.	43
—— maculicauda	South Brazil, Bolivia.	.....do	Contr. to Ornith., 1852, p. 20.	43
—— melanogenia......	South America....	.....do	Contr. to Ornith., 1852, p. 61.	45
Gallinago imperialis..	Colombia	Salvin-Godman Coll. in Brit. Mus.	Proc. Zool. Soc. London, 1860, p. 419.	479
—— nobilis	Bogota.............	Sclater Coll. in Brit. Mus.	Proc. Zool. Soc. London, 1856, p. 31.	84
Gallinula nesiotis.....	Tristan d'Acunha	.....do	Proc. Zool. Soc. London, 1861,pp. 209, 261, pl. xxx.	218, 221
Gazella naso..........	Somaliland	E. Lort Phillips Coll..	Proc. Zool. Soc. London, 1885, p. 504, pl. li.	1012
Geositta crassirostris.	Lima, Peru.......	Sclater Coll. in Brit. Mus.	Proc. Zool. Soc. London, 1866, p. 98.	376
Geothlypis semiflava..	Babahoyo, Ecuador.	.....do	Proc. Zool. Soc. London, 1860, p. 273.	180
—— speciosa..........	Mexico	.....do	Proc. Zool. Soc. London, 1858, p. 447.	130
Geotrygon chiriquensis.	Chiriqui	Sclater Coll...........	Proc. Zool. Soc. London, 1856, p. 143.	89
Gerygone dorsalis....	Larat, Lbetoe and Moloc, Tenimber Islands.	Brit. Mus.............	Proc. Zool. Soc. London, 1883, p. 190.	932
Glaucidium californicum.	(?)	Acad. of Nat. Sci., Philadelphia.	Proc. Zool. Soc. London, 1857, p. 4.	98
Glyphorhynchus major.	Choctum,Vera Paz	Sclater Coll. in Brit. Mus.	Cat. American Birds, p. 161 (1862).	8
—— pectoralis	Vera Paz, Guatemala.	Salvin-Godman Coll. in Brit.Mus.	Proc. Zool. Soc. London, 1860, p. 299.	182
Gracula kreffti.......	Solomon Islands..	Brit. Mus.............	Proc. Zool. Soc. London, 1869, p. 120, pl. ix.	464
Grallaria dignissima..	Sarayacu,Ecuador	Sclater Coll. and Salvin-Godman Coll. in Brit. Mus.	Proc. Zool. Soc. London, 1880, p. 160, pl. xvii.	848
—— erythroleuca	Huasampilla,Peru	Sclater Coll. in Brit. Mus.	Proc. Zool. Soc. London, 1873, p. 783.	633
—— erythrotis........	Tilotilo, Yungas, Bolivia.	Salvin-Godman Coll. in Brit. Mus.	Proc. Zool. Soc. London, 1876, p. 357.	723
—— ferrugineipectus .	Caracas, Venezuela.	Paris Mus.............	Proc. Zool. Soc. London, 1857, p. 129.	107
—— flavirostris.......	Rio Napo	Sclater Coll. in Brit. Mus.	Proc. Zool. Soc. London, 1858, p. 68	116
—— flavotincta.......	Antioquia	.....do	Ibis, 1877, p. 445, pl. ix.....	768
—— fulviventris......	Rio Napo.........	.....do	Proc. Zool. Soc. London, 1858, p. 68.	116
—— grisconucha......	Paramo de la Culata, Venezuela.	.....do	Proc. Zool. Soc. London, 1870, p. 786.	520

List of new species described—Continued.

Name.	Locality.	Location of type.	Place of description.	No. of paper.
Grallaria haplonota...	Venezuela	Sclater Coll. in Brit. Mus.	Ibis, 1877, p. 442	768
—— hypoleuca.........	Santa Fé di Bogota.	Jardin des Plantes Mus.	Proc. Zool. Soc. London, 1855, p. 88.	75
—— loricata	Caracas, Venezuela.	Paris Mus............	Proc. Zool. Soc. London, 1857, p. 129.	107
—— mexicana	Jalapa, Mexico....	Sclater Coll in Brit. Mus.	Proc. Zool. Soc. London, 1861, p. 381.	229
—— modesta..........	Santa Fé di Bogota.	Brit. Mus.............	Proc. Zool. Soc. London, 1855, p. 89, pl. xciv.	75
—— nuchalis	Rio Napo, Ecuador.	Sclater Coll. in Brit. Mus.	Proc. Zool. Soc. London, 1859, p. 441.	154
—— princeps.........	Veragua..........	Salvin-Godman Coll. in Brit. Mus.	Proc. Zool. Soc. London, 1869, p. 418.	470
—— regulus	Pallatanga, Ecuador.	Sclater Coll. in Brit. Mus.	Proc. Zool. Soc. London, 1860, p. 66.	103
—— ruficeps	Antioquia	....do	Proc. Zool. Soc. London, 1873, p. 729.	029
—— rufo-cinerea......	Santa Elena, Antioquia.	....do	Proc. Zool. Soc. London, 1879, p. 526.	825
Granatellus pelzelni..	Rio Madeira, Brazil.	......do	Proc. Zool. Soc. London, 1864, p. 606, pl. xxxvii, fig. 1.	326
Graucalus sublineatus.	New Ireland......	Brit. Mus.............	Proc. Zool. Soc. London, 1879, p. 448, pl. xxxvi.	822
—— unimodus	Larat, Tenimber Islands.	....do	Proc. Zool. Soc. London, 1883, p. 55.	926
Gymnocichla chiroleuca.	Costa Rica........	Salvin-Godman Coll. in Brit. Mus.	Proc. Zool. Soc. London, 1869, p. 417.	470
Gymnoglaux lawrencii.	Cuba	Smithsonian Institution.	Proc. Zool. Soc. London, 1868, p. 327, pl. xxix.	443
Hæmophila pulchra...	Rimac River, W. Peru.	Sclater Coll. in Brit. Mus.	Ibis, 1886, p. 259, pl. viii....	1016
Halmaturus luctuosus, D'Albertis MS.	S. E. New Guinea.	D'Albertis Coll......	Proc. Zool. Soc. London, 1874, pp. 110, 247, pl. xlii.	650, 656
Hapalocrcus acutipennis.	Bogota...........	Sclater Coll. in Brit. Mus.	Proc. Zool. Soc. London, 1873, p. 187.	612
Haplospiza uniformis.	Jalapa, Mexico....	Salvin-Godman Coll. in Brit. Mus.	Nomencl. Av. Neotrop. pp. 29, 157 (1873).	13
Harporhynchus ocellatus.	Oaxaca, Mexico...	Sclater Coll. in Brit. Mus.	Proc. Zool. Soc. London, 1862, p. 18, pl. iii.	240
Herpsilochmus frater.	Sarayacu, Ecuador	Sclater Coll. and Salvin-Godman Coll. in Brit. Mus.	Proc. Zool. Soc. London, 1880, p. 159.	848
—— pectoralis........	(?).................	Brit. Mus.............	Proc. Zool. Soc. London, 1857, p. 132.	107
Heterocercus aurantiivertex.	Sarayacu, Ecuador	Sclater Coll. and Salvin-Godman Coll. in Brit. Mus.	Proc. Zool. Soc. London, 1880, p. 157.	848
Heterocnemis albigularis.	Rio Napo.........	Sclater Coll. in Brit. Mus.	Proc. Zool. Soc. London, 1858, p. 67.	110
—— marginata........	Santa Fé di Bogota.	......do	Proc. Zool. Soc. London, 1855, p. 145.	77
—— simplex..........	R. Maroni, Surinam.	......do	Proc. Zool. Soc. London, 1868, p. 573.	454
Heteropelma amazonum.	Huallaga, Chamicuros, Peru.	......do	Proc. Zool. Soc. London, 1860, p. 466.	197
—— flavicapillum....	Brazil	......do	......do	197
—— igniceps..........	Oyapok, Cayenne.	......do	Proc. Zool. Soc. London, 1871, p. 750.	563
—— stenorhynchum ..	San Esteban, Venezuela.	Sclater Coll. and Salvin-Godman Coll. in Brit. Mus.	Proc. Zool. Soc. London, 1868, p. 632.	459
—— verœ-pacis	Vera Paz, Guatemala.	Salvin-Godman Coll. in Brit. Mus.	Proc. Zool. Soc. London, 1860, p. 300.	182
—— wallacii	Para...............	Sclater Coll. in Brit. Mus.	Proc. Zool. Soc. London, 1867, p. 579.	413
Hylophilus brunneiceps.	Ypanema, Brazil..	......do	Proc. Zool. Soc. London, 1866, p. 322.	387
—— cinereiceps	Vera Paz, Guatemala.	Salvin-Godman Coll. in Brit. Mus.	Proc. Zool. Soc. London, 1860, p. 299.	182
—— ferrugineifrons ..	Colombia	Sclater Coll. in Brit. Mus.	Proc. Zool. Soc. London, 1862, p. 110.	255
—— fuscicapillus.....	Sarayacu, Ecuador	Sclater Coll. and Salvin-Godman Coll. in Brit. Mus.	Proc. Zool. Soc. London, 1880, p. 155.	848
—— insularis	Tobago	Sclater Coll...........	Proc. Zool. Soc. London, 1861, p. 128.	215
—— luteifrons	Bartica Grove, British Guiana.	Salvin-Godman Coll. in Brit. Mus.	Ibis, 1881, p. 308	892

List of new species described—Continued.

Name.	Locality.	Location of type.	Place of description.	No. of paper.
Hylophilus muscicapinus.	Oyapok, Cayenne.	Sclater Coll. in Brit. Mus.	Nomencl. Av. Neotrop., pp. 12, 156 (1873).	13
—— ochraceiceps	Oaxaca, Mexico...	.....do	Proc. Zool. Sec. London, 1859, p. 375.	158
—— pectoralis	Matto Grosso, Brasil.	.....do	Proc. Zool. Soc. London, 1866, p. 322.	387
—— rubrifrons	River Amazon....	.....do	Proc. Zool. Soc. London, 1867, p. 509, pl. xxx, fig. 2.	413
—— semicinereus.....	Para..............	.....do	Proc. Zool. Soc. London, 1867, p. 570.	413
Hylophorba ruticilla..	Madagascar	Stevens Coll..........	Proc. Zool. Soc. London, 1865, p. 326, pl. xlii.	343
Hypocnemis elegans..	Bogota............	Sclater Coll. in Brit. Mus.	Proc. Zool. Soc. London, 1857, p. 47.	100
—— flavescens (Natt. MS.).	Marabitanas, Rio Negro.	.....do	Proc. Zool. Soc. London, 1864, p. 609.	328
—— hemileuca........	Lower Ucayali....	.....do	Proc. Zool. Soc. London, 1866, p. 186.	380
—— hypoxantha......	Upper Amazon ...	.....do	Proc. Zool. Soc. London, 1868, p. 573, pl. xliii.	454
—— lepidonota	Sarayacu, Ecuador	Salvin-Godman Coll. in Brit. Mus.	Proc. Zool. Soc. London, 1880, p. 160.	848
—— melanolæma	Chamicuros, Peru.	Sclater Coll. in Brit. Mus.	Proc. Zool. Soc. London, 1854. p. 254, pl. lxxii, fig.2.	64
—— melanopogon.....	Chamicuros, Peru.	.....do	Proc. Zool. Soc. London, 1857, p. 130.	107
—— melanosticta	Chamicuros, Peru.	.....do	Proc. Zool. Soc. London, 1854, p. 254, pl. lxxiii.	64
—— melanura	Upper Ucayali....	.....do	Proc. Zool. Soc. London, 1866, p. 186.	380
—— schistacea........	Rio Javarri, Upper Amazon.	Brit. Mus..........	Proc. Zool. Soc. London, 1858, p. 252.	122
—— stellata	Sarayacu, Ecuador	Salvin-Godman Coll. in Brit. Mus.	Proc. Zool. Soc. London, 1880, p. 160.	848
Hypotænidia saturata, Salvad. MS.	Salawatti Island, New Guinea.	Turin Mus. (?)........	Ibis, 1880, p. 310	863
Hypoxanthus atriceps	Huasampilla, Peru.	Salvin-Godman Coll. in Brit. Mus.	Proc. Zool. Soc. London, 1876, p. 254.	715
Icterus hauxwelli	Chamicuros, Peru.	Brit. Mus	Proc. Zool. Soc. London, 1885, p. 671.	985
—— laudabilis........	St. Lucia, West Indies.	Sclater Coll. in Brit. Mus.	Proc. Zool. Soc. London. 1871, p. 270, pl. xxi.	546
—— wagleri	Coahuila..........	Acad. of Nat. Sci. Philadelphia.	Proc. Zool. Soc. London, 1857, p. 7.	98
—— xanthomus, Scl. MS.	Mexico	Sclater Coll. in Brit. Mus.	Cat. American Birds, p. 131 (1862).	8
Iridornis porphyrocephala.	Colombia	Berlin Mus	Proc. Zool. Soc. London, 1855, p. 227, pl. cx.	81
—— reinhardti	East Peru	Copenhagen University Mus.	Ibis, 1865, p. 495, pl. xi	368
Lalage mœsta........	Tenimber Islands.	Brit. Mus.	Proc. Zool. Soc. London, 1883, p. 55.	926
Laletes osburni.......	Jamaica	Osburn Coll..........	Proc. Zool. Soc. London, 1861, p. 72. pl. xiv, fig. 2.	212
Lanio lawrencii.......	Trinidad	G. N. Lawrence Coll..	Ibis, 1885, p. 272, pl. vi, fig. 2.	995
Lanius uncinatus.....	Socotra	Brit. Mus.	Proc. Zool. Soc. London, 1881, p. 168.	870
Lathria cryptolopha..	Mongi, Ecuador..	Salvin-Godman Coll. in Brit. Mus.	Proc. Zool. Soc. London, 1877, p. 522.	759
—— uropygialis	Tilotilo, Yungas, Bolivia.	.....do	Proc. Zool. Soc. London, 1876, p. 355. pl. xxxii.	723
Lemur nigerrimus....	(?)	Zool. Soc. Menagerie..	Proc. Zool. Soc. London, 1880, p. 451.	855
Leptasthenura andicola.	Panza, Ecuador...	Sclater Coll. in Brit. Mus.	Proc. Zool. Soc. London, 1880, p. 636. pl.xlix, fig. 2.	495
—— paranensis.......	Argentina	.....do	Proc. Zool. Soc. London, 1861, p. 377.	229
—— pileata...........	Lima, Peru......	.....do	Proc. Zool. Soc. London, 1881, p. 487.	880
Leptopogon erythrops.	Colombia	.....do	Proc. Zool. Soc. London, 1862, p. 111.	255
—— godmani	E. Ecuador	Salvin-Godman Coll. in Brit. Mus.	Proc. Zool. Soc. London, 1887, p. 48.	1019
—— oustaleti	Bogota, Colombia.	Paris Mus...........	Proc. Zool. Soc. London, 1887, p. 48, pl. ix, fig. 2.	1019
—— peruvianus	Chyavetas, Peru..	Sclater Coll. in Brit. Mus.	Proc. Zool. Soc. London, 1867, p. 757.	417
—— pœcilotis.........	Colombia	.....do	Proc. Zool. Soc. London, 1862, p. 111.	255
—— tristis...........	Simacu, Bolivia...	Salvin-Godman Coll. in Brit. Mus.	Proc. Zool. Soc. London, 1876, p. 254.	715

List of new species described—Continued.

Name.	Locality.	Location of type.	Place of description.	No. of paper.
Leptoptila cervini-ventris.	Vera Paz, Guatemala.	Salvin-Godman Coll. in Brit. Mus.	Proc. Zool. Soc. London, 1868, p. 59.	431
—— chalcauchenia, Salvad. MS.	(?)	Salvadori Coll. (?).....	Proc. Zool. Soc. London, 1869, p. 633.	404
—— megalura	Tilotilo, Yungas, Bolivia.	Salvin-Godman Coll. in Brit. Mus.	Proc. Zool. Soc. London, 1879, p. 640.	828
—— plumboiceps	Vera Paz, Guatemala.	.....do	Proc. Zool. Soc. London, 1868, p. 59.	431
—— rufinucha........	Veragua...........	.....do	Nomencl. Av. Neotrop., pp. 134, 162 (1873).	13
Leptotriccus superciliaris.	Chitra,Veragua...	.....do	Proc. Zool. Soc. London, 1868, p. 389.	445
Leucippus chlorocercus, Gould MS.	Upper Ucayali....	Gould Coll............	Proc. Zool. Soc. London, 1866, p. 194.	380
Leucopeza semperi...	St. Lucia, West Indies.	Sclater Coll. in Brit. Mus.	Proc. Zool. Soc. London, 1876, p. 14, pl. ii.	711
Leucophantes brachyurus.	Atam, Arfak Mountains,New Guinea.	D'Albertis Coll.......	Proc. Zool. Soc. London, 1873, p. 691, pl. liii.	628
Leucopternis principeps.	Costa Rica........	Salvin-Godman Coll. in Brit. Mus.	Proc. Zool. Soc. London, 1865, p. 429, pl. xxiv.	346
Liosceles erithacus...	Sarayacu,Ecuador	Sclater Coll. and Salvin-Godman Coll. in Brit. Mus.	Cat. B. Brit. Mus., XV, p. 345 (1890).	22
Lipaugus holerythrus.	Vera Paz, Guatemala.	Salvin-Godman Coll. in Brit. Mus.	Proc. Zool. Soc. London, 1860, p. 300.	182
—— immundus	Oyapok, French Guiana.	Sclater Coll. in Brit. Mus.	Nomencl. Av. Neotrop., pp. 57, 159 (1873).	13
—— rufescens	Coban,Guatemala.	Derby Mus............	Proc. Zool. Soc. London, 1857, p. 276.	114
—— subalaris........	Rio Napo, Ecuador.	Brit. Mus.............	Proc. Zool. Soc. London, 1861, p. 210.	219
—— unirufus	Oaxaca,Mexico...	Sclater Coll. in Brit. Mus.	Proc. Zool. Soc. London, 1859, p. 385.	153
Lochmias sororia.....	Venezuela........	.....do	Proc. Zool. Soc. London, 1873, p. 511.	620
Lophostrix stricklandi.	Central America..	Strickland Coll.......	Ibis, 1859, p. 221............	150b
Loriculus chrysonotus.	Zebu, Philippines.	Brit. Mus............	Ibis, 1872, p. 324, pl. xi....	603
—— tener..............	Duke of York Island.	Tweeddale Coll. in Brit. Mus.	Proc. Zool. Soc. London, 1877, p. 107.	750
Lorius tibialis........	Molucca group(?).	Zool. Soc. Menagerie.	Proc. Zool. Soc. London, 1871, p. 499, pl. xl.	552
Macacus rheso-similis.	(?)..............	Zool. Soc. Menagerie..	Proc. Zool. Soc. London, 1872, p. 495, pl. xxv.	582
Macropus erubescens.	Lake Hope, South Australia.	.....do	Proc. Zool. Soc. London, 1870, p. 126, pl. x.	506
Macropygia browni...	Duke of York Island.	Tweeddale Coll. in Brit. Mus.	Proc. Zool. Soc. London, 1877, p. 110.	750
Malacocichla maculata (Verr. MS.).	Rio Napo..........	Sclater Coll. in Brit. Mus.	Proc. Zool. Soc. London, 1858, p. 64.	116
Malacoptila aspersa...	Venezuela	Brit. Mus............	Proc. Zool. Soc. London, 1853, p. 123.	55
—— frontalis	Colombia	.....do	Ann. and Mag. Nat. Hist., ser. 2, XIII, p. 479 (1854).	66
—— fulvogularis	Bolivia	Derby Mus............	Proc. Zool. Soc. London, 1853, p. 123.	55
—— nigrifusca	Santa Fé di Bogota.	Brit. Mus............	Proc. Zool. Soc. London, 1855, p. 195.	78
—— poliopis..........	Esmeraldas, Ecuador.	Sclater Coll. in Brit. Mus.	Proc. Zool. Soc. London, 1862, p. 86, pl. viii.	253
—— substriata........	Colombia	.....do	Proc. Zool. Soc. London, 1853, p. 123, pl. li.	55
—— veræ-pacis	Coban, Guatemala	Salvin-Godman Coll. in Brit. Mus.	Ibis, 1860, p. 40............	200
Malacothraupis dentata.	Tilotilo, Yungas, Bolivia.	.....do	Proc. Zool. Soc. London, 1876, p. 353, pl. xxxi.	729
Manucodia comrii....	Huan Gulf, New Guinea.	Lord Tweeddale Coll.	Proc. Zool. Soc. London, 1876, p. 459, pl. xlii.	728
Margarops sanctæ-luciæ.	St. Lucia, West Indies.	Sclater Coll. in Brit. Mus.	Ibis, 1880, p. 73............	862
Margarornis brunnescens.	Bogota	.....do	Proc. Zool. Soc. London, 1856, p. 27, pl. cxvi.	84
—— stellata	Quito, Ecuador...	Salvin-Godman Coll. in Brit. Mus.	Nomencl. Av. Neotrop., pp. 67, 160 (1873).	13
Maslus coronulatus...	Nanegal, Ecuador	Sclater Coll. in Brit. Mus.	Proc. Zool. Soc. London, 1860, p. 91.	165
Mecocerculus gratiosus.	Ecuador	.....do	Proc. Zool. Soc. London, 1862, p. 113.	256
Megalurus intercapularis.	Kabakada, New Britain.	Brit. Mus............	Proc. Zool. Soc. London, 1880, p. 65, pl. vi.	845

List of new species described—Continued.

Name.	Locality.	Location of type.	Place of description.	No. of paper.
Megapodius brazieri (this name was founded on an egg from Banka Island, New Hebrides).	....	....	Proc. Zool. Soc. London, 1869, p. 529.	488
— rubrifrous	Admiralty Islands	Challenger Coll.......	Proc. Zool. Soc. London, 1877, p. 556.	762
— tenimberensis....	Kirimoen and Loetoo, Tenimber Islands.	Brit. Mus............	Proc. Zool. Soc. London, 1883, p. 57.	926
Megarhynchus chrysogaster.	Babahoyo, Ecuador.	Sclater Coll. in Brit. Mus.	Proc. Zool. Soc. London, 1860, p. 281.	180
Melanerpes pulcher..	Bogota, Colombia.	......do	Proc. Zool. Soc. London, 1870, p. 330.	514
— rubrigularis......	Trinity Valley, Northern California.	.....do	Ann. and Mag. Nat. Hist., ser. 3, I, p. 127 (1858).	135
Melanoptila glabrirostris.	Omoa, Honduras......	.....do	Proc. Zool. Soc. London, 1857, p. 275.	114
Melidectes torquatus.	Atam, Arfak Mountains, New Guinea.	D'Albertis Coll.......	Proc. Zool. Soc. London, 1873, p. 604, pl. lv.	628
Melipotes gymnops...	.....do	.....do	Proc. Zool. Soc. London, 1873, p. 695, pl. lvi.	628
Mellivora leuconota..	West Africa......	Zool. Soc. Menagerie..	Proc. Zool. Soc. London, 1867, p. 98, pl. viii.	400
Merganetta turneri...	Tinta, Peru	Sclater Coll. in Brit. Mus.	Proc. Zool. Soc. London, 1869, p. 600.	491
Metopothrix aurantiacus.	Sarayacu, Amazon.	.....do	Proc. Zool. Soc. London, 1866, p. 190, pl. xviii.	380
Microbates torquatus.	Oyapok, Cayenne.	.....do	Nomencl. Av. Neotrop., pp. 72, 161 (1873).	13
Microcerculus squamulatus.	San Cristobal, Venezuela.	.....do	Proc. Zool. Soc. London, 1875, p. 37, pl. vi.	678
Micrœca hemixantha.	Larat and Loetoo, Tenimber Islands.	Brit. Mus............	Proc. Zool. Soc. London, 1883, p. 55.	926
Minuta decipiens.....	Larat, Tenimber Islands.	.....do	Proc. Zool. Soc. London, 1883, p. 199.	932
Mionectes assimilis ..	Cordova, Mexico..	Sclater Coll. in Brit. Mus.	Proc. Zool. Soc. London, 1859, p. 46.	139
Mitrephorus phœocercus.	.....do	.....do	Proc. Zool. Soc. London, 1859, p. 44.	139
Momotus microstephanus.	Columbia	.....do	Proc. Zool. Soc. London, 1857, p. 251.	112
— nattereri	Goyaz, Brazil....	.....do	.....do	112
— semirufus........	Santa Marta, Rio Javarri.	.....do	Rev. et Mag. de Zool.,1853, p. 489.	57
— subrufescens.....	Colombia	.....do	.....do	57
— swainsoni........	Trinidad, Tobago.	.....do	Cat. American Birds, p. 261 (1862).	8
Monarcha castus ...	Loetoe, Timor Laut.	Brit. Mus............	Proc. Zool. Soc. London, 1883, p. 53, pl. xii, fig. 1.	926
— frater	Atam, Arfak Mountains, New Guinea.	D'Albertis Coll.......	Proc. Zool. Soc. London, 1873, p. 691.	628
— infelix	Admiralty Islands.	Challenger Coll.......	Proc. Zool. Soc. London, 1877, p. 552.	762
— melanonotus	New Guinea......	(?)................	Proc. Zool. Soc. London, 1877, p. 100.	750
— mundus..........	Tenimber Islands.	Brit. Mus............	Proc. Zool. Soc. London, 1883, p. 54, pl. xii, fig. 2.	926
— verticalis	Duke of York Island.	.....do	Proc. Zool. Soc. London, 1877, p. 99, pl. xiv, fig. 1.	750
Monasa grandior.....	Angostura, Costa Rica.	Salvin-Godman Coll. in Brit. Mus.	Proc. Zool. Soc. London, 1868, p. 327.	443
— peruana, Bp. et Verr. MS.	Chamicuros	Sclater Coll. in Brit. Mus.	Proc. Zool. Soc. London, 1855, p. 194.	78
Munia forbesi........	New Ireland......	Brit. Mus............	Proc. Zool. Soc. London, 1879, p. 449, pl. xxxvii, fig. 3.	822
— melæna	Kabakadai, New Britain.	.....do	Proc. Zool. Soc. London, 1880, p. 66, pl. vii, fig. 2.	845
Muscisaxicola fluviatilis.	Lower Ucayali....	Sclater Coll. in Brit. Mus.	Proc. Zool. Soc. London, 1866, p. 187.	380
Muscivora mexicana (Kp.), Bp. MS.	Cordova, S. Mexico.	Salló Coll	Proc. Zool. Soc. London, 1856, p. 295.	92
— occidentalis......	Babahoyo, Ecuador.	Sclater Coll. in Brit. Mus.	Proc. Zool. Soc. London, 1860, p. 282.	180

List of new species described—Continued.

Name.	Locality.	Location of type.	Place of description.	No. of paper.
Myiadestes unicolor..	Cordova, S. Mexico.	Sallé Coll............	Proc. Zool. Soc. London, 1856, p. 299.	92
—— venezuelensis	Caracas, Venezuola.	Paris Mus............	Ann. and Mag. Nat. Hist., ser. 2, XVII, p. 468 (1856).	94
Myiagra fulviventris.	Larat, Tenimber Islands.	Brit. Mus............	Proc. Zool. Soc. London, 1883, p. 54.	926
Myiarchus apicalis....	Bogota, Colombia.	Sclater Coll. in Brit. Mus.	Ibis, 1881, p. 269............	891
—— erythrocercus, Scl. MS.	Bahia, Brazil.....	....do	Proc. Zool. Soc. London, 1868, p. 631.	459
—— nigriceps..........	Pallatanga, Ecuador.	.....do	Proc. Zool. Soc. London, 1860, p. 68.	163
—— phæocephalus....	Babahoyo, Ecuador.	....do	Proc. Zool. Soc. London, 1860, p. 281.	180
—— semirufus	Pacasmayo, Peru.	Steere Coll............	Proc. Zool. Soc. London, 1878, p. 138, pl. xi.	775
Myiobius auroiventris.	Cosnipata, Peru...	Sclater Coll. in Brit. Mus.	Proc. Zool. Soc. London, 1873, p. 782.	633
—— bellus............	Colombia	....do	Proc. Zool. Soc. London, 1862, p. 111.	255
—— crypterythrus....	Ecuador	....do	Proc. Zool. Soc. London, 1860, p. 464.	197
—— cryptoxanthus...	....do	....do	Proc. Zool. Soc. London, 1860, p. 465.	197
—— flavicans	Pallatanga, Ecuador.	.....do	Proc. Zool. Soc. London, 1860, p. 464.	197
—— nationi...........	Lima, Peru.......	....do	Proc. Zool. Soc. London, 1866, p. 99, pl. xi, fig. 1.	376
—— pulcher	Ecuador	....do	Proc. Zool. Soc. London, 1860, p. 464.	197
—— subochraceous	Bolivia	Salvin-Godman Coll. in Brit. Mus.	Proc. Zool. Soc. London, 1887, p. 50.	1019
—— villosus	Nanegal, Ecuador.	Sclater Coll. in Brit. Mus.	Proc. Zool. Soc. London, 1860, p. 93.	165
Myiochanes nigrescens.	Sarayacu, Ecuador	Sclater Coll. and Salvin-Godman Coll. in Brit. Mus.	Proc. Zool. Soc. London, 1880, p. 157.	848
Myiodynastes nobilis.	Santa Marta, Colombia.	Sclater Coll. in Brit. Mus.	Proc. Zool. Soc. London, 1859, p. 42.	139
Myrmeciza exsul	Isthmus of Panama.	Derby Mus	Proc. Zool. Soc. London, 1858, p. 540.	132
—— hemimelæna	Bolivia	Brit. Mus............	Proc. Zool. Soc. London, 1857, p. 48.	100
—— immaculata	Isthmus of Panama.	Salvin-Godman Coll. in Brit. Mus.	Proc. Zool. Soc. London, 1864, p. 357.	322
—— leucaspis.........	Chamicuros, Peru; Colombia; Rio Negro.	Sclater Coll. in Brit. Mus.	Proc. Zool. Soc. London, 1854, p. 253, pl. lxx.	64
—— margaritata	Chamicuros, Peru.	.....do	Proc. Zool. Soc. London, 1854, p. 253, pl. lxxi.	64
Myrmelastes nigerrimus.	Upper Amazon ...	Brit. Mus............	Proc. Zool. Soc. London, 1858, p. 275.	123
—— plumbeus	Rio Javarri, Upper Amazon.	Sclater Coll. in Brit. Mus.	Proc. Zool. Soc. London, 1858, p. 274, pl. cxliii.	123
Myrmotherula cinereiventris, Scl. MS.	Cayenne..........	....do	Proc. Zool. Soc. London, 1867, p. 756.	417
—— gutturalis........	Bartica Grove, British Guiana.	Sclater Coll. and Salvin-Godman Coll. in Brit. Mus.	Ibis, 1881, p. 269............	891
—— multostriata	Ucayali, Upper Amazon.	Sclater Coll. in Brit. Mus.	Proc. Zool. Soc. London, 1858, p. 234, pl. cxli, figs. 2, 3.	122
—— pyrrhonota.......	Rio Negro and Oyapok, Guiana.	....do	Nomencl. Av. Neotrop., pp. 72, 160 (1873).	13
—— spodionota.......	Sarayacu, Ecuador	Salvin-Godman Coll. in Brit. Mus.	Proc. Zool. Soc. London, 1880, p. 150.	848
Myzomela annabellæ .	Loetoe, Timor Laut.	Brit. Mus............	Proc. Zool. Soc. London, 1883, p. 56.	926
—— cineracea	New Britain......	....do	Proc. Zool. Soc. London, 1879, p. 448, pl. xxxvii, fig. 1.	822
—— pammelæna	Admiralty Islands.	Challenger Coll......	Proc. Zool. Soc. London, 1877, p. 553.	762
Nasiterna pusio	Solomon Islands..	Brit. Mus............	Proc. Zool. Soc. London, 1865, p. 620, pl. xxxv.	356
Nemosia albigularis ..	Santa Fé di Bogota.	Sclater Coll. in Brit. Mus.	Proc. Zool. Soc. London, 1855, p. 109, pl. xcix.	76
—— auricollis.........	Cayenne and E. Peru.	Brit. Mus............	Proc. Zool. Soc. London, 1856, p. 111.	86a
—— chrysopis	Sarayacu, Ecuador	Salvin-Godman Coll. in Brit. Mus.	Proc. Zool. Soc. London, 1880, p. 155.	848

List of new species described—Continued.

Name.	Locality.	Location of type.	Place of description	No. of paper.
Netuosia guirina......	Bogota and E. Peru.	Sclater Coll. in Brit. Mus.	Proc. Zool. Soc. London. 1856, p. 110.	86a
—— insignis..........	South Brazil.......	...do	...do	86a
—— ornata	Pallatanga, Ecuador.	...do	Proc. Zool. Soc. London, 1859, p. 138.	143
Neochleo brevipennis.	Orizaba, Mexico..	Botteri Coll..........	Proc. Zool. Soc. London, 1857, p. 213	109
Neomorphus geoffroyii.	Brazil.............	Armytage Coll	Proc. Zool. Soc. London. 1864, p. 249.	318
—— radiolosus........	Intaj, Ecuador	Salvin Godman Coll. in Brit. Mus.	Proc. Zool. Soc. London, 1878, p. 439, pl. xxvii.	786
—— rufipennis........	Guiana	Armytage Coll	Proc. Zool. Soc. London, 1864. p. 249.	318
—— salvini	Veragua	Salvin-Godman Coll. in Brit. Mus.	Proc. Zool. Soc. London, 1866, p. 60, pl. v.	372
Neopipo rubicunda ...	Chamicuros, Peru.	Sclater Coll. in Brit. Mus.	Proc. Zool. Soc. London, 1869, p. 438, pl. xxx, fig. 3.	483
Nigrita bicolor........	Casamanza, W. Africa.	Edward Wilson Coll..	Contr. to Ornith., 1852, p. 34, pl. lxxxiii.	44
Ninox forbesi........	Loetoe, Timor Laut.	Brit. Mus.	Proc. Zool. Soc. London, 1883, p. 52, pl. xl.	926
—— odiosa............	New Britain.....	....do	Proc. Zool. Soc. London, 1877, p. 108.	750
Nonnula brunnea.....	Sarayacu, Ecuador	Sclater Coll. and Salvin-Godman Coll. in Brit. Mus.	Ibis, 1881, p. 600	896
—— cinoracea	Upper Amazon..	Brit. Mus.............	Proc. Zool. Soc. London, 1881, p. 778.	885
Nothoprocta curvirostris.	Calacali and Puellaro, Ecuador.	Salvin Godman Coll. in Brit. Mus.; and Smithsonian Inst.	Nomencl. Av. Neotrop., pp. 153, 162 (1873).	13
—— taczanowskii.....	Maraynioc, Peru..	Warsaw Mus (?)......	Proc. Zool. Soc. London, 1874, p. 679, pl. lxxxiv.	671
Nycticorax pauper....	Indefatigable Island.	Salvin-Godman Coll. in Brit. Mus.	Proc. Zool. Soc. London, 1870, p. 327.	513
Nyctipithecus rufipes.	Nicaragua	Zool.Soc.Menagerie...	Proc. Zool. Soc. London, 1872, p. 3, pl. i.	577
Ochthodlœta fuscorufus.	Tilotilo, Yungas, Bolivia.	Salvin-Godman Coll. in Brit. Mus.	Proc. Zool. Soc. London, 1876, p. 354.	723
Ochthœca arenacea...	Bogota, Colombia.	......do	Proc. Zool. Soc. London, 1877, p. 20.	745
——citrinifrons.......	Ecuador	Sclater Coll. in Brit. Mus.	Proc. Zool. Soc. London, 1862, p. 113.	256
—— fumicolor........	Bogota.............	....do	Proc. Zool. Soc. London, 1856, p. 28, pl. cxvii.	84
—— leucometopa......	Peru...............	....do	Proc. Zool. Soc. London, 1877, p. 19.	745
—— murina..........	Oyapok, Cayenne..	....do	Proc. Zool. Soc. London, 1871, p. 749.	563
—— nigrita	Merida, Venezuela	....do	Proc. Zool. Soc. London, 1870, p. 787.	520
—— polionota........	Pitumarca, Peru..	....do	Proc. Zool. Soc. London, 1869, p. 590.	401
—— pulchella........	Tilotilo, Yungas, Bolivia.	Salvin-Godman Coll. in Brit. Mus.	Proc. Zool. Soc. London, 1876, p. 355.	723
—— superciliosa	Paramos of Merida, Venezuela.	Sclater Coll. in Brit. Mus.	Proc. Zool. Soc. London, 1870, p. 786.	520
Ocydromus sylvestris.	Lord Howe Island.	Gould Coll. in Brit. Mus.	Proc. Zool. Soc. London, 1869, p. 472, pl. xxxv.	486
Odontophorus hypospodius.	Antioquia, Colombia.	Salvin-Godman Coll. in Brit. Mus.	Nomencl. Av. Neotrop., pp. 138, 162 (1873).	13
Oreas livingstonii.....	Usagara E. Africa.	Speke Coll	Proc. Zool. Soc. London, 1864, p. 105.	306
Oreomanes fraseri....	Chimborazo, Ecuador.	Sclater Coll. in Brit. Mus.	Proc. Zool. Soc. London, 1860, p. 75, pl. clix.	164
Ortalida ruficrissa....	Valle Dupar, Colombia.	Salvin-Godman Coll. in Brit. Mus.	Proc. Zool. Soc. London, 1870, p. 538.	516
Ortygocichla rubiginosa.	New Britain......	Mus. Godeffroy.....	Proc. Zool. Soc. London, 1881, p. 452, pl. xxxix.	879
Oryzoborus œthiops..	Nanegal, Ecuador.	Sclater Coll. in Brit. Mus.	Proc. Zool. Soc. London, 1860, p. 88.	165
—— atrirostris........	Moyobamba, Peru.	Steere Coll..........	Proc. Zool. Soc. London, 1878, p. 136.	775
—— funereus	Oaxaca, Mexico...	Sclater Coll. in Brit. Mus.	Proc. Zool. Soc. London, 1859, p. 378.	153
—— melas	Pebas, Peru........	....do	Proc. Zool. Soc. London, 1867, p. 979.	423
—— occidentalis......	Bababoyo, Ecuador.	....do	Proc. Zool. Soc. London, 1860, p. 276.	180
Ostinops oleagineus..	Venezuela (?).....	....do	Ibis, 1883, p. 154, pl.vii.....	948
—— salmoni	Antioquia	....do	Ibis, 1883, p. 153, pl.vi....	948

List of new species described—Continued.

Name.	Locality.	Location of type.	Place of description.	No. of paper.
Otocorys peregrina....	Bogota.............	Sclater Coll. in Brit. Mus.	Proc. Zool. Soc. London, 1855, p. 110, pl. cii.	76
Oxyrhamphus frater..	Veragua...........	Salvin-Godman Coll. in Brit. Mus.	Proc. Zool. Soc. London, 1868, p. 326.	443
Pachycephala arctitorquis.	Larat, Tenimber Islands.	Brit. Mus.............	Proc. Zool. Soc. London, 1883, p. 55, pl. xiii.	926
—— fusco-flava........	....do	....do	Proc. Zool. Soc. London, 1883, p. 198, pl. xxviii.	932
—— rufinucha........	Atam, Arfak Mountains, New Guinea.	D'Albertis Coll.......	Proc. Zool. Soc. London, 1873, p. 692.	628
—— soror.............	....do.............	....do	....do	628
Pachyrhamphus albogriscus.	Bogota.............	Sclater Coll. in Brit. Mus.	Proc. Zool. Soc. London, 1857, p. 78.	102
—— cinereiventris, Scl. MS.	Santa Marta......	....do	Cat. American Birds, p. 242 (1862).	8
—— dorsalis, Scl. MS..	Bogota (?)	....do	Cat. American Birds, p. 243 (1862).	8
—— homochrous	Pallatanga, Ecuador.	....do	Proc. Zool. Soc. London, 1859, p. 142.	143
—— spodiurus........	Babahoyo, Ecuador.	....do	Proc. Zool. Soc. London, 1860, p. 279.	180
Paradisea raggiana...	Orangcisa Bay, New Guinea.	D'Albertis Coll.......	Proc. Zool. Soc. London, 1873, p. 559.	625
Paroaria cervicalis, Scl. MS.	Bolivia	Sclater Coll. in Brit. Mus.	Cat. American Birds, p. 108 (1862).	8
Parra intermedia (Bp.) Verr. MS.	Venezuela........	....do	Proc. Zool. Soc. London, 1856, p. 282.	91
—— melanopygia	Santa Marta, Colombia.	....do	Proc. Zool. Soc. London, 1856, p. 283.	91
Parus meridionalis....	El Jacale, S. Mexico.	Sallé Coll.............	Proc. Zool. Soc. London, 1856, p. 293.	92
Passer insularis	Socotra	Brit. Mus	Proc. Zool. Soc. London, 1881, p. 169, pl. xvi.	870
Pavo nigripennis.....	(?)	Zool. Soc. Menagerie..	Proc. Zool. Soc. London, 1860, p. 221.	173
Percnostola fortis	Pebas and Chyavotas, Peru.	Sclater Coll. in Brit. Mus.	Proc. Zool. Soc. London, 1867, p. 980.	423
Petrochelidon swainsoni, new name for Hirundo melanogaster, Swains.	....	....do	Proc. Zool. Soc. London, 1858, p. 296.	126
Peucæa notosticta....	South Mexico.....	Salvin-Godman Coll. in Brit. Mus.	Proc. Zool. Soc. London, 1868, p. 322.	443
Phacellodomus rufipennis.	Bolivia	Sclater Coll. in Brit. Mus.	Proc. Zool. Soc. London, 1889, p. 33.	1056
—— sibilatrix, Döring MS.	Argentina	Döring Coll............	Proc. Zool. Soc. London, 1879, p. 461.	824
Phacthornis adolphi (Sallé MS.).	South Mexico.....	Gould Coll.............	Proc. Zool. Soc. London, 1856, p. 287.	92
Phasianus principalis.	Murghab, central Asia.	Prince of Wales Coll...	Proc. Zool. Soc. London, 1885, p. 324, pl. xxii.	980
Pheucticus crissalis ..	Riobamba, Ecuador.	Sclater Coll. in Brit. Mus.	Proc. Zool. Soc. London, 1877, p. 19.	745
—— uropygialis.......	Colombia	....do	Proc. Zool. Soc. London, 1870, p. 840.	524
Philemon albitorques.	Admiralty Islands	Challenger Coll.......	Proc. Zool. Soc. London, 1877, p. 553.	762
—— cockerelli........	New Britain......	Brit. Mus.............	Proc. Zool. Soc. London, 1877, p. 104.	750
Philydor cervicalis ...	British Guiana ...	Sclater Coll. in Brit. Mus.	Proc. Zool. Soc. London, 1889, p. 33.	1056
—— consobrinus......	Colombia	....do	Proc. Zool. Soc. London, 1870, p. 328.	514
— — erythronotus.....	Bogota, Colombia.	....do	Nomencl. Av. Neotrop., pp. 66, 160 (1873).	13
—— pancrythrus	Colombia	....do	Proc. Zool. Soc. London, 1862, p. 110.	255
—— subfulvus........	Gualaquiza, Ecuador.	....do	Proc. Zool. Soc. London, 1861, p. 378.	229
Phlogœnas bartletti..	Philippines (?) ...	Brit. Mus.............	Proc. Zool. Soc. London, 1863, p. 377, pl. xxxiv.	294
Phlogœnas johanno...	Duke of York Island.	Tweeddale Coll. in Brit. Mus.	Proc. Zool. Soc. London, 1877, p. 112, pl. xvi.	750
Phœnicothraupis gutturalis.	Colombia	Brit. Mus.............	Ann. and Mag. Nat. Hist., ser 2, XIII p. 25 (1854).	65
Phœnicopterus jamesi	Tarapacá, Chili ...	H. B. James Coll. (Now in Brit. Mus.).	Proc. Zool. Soc. London, 1886, p. 309, pl. xxxvi.	1010
Phrygilus coracinus ..	....do	....do	Proc. Zool. Soc. London, 1891, p. 133, pl. xiii.	1110

List of new species described—Continued.

Name.	Locality.	Location of type.	Place of description.	No. of paper.
Phrygilus ocularis....	Cuenca, Ecuador..	Sclater Coll. in Brit. Mus.	Proc. Zool. Soc. London, 1858, p. 454, pl. cxlv.	131
Phyllomyias berlepschi.	S. E. Brazil	......do	Proc. Zool. Soc. London, 1887, p. 49.	1019
— griseocapilla (Lafr. MS.).	Brazil	......do	Proc. Zool. Soc. London, 1861, p. 382, pl. xxxvi, fig. 2.	229
— platyrhyncha	Goiaz, Brazil	......do	Nomencl. Av. Neotrop.. pp. 48, 150 (1873).	13
— semifusca........	Santa Marta, Colombia.	......do	Proc. Zool. Soc. London, 1861, p. 383, pl. xxxvi, fig. 1.	• 229
Piaya nigricrissa.....	Colombia	......do	Proc. Zool. Soc. London, 1860, p. 285.	180
— thermophila......	Jalapa, S. Mexico.	......do	Proc. Zool. Soc. London, 1859, p. 368.	152
Picolaptes layardi...	Para, Brazil	......do	Ibis, 1873, p. 386, pl. xiv....	636
— parvirostris......	S. E. Brazil	Salvin-Godman Coll. in Brit. Mus.	Proc. Zool. Soc. London, 1880, p. 34.	1056
— puncticeps	Guiana	Sclater Coll. in Brit. Mus.	Nomencl. Av. Neotrop., pp. 60, 160 (1873).	13
Pionus haematotis	Vera Paz, Guatemala.	Salvin-Godman Coll. in Brit. Mus.	Proc. Zool. Soc. London, 1860, p. 300.	182
Pipilo albicollis.......	San Miguel de las Peras, S. Mexico.	Sclater Coll. in Brit. Mus.	Proc. Zool. Soc. London, 1858, p. 304.	126
Pipilopsis flavigularis	Colombia	Mus. d'Hist. Nat. Paris.	Rev. et Mag.de Zool.,1852, p. 8.	• 49
Pipra coracina........	Bogota	Sclater Coll. in Brit. Mus.	Proc. Zool. Soc. London, 1856, p. 29.	84
— deliciosa	Nanegal, Ecuador.	......do	Proc. Zool. Soc. London, 1860, p. 90.	165
— flavicapilla.......	Colombia	Mus. d'Hist. Nat. Paris.	Rev. et Mag.de Zool.,1852, p. 9.	49
— flavicollis	Barra do Rio Negro	Sclater Coll. in Brit. Mus.	Contr. to Ornith., 1851, p. 143.	41
— flavo-tincta.......	Bogota	......do	Proc. Zool. Soc. London, 1852, p. 34, pl. xlviii.	53
— heterocerca	Upper Amazon...	(?)	Proc. Zool. Soc. London, 1860, p. 313.	184
— isidorei...........	Colombia	Mus. d'Hist. Nat. Paris.	Rev. et Mag.de Zool.,1852, p. 9.	49
— leucorrhoa	...do	Sclater Coll. in Brit. Mus.	Proc. Zool. Soc. London, 1863 p. 63, pl. x.	281
— mentalis	Cordova, S. Mexico	Sallé Coll............	Proc. Zool. Soc. London, 1856, p. 299, pl. cxxi.	92
— nattereri	Borba, Brazil.....	Vienna Mus..........	Proc. Zool. Soc. London, 1864, p. 611, pl. xxxix.	328
— pyrocephala......	....	Mus. d'Hist. Nat. Paris	Rev. et Mag.de Zool.,1852, p. 9.	49
Pipraeidia albiventris.	Colombia	......do	Rev. et Mag.de Zool.,1852, p. 8.	49
Pipreola jucunda.....	Cachi-Llacta, Ecuador.	Sclater Coll. in Brit. Mus.	Proc. Zool. Soc. London, 1860, p. 89, pl. clx (Euchloruis jucunda on plate).	165
— melanolaema	Caracas, Venezuela.	......do	Ann. and Mag. Nat. Hist., ser. 2, XVII, p.469 (1856).	94
Pipridea venezuelensis.	...do	Paris Mus...........	Proc. Zool. Soc. London, 1856, p. 205.	805
Pithys erythrophrys..	Colombia	Sclater Coll.........	Proc. Zool. Soc. London, 1854, p. 255, pl. lxxii, fig.1.	64
— lunulata	Sarayacu, Peru ...	Sclater Coll. in Brit. Mus.	Proc. Zool. Soc. London, 1873, p. 276, pl. xxvi.	614
— melanosticta	Sarayacu, Ecuador	Salvin-Godman Coll. in Brit. Mus.	Proc. Zool. Soc. London, 1880, p. 160.	848
Platyrhynchus albogularis.	Pallatanga, Ecuador.	Sclater Coll. in Brit. Mus.	Proc. Zool. Soc. London, 1860, p. 68.	163
— cancrominus	Vera Paz, Guatemala.	Salvin-Godman Coll. in Brit. Mus.	Proc. Zool. Soc. London, 1860, p. 299.	182
— coronatus, Verr. MS.	Rio Napo........	Sclater Coll. in Brit. Mus.	Proc. Zool. Soc. London, 1858, p. 71.	116
— flavigularis	Colombia	......do	Proc. Zool. Soc. London, 1861, p. 382.	229
— senex	Sarayacu, Ecuador	Salvin-Godman Coll. in Brit. Mus.	Proc. Zool. Soc. London, 1886, p. 156.	848
Plectropterus niger...	S. E. Africa (?)...	Zool. Soc. Menagerie..	Proc. Zool. Soc. London, 1877, p. 28, pl. vii.	749
— rüppellii	East Africa.......	Brit. Mus...........	Proc. Zool. Soc. London, 1859, p. 132, pl. cliii, fig.1.	142
Poecilodryas aethiops..	Kabakadai, New Britain.	......do	Proc. Zool. Soc. London, 1880, p. 66, pl. vii, fig. 1.	845

List of new species described—Continued.

Name	Locality.	Location of type.	Place of description.	No. of paper.
Pogonotriccus guala-quizæ, Scl. MS.	W. Ecuador.......	Sclater Coll. in Brit. Mus.	Proc. Zool. Soc. London, 1887, p. 48 (see also 1885, p. 89).	1019
Polioptila albiloris.. .	River Motagua, Guatemala.	Salvin-Godman Coll. in Brit Mus.	Proc. Zool. Soc. London, 1860, p. 298.	182
—— buffoni...........	Guiana	Sclator Coll. in Brit. Mus.	Proc. Zool. Soc. London, 1861, p. 127.	215
Polytmus leucorrhous, Gould MS.	Cobati, Rio Negro.	Gould Coll............	Proc. Zool. Soc. London, 1867, p. 584.	413
Poospiza bonapartii...	Lima, Peru.......	Sclater Coll. in Brit. Mus.	Proc. Zool. Soc. London, 1867, p. 341, pl. xx.	408
—— cæsar	Tinta, Peru	....do	Proc. Zool. Soc. London, 1869, p. 152, pl. xiii.	471
—— erythrophrys	Sierra de Totoral, Catamarca.	.....do	Ibis, 1881, p. 599..........	895
—— oxyrhyncha(Natt. MS.).	Curytiba, Brazil..	.....do	Proc. Zool. Soc. London, 1864, p. 608.	328
—— whitii...........	Cosquin, Cordova, Argentine Republic.	.....do	Proc. Zool. Soc. London, 1883, p. 43, pl. ix.	925
Porzana castaneiceps.	Rio Napo, Ecuador	Brit. Mus............	Proc. Zool. Soc. London, 1868, p. 453.	448
—— erythrops	Lima, Peru.......	Sclater Coll. in Brit. Mus.	Proc. Zool. Soc. London, 1867, p. 343, pl. xxi.	408
—— fasciata	Pebas, Peru......	Salvin-Godman Coll. in Brit. Mus.	Proc. Zool. Soc. London, 1867, p. 981.	423
—— hauxwelli........	Ucayali, Pebas, Chamicuros.	.....do	Exotic Ornith., p. 105, pl. liii (1868).	12
—— levraudi...........	Caracas, Venezuela.	Paris Mus............	Proc. Zool. Soc. London, 1868, p. 452, pl. xxxv.	448
—— œnops	Sarayacu, Ecuador	Salvin-Godman Coll. in Brit. Mus.	Proc. Zool. Soc. London, 1880, p. 161.	848
Prionochilus vincens..	Ceylon............	Legge Coll............	Proc. Zool. Soc. London, 1872, p. 729.	594
Procnias occidentalis.	Colombia	Sclater Coll. in Brit. Mus.	Proc. Zool. Soc. London, 1854, p. 249.	62
Psalidoprocne albi-ceps.	Uzinza	Speke Coll............	Proc. Zool. Soc. London, 1864, p. 108, pl. xiv.	307
Psophia napensis.....	Rio Napo, Ecuador.	Brit. Mus.............	Nomencl. Av. Neotrop., pp.141, 162 (1873).	13
Pteroglossus didymus.	Upper Amazon...	Salvin-Godman Coll. in Brit. Mus.	Proc. Zool. Soc. London, 1890, p. 403.	1091
Pteroptochus thoracicus.	Rio Madeira, Brazil.	Vienna Mus..........	Proc. Zool. Soc. London, 1864, p. 609, pl. xxxviii.	328
Pteropus formosus....	Formosa	Zool. Soc. Menagerie..	Proc. Zool. Soc. London, 1873, p. 193, pl. xxii.	613
Ptilochloris buckleyi.	Pindo, Ecuador...	Salvin-Godman Coll. in Brit. Mus.	Proc. Zool. Soc. London, 1880, p. 158, pl. xvi.	848
Ptilonopus bellus.....	Atam, Arfak Mountains, New Guinea.	D'Albertis Coll.......	Proc. Zool. Soc. London, 1873, p. 606, pl. lvii.	628
Ptilopus johannis	Admiralty Islands.	Challenger Coll.......	Proc. Zool. Soc. London, 1877, p. 556.	762
Ptilotis cinerea.......	Atam, Arfak Mountains, New Guinea	D'Albertis Coll.......	Proc. Zool. Soc. London, 1873, p. 693.	628
—— melanophrys.....	....do.............	....do	....do.............	628
Pyranga testacea.....	Chitra and Calovevora, Veragua.	Salvin-Godman Coll. in Brit. Mus.	Proc. Zool. Soc. London, 1868, p. 388.	445
Pyrgisoma cabanisi ...	San José, Costa Rica.	Sclater Coll. in Brit. Mus.	Proc. Zool. Soc. London, 1868, p. 324.	443
Pyriglena ellisiana ...	Santa Fé di Bogota.	Brit. Mus.............	Proc. Zool. Soc. London, 1855, p. 109, pl. c.	76
—— maculicaudis.....	Trinidad..........	Sclater Coll. in Brit. Mus.	Proc. Zool. Soc. London, 1858, p. 247.	122
—— serva.............	Rio Napo........,	....do	Proc. Zool. Soc. London, 1858, p. 66.	116
—— tyrannina........	Santa Fé di Bogota.	Brit. Mus.............	Proc. Zool. Soc. London, 1855, p. 90, pl. xci.	75
Pyrocephalus mexicanus.	Mexico	Sclater Coll. in Brit. Mus.	Proc. Zool. Soc. London, 1859, p. 45.	139
Querquedula andium.	Riobamba and Mocha, Ecuador.	Salvin-Godman Coll. in Brit. Mus.	Nomencl. Av. Neotrop., pp. 129, 162 (1873).	13
Quiscalus æquatorialis, Scl. MS.	Babahoyo.........	Sclater Coll. in Brit. Mus.	Cat. American Birds, p. 140 (1862).	8
—— assimilis, Scl. MS.	Bogota	....do	Cat. American Birds, p. 141 (1862).	8
—— graysoni	Mazatlan, Mexico.	Salvin-Godman Coll. in Brit. Mus.	Ibis, 1884, p. 157..........	969

List of new species described—Continued.

Name.	Locality.	Location of type.	Place of description.	No. of paper.
Rallus insignis........	Kabakadai, New Britain.	Brit. Mus.............	Proc. Zool. Soc. London, 1880, p. 66, pl. viii.	845
— intactus..........	Solomon Islands..	....do	Proc. Zool. Soc. London, 1869, p. 123, pl. x.	464
— semiplumbeus ...	Bogota	Sclater Coll. in Brit. Mus.	Proc. Zool. Soc. London, 1856, p. 31.	84
Rostes bennetti......	Atam, Arfak Mountains, New Guinea.	D'Albertis Coll......	Proc. Zool. Soc. London, 1873, p. 692.	628
Rhamphocænus albiventris.	San Esteban, Venezuela.	Sclater Coll. in Brit. Mus.	Ibis, 1883, p. 95...........	947
— cinereiventris....	Pasto, Colombia..	Derby Mus..........	Proc. Zool. Soc. London, 1855, p. 76, pl. lxxxvii	73
— sanctæ marthæ..	Santa Marta, Colombia.	Sclater Coll. in Brit. Mus.	Proc. Zool. Soc. London, 1861, p. 380.	229
Rhamphocelus dorsalis, Bp. MS.	Brazil	....do	Tanagrarum Catalogus Specificus, pp. 9, 15 (1854); Proc. Zool. Soc. London, 1854, p. 97.	2, 58
— ephippialis......	Upper Amazon........do		Proc. Zool. Soc. London, 1861, p. 130.	215
— unicolor..........	Bogota	Brit. Mus., and Sclater Coll. in Brit. Mus	Proc. Zool. Soc. London, 1856, p. 128.	86a
Rhea macrorhyncha..	South America....	Zool. Soc. Menagerie..	Proc. Zool. Soc. London, 1860, p. 207.	172
Rhinoceros bicornis holmwoodi.	Zanzibar	Holmwood Coll. (horns only).	Proc. Zool. Soc. London, 1893, p. 517.	1175
Rhinocrypta fusca....	Mendoza, Argentina.	Sclater Coll. in Brit. Mus.	Nomencl. Av. Neotrop., pp. 76, 161 (1873).	13
Rhipidura fusco-rufa.	Larat, Moloe and Loetoe, Teninber Islands.	Brit. Mus.............	Proc. Zool. Soc. London, 1883, p. 197, pl. xxvii.	932
— hamadryas......	Larat, Tenimber Islands.	....do	Proc. Zool. Soc. London, 1883, p. 54.	926
— opistherythra....	Larat and Maroe, Tenimber Islands.	....do	Proc. Zool. Soc. London, 1883, p. 197.	932
— semirubra........	Admiralty Islands.	Challenger Coll......	Proc. Zool. Soc. London, 1877, p. 552.	762
Rhynchocyclus viridiceps.	Upper Amazon...	Sclater Coll. in Brit. Mus.	Proc. Zool. Soc. London, 1873, p. 280.	614
Rhynchostruthus socotranus.	Socotra	Brit. Mus............	Proc. Zool. Soc. London, 1881, p. 170, pl. xvii.	870
Saltator atripennis...	Popayan, Colombia.	Acad. of Nat. Sci. Philadelphia.	Proc. Acad. Nat. Sci. Philadelphia, 1856, p. 261.	95
— flavidicollis......	Babahoyo, Ecuador.	Sclater Coll. in Brit. Mus.	Proc. Zool. Soc. London, 1860, p. 274.	180
— isthmicus........	Isthmus of Panama.	....do	Proc. Zool. Soc. London, 1861, p. 130.	215
— laticlavius	Tinta, Peru......	....do	Proc. Zool. Soc. London, 1860, p. 151.	471
Sayornis aquatica.....	Dueñas, Guatemala.	Salvin-Godman Coll. in Brit. Mus.	Ibis, 1859, p. 119...........	156a
Sclerurus brunneus...	Bogota	Sclater Coll. in Brit. Mus.	Proc. Zool. Soc. London, 1857, p. 17.	99
— mexicanus......	Cordova, S. Mexico.	Sallé Coll.............	Proc. Zool. Soc. London, 1856, p. 290.	92
Scops barbarus.......	Vera Paz, Guatemala.	Salvin-Godman Coll. in Brit. Mus.	Proc. Zool. Soc. London, 1868, p. 56.	431
— nata.............	Ega, Upper Amazon.	Norwich Mus.........	Proc. Zool. Soc. London, 1858, p. 132.	118
Scytalopus prosthelcucus.	Cordova, S. Mexico.	Sallé Coll............	Proc. Zool. Soc. London, 1856, p. 290.	92
Serpophaga albogrisea.	Sarayacu, Ecuador	Salvin-Godman Coll. in Brit. Mus.	Proc. Zool. Soc. London, 1880, p. 156.	848
— hypoleuca......	Lower Ucayali...	Sclater Coll. in Brit. Mus.	Proc. Zool. Soc. London, 1866, p. 188.	380
— pœcilocerca......	Ecuador and Colombia.	....do	Nomencl. Av. Neotrop., pp. 47, 158 (1873).	13
— subflava........	Para.............	....do	....do	13
Setophaga albifrons..	Merida, Venezuela.	....do	Proc. Zool. Soc. London, 1870, p. 784.	520
Spermophila corvina..	Oaxaca, Mexico...	....do	Proc. Zool. Soc. London, 1859, p. 379.	153
— ocellata	Nauta, Peru......	....do	Proc. Zool. Soc. London, 1866, p. 181.	380
— ophthalmica......	Babahoyo, Ecuador.	....do	Proc. Zool. Soc. London, 1860, p. 276.	180
— pileata, Natt. MS.	Borda do Matto, Brazil.	....do	Proc. Zool. Soc. London, 1864, p. 607.	328

List of new species described—Continued.

Name.	Locality.	Location of type.	Place of description.	No. of paper.
Sphenaeacus pycnopygius.	Damara Country, S. W. Africa.	Strickland Coll......	Contr. to Ornith., 1852, p. 148.	52
Sphenopsis ignobilis..	Brazil	Sclater Coll. in Brit. Mus.	Proc. Zool. Soc. London, 1861, p. 379.	229
Spodiornis jardini...	Ecuador	....do	Proc. Zool. Soc. London, 1866, p. 322.	387
Stenopsis ruficervix..	Colombia	....do	Proc. Zool. Soc. London, 1866, p. 140, pl. xiv.	378
Sterna cassini.	Falkland Islands.	Sclater Coll. in Brit. Mus. (?).	Proc. Zool. Soc. London, 1860, p. 391.	180
Strix sororcula.......	Larat, Tenimber Islands.	Brit. Mus..........	Proc. Zool. Soc. London, 1883, p. 52.	926
Sturnella ludoviciana hippocrepis.	Cuba	Salvin-Godman Coll. in Brit. Mus.	Ibis, 1884, p. 25............	908
—— meridionalis.	Venezuela........	Sclater Coll. in Brit. Mus.	Ibis, 1884, p. 26............	908
—— mexicana..	Mexico	....do	....do	908
—— neglecta....	North America...	.....do	Ibis, 1884, p. 25............	908
Sublegatus glaber.....	Venezuela........	.....do	Proc. Zool. Soc. London, 1868, pp. 171, 172, pl. xiii, fig. 2.	435
Sycalis chrysops......	S. Mexico........	....do	Proc. Zool. Soc. London, 1861, p. 376.	229
—— pelzelni	Buenos Aires	....do	Ibis, 1872, p. 42............	601
Synallaxis albigularis (Lafr. MS.).	Rio Napo........	Lafresnaye Coll.....	Proc. Zool. Soc. London, 1858, p. 63.	116
—— antisiensis	Cuenca, Ecuador..	Sclater Coll. in Brit. Mus.	Proc. Zool. Soc. London, 1858, p. 457.	131
—— arequipae	Arequipa, Peru...	....do	Proc. Zool. Soc. London, 1860, p. 417.	479
—— brunneicaudalis (Lafr. MS.).	Rio Napo........	Lafresnaye Coll.....	Proc. Zool. Soc. London, 1858, p. 62.	116
—— cauleops	Brazil	Eyton Coll.........	Proc. Zool. Soc. London, 1856, p. 98.	88
—— castanea	Caracas, Venezuela.	Brit. Mus..........	Ann. and Mag. Nat. Hist., ser. 2, XVII, p. 460(1856).	94
—— curtata	Colombia..........	Sclater Coll. in Brit. Mus.	Proc. Zool. Soc. London, 1869, p. 636, pl. xlix, fig. 1.	495
—— elegans	Bogota..........	....do	Proc. Zool. Soc. London, 1856, p. 25.	84
—— elegantior, nom. emend. pro elegans, Scl.	....	....	Cat. American Birds, p. 151 (1862).	8
—— erythrops	Pallatanga, Ecuador.	Sclater Coll. in Brit. Mus.	Proc. Zool. Soc. London, 1860, p. 66.	108
—— erythrothorax....	Central America, Coban, and Honduras.	Derby Mus..........	Proc. Zool. Soc. London, 1855, p. 75, pl. lxxxvi.	73
—— fusco-rufa........	San Sebastian, Colombia.	Salvin-Godman Coll. in Brit. Mus.	Proc. Zool. Soc. London, 1882, p. 578, pl. xliii, fig. 1.	915
—— graminicola	Junin, Peru.......	Warsaw Mus..........	Proc. Zool. Soc. London, 1874, p. 446, pl. lviii, fig. 2.	662
—— griseo-murina....	San Lucas, Ecuador.	Salvin-Godman Coll. in Brit. Mus.	Proc. Zool. Soc. London, 1882, p. 578, pl. xliii, fig. 2.	915
—— hudsoni..........	Conchitas, Buenos Ayres.	Sclater Coll. in Brit. Mus.	Proc. Zool. Soc. London, 1874, p. 25.	645
—— hypospodia	Bahia, Brazil......	....do	Proc. Zool. Soc. London, 1874, p. 10.	645
—— lemosticta	Colombia..........	....do	Proc. Zool. Soc. London, 1859, p. 192.	144
—— moesta	Bogota..........	....do	Proc. Zool. Soc. London, 1856, p. 26.	84
—— multo-striata....	Colombia..........	Paris Mus..........	Proc. Zool. Soc. London, 1857, p. 273.	114
—— mustelina, Natt. MS.	Rio Madeira......	Vienna Mus. (?)....	Proc. Zool. Soc. London, 1874, p. 14.	645
—— pudibunda	Obrajillo, Peru...	Warsaw Mus..........	Proc. Zool. Soc. London, 1874, p. 445, pl. lviii, fig. 1.	662
—— pudica	Colombia..........	Sclater Coll. in Brit. Mus.	Proc. Zool. Soc. London, 1859, p. 191.	144
—— rufipennis.......	Tilotilo, Bolivia..	Salvin-Godman Coll. in Brit. Mus.	Proc. Zool. Soc. London, 1879, p. 620.	828
—— scutata..........	Brazil	Brit. Mus..........	Proc. Zool. Soc. London, 1859, p. 191.	144
—— spixi	....do	Sclater Coll. in Brit. Mus.	Proc. Zool. Soc. London, 1856, p. 98.	88
—— stictothorax......	Guayaquil, Ecuador.	Brit. Mus..........	Proc. Zool. Soc. London, 1859, p. 191.	144
—— suberistata.......	Caracas, Venezuela.	Sclater Coll. in Brit. Mus.	Proc. Zool. Soc. London, 1874, p. 20, pl. iv, fig. 1.	645
—— subpudica........	Bogota, Colombia..	....do	Proc. Zool. Soc. London, 1874, p. 19.	645

List of new species described—Continued.

Name.	Locality.	Location of type.	Place of description.	No. of paper.
Synallaxis terricolor	Ucayali	Brit. Mus., Sclater Coll. and Salvin-Godman Coll. in Brit. Mus.	Proc. Zool. Soc. London, 1888 p. 362.	390
—— virgata	Junin, Peru	Warsaw Mus.	Proc. Zool. Soc. London, 1874, p. 446.	452
—— vulpecula	Ucayali	Brit. Mus., and Sclater Coll. in Brit. Mus.	Proc. Zool. Soc. London, 1888, p. 164.	390
—— whitii	Oran, Salta, Argentine Republic.	Sclater Coll. in Brit. Mus.	Ibis, 1881, p. 610.	885
—— wyatti	Paramo of Pamplona, Colombia.	....do	Proc. Zool. Soc. London, 1870, p. 845.	894
Syristes albocinereus	Bogota, Colombia	....do	Proc. Zool. Soc. London, 1880, p. 156.	445
Syrnium fulvescens	Guatemala	Salvin-Godman Coll. in Brit. Mus.	Proc. Zool. Soc. London, 1868, p. 56.	681
Tachyphonus chrysomelas.	Cordillera de Chucu, Veragua	....do	Proc. Zool. Soc. London, 1869, p. 440 pl. xxxii.	494
—— cristatellus. Scl. MS.	New Granada	Sclater Coll. in Brit. Mus.	Cat. American Birds, p. 86 (1862).	8
—— xanthopygius	Colombia	Brit. Mus.	Proc. Zool. Soc. London, 1854 p. 156, pl. lxix.	60
Taenioptera erythropygia.	Ecuador	Edward Wilson Coll.	Proc. Zool. Soc. London, 1861, p. 103, pl. xli.	42
—— holospodia	Bolivia	Brit. Mus.	Proc. Zool. Soc. London, 1867, p. 47.	1079
—— striaticollis	Ecuador	Sclater Coll. in Brit. Mus.	Proc. Zool. Soc. London, 1851 p. 193, pl. xlii.	62
Tanagra olivina. Natt. MS.	Cuyaba, Brazil.	....do	Proc. Zool. Soc. London, 1864 p. 607.	226
—— subcinerea	Venezuela	....do	Proc. Zool. Soc. London, 1861, p. 129.	215
Tanygnathus subaffinis.	Larat, Tenimber Islands.	Brit. Mus.	Proc. Zool. Soc. London, 1883, p. 52.	956
Tanyoiptera nigriceps	Duke of York Island.	Tweeddale Coll. in Brit. Mus.	Proc. Zool. Soc. London, 1877, p. 105.	736
Terenura humeralis	Sarayacu, Ecuador	Salvin-Godman Coll. in Brit. Mus.	Proc. Zool. Soc. London, 1880, p. 159.	644
—— spodioptila	Bartica Grove, British Guiana.	....do	Ibis, 1881, p. 270, pl. ix. fig. 1.	891
Testudo argentina, new name for T. chilensis, Gray.	Argentina	Zool. Soc. Menagerie	Ann. and Mag. Nat. Hist., ser. 4. VI. p. 471.	526
Tetragonops frantzii	Costa Rica	Smithsonian Inst.	Ibis, 1864, p. 371, pl. x.	223
Thamnistes aequatorialis.	Ecuador	Sclater Coll. in Brit. Mus.	Proc. Zool. Soc. London, 1862, p. 300.	259
—— anabatinus	Vera Paz, Guatemala.	Salvin-Godman Coll. in Brit. Mus.	Proc. Zool. Soc. London, 1868, p. 209.	102
Thamnophilus aethiops.	Rio Napo	Sclater Coll. in Brit. Mus.	Proc. Zool. Soc. London, 1858, p. 65.	116
—— albinuchalis	Guayaquil and Puna Island, Ecuador.	Brit. Mus.	Proc. Zool. Soc. London, 1855, p. 76.	70
—— amazonicus	Upper Amazon	Sclater Coll. in Brit. Mus.	Proc. Zool. Soc. London, 1858, p. 214, pl. cxxxix.	121
—— bridgesi	Chiriqui	Sclater Coll.	Proc. Zool. Soc. London, 1856, p. 141.	89
—— caesius (Cuv. MS.).	British Guiana	Paris Mus. and Sclater Coll. in Brit. Mus.	Proc. Zool. Soc. London, 1855, p. 19, pl. lxxxii.	70
—— capitalis	Rio Napo	Sclater Coll. in Brit. Mus.	Proc. Zool. Soc. London, 1858, p. 65.	116
—— leuchauchen	Chamicuros, E. Peru.	....do	Proc. Zool. Soc. London, 1855, p. 16, pl. lxxix.	70
—— maculipennis	Peruvian Amazons.	....do	Edinburgh New Phil. Journ. n. s. I. p. 347.	62
—— melanchrous	Huiro, Peru	Sclater Coll. and Salvin-Godman Coll. in Brit. Mus.	Proc. Zool. Soc. London, 1878, p. 18, pl. iii.	712
—— melanocrissus	Santecomapam, Mexico.	Sclater Coll. in Brit. Mus.	Proc. Zool. Soc. London, 1860, p. 252.	176
—— melanonotus	Santa Marta, Colombia.	....do	Proc. Zool. Soc. London, 1855, p. 19, pl. lxxx.	70
—— melanothorax	Central America	Brit. Mus.	Proc. Zool. Soc. London, 1857, p. 133.	167
—— murinus, Natt. MS.	Xeberos, Peru	Sclater Coll. in Brit. Mus.	Proc. Zool. Soc. London, 1857, p. 754.	417
—— nigriceps	Colombia	....do	Proc. Zool. Soc. London, 1868, p. 571.	454
—— nigrocinereus	Para, Brazil	Brit. Mus. and Sclater Coll. in Brit. Mus.	Proc. Zool. Soc. London, 1855, p. 19, pl. lxxxi.	70

List of new species described—Continued.

Name.	Locality.	Location of type.	Place of description.	No. of paper.
Thamnophilus simplex	Para, Brazil	Sclater Coll. in Brit. Mus.	Ibis, 1873, p. 387, pl. xv	636
— strenuus, Scl. MS.	Cayenne	....do	Cat. American Birds, p. 173 (1862).	8
— subfasciatus	Tilotilo, Yungas, Bolivia.	Salvin-Godman Coll. in Brit. Mus.	Proc. Zool. Soc. London, 1870, p. 753. pl. xxxiii.	723
— transandeanus	Guayaquil, Ecuador.	Brit. Mus	Proc. Zool. Soc. London, 1855, p. 18.	70
— tristis	Oyapok, French Guiana.	Sclater Coll. in Brit. Mus.	Nomencl. Av. Neotrop., pp. 69, 160 (1873).	13
— ventralis	South Brazil	....do	Edinburgh New Phil. Journ., n. s., I, p. 244.	82
Thaumantias bartletti, Gould MS.	Upper Ucayali	Gould Coll	Proc. Zool. Soc. London, 1866, p. 194.	360
Thaumasius taozanowskii.	Guajungo, Cajamarca, Peru.	Warsaw Mus	Proc. Zool. Soc. London, 1879, p. 146.	811
Thaumastura francesiæ, nom. emend. pro fanny, Less.			Cat. American Birds, p. 209 (1862).	8
— henicura, nom. emend. pro enicurus, Vieill.		....do		8
Thlypopsis amazonum.	Lower Ucayali	Sclater Coll. in Brit. Mus.	Cat. B. Brit. Mus., XI, p. 220 (1886).	19
Thripophaga fusciceps.	Bolivia	Brit. Mus	Proc. Zool. Soc. London, 1889, p. 33.	1056
— guttuligera	Colombia	Sclater Coll. in Brit. Mus.	Proc. Zool. Soc. London, 1864, p. 167.	311
Thryophilus fulvus	Huasampilla, Peru	....do	Proc. Zool. Soc. London, 1873, p. 781.	633
Thryothorus euophrys.	Lloa, Ecuador	....do	Proc. Zool. Soc. London, 1860, p. 74.	164
— felix	Oaxaca, Mexico	....do	Proc. Zool. Soc. London, 1859, p. 371.	153
— martinicensis	Martinique, West Indies.	....do	Proc. Zool. Soc. London, 1866, p. 321.	387
— mesoleucus	St. Lucia, West Indies.	....do	Proc. Zool. Soc. London, 1876, p. 14.	711
— mystacalis	Pallatanga, Ecuador.	....do	Proc. Zool. Soc. London, 1860, p. 64.	163
— nigricapillus	Nanegal, Ecuador	....do	Proc. Zool. Soc. London, 1860, p. 84.	165
— nisorius (Licht. MS.)	Real Arriba, Mexico.	Berlin Mus	Proc. Zool. Soc. London, 1869, p. 592, pl. xlv.	489
— pleurostictus	Vera Paz, Guatemala.	Sclater Coll. in Brit. Mus.	Ibis, 1860, p. 30	200
— rufiventris, Natt. MS.	Goyaz and Matto Grosso, Brazil.	....do	Proc. Zool. Soc. London, 1870, p. 328.	514
Tigrisoma salmoni	Cauca, Colombia	Salvin-Godman Coll. in Brit. Mus.	Proc. Zool. Soc. London, 1875, p. 38.	678
Tinamus boucardi, Sallé MS.	Oaxaca, Mexico	Sclater Coll. in Brit. Mus.	Proc. Zool. Soc. London, 1859, p. 392.	153
— castaneus	Bogota	....do	Proc. Zool. Soc. London, 1857, p. 277.	114
— meserythrus	Oaxaca, Mexico	....do	Proc. Zool. Soc. London, 1859, p. 392.	153
— robustus	S. Mexico	....do	Proc. Zool. Soc. London, 1860, p. 253.	178
— ruficeps	Western Ecuador, Panama, and Chiriqui.	Salvin-Godman Coll. in Brit. Mus.	Nomencl. Av. Neotrop., pp. 152, 162 (1873).	13
Todirostrum calopterum.	Rio Napo, Ecuador	Sir William Jardine Mus.	Proc. Zool. Soc. London, 1857, p. 82, pl. cxxv, fig. 1.	104
— capitale	....do	....do	Proc. Zool. Soc. London, 1857, p. 83, pl. cxxv, fig. 2.	104
— cinereigulare	Cordova, S. Mexico	Sallé Coll	Proc. Zool. Soc. London, 1856, p. 295.	92
— exile	Colombia	Sclater Coll. in Brit. Mus.	Proc. Zool. Soc. London, 1857, p. 83, pl. cxxv, fig. 3.	104
— gracilipes	Santa Fé di Bogota	Brit. Mus	Proc. Zool. Soc. London, 1855, p. 19.	77
— nigriceps, ♂, ♀	Santa Marta, Colombia.	Sclater Coll. in Brit. Mus.	Proc. Zool. Soc. London, 1855, p. 66, pl. lxxxiv, fig. 1.	72
— picatum	Rio Napo	....do	Proc. Zool. Soc. London, 1858, p. 70.	116
— pulchellum	Cosnipata, Peru	....do	Proc. Zool. Soc. London, 1873, p. 781.	633
— rufigene	Mongi, Ecuador	Salvin-Godman Coll. in Brit. Mus.	Proc. Zool. Soc. London, 1877, p. 522.	750
— signatum	Pebas and Yquitos, Peru.	....do	Ibis, 1881, p. 267	891

List of new species described—Continued.

Name.	Locality.	Location of type.	Place of description	No. of paper.
Tragelaphus gratus...	Gaboon	(?)	Proc. Zool. Soc. London, 1880, p. 452, pl. xliv.	856
—— spekii...........	Karagweh	Speke Coll...........	Proc. Zool. Soc. London, 1864, p. 103, pl. xii.	306
Tribonyx gouldi......	Tasmania.........	Zool. Soc. Menagerie..	Ann. and Mag. Nat. Hist., ser. 3, XX, p. 123 (1867).	427
Trichoglossus rubri gularis.	New Britain.....	Mus. Godeffroy......	Proc. Zool. Soc. London, 1881, p. 451.	879
—— subplacens.......	Naiabui, New Guinea.	D'Albertis Coll......	Proc. Zool. Soc. London, 1876, p. 519.	733
Troglodytes brunnei collis.	Parada, S. Mexico.	Sclater Coll. in Brit. Mus.	Proc. Zool. Soc. London, 1858, p. 297.	126
—— hypaëdon	S. Mexico.........	....do	Proc. Zool. Soc. London, 1861, p. 128.	215
—— solstitialis	Matos and Pinipi, Ecuador.	....do	Proc. Zool. Soc. London, 1858, p. 550.	134
Trogon chionurus.....	Panama...........	Salvin-Godman Coll. in Brit. Mus.	Proc. Zool. Soc. London, 1870, p. 843.	524
Turdus ephippialis ...	Colombia	Sclater Coll. in Brit. Mus.	Proc. Zool. Soc. London, 1862, p. 109.	255
—— fulviventris, Verr. MS.	Bogota, Colombia.	....do	Proc. Zool. Soc. London, 1857, p. 273.	114
—— hortulorum	Macao, China....	Swinhoe Coll........	Ibis, 1863, p. 196..........	298
—— ignobilis	Colombia	Sclater Coll. in Brit. Mus.	Proc. Zool. Soc. London, 1857, p. 273.	114
—— leucauchen.......	Guatemala........	....do	Proc. Zool. Soc. London, 1858, p. 447.	130
—— pinicola	Jalapa, S. Mexico.	....do	Proc. Zool. Soc. London, 1859, p. 334.	149
—— subcinereus......	Chili.............	....do	Proc. Zool. Soc. London, 1866, p. 320.	387
Turtur aldabranus....	Aldabra Island...	Cambridge Mus...	Proc. Zool. Soc. London, 1871, pp.623, 692, pl.lxxiii.	555
Tyranneutes brachy urus.	Bartica Grove, British Guiana.	Salvin-Godman Coll. in Brit. Mus.	Ibis, 1881, p. 269........	891
Tyranniscus gracili pes, Scl. MS.	Pebas, Peru......	Sclater Coll. in Brit. Mus.	Proc. Zool. Soc. London, 1867, p. 981.	423
—— griseiceps.......	Pallatanga and Ba bahoyo, Ecuador.	....do	Proc. Zool. Soc. London, 1870, p. 842.	524
—— improbus	Andes of Vene zuela and Colom bia.	....do	Proc. Zool. Soc. London, 1870, p. 841, pl. liii, fig. 3.	524
—— leucogonys.......	Colombia	....do	Proc. Zool. Soc. London, 1870, p. 841, pl. liii, fig. 1.	524
—— viridissimus	Cosnipata, Peru...	....do	Proc. Zool. Soc. London, 1873, p. 782.	633
Tyrannula phœnicura	Quijos, Ecuador...	Gould Coll...........	Proc. Zool. Soc. London, 1854, p.113, pl. lxvi, fig.1.	59
—— sulphureipygia ...	Cordova, S.Mexico	Salló Coll...........	Proc. Zool. Soc. London, 1856, p. 296.	92
Tyrannulus chrysops.	Gualaquiza and Zamora, Ecuador	Sclater Coll. in Brit. Mus.	Proc. Zool. Soc. London, 1858, p. 458.	131
—— cinereiceps.......	Pallatanga, Ecua dor.	....do	Proc. Zool. Soc. London, 1860, p. 69.	163
—— flavidifrons	....do	....do	....do	163
—— semiflavus	Vera Paz, Guate mala.	Salvin-Godman Coll. in Brit. Mus.	Proc. Zool. Soc. London, 1860, p. 300.	182
Tyrannus atrifrons...	Ecuador	Eyton Coll........	Proc. Zool. Soc. London, 1857, p. 274.	114
—— inca, Licht. MS...	Bolivia	Sclater Coll. in Brit. Mus.	Proc. Zool. Soc. London, 1861, p. 383.	229
—— niveigularis......	Babahoyo, Ecua dor.	....do	Proc. Zool. Soc. London, 1860, p. 281.	180
Upucerthia bridgesi ..	Bolivia	Brit. Mus........	Proc. Zool. Soc. London, 1889, p. 32.	1056
Urochroma dilectis sima.	Merida, Vene zuela.	Sclater Coll. in Brit. Mus.	Proc. Zool. Soc. London, 1870, p. 788, pl. xlvii.	520
—— stictoptera......	Colombia	....do	Proc. Zool. Soc. London, 1862, p. 112, pl. xl.	255
Urogalba amazonum..	N. Brazil, Para, and R. Amazon.	Sclater Coll.......	Proc. Zool. Soc. London, 1855, p. 14.	69
Ursus japonicus......	Japan	Zool. Soc. Menagerie..	Proc. Zool. Soc. London, 1862, pp. 187, 261, pl. xxxii.	264, 269
—— nasutus..........	South America (?).	....do	Proc. Zool. Soc. London, 1868, p. 73, pl. viii.	432
Vireo hypochryseus..	Mexico	Sclater Coll. in Brit. Mus.	Proc. Zool. Soc. London, 1862, p. 309, pl. xlvi.	272
—— josephæ	Pallatanga, Ecua dor.	....do	Proc. Zool. Soc. London, 1859, p. 137, pl. cliv.	143
—— modestus........	Jamaica	....do	Proc. Zool. Soc. London, 1860, p. 462.	197

List of new species described—Continued.

Name.	Locality.	Location of type.	Place of description.	No. of paper.
Vireolanius pulchellus	Central America..	Brit. Mus............	Ibis, 1859, p. 12............	156
Vireosylvia cobanensis...............	Guatemala........	Sclater Coll. in Brit. Mus.	Proc. Zool. Soc. London, 1860, p. 463.	197
Xenops littoralis.....	Esmeraldas, Ecuador.	.....do	Proc. Zool. Soc. London, 1861, p. 379.	229
—— mexicanus	Cordova, S. Mexico.	Sallé Coll............	Proc. Zool. Soc. London, 1856, p. 289.	92
Xiphocolaptes emigrans.	Central America..	Sclater Coll. in Brit. Mus.	Ibis, 1859, p. 118	156a
Xiphorhynchus pusillus.	Colombia	.....do	Proc. Zool. Soc. London, 1860, p. 278.	180
—— thoracicus	Babahoyo, Ecuador.	.....do	Proc. Zool. Soc. London, 1860, p. 277.	180
Zonotrichia botteri...	Orizaba, Mexico ..	Botteri Coll..........	Proc. Zool. Soc. London, 1857, p. 214.	109
—— boucardi	South Mexico	Sclater Coll. in Brit. Mus.	Proc. Zool. Soc. London, 1867, p. 1, pl. i.	398
—— quinquestriata...	Mexico	.....do	Proc. Zool. Soc. London, 1868, p. 323.	443
Zosterops griseiventris	Larat, Loetoe and Moloc, Teninber Islands.	Brit. Mus............	Proc. Zool. Soc. London, 1883, p. 199.	932

List of species figured—Continued.

Name.	Where figured.	No. of paper.
Babirussa alfurus	Proc. Zool. Soc. London, 1860, p. 443, pl. lxxxiii	194
——, young	Proc. Zool. Soc. London, 1883, p. 463, pl. xlvii	941
Balæniceps rex	Wolf's Zoological Sketches, II, pl. xliv	7
Basileuterus cinereicollis	Proc. Zool. Soc. London, 1865, p. 285, pl. ix, fig. 2	341
—— fraseri	Proc. Zool. Soc. London, 1883, p. 653, pl. lxi	946
—— mesoleucus	Proc. Zool. Soc. London, 1865, p. 286, pl. ix, fig. 1	341
—— semicervinus	Proc. Zool. Soc. London, 1865, p. 286, pl. x, fig. 1	341
—— uropygialis	Proc. Zool. Soc. London, 1865, p. 286, pl. x, fig. 2	341
Bassaris astuta	Wolf's Zoological Sketches, I, pl. xiv	7
Berlepschia rikeri	Ibis, 1889, p. 350, pl. xi	1079
Bernicla magellanica (Chloephaga pollocephala in text) ♂, ♀.	Wolf's Zoological Sketches, I, pl. xlix	7
Bolborhynchus aymara	Argentine Ornith., II, p. 46, pl. xv	21
Boa frontalis, ♀ adult and young...	Proc. Zool. Soc. London, 1882, p. 233, pl. x	900
——, young	Proc. Zool. Soc. London, 1866, p. 1, pl. i	368
Botaurus pinnatus	Exotic Ornith., p. 181, pl. xci	12
Brachygalba albigularis	Monogr. of Jacamars and Puff-birds, p. 45, pl. xiv	15
—— geringi, ♂, ♀	Monogr. of Jacamars and Puff-birds, p. 41, pl. xii	15
——— ♂, ♀	Proc. Zool. Soc. London, 1869, p. 253, pl. xviii	473
—— lugubris, ♂, ♀	Monogr. of Jacamars and Puff-birds. p. 39, pl. xi	15
—— melanosterna, ♂	Monogr. of Jacamars and Puff-birds, p. 47, pl. xv	15
—— salmoni	Monogr. of Jacamars and Puff-birds. p. 43, pl. xiii	15
Bradypus tridactylus	Wolf's Zoological Sketches, II, pl. xxv	7
Buarremon castaneifrons	Proc. Zool. Soc. London, 1875, p. 235, pl. xxxv, fig. 1	686
—— comptus	Cat. Bds. Brit. Mus., XI, p. 264, pl. xv	19
—— eleoprorus, egg	Proc. Zool. Soc. London, 1879, p. 504, pl. xlii, fig. 7	825
—— latinuchus	Ibis, 1879, p. 426, pl. x, fig. 1	838
—— leucopis	Cat. Bds. Brit. Mus., XI, p. 261, pl. xiv	19
—— leucopterus	Proc. Zool. Soc. London, 1855, p. 214, pl. cix	80
—— melanolæmus	Ibis, 1879, p. 425, pl. x, fig. 2	838
—— nationi	Proc. Zool. Soc. London, 1881, p. 485, pl. xlvi	880
—— taczanowskii	Proc. Zool. Soc. London, 1875, p. 236, pl. xxxv, fig. 2	686
—— tricolor	Cat. Bds. Brit. Mus., XI, p. 269, pl. xvi	19
Bubalis buselaphus	The Book of Antelopes, I, p. 7, pl. i (1894)	26
—— caama	The Book of Antelopes, I, p. 33, pl. iv (1894)	26
—— cokei	The Book of Antelopes, I, p. 27, pl. iii (1894)	26
—— lichtensteini	The Book of Antelopes, I, p. 45, pl. v (1894)	26
—— swaynei	The Book of Antelopes, I, p. 21, pl. ii (1894)	26
——, head	Proc. Zool. Soc. London, 1892, p. 100, pl. v	1137
Bubo fasciolatus	Proc. Zool. Soc. London, 1863, p. 376, pl. xxxiii	294
Bucco bicinctus	Synopsis of the Bucconidæ, p. 11, pl. ii	3
—— ——	Monogr. of Jacamars and Puff-birds, p. 91, pl. xxx	15
—— chacuru	Monogr. of Jacamars and Puff-birds, p. 103, pl. xxxiv	15
—— collaris, ♀	Monogr. of Jacamars and Puff-birds, p. 61, pl. xix	15
—— dysoni	Monogr. of Jacamars and Puff-birds, p. 67, pl. xxi	15
—— hyporhynchus	Monogr. of Jacamars and Puff-birds, p. 71, pl. xxii	15
—— ——	Proc. Zool. Soc. London, 1855, p. 193, pl. cv	78
—— lanceolatus	Synopsis of the Bucconidæ, p. 13, pl. iii	3
—— macrodactylus, ♀	Monogr. of Jacamars and Puff-birds, p. 85, pl. xxviii	15
—— macrorhynchus	Monogr. of Jacamars and Puff-birds, p. 65, pl. xx	15
—— maculatus	Monogr. of Jacamars and Puff-birds, p. 90, pl. xxxii	15
—— ordi	Monogr. of Jacamars and Puff-birds, p. 77, pl. xxv	15
—— pectoralis	Monogr. of Jacamars and Puff-birds, p. 75, pl. xxiv	15
—— pulmentum	Monogr. of Jacamars and Puff birds, p. 97, pl. xxxi, fig. 2	15
—— ——	Proc. Zool. Soc. London, 1855, p. 194, pl. cvi	78
—— radiatus, ♂, ♀	Monogr. of Jacamars and Puff-birds, p. 109, pl. xxxvi	15
—— ——	Proc. Zool. Soc. London, 1853, p. 122, pl. l	55
—— ruficollis	Synopsis of the Bucconidæ, p. 10, pl. i	3
—— ——	Monogr. of Jacamars and Puff-birds, p. 89, pl. xxix	15
—— striatipectus	Monogr. of Jacamars and Puff-birds, p. 101, pl. xxxiii	15
—— striolatus, ♀	Exotic Ornith., p. 153, pl. lxxvii	12
—— —— ♀	Monogr. of Jacamars and Puff-birds, p. 107, pl. xxxv	15
—— subtectus, ♂	Monogr. of Jacamars and Puff-birds, p. 83, pl. xxvii	15
—— swainsoni	Monogr. of Jacamars and Puff-birds, p. 73, pl. xxiii	15
—— tamatia, ♂	Monogr. of Jacamars and Puff-birds, p. 93, pl. xxxi, fig. 1	15
—— tectus	Monogr. of Jacamars and Puff-birds, p. 79, pl. xxvi	15
Buceros bicornis	Wolf's Zoological Sketches, II, pl. xxix	7
—— rhinoceros	Wolf's Zoological Sketches, II, pl. xxx	7
—— subcylindricus	Proc. Zool. Soc. London, 1870, p. 668, pl. xxxix	518
Buteo erythronotus (egg)	Ibis, 1860 p 25, pl. i, fig. 3	198
—— fuliginosus	Trans. Zool. Soc. London, IV, p. 267, pl. 62 (1858)	128
—— swainsoni	Argentine Ornith., II. p. 59. pl. xvi	21
—— zonocercus	Trans. Zool. Soc. London, IV p. 263, pl. 59 (1858)	119
Buthraupis arcæi	Proc. Zool. Soc. London, 1860, p. 439, pl. xxxi	484
—— chloronota	Proc. Zool. Soc. London, 1854, p. 97. pl. lxiv	58
Cacatua ducorpsii	Proc. Zool. Soc. London, 1862, p. 141. pl. xiv	259
—— ——	Proc. Zool. Soc. London, 1864, p. 180, pl. xvii. The species figured 1862. pl. xiv, under this name is C. ophthalmica.	259, 315
—— goffini	Proc. Zool. Soc. London, 1875, p. 61, pl. x	680
—— ophthalmica	Proc. Zool. Soc. London, 1864, p.188. Figured in Proc.Zool. Soc. London, 1862, pl. xiv, as C. ducorpsii.	259, 315

List of species figured—Continued.

Name.	Where figured.	No. of paper.
Caica xanthomera	Proc. Zool. Soc. London, 1879, p. 301, pl. xxviii	816
Calliste argentea	Monogr. of Genus Calliste, p. 75, pl. xxxiv	5
—— arthusi	Monogr. of Genus Calliste, p. 35, pl. xvi	5
—— aurulenta	Monogr. of Genus Calliste, p. 29, pl. xlv, fig. 2	5
—— argyrofenges	Proc. Zool. Soc. London, 1876, p. 354, pl. xxx, fig. 2	723
—— atricapilla, ♂, ♀	Monogr. of Genus Calliste, p. 73, pl. xxxiii	5
—— atricœrulea	Monogr. of Genus Calliste, p. 69, pl. xxxi	5
—— boliviana	Monogr. of Genus Calliste, p. 67, pl. xxx	5
—— brasiliensis	Monogr. of Genus Calliste, p. 61, pl. xxviii	5
—— cabanisi	Ibis, 1868, p. 71, pl. iii	460
—— cayana	Monogr. of Genus Calliste, p. 41, pl. xix	5
—— chrysophrys	Contr. to Ornithology, 1851, p. 24, pl. lxix, fig. 2	34
—— chrysotis	Monogr. of Genus Calliste, p. 97, pl. xlii	5
—— cœlicolor	Monogr. of Genus Calliste, p. 3, pl. i, fig. 2	5
—— cucullata	Monogr. of Genus Calliste, p. 45, pl. xx	5
—— cyaneicollis	Monogr. of Genus Calliste, p. 87, pl. xxxviii	5
—— cyaneiventris	Monogr. of Genus Calliste, p. 13, pl. vi	5
—— cyanescens	Monogr. of Genus Calliste, p. 79, pl. xxxv	5
—— cyanoptera	Monogr. of Genus Calliste, p. 53, pl. xxiv	5
—— cyanotis	Cat. American Birds, p. 71, pl. ix	8
—— ——	Ibis, 1876, p. 407, pl. xii, fig. 2	741
—— desmaresti	Monogr. of Genus Calliste, p. 59, pl. xxvii	5
—— dowii	Ibis, 1863, p. 451, pl. xii	300
—— fastuosa	Monogr. of Genus Calliste, p. 9, pl. iv	5
—— festiva	Monogr. of Genus Calliste, p. 11, pl. v	5
—— flava, ♂, ♀	Monogr. of Genus Calliste, p. 47, pl. xxi	5
—— flaviventris	Monogr. of Genus Calliste, p. 93, pl. xlix	5
—— florida	Proc. Zool. Soc. London, 1860, p. 416, pl. xxviii	479
—— fulvicervix	Proc. Zool. Soc. London, 1876, p. 354, pl. xxx, fig. 1	723
—— graminea	Monogr. of Genus Calliste, p. 25, pl. xii	5
—— guttata	Monogr. of Genus Calliste, p. 21, pl. x	5
—— gyrola	Monogr. of Genus Calliste, p. 55, pl. xxv	5
—— gyroloides	Monogr. of Genus Calliste, p. 57, pl. xxvi	5
—— icterocephala	Monogr. of Genus Calliste, p. 37, pl. xvii	5
—— ——	Contr. to Ornithology, 1851, p. 53, pl. lxx, fig. 1	35
—— inornata	Monogr. of Genus Calliste, p. 103, pl. xlv	5
—— labradorides	Monogr. of Genus Calliste, p. 89, pl. xxxix	5
—— larvata	Monogr. of Genus Calliste, p. 81, pl. xxxvi	5
—— lunigera	Monogr. of Genus Calliste, p. 95, pl. xlii	5
—— ——	Contr. to Ornithology, 1851, p. 65, pl. lxx, fig. 2	35
—— melanonota, ♂, ♀	Monogr. of Genus Calliste, p. 51, pl. xxiii	5
—— melanotis	Ibis, 1876, p. 408, pl. xii, fig. 1	741
—— nigricincta	Monogr. of Genus Calliste, p. 85, pl. xxxvii	5
—— parzudakii	Monogr. of Genus Calliste, p. 93, pl. xli	5
—— pretiosa	Monogr. of Genus Calliste, p. 49, pl. xxii	5
—— pulchra	Monogr. of Genus Calliste, p. 33, pl. xv	5
—— punctata	Monogr. of Genus Calliste, p. 19, pl. ix	5
—— ruficervix	Monogr. of Genus Calliste, p. 71, pl. xxxii	5
—— rufigenis	Monogr. of Genus Calliste, p. 91, pl. xl	5
—— rufigula (C. rufigularis in text)	Monogr. of Genus Calliste, p. 27, pl. xiii	5
—— schranki	Monogr. of Genus Calliste, p. 17, pl. viii	5
—— sclateri	Monogr. of Genus Calliste, p. 31, pl. xiv, fig. 1	5
—— tatao	Monogr. of Genus Calliste, p. 1, pl. i, fig. 1	5
—— thoracica	Monogr. of Genus Calliste, p. 15, pl. vii	5
—— tricolor	Monogr. of Genus Calliste, p. 7, pl. iii	5
—— venusta	Monogr. of Genus Calliste, p. 101, pl. xliv, fig. 2	5
—— virescens	Contr. to Ornithology, 1851, p. 22, pl. lxix, fig. 1	34
—— vitriolina	Monogr. of Genus Calliste, p. 39, pl. xviii	5
—— ——, egg	Proc. Zool. Soc. London, 1879, p. 498, pl. xlii, fig. 2	825
—— xanthocephala	Monogr. of Genus Calliste, p. 99, pl. xliv, fig. 1	5
—— xanthogastra	Monogr. of Genus Calliste, p. 23, pl. xi	5
—— yeni	Monogr. of Genus Calliste, p. 5, pl. ii	5
Callithrix, sp	Quart. Journ. of Sci., London, II, p. 621, pl. 8 (1865)	367
Calornis crassa, ♂, ♀	Proc. Zool. Soc. London, 1883, p. 56, pl. xiv	926
Campephaga aurulenta	Proc. Zool. Soc. London, 1873, p. 692, pl. liv	628
Camptostoma imberbe	Ibis, 1859, p. 444, pl. xiv, fig. 1	150
Campylorhynchus jocosus	Cat. American Birds, p. 17, pl. iii	8
Canis azarœ	Wolf's Zoological Sketches, I, pl. xvi	7
—— cerdo	Wolf's Zoological Sketches, II, pl. iv	7
—— chama	Proc. Zool. Soc. London, 1875, p. 81, pl. xvii	681
—— jubata	Proc. Zool. Soc. London, 1877, p. 806, pl. lxxxi	765
—— lateralis	Proc. Zool. Soc. London, 1870, p. 279, pl. xxiii	512
—— microtis	Proc. Zool. Soc. London, 1882, p. 631, pl. xlvii	917
—— niger, ♂, ♀	Proc. Zool. Soc. London, 1874, p. 655, pl. lxxviii	667
Capito maculicoronatus, ♂, ♀	Ibis, 1862, p. 1, pl. i	274
—— steerii	Proc. Zool. Soc. London, 1878, p. 140, pl. xvi	775
Capra ægagrus, ♂	Proc. Zool. Soc. London, 1886, p. 315, pl. xxxi	1006
—— jemlaica	Wolf's Zoological Sketches, I, pl. xxv	7
—— megaceros	Wolf's Zoological Sketches, II, pl. xx	7
—— picta, ♀	Proc. Zool. Soc. London, 1872, 689, pl. lviii	592
—— sinaitica, ♂	Proc. Zool. Soc. London, 1880, p. 316, pl. xxxii	1006

List of species figured—Continued.

Name.	Where figured.	No. of paper.
Cardinalis phœniceus, ♂, ♀	Exotic Ornith., p. 125, pl. lxiii................	12
Carpophaga melanochroa.........	Proc. Zool. Soc. London, 1878, p. 672, pl. xlii	796
Casarca cana × Tadorna vulpanser, hybrid, ♂, ♀.	Proc. Zool. Soc. London, 1859, p. 442, pl. clviii	155
—— leucoptera (Anas scutulata in text).	Wolf's Zoological Sketches, II, pl. xlix...................	7
Casuarius beccarii (head).........	Proc. Zool. Soc. London, 1875, p. 527, pl. lviii............	695
—— bennettii, ♂, ♀	Wolf's Zoological Sketches, I, pl. xliii	7
——	Trans. Zool. Soc. London, IV, p. 359, pl. lxxii (1862).........	276
—— ——, young............	Proc. Zool. Soc. London, 1863, p. 518, pl. xlii...........	296
—— bicarunculatus..............	Trans. Zool. Soc. London, IV, p. 358, pl. lxxiii (1862).........	276
—— ——	Proc. Zool. Soc. London, 1872, p. 495, pl. xxvi	582
—— galeatus	Trans. Zool. Soc. London, IV, p. 358, pl. lxxi(1862).........	276
—— kaupi	Proc. Zool. Soc. London, 1872, p. 149, pl. ix..........	579
—— picticollis (head)............	Proc. Zool. Soc. London, 1875, p. 85, pl. xviii.........	684
—— uniappendiculatus............	Trans. Zool. Soc. London, IV, p. 350, pl. lxxiv (1862)	276
—— ——	Proc. Zool. Soc. London, 1875, p. 85, pl. xx	684
—— westormanni (head)..........	Proc. Zool. Soc. London, 1875, p. 85, pl. xix..........	684
Catharopeza bishopi, ♀ adult and ♂ jr.	Ibis, 1880, p. 73, pl. i................	862
Cathartes californianus (egg).....	Ibis, 1800, p. 278, pl. viii...................	202
—— —— (young).................	Ibis, 1800, p. 278, pl. ix	202
Cebus, sp...................	Quart. Journ. of Sci., London, II, p. 621, pl. 8 (1865)	367
Coleus kerri, ♂, ♀	Ibis, 1892, p. 136, pl. iii.............	1156
Centrites orcas.............	Exotic Ornith., p. 191, pl. xcvi...............	12
Centropelma micropterum........	Exotic Ornith., p. 189, pl. xcv...............	12
Centropsar mirus................	Proc. Zool. Soc. London, 1874, p. 176, pl. xxvi.........	653
Cephalophus dorsalis...........	Proc. Zool. Soc. London, 1869, p. 505, pl. xlvi...........	490
Cephalopterus penduliger	Ibis, 1859, p. 114, pl. iii	143
Ceratopipra iracunda.............	Cat. Bds. Brit. Mus., XIV, p. 288, pl. xix	20
Cercoleptes caudivolvulus........	Quart. Journ. of Sci., London, II, p. 621, pl. 8 (1865)	367
Cercopithecus brazzæ	Proc. Zool. Soc. London, 1893, p. 443, pl. xxxiii	1172
—— martini	Proc. Zool. Soc. London, 1884, p. 176, pl. xiv.........	956
—— moloneyi...............	Proc. Zool. Soc. London, 1893, p. 252, pl. xvii..........	1166
—— pluto (C. stangeri on plate)....	Wolf's Zoological Sketches, I, pl. ii................	7
—— schmidti	Proc. Zool. Soc. London, 1893, p. 245, pl. xvi..........	1166
—— stairsi	Proc. Zool. Soc. London, 1892, p. 580, pl. xl...........	1152
—— stangeri (C. pluto in text)....	Wolf's Zoological Sketches, I, pl. ii................	7
Ceriornis blythii	Proc. Zool. Soc. London, 1870, p. 163, pl. xv..........	509
—— melanocephala..............	List of Species of Phasianidæ, p. 10, pl. x...........	10
—— satyra, ♂, ♀	Wolf's Zoological Sketches, II, pl. xxxix...........	7
—— ——, egg.................	Proc. Zool. Soc. London, 1879, p. 117, pl. viii, fig. 4.........	810
—— temmincki	List of Species of Phasianidæ, p. 11, pl. xi	10
—— ——, egg.................	Proc. Zool. Soc. London, 1879, p. 117, pl. viii, fig. 3.........	810
Certhiola dominicana............	Cat. Bds. Brit. Mus., XI, p. 44, pl. v, fig. 2	19
—— martinicana (C. martinicensis on plate).	Cat. Bds. Brit. Mus., XI, p. 46, pl. v, fig. 1	19
Cervulus crinifrons...............	Proc. Zool. Soc. London, 1885, p. 1, pl. i	971
—— micrurus...................	Proc. Zool. Soc. London, 1875, p. 421, pl. li, fig. 1..........	692
—— reevesi, young.............	Proc. Zool. Soc. London, 1875, p. 422, pl. li, fig. 2..........	692
Cervus alfredi..................	Proc. Zool. Soc. London, 1870, p. 381, pl. xxviii.........	515
—— canadensis, ♂, ♀	Wolf's Zoological Sketches, I, pl. xix...............	7
—— cashmeerianus, ♂.........	Trans. Zool. Soc. London, VII, p. 339, pl. xxx (1871)	569
—— davidianus, ♂, ♀.........	Trans. Zool. Soc. London, VII, p. 333, pl. xxviii (1871)	569
—— duvaucelli, ♂, ♀ in summer dress.	Trans. Zool. Soc. London, VII, p. 346, pl. xxxvi (1871)	569
—— eldi, ♂ in summer dress.......	Trans. Zool. Soc. London, VII, p. 348, pls. xxxvii, xxxviii (1871).	569
—— humilis	Wolf's Zoological Sketches, II, pl. xviii	7
—— leucurus, ♂, ♀...........	Wolf's Zoological Sketches, I, pl. xx	7
—— manchuricus, ♂, ♀	Wolf's Zoological Sketches, II, pl. xiii	7
—— ——, in summer and winter dress.	Trans. Zool. Soc. London, VII, p. 344, pl. xxxi, in summer dress; pl. xxxii, in winter dress (1871).	569
—— maral (C. wallichii on plate), ♂, ♀ and young.	Wolf's Zoological Sketches, II, pl. xii	7
—— ——, ♂, ♀ in winter dress, and young.	Trans. Zool. Soc. London, VII, p. 336, pl. xxix (1871)........	569
—— pudu, ♂, ♀	Proc. Zool. Soc. London, 1871, p. 238, pl. xvii	543
—— rusa, ♂, ♀...................	Wolf's Zoological Sketches, II, pl. xvi	7
—— savannarum, ♂...........	Proc. Zool. Soc. London, 1872, p. 690, pl. lix	592
—— sika, ♂, ♀...................	Wolf's Zoological Sketches, II, pl. xv	7
—— ——, in summer dress.....	Trans. Zool. Soc. London, VII, p. 346, pl. xxxv (1871)	569
—— swinhoii	Wolf's Zoological Sketches, II, pl. xvii...............	7
—— ——................?..	Proc. Zool. Soc. London, 1862, p. 152, pl. xvii..............	260
—— ——, ♂, ♀ in winter dress.....	Trans. Zool. Soc. London, VII, p. 349, pl. xxxix (1871)	569
—— tcevanus..................	Proc. Zool. Soc. London, 1862, p. 152, pl. xvi.............	260
—— ——, ♂ in summer dress and ♀ and young.	Trans. Zool. Soc. London, VII, p. 345, pl. xxxiii, ♂ in summer dress; xxxiv, ♂ and young (1871).	569
—— ——..............	Wolf's Zoological Sketches, II, pl. xiv	7
—— wallichii (C. maral in text),♂, ♀, young.	Wolf's Zoological Sketches, II, pl. xii	7

List of species figured—Continued.

Name.	Where figured.	No. of paper.
Chætocercus burmeisteri.........	Argentine Ornith., II, p. 2, pl. xi	21
Chætura biscutata.................	Proc. Zool. Soc. London, 1865, p. 609, pl. xxxiv	354
—— brachycerca.................	Proc. Zool. Soc. London, 1867, p. 758, pl. xxxiv	417
—— cassinii	Proc. Zool. Soc. London, 1863, p. 205, pl. xlv, fig. 2	287
—— cinereiventris	Proc. Zool. Soc. London, 1863, p. 101, pl. xlv, fig. 1	283
—— rutila, ♂, ♀	Ibis, 1860, p. 37, pl. iii	200
—— semicollaris	Exotic Ornith., p. 103, pl. lii	12
Chamæza mollissima.............	Proc. Zool. Soc. London, 1855, p. 89, pl. xcv	
Chasiempis sandwichensis, ♂, ♀ ...	Ibis, 1885, p. 18, pl. i..........................	994
Chasmorhynchus nudicollis........	Intellectual Observer, X, p. 401, pl. xi................	428
Chauna nigricollis...............	Proc. Zool. Soc. London, 1864, p. 75, pl. xi..............	305
Chelidoptera albipennis...........	Synopsis of the Bucconidæ, p. 24, pl. iv..............	3
—— brasiliensis	Monogr. of Jacamars and Puff-birds, p. 165, pl. lv, fig. 2 ..	15
—— tenebrosa	Monogr. of Jacamars and Puff-birds, p. 161, pl. lv, fig. 1 ..	15
—— (egg)	Monogr. of Jacamars and Puff-birds, p. 162, pl. lv	15
Chiromachæris manacus, egg......	Proc. Zool. Soc. London, 1879, p. 517, pl. xlii, fig. 11......	825
—— vitellina, egg..............	Proc. Zool. Soc. London, 1879, p. 517, pl. xlii, fig. 10......	825
Chiromyia madagascariensis	Wolf's Zoological Sketches, II, pl. iii..................	7
	Quart. Journ. of Sci., London, I, p. 216, pl. ii (1864)	335
Chiroxiphia regina..............	Cat. American Birds, p. 251, pl. xx...................	8
Chlœphaga magellanica, ♂, ♀	Wolf's Zoological Sketches, II, pl. xlviii	7
—— poliocephala, ♂, ♀ (Bernicla magellanica on plate).	Wolf's Zoological Sketches, I, pl. xlix..............	7
—— rubidiceps	Proc. Zool. Soc. London, 1860, p. 387, pl. clxxiii	189
Chlorochrysa calliparæa...........	Contr. to Ornithology, 1851, p. 99, pl. lxxiii, fig. 1	39
—— nitidissima..............	Ibis, 1875, p. 466, pl. x..........................	704
—— phœnicotis................	Contr. to Ornithology, 1851, p. 100, pl. lxxiii, fig. 2.......	39
Chloronerpes dignus, ♂	Proc. Zool. Soc. London, 1877, p. 20, pl. i............	745
Chlorophanes purpurascens, ♂	Cat. Bds. Brit. Mus., XI, p. 31, pl. iv..............	19
Chlorophonia calophrys, ♂, ♀	Exotic Ornith., p. 135, pl. lxviii...................	12
—— flavirostris, ♀..........	Cat. Bds. Brit. Mus., XI, p. 56, pl. vi, fig. 2.........	19
—— frontalis	Exotic Ornith., p. 81, pl. xli, fig. 1.................	12
—— longipennis	Exotic Ornith., p. 82, pl. xli, fig. 2.................	12
—— occipitalis, ♂, ♀.........	Exotic Ornith., p. 83, pl. xlii	12
—— roraimæ, ♂	Cat. Bds. Brit. Mus., XI, p. 56, pl. vi, fig. 1.........	19
Chlorospingus castaneicollis.......	Cat. American Birds, p. 90, pl. x.................	8
—— flavipectus, egg..........	Proc. Zool. Soc. London, 1879, p. 503, pl. xlii, fig. 6.......	825
—— goeringi.................	Proc. Zool. Soc. London, 1870, p. 784, pl. xlvi, fig. 1.......	520
—— melanotis	Proc. Zool. Soc. London, 1854, p. 157, pl. lxviii........	60
—— phæocephalus	Proc. Zool. Soc. London, 1877, p. 521, pl. lii, fig. 2	759
Cholopus didactylus.............	Quart. Journ. of Sci., London, II, p. 621, pl. 8 (1865)	367
	Proc. Zool. Soc. London, 1872, p. 861, pl. lxxii, pl. 2.......	599
—— hoffmanni.............	Proc. Zool. Soc. London, 1872, p. 861, pl. lxxii, pl. 1.......	599
Chrysotis bouqueti	Proc. Zool. Soc. London, 1875, p. 61, pl. xi	080
—— cœligena	Proc. Zool. Soc. London, 1880, p. 68, pl. ix, fig. 1	846
—— dufresniana	Proc. Zool. Soc. London, 1880, p. 68, pl. ix, fig. 2	846
—— erythrura	Proc. Zool. Soc. London, 1880, p. 23, pl. ii	842
—— finschi	Proc. Zool. Soc. London, 1874, p. 200, pl. xxxiv........	655
—— xantholora..............	Proc. Zool. Soc. London, 1875, p. 157, pl. xxvi........	685
Chunga burmeisteri	Proc. Zool. Soc. London, 1870, p. 666, pl. xxxvi........	518
Ciccaba nigrolineata............	Trans. Zool. Soc. London, IV, p. 268, pl. 63 (1859)	141
Cichlopsis leucogonys	Exotic Ornith., p. 37, pl. xix......................	12
Ciconia boyciana...............	Proc. Zool. Soc. London, 1874, p. 2, pl. i.............	644
—— senegalensis (Mycteria senegalensis on plate).	Wolf's Zoological Sketches, II, pl. xliii............	7
Cinclocerthia gutturalis	Exotic Ornith., p. 23, pl. xii......................	12
—— macrorhyncha	Exotic Ornith., p. 21, pl. xi.......................	12
—— ruficauda	Exotic Ornith., p. 19, pl. x.......................	12
Cinclus leuconotus	Cat. American Birds, p. 10, pl. ii.................	8
—— schulzi................	Argentine Ornith., I, p. 11, pl. ii..................	21
Cinnyris balfouri, bird and nest...	Proc. Zool. Soc. London, 1881, p. 169, pl. xv, fig. 2......	870
Circus maillardi, ♂, ♀	Ibis, 1863, p. 163, pl. iv	297
Cisticola incana................	Proc. Zool. Soc. London, 1881, p. 166, pl. xv, fig. 1........	870
Clemmys unicolor...............	Proc. Zool. Soc. London, 1873, p. 517, pl. xliv.........	621
Clotho nasicornis	Wolf's Zoological Sketches, II, pl. l.................	7
Cnemophilus macgregorii.........	Ibis, 1891, p. 414, pl. x..........................	1127
Cnipodectes subbrunneus........	Cat. Bds. Brit. Mus., XIV, p. 107, pl. xvi..............	20
Cnipolegus hudsoni, ♂	Proc. Zool. Soc. London 1872, p. 541, pl. xxxi........	584
Cobus ellipsiprymnus, ♀ and young.	Proc. Zool. Soc. London, 1803, p. 505, pl. xxxix.........	1173
Coccothraustes maculipennis, ♂, ♀.	Proc. Zool. Soc. London, 1868, p. 251, pl. clxiii.........	178
Coccyzus cinereus	Argentine Ornith., II, p. 38, pl. xiii	21
Colius castanonotus	Proc. Zool. Soc. London, 1876, p. 413, pl. xxxv.........	725
—— erythromelon	Proc. Zool. Soc. London, 1884, p. 475, pl. xlv, figs. 2, 3......	962
—— nigricollis	Proc. Zool. Soc. London, 1884, p. 530, pl. xlv, fig. 1......	964
Colobus ferrugineus............	Proc. Zool. Soc. London, 1860, p. 590, pl. xlviii.........	1098
Conirostrum ferrugineiventre	Proc. Zool. Soc. London, 1855, p. 74, pl. xxxv.........	73
—— fraseri, ♂	Cat. Bds. Brit. Mus., XI, p. 15, pl. ii, fig. 1..........	19
Conopophaga cucullata...........	Proc. Zool. Soc. London, 1856, p. 29, pl. cxix.........	84
Conurus egregius	Ibis, 1881, p. 130, pl. iv.........................	890
—— hoffmanni..............	Exotic Ornith., p. 161, pl. lxxxi..................	12
—— molinæ	Argentine Ornith., II, p. 43, pl. xiv................	21

List of species figured—Continued.

Name.	Where figured.	No. of paper.
Conurus rhodogaster	Proc. Zool. Soc. London, 1864, p. 298, pl. xxiv	320
—— rubritorquis	Proc. Zool. Soc. London, 1886, p. 539, pl. lvi	1013
Corvus capellanus	Proc. Zool. Soc. London, 1876, p. 694, pl. lxvi	734
Coryphistera alaudina	Proc. Zool. Soc. London, 1870, p. 57, pl. iii	501
Corythaix leucolopha	Student and Intellectual Observer, II, p. 4, pl. i (1860)	498
Cosmetornis vexillarius	Ibis, 1864, p. 114, pl. ii	330
Cotinga porphyroluema	Contr. to Ornithology, 1852, p. 130, pl. xcvi	51
Crax alberti, ♂, ♀	Trans. Zool. Soc. London, IX, p. 280, pl. xlviii (1875)	705
—— alector, ♂, ♀	Trans. Zool. Soc. London, IX, p. 277, pl. xliii (1875)	705
—— carunculata, ♂, ♀	Trans. Zool. Soc. London, IX, p. 279, pl. xlvii (1875)	705
—— daubentoni, ♂, ♀	Trans. Zool. Soc. London, IX, p. 276, pl. xli, xlii (1875)	705
—— erythrognatha, ♂, ♀	Trans. Zool. Soc. London, X, p. 543, pl. xc (1879)	839
—— globicera, ♂, ♀	Trans. Zool. Soc. London, IX, p. 274, pl. xl (1875)	705
——, ♀	Trans. Zool. Soc. London, X, p. 543, pl. lxxxix (1879)	839
—— globulosa, ♂, ♀	Trans. Zool. Soc. London, IX, p. 270, pl. xlvi (1875)	705
——, ♀	Trans. Zool. Soc. London, X, p. 544, pl. xci (1879)	839
—— incommoda, ♀	Trans. Zool. Soc. London, IX, p. 281, pl. xlix (1875)	705
——	Trans. Zool. Soc. London, X, p. 544, pl. xciii (1879)	839
—— sclateri, ♂, ♀	Trans. Zool. Soc. London, IX, p. 278, pl. xliv, xlv (1875)	705
—— viridirostris	Trans. Zool. Soc. London, X, p. 544, pl. xcii (1879)	839
Creurgops verticalis	Proc. Zool. Soc. London, 1858, p. 72, pl. cxxxii, fig. 2	116
Crossoptilon auritum	List of Species of Phasianidæ, p. 6, pl. v	10
—— mantchuricum, egg	Proc. Zool. Soc. London, 1879, p. 118, pl. viii, fig. 5	810
—— tibetanum	List of Species of Phasianidæ, p. 6, pl. iv	10
Crypturus boucardi, ♂, ♀	Exotic Ornith., p. 91, pl. xlvi	12
—— meserythrus	Exotic Ornith. p. 93, pl. xlvii	12
—— sallæi, ♂, ♀	Exotic Ornith. p. 89, pl. xlv	12
—— transfasciatus	Proc. Zool. Soc. London, 1878, p. 141, pl. xiii	775
Culicivora boliviana	Proc. Zool. Soc. London, 1852, p. 34, pl. xlvii	53
Cyanocitta melanocyanea (egg)	Ibis, 1859, p. 21, pl. v, fig. 6	156a
Cyanorhamphus saisseti	Proc. Zool. Soc. London, 1882, p. 630, pl. xlvi	917
Cyclopsitta suavissima, ♂, ♀	Proc. Zool. Soc. London, 1876, p. 520, pl. liv	733
Cyclorhis altirostris	Argentine Ornith., I, p. 24, pl. iii, fig. 2	21
—— atrirostris	Ibis, 1887, p. 324, pl. x	1037
—— ochrocephala	Argentine Ornith., I, p. 23, pl. iii, fig. 1	21
—— virenticeps	Proc. Zool. Soc. London, 1860, p. 274, pl. clxiv	180
Cygnus nigricollis, adult and young	Wolf's Zoological Sketches, I, pl. xlviii	7
——	Argentine Ornith., II, p. 124, pl. xviii	21
Cyphorinus albigularis	Proc. Zool. Soc. London, 1855, p. 76, pl. lxxxviii	73
—— dichrous	Proc. Zool. Soc. London, 1879, p. 492, pl. xli	825
—— lawrencii	Exotic Ornith., p. 41, pl. xxi	12
—— phæocephalus	Exotic Ornith., p. 43, pl. xxii	12
Cypselus squamatus, bird and nest	Proc. Zool. Soc. London, 1865, p. 605, pl. xxxiii	354
Dacnis analis (D. speciosa in text)	Contr. to Ornithology, 1852, p. 101, pl. xciii, fig. 2	47
—— cœruleicolor, ♂, ♀	Cat. Bds. Brit. Mus., XI, p. 21, pl. iii	19
——	Contr. to Ornithology, 1852, p. 102, pl. xciii, fig. 1	47
—— egregia, ♂, ♀	Cat. American Birds, p. 51, pl. vii	8
—— pulcherrima	Cat. American Birds, p. 51, pl. viii	8
—— salmoni, ♀	Cat. Bds. Brit. Mus, XI, p. 27, pl. ii, fig. 2	19
—— speciosa (D. analis on plate)	Contr. to Ornithology, 1852, p. 101, pl. xciii, fig. 2	47
—— venusta, ♂, ♀	Ibis, 1863, p. 315, pl. vii	299
Dafila spinicauda	Proc. Zool. Soc. London, 1870, p. 666, pl. xxxviii	518
Damalis hunteri, ♀	Proc. Zool. Soc. London, 1889, p. 372, pl. xlii	1072
Damaliscus hunteri	The Book of Antelopes, I, p. 53, pl. vi (1894)	26
Dasyprocta antillensis	Proc. Zool. Soc. London, 1874, p. 666, pl. lxxxii	668
Dendrocolaptes cytoni	Proc. Zool. Soc. London, 1853, p. 69, pl. lii	54
—— puncticollis	Proc. Zool. Soc. London, 1868, p. 54, pl. v	431
Dendrolagus bennettianus	Proc. Zool. Soc. London, 1894, p. 693, pl. xlvi	1223
Dendrornis polysticta	Cat. Bds. Brit. Mus., XV, p. 135, pl. x	22
Dicæum eximium	Proc. Zool. Soc. London, 1877, p. 102, pl. xiv, fig. 2	750
Dicotyles torquatus, adult and young.	Wolf's Zoological Sketches, II, pl. xxiii	7
Diglossa albilateralis, ♂, ♀	Ibis, 1875, p. 216, pl. v	702
—— gloriosa	Proc. Zool. Soc. London, 1870, p. 784, pl. xlvi, fig. 2	520
—— indigotica	Cat. American Birds, p. 49, pl. vi	8
—— mystacalis	Cat. Bds. Brit. Mus., XI, p. 6, pl. i	19
—— pectoralis	Ibis, 1875, p. 219, pl. iv	702
—— personata, egg	Proc. Zool. Soc. London, 1879, p. 496, pl. xlii, fig. 1	825
Donacicola spectabilis	Proc. Zool. Soc. London, 1879, p. 449, pl. xxxvii, fig. 2	822
Drepanornis albertisi, ♂, ♀	Proc. Zool. Soc. London, 1873, pp. 558, 560, pl. xlvii	625
Dromæus irroratus	Trans. Zool. Soc. London, IV, p. 360, pl. lxxvi (1862)	276
—— novæ hollandiæ	Trans. Zool. Soc. London, IV, p. 360, pl. lxxv (1862)	276
Drymornis bridgesi	Argentine Ornith., I, p. 109, pl. x	21
Dysithamnus leucostictus	Proc. Zool. Soc. London, 1858, p. 223, pl. cxl	121
—— semicinereus	Proc. Zool. Soc. London, 1855, p. 90, pl. xcvii	75
—— unicolor, egg	Proc. Zool. Soc. London, 1879, p. 525, pl. xliii, fig. 9	825
Echidna hystrix	Quart. Journ. of Sci., London, II, p. 19, pl. 5 (1865)	366
Echinogale telfairi	Quart. Journ. of Sci., London, I, p. 219, pl. ii (1864)	335
Eclectus riedeli, ♂, ♀	Proc. Zool. Soc. London, 1883, p. 195, pl. xxvi	932
Elainia griseigularis	Proc. Zool. Soc. London, 1858, p. 554, pl. cxlvi, fig. 1	134
—— olivina	Cat. Bds. Brit. Mus., XIV, p. 146, pl. xii	20

List of species figured—Continued.

Name.	Where figured.	No. of paper.
Elainia pallatangæ	Proc. Zool. Soc. London, 1861, p. 407, pl. xli	233
— placens	Ibis, 1859, p. 123, pl. iv, fig. 2	156a
— atictoptera	Proc. Zool. Soc. London, 1858, p. 554, pl. cxlvi, fig. 2	134
— vilissima	Ibis, 1859, p. 122, pl. iv, fig. 1	156a
Elephas africanus, adults and young.	Wolf's Zoological Sketches, II, pl. xxiv	7
Embernagra chrysoma	Cat. American Birds, p. 117, pl. xi	8
Equus asinus africanus	Proc. Zool. Soc. London, 1884, p. 542, pl. l, fig. 2	965
— — somalicus	Proc. Zool. Soc. London, 1884, p. 542, pl. l, fig. 1	965
Erythrura regia	Ibis, 1881, p. 544, pl. xv, fig. 2	894
— serena	Ibis, 1881, p. 544, pl. xv, fig. 1	894
Euchlornis jucunda	Proc. Zool. Soc. London, 1860, p. 89, pl. clx. Pipreola jucunda in text.	165
Euchrœtes coccineus	Proc. Zool. Soc. London, 1858, p. 73, pl. cxxxii, fig. 1	116
Eucometis cassinii	Proc. Zool. Soc. London, 1864, p. 351, pl. xxx	322
Eupetes leucostictus	Proc. Zool. Soc. London, 1873, p. 690, pl. lii	628
Euphonia chrysopasta, ♂, ♀	Proc. Zool. Soc. London, 1860, p. 438, pl. xxx, figs. 1, 2	483
— concinna, ♂, ♀	Cat. Bds. Brit. Mus., XI, p. 69, pl. vii	19
	Proc. Zool. Soc. London, 1854, p. 98, pl. lxv, fig. 2	58
— finschi, ♂	Cat. Bds. Brit. Mus., XI, p. 70, pl. viii, fig. 1	19
— gouldi, ♂, ♀	Proc. Zool. Soc. London, 1857, p. 66, pl. cxxiv	101
— hirundinacea	Proc. Zool. Soc. London, 1854, p. 98, pl. lxv, fig. 1	58
— insignis	Proc. Zool. Soc. London, 1877, p. 521, pl. lii, fig. 1	759
— melanura, ♂, ♀	Cat. Bds. Brit. Mus., XI, p. 78, pl. ix	19
— nigricollis	Contr. to Ornithology, 1851, p. 83, pl. lxxv, fig. 1	36
— pyrrhophrys	Contr. to Ornithology, 1851, p. 89, pl. lxxv, fig. 2	36
— saturata, ♂	Cat. Bds. Brit. Mus., XI, p. 70, pl. viii, fig. 2	19
— vittata, ♂	Cat. Bds. Brit. Mus., XI, p. 80, pl. x	19
Euplocamus erythrophthalmus, ♂, ♀.	Wolf's Zoological Sketches, II, pl. xxxiv	7
	List of Species of Phasianidæ, p. 7, pl. viii	10
— lineatus, ♂, ♀	Wolf's Zoological Sketches, II, pl. xxxviii	7
	List of Species of Phasianidæ, p. 8, pl. ix	10
— nobilis	Proc. Zool. Soc. London, 1863, p. 119, pl. xvi	285
— prælatus, ♂, ♀	Wolf's Zoological Sketches, II, pl. xxxv	7
	List of Species of Phasianidæ, p. 6, pl. vi	10
— swinhoii, ♂, ♀	Wolf's Zoological Sketches, II, pl. xxxvii	7
— vieillotii (Gallophasis vieilloti on plate).	Wolf's Zoological Sketches, II, pl. xxxvi	7
	List of Species of Phasianidæ, p. 6, pl. vii	10
Euscarthmus agilis	Proc. Zool. Soc. London, 1856, p. 28, pl. cxviii	84
— apicalis	Proc. Zool. Soc. London, 1887, p. 47, pl. ix, fig. 1	1019
— impiger	Cat. Bds. Brit. Mus., XIV, p. 84, pl. ix, fig. 2	20
	Proc. Zool. Soc. London, 1868, p. 171, pl. xlii, fig. 1	435
— russatus	Cat. Bds. Brit. Mus., XIV, p. 82, pl. ix, fig. 1	20
Falco circumcinctus	Ibis, 1862, p. 23, pl. ii	275
— dickinsoni	Ibis, 1864, p. 305, pl. viii	332
— groenlandicus	Wolf's Zoological Sketches, I, pl. xxxiv	7
— islandicus	Wolf's Zoological Sketches, I, pl. xxxv	7
— sacer, ♂, ♀	Wolf's Zoological Sketches, I, pl. xxxiii	7
Felis aurata	Proc. Zool. Soc. London, 1867, p. 816, pl. xxxvi	418
	Proc. Zool. Soc. London, 1873, p. 311, pl. xxvii	615
— canadensis (Lynx canadensis in text).	Wolf's Zoological Sketches, I, pl. xii	7
— caracal (red and dark varieties)	Wolf's Zoological Sketches, I, pls. x, xi	7
— chaus	Wolf's Zoological Sketches, I, pl. ix	7
— eyra	Wolf's Zoological Sketches, I, pl. vi	7
— jubata	Wolf's Zoological Sketches, I, pl. xiii	7
— lanea, ♂	Proc. Zool. Soc. London, 1877, p. 532, pl. lv	760
— leo (♀ and young)	Wolf's Zoological Sketches, I, pl. iii	7
— leopardus (black and spotted varieties).	Wolf's Zoological Sketches, I, pl. iv	7
— lynx	Wolf's Zoological Sketches, II, pl. vi	7
— macroscelis	Wolf's Zoological Sketches, I, pl. vii	7
— onca	Quart. Journ. of Sci., London, II, p. 621, pl. 8 (1865)	367
— picta	Wolf's Zoological Sketches, I, pl. v	7
— serval	Wolf's Zoological Sketches, I, pl. viii	7
— servalina	Proc. Zool. Soc. London, 1874, p. 495, pl. lxiii	663
— viverrina	Wolf's Zoological Sketches, II, pl. vii	7
— yaguarundi	Wolf's Zoological Sketches, II, pl. v	7
Formicivora boucardi, ♂, ♀	Cat. American Birds, p. 183, pl. xvi	8
— callinota	Proc. Zool. Soc. London, 1855, p. 89, pl. xcvi	75
— caudata, ♂, ♀	Proc. Zool. Soc. London, 1854, p. 254, pl. lxxiv	64
— erythrocera	Proc. Zool. Soc. London, 1858, p. 240, pl. cxlii	122
— hauxwelli	Proc. Zool. Soc. London, 1857, p. 131, pl. cxxvi, fig. 2	107
— strigilata, ♂, ♀	Exotic Ornith., p. 159, pl. lxxx	12
— urosticta	Proc. Zool. Soc. London, 1857, p. 130, pl. cxxvi, fig. 1	107
Fulica ardesiaca	Exotic Ornith., p. 113, pl. lvii	12
— armillata	Exotic Ornith., p. 115, pl. lviii	12
— leucoptera	Exotic Ornith., p. 119, pl. lx	12
— leucopyga	Exotic Ornith., p. 117, pl. lix	12

List of species figured—Continued.

Name.	Where figured.	No. of paper.
Fuligula nationi, ♂, ♀	Proc. Zool. Soc. London, 1878, p. 477, pl. xxxii	788
Furnarius torridus	Exotic Ornith., p. 7, pl. iv	12
—— ——	Cat. Bds. Brit. Mus., XV, p. 15, pl. ii	22
Galago alleni	Proc. Zool. Soc. London, 1863, p. 375, pl. xxxii	294
—— garnetti	Proc. Zool. Soc. London, 1864, p. 711, pl. xl	329
Galbalcyrhynchus leucotis, ♂, ♀	Monogr. of Jacamars and Puff-birds, p. 53, pl. xvii	15
Galbula albirostris, ♂, ♀	Monogr. of Jacamars and Puff-birds, p. 27, pl. vii	15
—— chalcothorax, ♂	Monogr. of Jacamars and Puff-birds, p. 37, pl. x	15
—— cyaneicollis, ♂	Monogr. of Jacamars and Puff-birds, p. 31, pl. viii	15
—— fuscicapilla	Proc. Zool. Soc. London, 1855, p. 13, pl. lxxvii	69
—— leucogastra, ♂, ♀	Monogr. of Jacamars and Puff-birds, p. 33, pl. ix	15
—— melanogenia, ♂, ♀	Monogr. of Jacamars and Puff-birds, p. 19, pl. v	15
—— ——	Contr. to Ornithology, 1852, p. 93, pl. xc	46
—— ruficauda, ♂, ♀	Monogr. of Jacamars and Puff-birds, p. 15, pl. iv	15
—— rufoviridis, ♂, ♀	Monogr. of Jacamars and Puff-birds, p. 11, pl. iii	15
—— tombacea, ♂, ♀	Monogr. of Jacamars and Puff-birds, p. 23, pl. vi	15
—— viridis, ♂, ♀	Monogr. of Jacamars and Puff-birds, p. 7, pl. ii	15
Galidictis vittata	Quart. Journ. of Sci., London, I, p. 219, pl. ii (1864)	335
Gallinago imperialis	Exotic Ornith., p. 193, pl. xcvii	12
—— nobilis	Exotic Ornith., p. 195, pl. xcviii	12
Gallinula nesiotis	Proc. Zool. Soc. London, 1861, p. 261, pl. xxx	221
Galloperdix lunulosa, ♂, ♀	Wolf's Zoological Sketches, I, pl. xli	7
Gallophasis horsfieldii	Wolf's Zoological Sketches, I, pl. xxxix	7
—— vieilloti (Euplocamus vieillotii in text)	Wolf's Zoological Sketches, II, pl. xxxvi	7
Gazella granti, ♂, ♀	Proc. Zool. Soc. London, 1875, p. 527, pl. lix	695
—— naso, head	Proc. Zool. Soc. London, 1886, p. 504, pl. li	1012
—— sœmmerringi	Proc. Zool. Soc. London, 1867, p. 817, pl. xxxvii	418
—— subgutturosa, ♂, ♀	Wolf's Zoological Sketches, I, pl. xxii	7
—— walleri, skin and head	Proc. Zool. Soc. London, 1884, p. 539, pl. xlix	965
Geobates pœcilopterus	Proc. Zool. Soc. London, 1866, p. 205, pl. xxi	383
Geositta crassirostris	Cat. Bds. Brit. Mus., XV, p. 10, pl. i	22
Geotrygon albifacies (figured as G. chiriquensis).	Exotic Ornith., p. 77, pl. xxxix	12
—— bourcieri	Exotic Ornith., p. 79, pl. xl	12
—— chiriquensis (error for G. albifacies).	Exotic Ornith., p. 77, pl. xxxix	12
—— ——	Exotic Ornith., p. 123, pl. lxii	12
Golunda pulchella	Proc. Zool. Soc. London, 1864, p. 100, pl. xiii	306
Gracula kreffti	Proc. Zool. Soc. London, 1860, p. 120, pl. ix	464
Grallaria dignissima	Proc. Zool. Soc. London, 1880, p. 160, pl. xvii	848
—— erythrotis	Cat. Bds. Brit. Mus., XV, p. 319, pl. xviii	22
—— flavotincta	Ibis, 1877, p. 445, pl. ix	768
—— fulviventris	Cat. Bds. Brit. Mus., XV, p. 323, pl. xx	22
—— haplonota	Cat. Bds. Brit. Mus., XV, p. 315, pl. xvi	22
—— modesta	Proc. Zool. Soc. London, 1855, p. 89, pl. xciv	75
—— ruficapilla, egg	Proc. Zool. Soc. London, 1879, p. 527, pl. xliii, fig. 6	825
—— ruficeps	Ibis, 1877, p. 444, pl. viii	768
—— ——, egg	Proc. Zool. Soc. London, 1879, p. 526, pl. xliii, fig. 5	825
—— rufo-cinerea	Cat. Bds. Brit. Mus., XV, p. 317, pl. xix	22
Granatellus pelzelni	Proc. Zool. Soc. London, 1864, p. 606, pl. xxxvii, fig. 1	328
—— sallæi	Proc. Zool. Soc. London, 1856, p. 292, pl. cxx	92
—— venustus	Proc. Zool. Soc. London, 1864, p. 607, pl. xxxvii, fig. 2	328
Graucalus sublineatus	Proc. Zool. Soc. London, 1879, p. 448, pl. xxxvi	822
Grus japonensis (G. montignesia in text).	Wolf's Zoological Sketches, I, pl. xlvi	7
—— montignesia (G. japonensis on plate).	......do	7
Gymnoglaux lawrencii	Proc. Zool. Soc. London, 1868, p. 327, pl. xxix	443
Gypohierax angolensis (immature examples).	Wolf's Zoological Sketches, I, pl. xxxvi	7
Hadrostomus homochrous, ♂, ♀	Cat. Bds. Brit. Mus., XIV, p. 334, pl. xxiv	20
—— ——, egg	Proc. Zool. Soc. London, 1879, p. 517, pl. xlii, fig. 12	825
Hæmophila pulchra, ♂	Ibis, 1886, p. 259, pl. viii	1016
Halmaturus luctuosus	Proc. Zool. Soc. London, 1874, p. 247, pl. xlii	656
Hapale melanura	Proc. Zool. Soc. London, 1875, p. 419, pl. i	692
Hapaloptila castanea	Monogr. of Jacamars and Puff-birds, p. 143, pl. xlvii	15
Harporhynchus ocellatus	Proc. Zool. Soc. London, 1862, p. 18, pl. iii	249
Heterocercus aurantiivertex	Cat. Bds. Brit. Mus., XIV, p. 325, pl. xxiii	20
Heteropelma flavicapillum	Cat. Bds. Brit. Mus., XIV, p. 321, pl. xxi	20
—— igniceps	Cat. Bds. Brit. Mus., XIV, p. 322, pl. xxii	20
—— wallacii	Cat. Bds. Brit. Mus., XIV, p. 319, pl. xx	20
Hippopotamus amphibius	Wolf's Zoological Sketches, I, pl. xxvii	7
Hippotragus bakeri, young ♂	Proc. Zool. Soc. London, 1868, p. 214, pl. xvi	439
Hirundinea bellicosa	Ibis, 1860, p. 196, pl. v, fig. 1	496
—— ferruginea	Ibis, 1860, p. 196, pl. v, fig. 2	496
—— rupestris	Ibis, 1860, p. 198, pl. v, fig. 3	496
Homorus lophotes	Argentine Ornith., I, p. 195, pl. ix	21
Hydrochœrus capybara	Quart. Journ. of Sci., London, II, p. 621, pl. 8 (1865)	367
Hydropsalis furcifera	Argentine Ornith., II, p. 15, pl. xii	21
Hylactes castaneus	Exotic Ornith., p. 57, pl. xxix	12

List of species figured—Continued.

Name.	Where figured.	No. of paper.
Hylobates hoolock	Proc. Zool. Soc. London, 1870, p. 86, pl. v, fig. 2	502
—— lar	Proc. Zool. Soc. London, 1870, p. 86, pl. v, fig. 1	502
—— leucogenys	Proc. Zool. Soc. London, 1877, p. 679, pl. lxx	703
Hylophilus brunneiceps	Ibis, 1881, p. 305, pl. xi, fig. 1	892
—— ferrugineifrons	Ibis, 1881, p. 307, pl. xi, fig. 2	892
—— fuscicapillus	Ibis, 1881, p. 303, pl. x, fig. 2	892
—— muscicapinus	Ibis, 1881, p. 299, pl. x, fig. 1	892
—— ochraceiceps	Cat. American Birds, p. 44, pl. v	6
—— rubrifrons	Proc. Zool. Soc. London, 1867, p. 569, pl. xxx, fig. 1	413
—— semicinereus	Proc. Zool. Soc. London, 1867, p. 570, pl. xxx, fig. 2	413
Hypocnemis hypoxantha	Proc. Zool. Soc. London, 1868, p. 573, pl. xliii	454
—— lepidonota, ♂, ♀	Cat. Bds. Brit. Mus., XV, p. 287, pl. xvi	22
—— melanosticta	Proc. Zool. Soc. London, 1854, p. 254, pl. lxxii, fig. 2	64
—— melanosticta, ♂, ♀	Proc. Zool. Soc. London, 1854, p. 254, pl. lxxiii	64
Hypocolius ampelinus, ♂	Proc. Zool. Soc. London, 1890, p. 147, pl. xv	1088
Hypopyrrhus pyrrhogaster, egg	Proc. Zool. Soc. London, 1879, p. 510, pl. xliii, fig. 4	825
Hypotaenidia sulcirostris	Ibis, 1880, p. 311, pl. vi	863
Hypotriorchis castanonotus	Ibis, 1861, p. 346, pl. xii	239
Hystrix malabarica	Proc. Zool. Soc. London, 1865, p. 353, pl. xvi	344
Ibis aethiopica, young and egg	Ibis, 1878, p. 449, pl. xii	805
Icterus abeillei, ♂, ♀	Exotic Ornith., p. 187, pl. xciv	12
—— graceannae, ♀	Ibis, 1863, p. 366, pl. xi	949
—— hauxwelli	Cat. Bds. Brit. Mus., XI, p. 377, pl. xviii	19
—— laudabilis	Proc. Zool. Soc. London, 1871, p. 270, pl. xxi	546
—— pustulatus, ♂, ♀	Exotic Ornith., p. 47, pl. xxiv	12
Idiopsar brachyurus	Ibis, 1884, p. 240, pl. vii	970
Iodopleura leucopygia	Cat. Bds. Brit. Mus., XIV, p. 393, pl. xxvi	20
Iridornis porphyrocephala	Proc. Zool. Soc. London, 1855, p. 227, pl. cx	81
—— reinhardti	Ibis, 1865, p. 495, pl. xi	363
Jacamaralcyon tridactyla, ♂	Monogr. of Jacamars and Puff-birds, p. 49, pl. xvi	15
Jacamerops grandis, ♂, ♀	Monogr. of Jacamars and Puff-birds, p. 57, pl. xviii	15
Lagothrix humboldtii, adult and young.	Proc. Zool. Soc. London, 1863, p. 374, pl. xxxi	294
Laletes osburni	Proc. Zool. Soc. London, 1861, p. 72, pl. xiv, fig. 2	212
Lanio aurantius, ♂, ♀	Exotic Ornith., p. 61, pl. xxxi	12
—— lawrencii, young	Ibis, 1865, p. 272, pl. vi, fig. 2	995
—— leucothorax, ♂, ♀	Exotic Ornith., p. 63, pl. xxxii	12
Lathria uropygialis	Proc. Zool. Soc. London, 1876, p. 355, pl. xxxii	723
Lemur catta	Quart. Journ. of Sci., London, I, p. 219, pl. ii (1864)	335
—— leucomystax	do	335
—— mongoz, ♂, ♀	Proc. Zool. Soc. London, 1871, p. 230, pl. xvi	543
—— nigrifrons (adult and young)	Wolf's Zoological Sketches, II, pl. ii	7
—— varius	Quart. Journ. of Sci., London, I, p. 219, pl. ii (1864)	335
—— xanthomystax	do	335
Leptasthenura andicola	Proc. Zool. Soc. London, 1869, p. 636, pl. xlix, fig. 2	495
Leptopogon erythrops	Cat. Bds. Brit. Mus., XIV, p. 119, pl. x	20
—— oustaleti	Proc. Zool. Soc. London, 1887, p. 48, pl. ix, fig. 2	1019
Leucopeza semperi	Proc. Zool. Soc. London, 1876, p. 14, pl. vi	711
Leucophantes brachyurus	Proc. Zool. Soc. London, 1873, p. 601, pl. liii	628
Leucopternis palliata	Exotic Ornith., p. 97, pl. xlix	12
—— princeps	Proc. Zool. Soc. London, 1865, p. 429, pl. xxiv	346
—— semiplumbea	Exotic Ornith., p. 121, pl. lxi	12
—— superciliaris	Exotic Ornith., p. 75, pl. xxxviii	12
Lipaugus rufescens	Exotic Ornith., p. 5, pl. iii	12
—— subalaris	Exotic Ornith., p. 3, pl. ii	12
—— unirufus	Exotic Ornith., p. 1, pl. i	12
Loblophasis bulweri	Proc. Zool. Soc. London, 1876, p. 465, pl. xliv	731
Lophophorus l'huysi	Proc. Zool. Soc. London, 1868, p. 1, pl. i	430
—— sclateri	Proc. Zool. Soc. London, 1870, p. 163, pl. xiv	509
Loriculus aurantifrons, ♀	Rowley's Ornith. Miscell., I, p. 376, pl. lxxii, fig. 1 (1877)	769
—— chrysonotus, ♂, ♀	Ibis, 1872, p. 324, pl. xi	603
—— tener, ♀	Rowley's Ornith. Miscell., II, p. 376, pl. lxxii, figs. 2, 3 (1877)	769
Lorius chlorocercus	Proc. Zool. Soc. London, 1807, p. 183, pl. xvi	402
—— tibialis	Proc. Zool. Soc. London, 1871, p. 499, pl. xl	552
Loxioides bailleui	Ibis, 1879, p. 90, pl. ii	834
Lynx canadensis (Felis canadensis on plate).	Wolf's Zoological Sketches, I, pl. xii	7
Macacus leoninus	Proc. Zool. Soc. London, 1870, p. 664, pl. xxxv	518
—— ocreatus	Wolf's Zoological Sketches, II, pl. i	7
—— ——	Proc. Zool. Soc. London, 1860, p. 420, pl. lxxxii	192
—— rheso similis	Proc. Zool. Soc. London, 1872, p. 495, pl. xxv	582
—— rufescens	Proc. Zool. Soc. London, 1872, p. 495, pl. xxiv	582
—— speciosus	Proc. Zool. Soc. London, 1875, p. 418, pl. xlvii	692
Malacoptila fulvigularis	Monogr. of Jacamars and Puff-birds, p. 127, pl. xlii	15
—— fusca, ♂	Monogr. of Jacamars and Puff-birds, p. 111, pl. xxxvii	15
—— inornata, ♂, ♀	Monogr. of Jacamars and Puff-birds, p. 125, pl. xli	15
—— panamensis, ♂, ♀	Monogr. of Jacamars and Puff-birds, p. 119, pl. xl	15
—— poliopis	Proc. Zool. Soc. London, 1882, p. 86, pl. viii	253
—— rufa	Monogr. of Jacamars and Puff-birds, p. 115, pl. xxxviii	15
—— substriata	Monogr. of Jacamars and Puff-birds, p. 129, pl. xliii	15
—— ——	Proc. Zool. Soc. London, 1853, p. 123, pl. 21	55

List of species figured—Continued.

Name.	Where figured.	No. of paper.
Malacoptila torquata	Monogr. of Jacamars and Puff-birds, p. 117, pl. xxxix	15
Malacothraupis dentata	Proc. Zool. Soc. London, 1876, p. 353, pl. xxxi	723
Macropus erubescens, young	Proc. Zool. Soc. London, 1870, p. 126, pl. x	506
—— major	Quart. Journ. of Sci., London, II, p. 19, pl. 5 (1865)	366
—— rufus	Wolf's Zoological Sketches, II, pl. xxvi	7
Manucodia comrii	Proc. Zool. Soc. London, 1876, p. 459, pl. xlii	728
Margarornis brunnescens	Proc. Zool. Soc. London, 1850, p. 27, pl. cxvi	84
Maslus coronulatus	Cat. American Birds, p. 247, pl. xix	8
Megalaima asiatica	Intellectual Observer, XII, p. 243, pl. viii	429
Megalurus interscapularis	Proc. Zool. Soc. London, 1880, p. 65, pl. vi	845
Megapodius macgillivrayii	Proc. Zool. Soc. London, 1876, p. 460, pl. xliii	728
Melanerpes rubrigularis	Proc. Zool. Soc. London, 1858, p. 2, pl. cxxxi	115
Melanotis hypoleucus, adult and young.	Exotic Ornith., p. 85, pl. xliii	12
Moleagris ocellata, ♂, ♀ (heads)	Proc. Zool. Soc. London, 1861, p. 402, pl. xl	232
Melidectes torquatus	Proc. Zool. Soc. London, 1873, p. 694, pl. lv	628
Molipotes gymnops	Proc. Zool. Soc. London, 1873, p. 695, pl. lvi	628
Mellivora capensis	Wolf's Zoological Sketches, II, pl. ix	7
—— indica	......do	7
—— leuconota	Proc. Zool. Soc. London, 1867, p. 98, pl. viii	400
Mephitis humboldtii	Wolf's Zoological Sketches, I, pl. xv	7
Morganetta turneri, ♂, ♀	Exotic Ornith., p. 199, pl. c	12
Metoplana peposaca, ♂, ♀	Proc. Zool. Soc. London, 1870, p. 666, pl. xxxvii	518
Metopothrix aurantiacus	Proc. Zool. Soc. London, 1866, p. 190, pl. xviii	380
Microbates collaris	Ibis, 1883, p. 96, pl. iii (Rhamphocaenus collaris in text)	947
Microcerculus squamulatus	Proc. Zool. Soc. London, 1875, p. 37, pl. vi	678
Micromonacha lanceolata	Monogr. of Jacamars and Puff-birds, p. 131, pl. xliv	15
Midas devillii, ♂	Proc. Zool. Soc. London, 1871, p. 220, pl. xiii	542
—— geoffroi	Proc. Zool. Soc. London, 1871, p. 478, pl. xxxviii	549
Milvago australis (egg), 2 figures	Ibis, 1860, p. 25, pl. i, figs. 1, 2	198
—— carunculatus	Ibis, 1861, p. 19, pl. i	234
Mimus triurus	Argentine Ornith., I, p. 8, pl. i	21
Mitrephorus phæocercus	Ibis, 1859, p. 442, pl. xiv, fig. 2	159
Mitua salvini, ♀	Trans. Zool. Soc. London, X, p. 545, pl. xcv (1879)	839
—— tomentosa	Trans. Zool. Soc. London, IX, p. 284, pl. lii (1875)	705
—— tuberosa	Trans. Zool. Soc. London, IX, p. 283, pl. li (1875)	705
Molothrus badius	Argentine Ornith., I, p. 95, pl. vi, fig. 1	21
—— rufo-axillaris, pull	Argentine Ornith., I, p. 86, pl. vi, fig. 2	21
Monacha flavirostris	Monogr. of Jacamars and Puff-birds, p. 149, pl. xlix	15
—— grandior, ♀	Monogr. of Jacamars and Puff-birds, p. 155, pl. lii	15
—— morpheus	Monogr. of Jacamars and Puff-birds, p. 151, pl. l	15
—— nigra	Monogr. of Jacamars and Puff-birds, p. 145, pl. xlviii	15
—— nigrifrons, ♂	Monogr. of Jacamars and Puff-birds, p. 159, pl. liv	15
—— pallescens	Monogr. of Jacamars and Puff-birds, p. 157, pl. liii	15
—— peruana	Monogr. of Jacamars and Puff-birds, p. 153, pl. li	15
Monarcha castus	Proc. Zool. Soc. London, 1883, p. 53, pl. xii, fig. 1	926
—— mundus	Proc. Zool. Soc. London, 1883, p. 54, pl. xii, fig. 2	926
—— verticalis	Proc. Zool. Soc. London, 1877, p. 99, pl. xiv. fig. 1	750
Munia forbesi	Proc. Zool. Soc. London, 1879, p. 449, pl. xxxvii, fig. 3	822
—— melæna	Proc. Zool. Soc. London, 1880, p. 66, pl. vii, fig. 2	845
Muscisaxicola rubricapilla	Proc. Zool. Soc. London, 1867, p. 986, pl. xlvi	424
Muscivora occidentalis, ♂, ♀	Cat. Bds. Brit. Mus., XIV, p. 194, pl. xv	20
Mycteria australis	Wolf's Zoological Sketches, I, pl. xlvii	7
—— senegalensis (Ciconia senegalensis in text).	Wolf's Zoological Sketches, II, pl. xliii	7
Myiadestes elisabethæ	Exotic Ornith., p. 55, pl. xxviii	12
—— obscurus	Exotic Ornith., p. 49, pl. xxv	12
—— ralloides, adult and young	Exotic Ornith., p. 53, pl. xxvii	12
—— unicolor	Exotic Ornith., p. 51, pl. xxvi	12
Myiarchus semirufus	Proc. Zool. Soc. London, 1878, p. 138, pl. xi	775
Myiobius flavicans	Cat. Bds. Brit. Mus., XIV, p. 205, pl. xvii	20
—— nationi	Proc. Zool. Soc. London, 1866, p. 99, pl. xi, fig. 1	376
—— pulcher	Proc. Zool. Soc. London, 1866, p. 100, pl. xi, fig. 2	376
—— roraimæ	Cat. Bds. Brit. Mus., XIV, p. 208, pl. xviii	20
Myiozetetes texensis (egg)	Ibis, 1859, p. 123, pl. v, fig. 5	156a
Myrmeciza loricaspis	Proc. Zool. Soc. London, 1854, p. 253, pl. lxx	64
—— margaritata, ♂, ♀	Proc. Zool. Soc. London, 1854, p. 253, pl. lxxi	64
Myrmecophaga jubata	Wolf's Zoological Sketches, I, pl. xxx	7
	Quart. Journ. of Sci., London, II, p. 621, pl. 8 (1865)	367
Myrmelastes plumbeus, ♂, ♀	Proc. Zool. Soc. London, 1858, p. 275, pl. cxliii	121
Myrmotherula erythrura, ♂, ♀	Cat. Bds. Brit. Mus., XV, p. 236, pl. xv	22
—— multostriata, ♂, ♀	Proc. Zool. Soc. London, 1858, p. 234, pl. cxli, figs. 2, 3	122
—— ornata, ♂, ♀	Cat. American Birds, p. 179, pl. xv	8
—— surinamensis	Proc. Zool. Soc. London, 1858, p. 234, pl. cxli, fig. 1	122
Myzomela cineracea	Proc. Zool. Soc. London, 1879, p. 449, pl. xxxvii, fig. 1	822
Nasiterna pusio	Proc. Zool. Soc. London, 1865, p. 620, pl. xxxv	356
Nemosia albigularis, ♂, ♀	Cat. Bds. Brit. Mus., XI, p. 227, pl. xii	19
	Proc. Zool. Soc. London, 1855, p. 109, pl. xcix	76
Neomorphus radiolosus	Proc. Zool. Soc. London, 1878, p. 439, pl. xxvii	786
—— salvini	Proc. Zool. Soc. London, 1866, p. 60, pl. v	372
Neopipo rubicunda	Proc. Zool. Soc. London, 1869, p. 438, pl. xxx, fig. 3	483

List of species figured—Continued.

Name.	Where figured.	No. of paper.
Neorhynchus nasesus (masons on plate).	Proc. Zool. Soc. London, 1869, p. 147, pl. xii.	407
Nigrita bicolor.	Contr. to Ornithology, 1852, p. 34, pl. lxxxiii.	44
Ninox forbesi.	Proc. Zool. Soc. London, 1883, p. 52, pl. xi.	926
Nothocrax urumutum.	Trans. Zool. Soc. London, IX, p. 282, pl. l (1875).	705
——	Trans. Zool. Soc. London, X, p. 545, pl. xciv (1879).	839
Nonnula brunnea.	Monogr. of Jacamars and Puff-birds, p. 141, pl. xlvi, fig. 2.	15
—— cineracea.	Monogr. of Jacamars and Puff-birds, p. 135, pl. xlv, fig. 2.	15
—— rubecula.	Monogr. of Jacamars and Puff-birds, p. 133, pl. xlv, fig. 1.	15
—— ruficapilla.	Monogr. of Jacamars and Puff-birds, p. 137, pl. xlvi, fig. 1.	15
Nothoprocta taczanowskii.	Proc. Zool. Soc. London, 1874, p. 679, pl. lxxxiv.	671
Nothura darwini.	Argentine Ornith., II, p. 213, pl. xx.	21
Numida, sp., head and neck.	Proc. Zool. Soc. London, 1890, p. 86, pl. xii.	1085
Nyctereutes procynides.	Proc. Zool. Soc. London, 1874, p. 323, pl. l.	660
Nyctibius bracteatus.	Exotic Ornith., p. 39, pl. xx.	12
Nyctipithecus rufipes.	Proc. Zool. Soc. London, 1872, p. 3, pl. i	577
Nymphicus cornutus.	Proc. Zool. Soc. London, 1879, p. 550, pl. xliv.	826
Ochthodiæta fusco-rufus.	Cat. Bds. Brit. Mus., XIV, p. 18, pl. v.	20
Ochthœca citrinifrous.	Cat. Bds. Brit. Mus., XIV, p. 22, pl. vii, fig. 1	20
—— fumicolor.	Proc. Zool. Soc. London, 1856, p. 28, pl. cxvii.	84
—— leucometopa.	Cat. Bds. Brit. Mus., XIV, p. 21, pl. vi.	20
—— pulchella.	Cat. Bds. Brit. Mus., XIV, p. 22, pl. vii, fig. 2.	20
Ocyalus wagleri, egg.	Proc. Zool. Soc. London, 1879, p. 508. pl. xliii, fig. 3.	825
Ocydromus australis, ♂, ♀.	Wolf's Zoological Sketches, II, pl. xlii.	7
—— sylvestris.	Proc. Zool. Soc. London, 1869, p. 472, pl. xxxv.	480
Œdicnemus superciliaris.	Exotic Ornith., p. 59, pl. xxx.	12
Oncostoma cinereigulare.	Cat. American Birds, p. 208, pl. xviii, fig. 1.	8
Oreas canna (young).	Wolf's Zoological Sketches, I, pl. xxi.	7
Oreomanes fraseri.	Proc. Zool. Soc. London, 1860, p. 75, pl. clix.	164
Ortygocichla rubiginosa, bird and egg.	Proc. Zool. Soc. London, 1881, p. 452, pl. xxxix.	879
Oryx beisa, ♀ adult and young.	Proc. Zool. Soc. London, 1881, p. 626, pl. liv.	881
—— leucoryx, ♂, ♀.	Wolf's Zoological Sketches, I, pl. xxiii.	7
——, young.	Wolf's Zoological Sketches, II, pl. xix.	7
Ostinops atrocastaneus, egg.	Proc. Zool. Soc. London, 1879, p. 509, pl. xliii, figs. 1, 2.	825
—— oleagineus.	Ibis, 1883, p. 154, pl. vii.	948
—— salmoni.	Ibis, 1883, p. 153, pl. vi.	948
Otaria hookeri.	Wolf's Zoological Sketches, II, pl. xi.	7
Otis tarda.	Wolf's Zoological Sketches, I, pl. xlv.	7
Otocorys peregrina.	Proc. Zool. Soc. London, 1855, p. 110, pl. cii.	76
Ovis cycloceros (O. vignei on plate).	Wolf's Zoological Sketches, I, pl. xxiv.	7
——, ♂, ♀.	Proc. Zool. Soc. London, 1860, p. 128, pl. lxxx.	107
—— tragelaphus, ♂, ♀ and young.	Wolf's Zoological Sketches, II, pl. xxi.	7
—— vignei (O. cycloceros in text), ♂, ♀ and young.	Wolf's Zoological Sketches, I, pl. xxiv.	7
——	Proc. Zool. Soc. London, 1860, p. 127, pl. lxxix.	167
Oxyrhamphus frater, ♀ adult and young.	Exotic Ornith., p. 131, pl. lxvi.	12
Oxyurus masafueræ.	Ibis, 1871, p. 180, pl. vii, fig. 2.	566
Pachycephala arctitorquis, ♂, ♀.	Proc. Zool. Soc. London, 1883, p. 55, pl. xiii.	926
—— fusco-flava, ♂, ♀.	Proc. Zool. Soc. London, 1883, p. 198, pl. xxviii.	932
Pachyrhamphus spodiurus, ♂, ♀.	Cat. Bds. Brit. Mus., XIV, p. 341, pl. xxv.	20
Paradoxurus prehensilis.	Proc. Zool. Soc. London, 1877, p. 681, pl. lxxi.	763
Paramythia montium.	Ibis, 1893, p. 244, pl. vii.	1188
Passer insularis, ♂, ♀.	Proc. Zool. Soc. London, 1881, p. 160, pl. xvi.	870
Pauxi galeata.	Trans. Zool. Soc. London, IX, p. 285, pl. liii, fig. 1 (1875).	705
—— var. rubra.	Trans. Zool. Soc. London, IX, p. 285, pl. liii, fig. 2 (1875).	705
Pelecanus fuscus, two individuals in different plumages.	Proc. Zool. Soc. London, 1868, p. 268, pl. xxvi.	441
—— rufescens, two young birds in different plumages.	Proc. Zool. Soc. London, 1868, p. 267, pl. xxvi.	441
—— sharpii.	Proc. Zool. Soc. London, 1871, p. 632, pl. li.	557
—— trachyrhynchus.	Proc. Zool. Soc. London, 1883, p. 463, pl. xlvi.	941
Percnostola funebris, ♂, ♀.	Proc. Zool. Soc. London, 1867, p. 980, pl. xlv.	423
Petaurus, sp.	Quart. Journ. of Sci., London, II, p. 19, pl. 5 (1865).	366
—— tagunnoides.	...do...	366
Phacelodomus ruffipennis.	Cat. Bds. Brit. Mus., XV, p. 83, pl. v.	22
Phacochœrus æliani, ♀.	Proc. Zool. Soc. London, 1869, p. 276, pl. xx.	474
Phascolarctos cinereus.	Quart. Journ. of Sci., London, II, p. 19, pl. 5 (1865).	366
Phascolomys lasiorhinus (P. latifrons in text).	Wolf's Zoological Sketches, II, pl. xxvii.	7
—— latifrons (P. lasiorhinus on plate).	Quart. Journ. of Sci., London, II, p. 19, pl. 5 (1865).	366
—— ——	Wolf's Zoological Sketches, II, pl. xxvii.	7
—— wombat adult and young.	Wolf's Zoological Sketches, I, pl. xxxii.	7
Phasianus principalis, ♂.	Proc. Zool. Soc. London, 1885, p. 324, pl. xxii.	980
—— reevesi, ♂, ♀.	Wolf's Zoological Sketches, II, pl. xxxiii.	7
——	List of Species of Phasianidæ, p. 5, pl. i.	10
—— sœmmerringii, ♂, ♀.	Wolf's Zoological Sketches, II, pl. xxxii.	7
——	List of Species of Phasianidæ, p. 5, pl. ii.	10
—— torquatus, ♂, ♀.	Wolf's Zoological Sketches, I, pl. xxxvii.	7

List of species figured—Continued.

Name.	Where figured.	No. of paper.
Phasianus versicolor, ♂, ♀, and young.	Wolf's Zoological Sketches, I, pl. xxxviii	7
Philydor consobrinus	Cat. Bds. Brit. Mus., XV, p. 98, pl. ix	22
—— erythronotus	Cat. Bds. Brit. Mus., XV, p. 99, pl. viii	22
Philogænas bartletti	Proc. Zool. Soc. London, 1863, p. 377, pl. xxxiv	294
—— johannæ	Proc. Zool. Soc. London, 1877, p. 112, pl. xvi	750
Phlogopsis macleannani	Exotic Ornith., p. 17, pl. ix	12
Phœnicopterus jamesi	Proc. Zool. Soc. London, 1886, p. 309, pl. xxxvi	1010
Phœnicothraupis gutturalis, ♂	Cat. Bds. Brit. Mus., XI, p. 201, pl. xi	19
——, egg	Proc. Zool. Soc. London, 1879, p. 502, pl. xlii, fig. 4	825
Phrygilus coracinus	Proc. Zool. Soc. London, 1891, p. 133, pl. xiii	1110
—— ocularis, ♂, ♀	Proc. Zool. Soc. London, 1858, p. 454, pl. cxlv	131
Phyllomyias griseocapilla	Proc. Zool. Soc. London, 1861, p. 382, pl. xxxvi, fig. 2	229
—— semifusca	Proc. Zool. Soc. London, 1861, p. 383, pl. xxxvi, fig. 1	229
Phytotoma rutila, ♂, ♀	Argentine Ornith., I, p. 104, pl. viii	21
Picolaptes layardi	Ibis, 1873, p. 385, pl. xiv	636
Pionus corallinus	Rowley's Ornith. Miscell., III, p. 6, pl. lxxx (1877)	770
—— hæmatotis	Ibis, 1860, p. 401, pl. xiii	200b
—— tumultuosus	Rowley's Ornith. Miscell., III, p. 6, pl. lxxxi (1877)	770
Pipilopsis flavigularis	Contr. to Ornithology, 1852, p. 131, pl. xcviii	51
Pipra flavicapilla	Contr. to Ornithology, 1852, p. 132, pl. xcvii, fig. 2	51
—— flavo-tincta	Proc. Zool. Soc. London, 1852, p. 34, pl. xlviii	53
—— isidorei	Contr. to Ornithology, 1852, p. 132, pl. c, fig. 1	51
—— leucorrhoa	Proc. Zool. Soc. London, 1863, p. 63, pl. x	281
—— mentalis, ♂, ♀	Proc. Zool. Soc. London, 1856, p. 299, pl. cxxi	92
—— nattereri, ♂, ♀	Proc. Zool. Soc. London, 1864, p. 611, pl. xxxix	328
—— pyrocephala	Contr. to Ornithology, 1852, p. 132, pl. xcvii, fig. 1	51
Pipræidea albiventris	Contr. to Ornithology, 1852, p. 131, pl. c, fig. 2	51
Pipreola frontalis	Ibis, 1878, p. 109, pl. vi	803
—— jucunda	Proc. Zool. Soc. London, 1860, p. 89, pl. clx (Euchlornis jucunda on plate).	165
—— riefferii, egg	Proc. Zool. Soc. London, 1879, p. 519, pl. xliii, fig. 8	825
Pitangus derbianus (egg)	Ibis, 1859, p. 120, pl. v, fig. 3	150a
Pithecia, sp.	Quart. Journ. of Sci., London, II, p. 621, pl. 8 (1865)	367
—— albinasa	Proc. Zool. Soc. London, 1881, p. 258, pl. xxix	872
—— satanas, young	Proc. Zool. Soc. London, 1864, p. 712, pl. xii	329
Pithys erythrophrys	Proc. Zool. Soc. London, 1854, p. 255, pl. lxxii, fig. 1	64
—— lunulata, ♀	Proc. Zool. Soc. London, 1873, p. 276, pl. xxvi	614
Pitylus humeralis	Exotic Ornith., p. 167, pl. lxxxiv	12
Platyrhynchus albogularis	Cat. Bds. Brit. Mus., XIV, p. 67, pl. viii, fig. 2	20
—— coronatus	Cat. American Birds, p. 207, pl. xvii	8
—— flavigularis	Cat. Bds. Brit. Mus., XIV, p. 65, pl. viii, fig. 1	20
Plectropterus gambensis, ♂	Proc. Zool. Soc. London, 1859, p. 132, pl. cliii, fig. 2	142
—— rüppelli, ♂	Proc. Zool. Soc. London, 1859, p. 132, pl. cliii, fig. 1	142
Pœcilodryas æthiops	Proc. Zool. Soc. London, 1880, p. 66, pl. vii, fig. 1	845
Pœocephalus rueppelli, ♂, ♀	Proc. Zool. Soc. London, 1882, p. 577, pl. xlii	914
Polyborus tharus, var.	Proc. Zool. Soc. London, 1876, p. 333, pl. xxv	722
Polychlorus westermauni	Proc. Zool. Soc. London, 1857, p. 226, pl. cxxvii	110
Polyplectron bicalcaratum, ♂, ♀	List of Species of Phasianidæ, p. 12, pl. xii	10
—— chinqius, egg	Proc. Zool. Soc. London, 1879, p. 116, pl. viii, fig. 2	810
Poospiza bonapartii, ♂, ♀	Proc. Zool. Soc. London, 1867, p. 341, pl. xx	408
—— cæsar	Proc. Zool. Soc. London, 1869, p. 152, pl. xiii	471
—— erythrophrys	Ibis, 1881, p. 599, pl. xvii, fig. 1	895
—— whitii, ♂, ♀	Proc. Zool. Soc. London, 1883, p. 43, pl. ix	925
Porcula salvania	Proc. Zool. Soc. London, 1882, p. 546, pl. xxxvii	912
——, young	Proc. Zool. Soc. London, 1883, p. 388, pl. xliii	940
Porzana albigularis, ♂, ♀	Exotic Ornith., p. 109, pl. lv	12
—— castaneiceps	Exotic Ornith., p. 155, pl. lxxviii	12
—— erythrops	Proc. Zool. Soc. London, 1867, p. 343, pl. xxi	408
—— hauxwelli	Exotic Ornith., p. 105, pl. liii	12
—— leucopyrrha	Exotic Ornith., p. 111, pl. lvi	12
—— levraudi	Proc. Zool. Soc. London, 1868, p. 452, pl. xxxv	448
—— melanophæa	Exotic Ornith., p. 107, pl. liv	12
—— rubra	Exotic Ornith., p. 31, pl. xvi	12
Potamochœrus africanus	Wolf's Zoological Sketches, I, pl. xxviii	7
—— penicillatus	Wolf's Zoological Sketches, I, pl. xxix	7
——, ♀ and young	Proc. Zool. Soc. London, 1861, p. 62, pl. xii	211
Prionirhynchus carinatus	Proc. Zool. Soc. London, 1857, p. 257, pl. cxxviii	112
Prionochilus melanoxanthus	Ibis, 1874, p. 3, pl. i, fig. 3	672
—— vincens, ♂, ♀	Ibis, 1874, p. 2, pl. i, figs. 1, 2	672
Psalidoprocne albiceps	Proc. Zool. Soc. London, 1864, p. 108, pl. xiv	307
Psittospiza riefferi, egg	Proc. Zool. Soc. London, 1879, p. 504, pl. xlii, fig. 8	825
Pteroglossus didymus	Cat. Bds. Brit. Mus., XIX, p. 147, pl. vi	24
Pteromys magnificus	Proc. Zool. Soc. London, 1872, p. 635, pl. i	588
Pteroplochus thoracicus	Proc. Zool. Soc. London, 1864, p. 609, pl. xxxviii	328
Pteropus formosus	Proc. Zool. Soc. London, 1873, p. 193, pl. xxii	613
Ptilochloris buckleyi, adult and young.	Proc. Zool. Soc. London, 1880, p. 158, pl. xvi	848
Ptilogonys caudatus, ♂, ♀	Exotic Ornith., p. 11, pl. vi	12
Ptilonopus bellus	Proc. Zool. Soc. London, 1873, p. 696, pl. lvii	628
Ptilonorhynchus holosericeus, ♂, ♀, and immature.	Wolf's Zoological Sketches, II, pl. xxviii	7

List of species figured—Continued.

Name.	Where figured.	No. of paper.
Pyranga roseogularis	Ibis, 1873, p. 125, pl. iii	634
Pyrgisoma biarcuatum (egg)	Ibis, 1859, p. 18, pl. v, fig. 2	156a
— cabanisi	Exotic Ornith., p. 129, pl. lxv, fig. 1	12
— kieneri	Exotic Ornith., p. 130, pl. lxv, fig. 2	12
— leucote	Exotic Ornith., p. 128, pl. lxiv, fig. 2	12
— rubricatum	Exotic Ornith., p. 127, pl. lxiv, fig. 1	12
Pyriglena ellisiana	Proc. Zool. Soc. London, 1855, p. 109, pl. c	76
— tyrannina, ♂, ♀	Proc. Zool. Soc. London, 1855, p. 90, pl. xcviii	75
Pyroderus orenocensis, egg	Proc. Zool. Soc. London, 1879, p. 520, pl. xliii, fig. 7	825
Querquedula angium	Proc. Zool. Soc. London, 1876, p. 387, pl. xxxiv	724
— falcata × Tadorna casarca	Proc. Zool. Soc. London, 1890, p. 1, pl. i	1083
— puna	Exotic Ornith., p. 107, pl. xcix	12
Quiscalus tenuirostris	Ibis, 1884, p. 157, pl. v	969
Rallus antarcticus	Exotic Ornith., p. 103, pl. lxxxii	12
— fusigula	Proc. Zool. Soc. London, 1880, p. 66, pl. viii	845
— intactus	Proc. Zool. Soc. London, 1869, p. 123, pl. x	464
— maculatus	Argentine Ornith., II, p. 184, pl. xix	21
— semiplumbeus	Exotic Ornith., p. 105, pl. lxxxiii	12
Rhamphocaenus cinereiventris	Proc. Zool. Soc. London, 1855, p. 76, pl. lxxxvii	73
— collaris	Ibis, 1883, p. 96, pl. iii (Microbates collaris on plate)	947
Rhamphocelus flammigerus, egg	Proc. Zool. Soc. London, 1879, p. 501, pl. xlii, fig. 3	825
Rhea americana	Trans. Zool. Soc. London, IV, p. 355, pl. lxviii (1862)	276
— — (young)	Wolf's Zoological Sketches, I, pl. xlii	7
— darwinii	Trans. Zool. Soc. London, IV, p. 357, pl. lxx (1862)	276
— macrorhyncha	Trans. Zool. Soc. London, IV, p. 356, pl. lxix (1862)	276
Rhinoceros bicornis, ♂	Trans. Zool. Soc. London, IX, p. 655, pl. xcix (1876)	742
— —, ♂ jr	Student and Intellectual Observer, IV, p. 321, pl. xi (1870)	531
— —, young	Proc. Zool. Soc. London, 1868, p. 529, pl. xli	449
— —, head	Proc. Zool. Soc. London, 1886, p. 144, pl. xvi, fig. 2	1002
— lasiotis, ♀	Proc. Zool. Soc. London, 1872, p. 493, pl. xxiii	582
— —	Trans. Zool. Soc. London, IX, p. 652, pl. xcviii (1876)	742
— simus, head	Proc. Zool. Soc. London, 1886, p. 143, pl. xvi, fig. 1	1002
— sondaicus, ♂	Trans. Zool. Soc. London, IX, p. 649, pl. xcvi (1876)	742
— —	Proc. Zool. Soc. London, 1874, p. 182, pl. xxviii	654
— sumatrensis, ♀	Proc. Zool. Soc. London, 1872, p. 790, pl. lxvii	595
— —	Trans. Zool. Soc. London, IX, p. 650, pl. xcvii (1876)	742
— unicornis, ♂	Trans. Zool. Soc. London, IX, p. 645, pl. xcv (1876)	742
Rhinochetus jubatus	Wolf's Zoological Sketches, II, pl. xlv	7
Rhinocrypta fulva (fusca in text)	Ibis, 1874, p. 198, pl. viii	674
— fusca (fulva on plate)	.....do	674
Rhipidura fusco-rufa	Proc. Zool. Soc. London, 1883, p. 197, pl. xxvii	932
Rhynchocyclus fulvipectus	Cat. Bds. Brit. Mus., XIV, p. 167, pl. xli	20
Rhynchostruthus socotranus	Proc. Zool. Soc. London, 1881, p. 170, pl. xvii	870
Rupicola sanguinolenta	Exotic Ornith., p. 29, pl. xv	12
Saiga tartarica, ♂, ♀	Proc. Zool. Soc. London, 1867, p. 240, pl. xvii	403
Saltator albicollis, egg	Proc. Zool. Soc. London, 1879, p. 505, pl. xlii, fig. 9	825
— arremonops	Proc. Zool. Soc. London, 1855, p. 84, pl. xcii	74
Saltatricula multicolor	Argentine Ornith., I, p. 61, pl. v	21
Sarcidiornis carunculata, ♂, ♀	Proc. Zool. Soc. London, 1876, p. 695, pl. lxviii	734
— melanonota, ♂, ♀	Proc. Zool. Soc. London, 1876, p. 694, pl. lxvii	734
Sarcorhamphus aequatorialis	Proc. Zool. Soc. London, 1883, p. 349, pl. xxxv	939
Sclerurus mexicanus	Cat. American Birds, p. 140, pl. xii	8
Scops barbarus (in normal and abnormal plumages)	Exotic Ornith., p. 101, pl. li	12
— flammeola	Exotic Ornith., p. 99, pl. l	12
— usta	Trans. Zool. Soc. London, IV, p. 265, pl. 61 (1858)	119
Semioptera wallacii, ♂, ♀	Ibis, 1860, p. 26, pl. ii	199
Sibia auricularis	Proc. Zool. Soc. London, 1866, p. 109, pl. iv	394
Siptornis subcristata (Synallaxis subcristata on plate)	Cat. Bds. Brit. Mus., XV, p. 62, pl. iv	22
Sirystes albocinereus	Cat. Bds. Brit. Mus., XIV, p. 181, pl. xiv	20
Sitta krueperi	Ibis, 1865, p. 307, pl. vii	362
Spermophila aurita, ♂	Ibis, 1871, p. 14, pl. ii, figs. 1, 2	565
— nigro-rufa, ♂, ♀	Ibis, 1871, p. 6, pl. i, figs. 1, 2	565
— ocellata, ♀	Ibis, 1871, p. 14, pl. ii, fig. 3	565
— pileata, ♂	Ibis, 1871, p. 5, pl. i, fig. 3	565
Sphingurus spinosus	Proc. Zool. Soc. London, 1884, p. 389, pl. xxxiii	959
Stenopsis ruficervix	Proc. Zool. Soc. London, 1866, p. 140, pl. xiv	378
Stephanophorus leucocephalus	Argentine Ornith., I, p. 38, pl. iv	21
Strepsiceros imberbis	Proc. Zool. Soc. London, 1884, p. 45, pl. iv	953
Struthio camelus	Trans. Zool. Soc. London, IV, p. 355, pl. lxviia (1862)	276
— —, young	Wolf's Zoological Sketches, II, pl. xli	7
Sublegatus glaber	Proc. Zool. Soc. London, 1868, pp. 171, 172, pl. xiii, fig. 2	435
Sus andamanensis	Wolf's Zoological Sketches, II, pl. xxii	7
Sycalis aureiventris, ♂, ♀	Ibis, 1872, p. 47, pl. iii	601
— chrysops	Ibis, 1872, p. 45, pl. ii, fig. 1	601
— lutea	Ibis, 1872, p. 45, pl. ii, fig. 2	601
Synallaxis adusta	Cat. Bds. Brit. Mus., XV, p. 55, pl. iii	22
— candei	Proc. Zool. Soc. London, 1874, p. 15, pl. iii, fig. 2	645
— castanea	Cat. American Birds, p. 152, pl. xiii	8
— curtata	Proc. Zool. Soc. London, 1869, p. 636, pl. xlix, fig. 1	495

List of species figured—Continued.

Name.	Where figured.	No. of paper.
Synallaxis erythrothorax..........	Proc. Zool. Soc. London, 1855, p. 75, pl. lxxxvi	73
—— fusco-rufa...................	Proc. Zool. Soc. London, 1882, p. 578, pl. xliii, fig. 1........	915
—— graminicola.................	Proc. Zool. Soc. London, 1874, p. 440, pl. lviii, fig. 2.........	662
—— griseo-murina..............	Proc. Zool. Soc. London, 1882, p. 578, pl. xliii, fig. 2........	915
—— hyposticta	Proc. Zool. Soc. London, 1874, p. 20, pl. iv, fig. 2	645
—— kollari	Proc. Zool. Soc. London, 1874, p. 15, pl. iii, fig. 1..........	645
—— pudibunda.................	Proc. Zool. Soc. London, 1874, p. 445, pl. lviii, fig. 1........	662
—— scutata....................	Proc. Zool. Soc. London, 1874, p. 13, pl. ii, fig. 2..........	645
—— stictothorax...............	Proc. Zool. Soc. London, 1874, p. 12, pl. ii, fig. 1..........	645
—— subcristata................	Proc. Zool. Soc. London, 1874, p. 20, pl. iv, fig. 1..........	645
—— —— (Siptornis subcristata in text).	Cat. Bds. Brit. Mus., XV, p. 62, pl. iv................	22
—— whitii....................	Ibis, 1881, p. 600, pl. xvii, fig. 2	895
Syrnium albitarse............	Trans. Zool. Soc. London, IV, p. 263, pl. 60 (1858)	119
Tachyphonus chrysomelas, ♂, ♀ ..	Proc. Zool. Soc. London, 1860, p. 440, pl. xxxii............	484
—— delattrii, ♂, ♀	Exotic Ornith., p. 67, pl. xxxiv................	12
—— melaleucus, egg...........	Proc. Zool. Soc. London, 1879, p. 503, pl. xlii, fig. 5........	825
—— nattereri, ♂...............	Ibis, 1885, p. 273, pl. vi. fig. 1..................	905
—— phœniceus, ♂, ♀	Exotic Ornith., p. 65, pl. xxxiii................	12
—— xanthopygius..............	Proc. Zool. Soc. London, 1854, p. 158, pl. lxix............	60
——, ♂	Proc. Zool. Soc. London, 1855, p. 83, pl. xc...........	74
Tadorna casarca × Querquedula falcata.	Proc. Zool. Soc. London, 1890, p. 1, pl. i............	1083
—— tadornoides, ♂, ♀	Proc. Zool. Soc. London, 1864, p. 191, pl. xviii..........	316
—— variegata, ♂, ♀	Proc. Zool. Soc. London, 1864, p. 191, pl. xix...........	316
—— vulpanser × Casarca cana, hybrid, ♂, ♀	Proc. Zool. Soc. London, 1859, p. 442, pl. clviii..........	155
Tænioptera erythropygia........	Proc. Zool. Soc. London, 1851, p. 193, pl. xli...........	42
—— holospodia	Cat. Bds. Brit. Mus, XIV, p. 14, pl. iv............	20
—— rubetra...................	Argentine Ornith., I, p. 120, pl. vii................	21
—— striaticollis	Proc. Zool. Soc. London, 1851, p. 193, pl. xlii...........	42
Talegalla lathami..............	Wolf's Zoological Sketches, II, pl. xl................	7
Tamandua tetradactyla.........	Proc. Zool. Soc. London, 1871, p. 546, pl. xliii....	553
—— tridactyla	Quart. Journ. of Sci., London, II, p. 621, pl. 8 (1865)	367
Tanagra notabilis..............	Proc. Zool. Soc. London, 1855, p. 84, pl. xci...........	74
—— olivina	Proc. Zool. Soc. London, 1873, p. 186, pl. xxi...........	612
—— vicarius (egg)	Ibis, 1859, p. 16, pl. v, fig. 1..................	156a
Tanagrella calophrys...........	Contr., to Ornithology, 1851, p. 98, pl. xxiv............	38
Tantalus ibis..................	Wolf's Zoological Sketches, II, pl. xlvi................	7
—— leucocephalus.............	Wolf's Zoological Sketches, II, pl. xlvii................	7
Tapirus americanus............	Quart. Journ. of Sci., London, II, p. 621, pl. 8 (1865)	367
—— bairdi, young..............	Proc. Zool. Soc. London, 1871, p. 626, pl. l............	555
—— —— ——.................	Proc. Zool. Soc. London, 1872, p. 635, pl. li...........	588
—— dowi	Proc. Zool. Soc. London, 1882, p. 391, pl. xxiii..........	907
—— roulini, ♂ jr..............	Proc. Zool. Soc. London, 1878, p. 631, pl. xxxix..........	790
—— terrestris, ♀, adult........	Proc. Zool. Soc. London, 1872, p. 636, pl. lii...........	588
Tarsipes, sp..................	Quart. Journ. of Sci., London, II, p. 19, pl. 5 (1865)	366
Tereucura humeralis, ♂, ♀	Ibis, 1881, p. 271, pl. ix, figs. 2, 3................	891
—— apodioptila...............	Ibis, 1881, p. 270, pl. ix, fig. 1................	891
Tetragonops frantzii	Ibis, 1864, p. 371, pl. x....................	333
—— ramphastinus.............	Ibis, 1801, p. 184, pl. vi...................	236
Tetraogallus caspius...........	Wolf's Zoological Sketches, I, pl. xl................	7
Thamnophilus æthiops, ♂, ♀	Cat. Bds. Brit. Mus., XV, p. 190, pl. xi............	22
—— albinuchalis, ♂, ♀	Cat. Bds. Brit. Mus., XV, p. 204, pl. xiv............	22
—— amazonicus, ♂, ♀	Proc. Zool. Soc. London, 1858, p. 214, pl. cxxxix..........	121
—— cæsius, ♂, ♀	Proc. Zool. Soc. London, 1855, p. 19. pl. lxxxii..........	70
—— insignis, ♂, ♀	Cat. Bds. Brit. Mus., XV, p. 199. pl. xiii............	22
—— leuchauchen, ♂, ♀	Proc. Zool. Soc. London, 1855, p. 18, pl. lxxix..........	70
—— melanchrous	Proc. Zool. Soc. London, 1876, p. 18, pl. iii............	712
—— melanonotus	Proc. Zool. Soc. London, 1855, p. 19. pl. lxxx..........	70
—— nigriceps.................	Cat. Bds. Brit. Mus., XV, p. 194, pl. xii............	22
—— nigrocinereus	Proc. Zool. Soc. London, 1855, p. 19, pl. lxxxi..........	70
—— simplex, ♂, ♀	Ibis, 1873, p. 387, pl. xv...................	636
—— subfasciatus, ♂, ♀	Proc. Zool. Soc. London, 1876, p. 357, pl. xxxiii..........	723
Thaumalea amherstiæ	List of Species of Phasianidæ, p. 5, pl. iii............	10
Thlypopsis inornata, ♂.........	Cat. Bds. Brit. Mus., XI, p. 230, pl. xiii, fig. 2..........	19
—— ornata, ♂................	Cat. Bds. Brit. Mus., XI, p. 230, pl. xiii, fig. 1.........	19
Thripadectes flammulatus.......	Exotic Ornith., p. 185, pl. xciii................	12
Thryothorus nisorius...........	Proc. Zool. Soc. London, 1860, p. 592, pl. xlv............	489
—— pleurostictus.............	Cat. American Birds, p. 21, pl. iv................	8
Thylacinus cynocephalus.......	Wolf's Zoological Sketches, I, pl. xxxi............	7
Thyrorhina schomburgki........	Exotic Ornith., p. 133, pl. lxvii................	12
Tigrisoma cabanisi, adult and young.	Exotic Ornith., p. 95, pl. xlviii	12
—— fasciatum, immature.........	Exotic Ornith., p. 183, pl. xcii................	12
Tinamus robustus	Exotic Ornith., p. 87, pl. xliv................	12
Todirostrum calopterum.........	Proc. Zool. Soc. London, 1857, p. 82, pl. cxxv, fig. 1........	104
—— capitale	Proc. Zool. Soc. London, 1857, p. 83, pl. cxxv, fig. 2........	104
—— exile	Proc. Zool. Soc. London, 1857, p. 83, pl. cxxv, fig. 3........	104
—— nigriceps, ♂, ♀	Proc. Zool. Soc. London, 1855, p. 66, pl. lxxxiv, fig. 1........	72
—— schistaceiceps.............	Cat. American Birds, p. 208, pl. xviii, fig. 2.........	8

List of species figured—Continued.

Name.	Where figured.	No. of paper.
Todirostrum apiciferum	Proc. Zool. Soc. London, 1855, p. 67, pl. lxxxiv, fig. 2	72
Tolypeutes tricinctus	Quart. Journ. of Sci., London, II, p. 621, pl. 8 (1865)	367
Tragelaphus gratus, ♂, ♀	Proc. Zool. Soc. London, 1863, p. 34, pl. viii	924
—— spekii	Proc. Zool. Soc. London, 1864, p. 103, pl. xii	306
——, ♀	Proc. Zool. Soc. London, 1890, p. 500, pl. xlvii	1098
Trichecus rosmarus	Wolf's Zoological Sketches, I, pl. xviii	7
Trichoglossus mitchelli	Proc. Zool. Soc. London, 1871, p. 499, pl. xli	552
Tringa acuminata	Ibis, 1893, p. 183, pl. v	1187
Troglodytes brunneicollis	Exotic Ornith., p. 46, pl. xxiii, fig. 2	12
—— gorilla	Proc. Zool. Soc. London, 1877, p. 803, pl. xxxv	756
—— niger	Wolf's Zoological Sketches, I, pl. f	7
—— solstitialis	Exotic Ornith., p. 45, pl. xxiii, fig. 1	12
Turdus albicollis	Exotic Ornith., p. 141, pl. lxxi	12
—— albiventris	Exotic Ornith., p. 147, pl. lxxv	12
—— crotopezus	Exotic Ornith., p. 145, pl. lxxiii	12
—— fulviventris	Ibis, 1861, p. 277, pl. viii	237
—— gigas	Exotic Ornith., p. 139, pl. lxx	12
—— grayii (egg)	Ibis, 1859, p. 5, pl. v, fig. 7	156a
—— gymnophthalmus	Exotic Ornith., p. 151, pl. lxxvi	12
—— javanicus	Ibis, 1875, p. 346, pl. viii	703
—— leucomelas	Exotic Ornith., p. 143, pl. lxxii	12
—— phœopygus, adult and young	Exotic Ornith., p. 149, pl. lxxv	12
——, juv	Proc. Zool. Soc. London, 1867, p. 508, pl. xxix	413
—— pinicola	Cat. American Birds, p. 6, pl. i	8
Turtur aldabranus	Proc. Zool. Soc. London, 1871, p. 692, pl. lxxii	559
Tyranniscus cinereiceps	Cat. Bds. Brit. Mus., XIV, p. 131, pl. xi, fig. 1	20
——	Proc. Zool. Soc. London, 1870, p. 842, pl. liii, fig. 2	524
—— gracilipes	Cat. Bds. Brit. Mus., XIV, p. 133, pl. xi, fig. 2	20
—— improbus	Proc. Zool. Soc. London, 1870, p. 841, pl. liii, fig. 3	524
—— leucogonys	Proc. Zool. Soc. London, 1870, p. 841, pl. liii, fig. 1	524
Tyrannula ornata	Proc. Zool. Soc. London, 1854, p. 113, pl. lxvi, fig. 2	59
—— phœnicura	Proc. Zool. Soc. London, 1854, p. 113, pl. lxvi, fig. 1	59
Tyrannus melancholicus (egg)	Ibis, 1859, p. 121, pl. v, fig. 4	156a
—— niveigularis	Proc. Zool. Soc. London, 1880, p. 28, pl. iii	844
Urochroma dilectissima	Proc. Zool. Soc. London, 1870, p. 786, pl. xlvii	520
—— stictoptera	Proc. Zool. Soc. London, 1862, p. 312, pl. xi	255
Urogalba amazonum	Monogr. of Jacamars and Puff-birds, p. 5, pl. i, fig. 2	15
—— paradisea, ♀	Monogr. of Jacamars and Puff-birds, p. 1, pl. i, fig. 1	15
Ursus japonicus	Proc. Zool. Soc. London, 1862, p. 261, pl. xxxii	269
—— nasutus	Proc. Zool. Soc. London, 1868, p. 73, pl. viii	432
—— syriacus	Wolf's Zoological Sketches, I, pl. xvii	7
Urubitinga schistacea	Trans. Zool. Soc. London, IV, p. 261, pl. 58 (1856)	119
Vireo hypochryseus	Proc. Zool. Soc. London, 1862, p. 369, pl. xlvi	272
—— josephæ, ♂, ♀	Proc. Zool. Soc. London, 1859, p. 137, pl. cliv	143
—— modestus	Proc. Zool. Soc. London, 1861, p. 72, pl. xiv, fig. 1	212
Vireolanius icterophrys	Proc. Zool. Soc. London, 1855, p. 151, pl. ciii	77
—— melitophrys	Exotic Ornith., p. 13, pl. vii	12
—— pulchellus, ♂, ♀	Exotic Ornith., p. 15, pl. viii	12
Viverra civetta	Proc. Zool. Soc. London, 1871, p. 290, pl. xxix	547
Viverricula malaccensis	Wolf's Zoological Sketches, II, pl. viii	7
Xenopsaris albinucha	Proc. Zool. Soc. London, 1893, p. 166, pl. vii	1162
Xiphocolaptes emigrans	Exotic Ornith., p. 69, pl. xxxv	12
—— major	Exotic Ornith., p. 71, pl. xxxvi	12
Xipholena atropurpurea, ♂, ♀	Exotic Ornith., p. 9, pl. v	12
Xiphosoma caninum	Wolf's Zoological Sketches, I, pl. l	7
Zonotrichia boucardi	Proc. Zool. Soc. London, 1867, p. 1, pl. i	393
—— canicapilla	Ibis, 1877, p. 47, pl. i, fig. 1	766
—— strigiceps	Ibis, 1877, p. 47, pl. i, fig. 2	766

INDEX TO THE SUBJECTS OF THE SEPARATE WORKS AND PAPERS CATALOGUED IN PARTS I AND II.

LIST OF SEPARATE WORKS AND PAPERS PUBLISHED SUBSEQUENT TO DECEMBER, 1894, AND NOT INCLUDED IN PARTS I TO VI.

1240

Guide to the Gardens of the Zoological Society of London, 48th edition, 8vo, London, 1896.

1241

The Book of Antelopes. By P. L. Sclater, M. A., F. R. S., and Oldfield Thomas, F. Z. S., F. R. G. S. Illustrated by Joseph Wolf, F. Z. S., and J. Smit. Parts II–IV, pp. 59–220, pls. vii–xxiv (1895), and Part V, pp. 1–92, pls. xxv–xxxi (1896), 4to, London, 1895–96.

Part II contains figures and descriptions of *Damaliscus korrigum, D. pygargus, D. albifrons, D. lunatus, Connochœtes taurinus,* and *C. gnu,* and descriptions of *Damaliscus tiang, D. jimela,* and *Connochœtes albojubatus.* The last mentioned species, previously recognized as a subspecies, is given specific rank.

Part III contains figures and descriptions of *Cephalophus sylvicultrix* (2 figures), *C. jentinki, C. natalensis, C. harveyi, C. nigrifrons, C. dorsalis, C. ogilbyi,* and *C. rufilatus,* and descriptions of *C. spadix, C. leucogaster,* and *C. callipygus.*

Part IV contains figures and descriptions of *Cephalophus doriæ, C. niger, C. maxwelli, C. monticola, C. coronatus, C. abyssinicus, C. grimmi,* and *Tetraceros quadricornis,* and descriptions of *C. melanorheus,* and *C. æquatorialis.* This part concludes the first volume, and a temporary title-page and contents are issued with it.

Part V contains descriptions of *Oreotragus saltator, Ourebia scoparia, O. hastata, O. nigricaudata, O. montana, O. haggardi, Raphicerus melanotis, R. campestris, R. neumanni, Nesotragus moschatus, N. livingstonianus, Neotragus pygmæus, Madoqua saltiana, M. swaynei, M. phillipsi, M. damarensis, M. kirki,* and *M. guentheri.* The following species are figured: *Oreotragus saltator, Ourebia nigricaudata, Raphicerus melanotis, R. campestris, Nesotragus moschatus, Neotragus pygmæus, Madoqua saltiana, M. phillipsi,* and *M. guentheri.*

Each of the five parts is illustrated with several wood-cuts of the heads, horns, skulls, etc.

1242

[Report on the additions to the Society's Menagerie in December, 1894.]

Proc. Zool. Soc. London, 1895, p. 1.

1243

[Remarks upon two Tapirs deposited in the Society's Gardens by the Hon. W. Rothschild.]

Proc. Zool. Soc. London, 1895, p. 1.

1244

On the occurrence of the Barbary Sheep in Egypt.

Proc. Zool. Soc. London, 1895, pp. 85, 86.

Evidence is given of the occurrence in Egypt of *Ovis tragelaphus.*

1245

Note on the Breeding of the Surinam Water-Toad (*Pipa surinamensis*) in the Society's Reptile House.

Proc. Zool. Soc. London, 1895, pp. 86–88.

1246

[Report on the additions to the Society's Menagerie in January, 1895.]

Proc. Zool. Soc. London, 1895, p. 89.

1247

[Report on the additions to the Society's Menagerie in April, 1895.]

Proc. Zool. Soc. London, 1865, pp. 337, 338.

1248

[Remarks on the Pacific Rat (*Mus exulans*).]

Proc. Zool. Soc. London, 1895, p. 338.

Exhibition of and notes on specimens which had been obtained on Sunday Island, Kermadec group.

1249

[Remarks upon the Zoological Institutions which Mr. Sclater had recently visited in Egypt.]

Proc. Zool. Soc. London, 1895, pp. 400, 401.

1250

[Report on the additions to the Society's Menagerie in May, 1895.]

Proc. Zool. Soc. London, 1895, pp. 520, 521.

1251

[Exhibition of and remarks upon the head of a Barbary Sheep from Egypt.]

Proc. Zool. Soc. London, 1895, p. 521.

1252

[Exhibition of and remarks upon a skin of a Humming Bird (*Anthocephala berlepschi*) from Colombia.]

Proc. Zool. Soc. London, 1895, p. 521.

1253

[Exhibition of and remarks upon the skin and skull of a Loder's Gazelle (*Gazella loderi*) from Egypt.]

Proc. Zool. Soc. London. 1895, pp. 522, 523.

1254

[On the additions to the Society's Menagerie in June, July, August, and September, 1895.]

Proc. Zool. Soc. London, 1895, pp. 686, 687.

1255

[Remarks on the Principal Animals noticed in the Jardin d' Acclimatation and Jardin des Plantes, Paris, during a recent visit.]

Proc. Zool. Soc. London. 1895, p. 688.

1256

[Exhibition of and remarks upon a Zebra from the Henga Country, British Central Africa.]

Proc. Zool. Soc. London, 1895, pp. 688–690.

1257

[Exhibition of and remarks upon a pair of Horns of a male Livingstone's Eland offered to the Society by Sir Henry H. Johnston, K. C. B.]

Proc. Zool. Soc. London, 1895, pp. 690, 691.

The skull and horns of the Antelope (*Oreas canna livingstonii*) are figured in the text.

1258

[Report on the additions to the Menagerie in October and November, 1895.]

Proc. Zool. Soc. London, 1895, p. 827.

1259

[Exhibition of and remarks upon the head of an Antelope from British East Africa.]

Proc. Zool. Soc. London. 1895, pp. 868–870.

Cobus thomasi is remarked upon and the head figured in the text.

1260

The "*Scomber-scomber*" Principle.

Ibis, 1895, p. 168.

Letter from a correspondent pointing out that the name of the so-called *Scomber-scomber* principle probably originated in a printer's error.

1261

The Bird Collection of Zurich.

Ibis, 1895, pp. 168, 169.

Observations on the collection of birds in the Polytechnicum of Zurich.

1262

Field Notes on the Birds of the Estancia Sta. Elena, Argentine Republic. By A. H. Holland. With remarks by P. L. Sclater.

Ibis, 1895, pp. 213–217.

Remarks on 15 species of birds.

1263

On the Bower Bird recently described by Mr. C. W. De Vis as *Cnemophilus marvæ*.

Ibis. 1895, pp. 343, 344, pl. viii.

Remarks on and characters of the male and female of *Cnemophilus marvæ*; both sexes are figured.

1264

[Exhibition of a pair of Darwin's Tinamou (*Nothura darwini*) from Patagonia.]

Bull. Brit. Orn. Club, IV. p. xix (1895).

1265

[Extracts of letters received from Mr. Sclater on birds observed up the Nile, and on the mode of carriage of the legs in the Egyptian Kite.]

Bull. Brit. Orn. Club, IV, p. xxv (1895).

1266

[Abstract of an account of a tour up the Nile from Cairo to Wadi Halfeh and back.]

Bull. Brit. Orn. Club, IV, p. xxxi (1895).

1267

[Exhibition of skins of *Falco richardsoni* obtained in Larimer County, Colo.]

Bull. Brit. Orn. Club, IV, p. xlii (1895).

1268

[Exhibition of a Nest and two Eggs of *Ptyonoprogne obsoleta* taken from the smaller rock-temple of Abu Simbel, Upper Egypt.]

Bull. Brit. Orn. Club, IV, p. xlii (1895).

1269

[Chairman's address on opening the fourth session of the British Ornithologists' Club, 1895.]

Bull. Brit. Orn. Club, V, pp. 1–4 (1895).

1270

[Remarks on a specimen of the Spotted Redshank (*Totanus fuscus*) living in the Zoological Society's Gardens.]

Bull. Brit. Orn. Club, V, p. v (1895).

1271

[Remarks on the death of Mr. Henry Seebohm.]

Bull. Brit. Orn. Club, V, p. ix (1895).

1272

"*Dendrexetastes capitoides*."

Nature, LIII, pp. 102, 103 (1895).

Letter in reply to Dr. H. O. Forbes, respecting the typical specimen of *Dendrexetastes capitoides* in the Derby Museum.

1273

The "Exposition de Madagascar" at the Jardin des Plantes.

Natural Science, VII, pp. 251, 252.

Note on a representative collection of the Malagasy fauna in the Musée d'Histoire Naturelle, Paris.

1274

[Report on the additions to the Society's Menagerie in December, 1895.]

Proc. Zool. Soc. London, 1896, p. 1.

1275

[Report on the additions to the Society's Menagerie in January, 1896.]

Proc. Zool. Soc. London, 1896, p. 212.

1276

[Report on the additions to the Society's Menagerie in February, 1896.]

Proc. Zool. Soc. London. 1896, pp. 303, 304.

1277

Remarks on the Divergencies between the "Rules for Naming Animals" of the German Zoological Society and the Strick-landian Code of Nomenclature.

Proc. Zool. Soc. London, 1896, pp. 306–322.

1278

[Remarks on the Prospectus of the new German Work, "Das Thierreich."

Proc. Zool. Soc. London, 1896, pp. 400, 401.

1279

[Report on the additions to the Society's Menagerie in March, 1896.]

Proc. Zool. Soc. London, 1896, pp. 505, 506.

Among the additions, special attention is drawn to a specimen of a young female gorilla. The head and shoulders of the animal are figured in the text.

1280

[Exhibition of and remarks upon Natural-History specimens from Myasaland sent home by Sir H. H. Johnston, K.C.B.]

Proc. Zool. Soc. London, 1896, p. 506.

1281

[Exhibition of and remarks upon a pair of horns of the so-called *Antelope triangularis*.]

Proc. Zool. Soc. London, 1896, p. 506.

These horns were supposed to be an abnormal pair of a female Eland, *Oreas canna.*

1282

On a collection of Birds from Mount Chiradzulu, in the Shiré Highlands, Myasaland. By Capt. G. E. Shelley, F. Z. S. With prefatory remarks by P. L. Sclater.

Ibis. 1896, pp. 177 184.

1283

Field Notes on the Birds of the Estancia Sta. Elena, Argentine Republic, Part III. By A. H. Holland. With remarks by P. L. Sclater.

Ibis, 1896, pp. 315–318

Remarks on 11 species of birds. *Hapalocereus hollandi* is described as new, and its head, wing, and foot figured in the text.

1284

[Outlines of a scheme for a new general work on Birds.]

Bull. Brit. Orn. Club, V, pp. xvii, xviii, (1896).

1285

[Exhibition of some bird skins sent from British Guiana by Mr. J. J. Quelch.]

Bull. Brit. Orn. Club, V, p. xxiii (1896).

1286

[Remarks on the completion of the first volume of Captain Shelley's "Birds of Africa."]

Bull. Brit. Orn. Club, V, pp. xxiii, xxiv, (1896).

1287

Count von Götzen's Journey across Africa.

Natural Science, IX, pp. 58-60.

A review of Count G. A. von Götzen's "Durch Afrika von Ost nach West."